The picture that I

"The Father"

plagued New Guinea during WW2.

Known as "The Father of the Loniu," the saltwater crocodile was finally brought down by soldiers who found more than 30 bullets embedded in its thick hide.

"On a trip to the savage island, I encountered a picture that would change my life. 'The Father' began to swim through the murky recesses of my imagination. The result is this book."

—Timothy James Dean

Acknowledgement: South Pacific Magazine, Mike Coutts; PNG War Museum;Australia War Memorial.

Reader Raves

“**TEETH** has more hooks than a fisherman’s tackle box. Get ready to make some new ‘best mates’ and go reeling with them on a wild, wild ride! I am always in transit, and I devour at least three bestsellers a week. Because I have to carry it, I rate each book on whether it was worth its weight. I must tell you, **TEETH** is worth every ounce! I have a special love of fiction that entertains, while it informs me about real events and places in our world. **TEETH** is the work of a master storyteller. "

—Sharon Noe, Executive VP, USA

"**TEETH** is a fascinating read. A monster crocodile, soldiers, surfers, cannibals, headhunters, alluring women, mortal enemies and best of friends. It’s an epic story, brilliantly conceived and executed. It’s set primarily in New Guinea—a real place. Our heroes fight for their lives against the sweep of world events at the close of WW2. **TEETH** informed, enthralled, and moved me. Mr. Dean’s research is voluminous, insightful and meticulous. Before **TEETH**, I did not know much about the ‘Cargo Cult,’ MacArthur’s ‘forgotten war,’ or Catholicism in Japan. **TEETH** has everything going for it."

—David Williams, Reviewer, Canada

"I must say, **TEETH** is a masterpiece. It is one of the greatest books I have ever read. The whole thing is gripping. The beautiful language helps the reader envision every scene. This is the trait of a great novel. Timothy has visited Japan and studied our culture. I do not know of another novel that shows American and Japanese soldiers learning to respect and appreciate one another, and become friends. Healing the wounds of war goes on to this day.

Now I want to see the movie!"

—Yasuyuki Kasai, Samurai Descendant,
Author, “Dragon of the Mangroves”

Dedication

To Deborah,
who made this book possible.

For my parents,
Dr. Jim and Glady Dean,
who took me to New Guinea
and let me roam free.

And to the native people
of the Island of
New Guinea
— may you remember the face
of your mother and father.
Prosper, "one-talks,"
and live long!

The South Pacific
Japan
South Pacific Ocean
The Philippines
New Guinea
Australia
In 1945, the Island of New Guinea was the Territories of New Guinea and Papua on the right - now "Papua New Guinea," or PNG. And Dutch New Guinea on the left, is now claimed by Indonesia, known as "Papua" and "West Papua"

TEETH—The Epic Novel with Bite
is a work of fiction. Apart from well known actual people and major events and places that occur in the narrative, all characters names, places and incidents are figments of the author's imagination and are used fictitiously.
Any resemblance to current places and persons living or dead is unintentional and coincidental.

Published by
Readr Books
An imprint of

Readr Publishing, LLC
Las Vegas, Nevada

Save a tree! Please do not use snail mail.
All inquiries:
www.readrbooks.com

ISBN: 978-0-9825398-0-4
World War 2, 1945, South Pacific, Papua New Guinea, Philippines, Saltwater Crocodile Attack, Fiction

Printed in the United States of America
By Bookmasters, Inc., Idaho

Cover design: Dwight Kirkland ✦ www.BlackleafStudios.com

First Edition

TEETH

The Epic Novel With Bite

To Tara ...
another story to share
all my love, Dad
11-19-09

by

Timothy James Dean

#3/3000

READR BOOKS

An Imprint of
Readr Publishing, LLC
Las Vegas, Nevada
USA

www.readrbooks.com

Prologue

It begins as a stream that leaps laughing from the mountains and bounds down through the canyons, chuckling in wide rapids. A torrent at last, grown in silent strength, it loops across the tropical wilderness. Mighty as it is, the river is swallowed whole by the mangrove swamps, but oozes forth again in fat fingers across the delta. At last the café au lait waters stain the sultry blue South Pacific Ocean, forming a plume visible far out to sea.

The largest delta waterway is sixty yards across. Its banks are choked with jungle, except where the vegetation has been worn away by huge claws and dragging bodies.

A brilliant blue butterfly dances down the foliage. A fish jumps at it and falls back in the shallows. The butterfly flits over a clearing and flutters down to perch on a stone. It is newly cracked from its cocoon, and flares its wings to harden in the sun.

A tongue flicks out and the wings fold sideways and jerk into a cave that opens in thin air. A bullfrog galumphs forward, detaching from the background, the wingtips a gaudy fringe around its lips. One gulp and another, and the butterfly's brief life is done.

Its erstwhile perch begins to shake. The frog cocks its head and watches cracks web across the surface. This, it seems, is no rock. An end falls off, trailing mucus. A snout shoots from the gel. Yellow eyes with vertical irises fly open. The frog pulls its head into its chins while the newcomer struggles to birth itself.

With only its tail stuck, four clawed legs raking the mud, the hatchling attempts to walk away, but the past is not yet done with it. The infant pauses and pants while the frog grows sleepy.

At last the little one goes into a paroxysm of lashing and flings the shell off. The bullfrog sees a scaly olive back, creamy throat, and jaws lined with sharp teeth. It does not perceive this as food, and it turns on its haunches to leap into the river.

Its movement attracts attention. The hatchling comes at it on unsure legs. The frog dips its head while the other lifts its snout.

They sniff.

The baby leaps up, rising on its tail, and bites across the frog's head, sealing its nostrils. Needles sink through green flesh and agony blossoms in the amphibian brain. Now how it bucks, but its rider hangs on. Again and again, the two somersault up and crash to earth. The frog cannot breathe, and in mounting panic, it tries to shake its tormentor off. The baby whips but will not let go.

The frog gathers its hind legs and makes its most prodigious leap. The combatants cartwheel across the sky. They fall together and the hatchling strikes its head on a sharp ridge of rock, the full weight of the frog hammering down on it. The baby is slashed across an eye to the bone. But still, it will not let loose.

The bullfrog walks toward the river, dragging its terrible appendage. Its throat spasms continually and it stares at the water, so close, but forever out of reach. Its jade eyes bulge and the world goes dim. It topples on its side. The hatchling is dragged with it and rolls hard, which flops the amphibian on its back. The baby embraces the frog until the long legs scissor out, tremble, and go still.

Only now does the hatchling release its grip. It trots down the corpse's flank and stops where a leg attaches. It positions its jaws and bites again. Blood gurgles down its throat and the baby achieves its first ecstasy. It jerks its head from side to side, mewling, as the frog belly slops. The leg pops off, trailing tendons. The hatchling turns it in its mouth. In the way of its kind, it does not chew, just chomps and swallows. The limb slides down its gullet. When one end is in its stomach and a webbed foot droops from its snout, the infant rests again.

A basso rumble comes from the sky. It is so loud, the puddles tremble. The hatchling is terrified as a head a thousand times its size descends. A great fence of teeth settles on the mud. But once more, instinct comes to its aid. The little one is staring into the eye of its enormous mother. It sees her with stereoscopic vision. The slice across its head has not hurt its eye.

For a time, the two are lost in reptilian love.

At last the baby chokes down the frog foot, and in the aftermath of the kill, it turns to the river to bellow its triumph. It opens its jaws, but only a squeak emerges. Then its mother joins in, a guttural roar that makes storks defecate and mount the air. For this is the call of **Crocodylus porosus***, the giant saltwater crocodile, and the largest* *reptile on Earth.*

Upon hearing this sound the bones of all animals, including man, turn to water, for this predator feeds on their kind. It is the sly hunter that spies on them from the river, and the nightmare that surges up, seizes them in pitiless teeth and drags them down to their doom.

But at this moment, the female belies that reputation. Her twelve-foot body draped on the riverbank, she is the epitome of fond motherhood. Behind her stands a nest, a mound of clawed up mud and foliage. In it are scores of pale eggs, some whole, others in shards. This morning, upon hearing the chorus of chirps and taps from within, she gently nuzzled and scraped away the covering.

Across the clearing, a dozen miniature crocodiles take their first steps. Curiously, every one is male, but this, too, is the way of the species. The precise temperature at which they incubated determined their sex. A degree or two either way, and the entire brood would have been female.

Of them all, only the largest has killed and eaten. The baby bull still rests beside its mother. A sibling approaches, lured by the reek of death, and begins to tug at the corpse. Its brother is consumed by new sensations—rivalry and territorial rage. It charges the interloper and bites, and the two twist across the mud. The mother raises her head and grunts approval, for in her world, all is as it should be.

In the nearby jungle, her call makes the bristles rise on a wild boar. It snorts and charges off, tossing its tusks. An arrow flashes across the light and skewers the pig. It topples squealing on its side and the projectile stands. This is long as a spear, featherless, with a hollow bamboo point. The boar roots at its torment while its lifeblood pumps through the tube.

A brown man steps from the foliage. He is brawny and young and carries a black longbow and a clutch of pig arrows. White beads are woven in his kinky hair, and in the hole punched through his nasal septum are two crocodile teeth, bound together, points out. He is naked except for the cucumber-size gourd that encases his genitals, tied around his waist with bark string. A stone knife presses against his side.

The pig hunter places a foot on the boar and pulls out his arrow. He crouches with his knife and cuts the throat from ear to ear.

The boar thrashes, and the man speaks soothing words until it dies. Then he grasps the trotters and slings it around his neck. He takes his weapons and stands. Hog blood spills and he looks down at it.

An arrow slams into his chest and emerges from his back. The hunter's features contort as he sees the hardwood tip, carved in backswept barbs. His own blood flows with the boar's.

Five more Negroid warriors step from the jungle. These look so different than their victim, they might almost be a different species. Their facial features are broad, and their bodies shine coal-black. Patterns in red, white and yellow mark their faces, torsos and thighs. Through their noses are paired pig tusks, turned up towards the eyes, signifying war. Floating over them are headdresses of white egret feathers, incongruous in their delicate beauty.

These men carry longbows, but with arrows of the kind for killing men. Some wield stone-headed axes and cudgels. They, too, are naked but for their penis gourds, but these are yellow and long, leave the testes exposed, and curl in outlandish shapes.

Two of the newcomers wear especially grisly trophies. Freshly cut human heads dangle from their necks. The dead faces resemble the pig hunter—the same beads in the hair and crocodile teeth through the noses. The stricken man's eyes fix on his kin while his knees buckle. The attackers seize his arms to hold him up. One jerks the boar off his neck and runs an admiring finger along a tusk.

The most powerful of the headhunters steps to the victim. This is the Mambu-ato, *the war chief, and it is his arrow that skewers the man. He reaches a finger to the place where it punctures the ribs, dips it in hot blood, and sucks it. He flashes a grin of ebony teeth.*

He grabs the knife from his victim's fingers and carves a slice off the shoulder. The hunter jerks back, but is held firm. The chief folds the meat into his mouth and smacks his lips. His warriors shout with cruel laughter. The last thing the pig hunter sees is his own body being consumed. He jitters as his eyelids close.

His killer nestles the skull into his armpit and saws at the neck. His warriors hold the body while the chief removes the head. They chatter lightheartedly, as men will do after a successful hunt.

The mother crocodile rests near the river, jaws agape. Her son guards his kill as he stares at the muddy swirling water. A crust of blood has dried across his eye in the shape of a crescent moon.

The river spills endlessly into the sea.

Part 1
Operation Teeth

☽

"Yea, and if some god shall wreck me in the wine-dark deep,
even so I will endure...
For already have I suffered full much,
and much have I toiled in perils of waves and war.
Let this be added to the tale of those."
– Homer, The Odyssey

☼

"They died hard, those savage men—like wounded wolves at bay.
They were filthy, and they were lousy, and they stunk.
And I loved them."
– General Douglas MacArthur

❍

"*You may not be interested in war, but war is interested in you.*"
– Leon Trotsky

CHAPTER 1

PORT MORESBY ON THE SOUTHERN COAST OF NEW GUINEA - July, 1945

"Operation Teeth" is a good name.

The sixty-seven year old Commander stared through the window at the sunlight winking on the harbor. *We will show the Japs when they threaten Americans and our Allies—especially priests—they do so at their peril!* His own war was in its final days. In less than a month he'd be on the family estate halfway around the world.

Charleston, South Carolina. Put out to pasture like the old warhorse I am, he thought ruefully. *But before I go, I will see this last action through. Now, who can I send with the Major?*

Dingo Hawsey, a senior Australian officer, had volunteered to lead the Colonel's mission. *He's the ideal man. He ran his plantations before the war and he can handle the locals—speaks several of the barbaric languages. He's a veteran of the Kokoda Trail, some of the fiercest fighting seen in New Guinea. And he's as tough as a hickory axe handle.*

"Two man crew. One of ours—that's me, Henry," Dingo had said in this very office, "and one of yours. A proper Allied operation. Just make sure the bloke's not too wet behind the ears. Give me someone who's been in a scrap or two in the bush, will you?"

So who do I have? Henry asked himself. He went through a mental list, but for one reason or another, was not satisfied. Here in mid-1945, the battle had moved further and further from Port Moresby. The best of the American soldiers were gone. Certainly, hundreds of thousands of enemy remained on the vast island, but it would be up to the Aussies to round them up. Most American fighting men had departed with the Colonel's famous predecessor,

Supreme Commander and five-star General Douglas MacArthur.

Hard though it was for Henry to believe, only two months before, the Germans had surrendered. America's "Operation Overlord" had prevailed, and the Nazis had been put down. In May, a stunned peace settled across war-numbed Europe. But here in the South Pacific, World War Two beat on, hammer-and-tongs. Still, the Japanese were being driven ever closer to their homeland.

At this moment, Supreme Commander MacArthur was in Manila. He had made good his promise to liberate the Philippines. Henry Chambers pictured the General, face fierce as the American eagle emblazoned on his cap, staring north across the Pacific. The scuttlebutt was that MacArthur's "Operation Downfall," the invasion of the Japanese islands, would begin within months.

And it was thinking about the Commander that gave Henry the answer to his own, more modest, challenge. *The soldier's hell-bent on getting back to the General in time for the invasion. He might only be twenty, but he's no greenhorn. He's been fighting in these hellish jungles since he was seventeen. Dingo will like that. He's a sniper, an ace with a rifle, and that will be useful.*

The soldier was only in Port Moresby because he'd been wounded. He'd been shot through the chest and almost died. But as soon as he was mobile again, he'd started clamoring to get back in the fight.

As if the Jap Invasion is his personal war! All right, Henry decided. *I'll give him the chance to show he's fit. If he can rescue these priests, eliminate the Japs, and stay away from the crocodile—well, I'll ship him back to MacArthur. He'll get his fight.*

A beetle whizzed at him through the window. Metallic green wingcases spread wide, it struck the glass and bounced down. Unfortunately for the bug, it landed in a web. A black spider hung there, abdomen as big as a fifty-cent piece. Henry often watched these arachnids. They liked the harbor-side windows of the American compound. They wove a lacy "x" into their webs that marked dead center, where they waited. The instant the beetle tangled, the spider ran at it. As Henry watched, faintly appalled, the predator loomed and the bug redoubled its efforts to break loose. But the spider pounced and sank in its fangs. The beetle's wings drooped. The hunter touched its abdomen to it and a strand of web glistened. It spun the beetle until it was wrapped like a mummy.

This country! Something is always eating something else. Henry shuddered and returned to his desk.

"Operation Teeth" will kill two birds with one stone. I give the Major an experienced fighter, and get the gung-ho boy out of my hair for a few days. The Colonel had a flash of inspiration. *On top of that, I just may get a personal anecdote for the Foreword to my book. I have been a man of action!*

The Colonel hollered and an aide came running.

"Take my jeep to the hospital," the Commander ordered. "Find old Doc Mac. Tell him I got the message about our young American. Have him send the Private to see me at once."

"Yes Sir!" The 2nd Lieutenant was already on his way.

– ☽ –

– *Three Hours Earlier*

Johnny had thought that this time, his wound would not heal. Now, while he knew he was going to make it, it was the throb in his chest that woke him. He lay on his canvas cot, already sweating, while the feathered orchestra tuned up over the tent. His fingers massaged the welt on his chest. *It aches something fierce this morning.*

It was an important day. He had a meeting with the man who controlled his future. If Johnny had anything to do with it, that future lay north, across the Pacific Ocean. He was going to be there for the invasion of Japan. It was already mid-July, 1945, and he figured the Army would be on the move from the Philippines to Okinawa any day. For sure, the fighting would be hand-to-hand, between the houses of the enemy cities, before the year was out.

Johnny had sworn by things he held sacred to help bring down the enemy Empire. His hatred of "the Japs" ran deep, and his reasons were personal, held close to his chest.

The challenge was, he had to get himself back across the ocean to the Philippines. And here he was, languishing in hospital. He would not forgive himself if, after everything he'd been through in these three years of ferocious war, he missed the Big One.

The light gradually intensified behind the canvas wall of the shelter he shared with five other injured men. He sat up and ran his fingers through his longish dark hair, then stretched without thinking. The stab pierced him and he stifled a groan and dropped his arms.

Fight to live, he encouraged himself fiercely. *Live to fight!*

The words had echoed through his mind during the long dog-days of suffering back in the Philippines and here in New Guinea. Those were the lost months when even the doctors didn't seem to expect him to live.

Live to fight, fight to live! He didn't know where he'd come up with the chant, but he'd repeated it as if his life depended on it, and maybe it had.

During his years under General MacArthur, Johnny had been shot three times and bayoneted once. He'd taken a bullet through the thigh, one in the forearm, and there'd been the stabbing. He had a nifty scar that zigzagged down his ribcage, but at least the knife had not killed him. It was this last bullet that had almost done the trick. It had gone through his chest and out his back. That had been four months ago.

Last night, Johnny had stretched out as usual under the mosquito netting, wearing only his boxer shorts in the heat. But every time he shifted, the pain woke him up. At last he must have slept, because when next he came to, someone was whimpering. Gradually, he realized he was the source of the pitiful sounds, and he choked them off. He hoped he hadn't bothered the other guys.

Just one of my nightmares. Like most soldiers who'd fought in New Guinea, Johnny had malaria. It lived in his bloodstream and there was no cure. Every once in a while it came knocking so hard, his teeth rattled. This time the night terror had been so bad, he worried a bout of the fever was coming on, and that was the last thing he needed today.

Johnny's nightmare had been about the dead men again—the ones who died at his side, and the others he had killed. In life, they had been on opposite sides, but in death they came together.

The nightmare that woke him up this time was one of the worst. Walt, the buddy he'd arrived with in New Guinea, was bayoneted again. It had happened in the opening minutes of Johnny's first firefight, in the stinking swamps of Buna on the north coast.

The Jap runs. The scream, the scowl, the crooked tooth. The rifle and knife.

Johnny and Walt had been seventeen. Like tens of thousands of American teenagers, they'd lied about their age and joined the

Army. That particular morning, after a terrible trek across the New Guinea mountains that took more than forty days, they'd arrived at Buna. At once, their column had been ordered into the swamp towards an enemy machine gun. Walt was already sick, out of his mind with fever. He'd fallen facedown in the murk and lost his glasses.

The bayonet went deep into Walt's chest. In his dream Johnny saw Walt's mouth form the "oh!" of his death. Again, he swung his own rifle with the big knife on it and saw it pop through the enemy's neck. Both skewered men fell to the mud.

But that was where reality and the nightmare diverged. Walt and the enemy soldier had died right there, but in the nightmare they lived on. They writhed and choked and sliced their hands on the piercing steel.

"Why?" Walt asked Johnny, staring with his mild blue eyes while the blood bubbled on his lips. "Why? Why?" The sheer misery of it woke Johnny up. He lay still and waited for the images to fade. He reached under the cot for his Springfield rifle and laid it beside him. He'd acquired it the day Walt had died, all that eternity ago, back in the fall of '42. Johnny's carbine had taken a bath in the swamp that day and was useless. He saw the Springfield .30-06 in the hands of a dead GI and the shape called to the game hunter in him. It was the ideal firearm for the sniper he became.

Walt was long gone in the New Guinea mud, but Johnny still had the Springfield M1903. It had saved his life countless times, and the touch of it always brought him comfort.

The light was bright enough for him to get up. The others could sleep, but he had plans. In order to convince the brass to send him back to battle, he had to flog himself into shape. For the last two weeks, ever since he could get about well enough, he'd taken ever-longer walks through the town. And for five days, he'd even managed a little running. *If you could call it that. More of a shuffle, gasping like some broken down geezer. Maybe,* the forlorn thought entered his mind, *this time I won't bounce back.*

At once, Johnny heard from the tough-as-nails soldier in his head. This was the part of him that had done most of his thinking during the war years. *No whining! Today, you'll run the whole way!*

"Now let's hear those feet hit the deck!" as his father used to say. Johnny sighed and sat up. He pulled a thin-strapped under-

shirt over his head and tugged it down over his dog tags. He pulled on camo trousers, socks, and grabbed the worn canvas sneakers from under his bed. He'd scrounged these at the hospital. *A dead man's shoes.* He knocked them out to make sure no spiders or centipedes had taken up residence overnight, and slid in his feet. He stuffed his Zippo and a box of smokes in a pocket and went out through the screen door on its spring, catching it so it wouldn't bang and wake the others.

Just as he stepped out, the sun sailed up over the trees and drenched in gold the canvas edifices and Quonset huts that made up the Port Moresby Military Hospital. In the big tree over the tent, the birds burst into their full-throated paean to the new day. Johnny glanced around and saw only a few other people this early, medics and native orderlies coming off shift. His tent was out on the fringe. *Which is good—means I'm about done with the place.*

All his life, Johnny had been athletic. In San Diego, he'd been a pass receiver on the football team, and his track-and-field events were sprints and the long jump. He'd been fast! But then in the Territory of Hawaii, he thought the football team was lame, and he'd transferred all his considerable enthusiasm to ocean sports. He'd been sixteen when he got there, and right away, he'd admired the beachboys and their long boards. Honolulu was a growing town that attracted more and more mainland vacationers, especially since the advent of service by Pan Am, with their huge Flying Boats, the Clippers. Johnny saw that the surfers attracted the prettiest girls. During his year on Oahu, Johnny had joined their ranks. Egged on by his new friends, he'd even become an adept rider of the water mountains that thundered onto the island's north shore.

But after months in hospital, his strength had been stolen away. Somehow, he had to get it back. As he stretched out his hamstrings against the tree, he thought for the umpteenth time, *I shouldn't even be in New Guinea! What bad break brought me back here?* He figured he'd left the steaming jungles and swamps behind him for good.

And then there's Gwyndolyn. The lovely nurse bothered him! She gave him the hope there was a better, softer world. But the hard soldier was quick to bust up that illusion. *A fellow whose job is killing other men has no business feeling hope, or much of anything.*

Forget about Gwyn, the voice told him. *Remember your promise! Get back to the fight.*

Johnny headed along the muddy road towards the harbor, mustering the will to run. But on that sultry Saturday in July, Johnny had no way of knowing that in a handful of days, he'd think back on this and wonder how his plans had gone so wrong. By then, he was lost in the unexplored heart of the island, running from a great predator directly for the most bloodthirsty cannibal nation on the island.

But Johnny was sheltered from that knowledge by an ineluctable fact of the human condition. In the present, our sight is a marvelous thing, showing even the far horizon. And hindsight, as they say, is "twenty-twenty." But in the crucial direction, the one from which both destiny and destruction rush at us, we are as blind as newborns.

When it comes to peering into the future, even lofty intellects that can describe the births and deaths of galaxies at the far edge of the Universe are as nearsighted as anyone. Take Albert Einstein, one of the greatest of geniuses. Back in 1905 when he published his famous equation, $E=mc^2$ (energy = mass, multiplied by the speed of light, squared), he did not even glimpse that the Nazis would soon rise up and win Germany. Nor did he get the faintest glimmer that Hitler's henchmen would seize upon his work as their best hope for world dominion. He did not have an inkling that it would be his new home, America, that would win the desperate race to create atomic weapons of mass destruction.

On this particular Saturday morning (which, in time's relativity, was Friday night in New Jersey where Albert stood in his moosehead pajamas, brushing his teeth for bed), the physicist could not part the veil of days to the time when the practical application of his theory would alter Planet Earth forever.

"If only I had known," the physicist would one day sigh, "I should have become a watchmaker."

So, as Johnny broke into a jog, dodging the groups of natives, he did not know that the future he desperately wanted had already cut him adrift, left him behind.

Fight to live, he chanted as he quickened his pace. *Live to fight!*

CHAPTER 2

It was going to be another blistering day in Port Moresby, capital of the Territory of Papua, and the largest urban center on the island of New Guinea. "Capital," however, was a rather grandiose description for what was in truth a rough town on the edge of a savage frontier. The reason for its existence was its fine harbor, just across the gulf from the north-pointing beak of Australia.

The Equatorial sun winked on the waves and glared from the metal roofs of the buildings clustered along the shore. It glanced blindingly off the thousand puddles that pocked the roads, the legacy of the downpour of the previous afternoon. The rays burnished the dusky skin of hundreds of natives who strolled the streets, flowing among the military vehicles and vintage cars from the pre-war period.

A jeep splashed by, honking at the pedestrians. The Australian officer in the passenger seat shouted to get out of the way! Grudgingly, they obliged. *Why is the white man always in a rush?* The fenders brushed by. The Major had urgent business with the Commander of all US forces in the New Guinea Territories.

The natives' dark skin and kinky hair attested to their distant African heritage. They were thickly muscled, outfitted in tribal regalia and the brilliant trade store cloth they favored. Men and most women were bare-chested. The warriors carried homemade weapons—bamboo longbows, arrows, axes of stone and steel, and wooden clubs. Even though World War Two had brought millions of guns to New Guinea, the natives did not possess them—at least not overtly, and never in town, for these were strictly forbidden by the Australian authorities. The men carried their traditional weapons this day, not because they spoiled for a fight, but simply because they never left home without them. In fact, they were in a festive mood. Saturday was market day!

The jeep braked at an office compound. Buildings of white weatherboard were separated by plots of trimmed grass and crushed coral walkways. Beneath the Stars and Stripes, the sign indicated that this was American Army Headquarters.

The jeep's passenger, Major D. Hawsey, climbed out, grabbed his worn crocodile-skin briefcase, and headed for the entrance. The "D" stood for "Dwayne," a name the Major had loathed since he'd had to defend it with his fists in school. As far as even his closest mates knew, the "D" stood for "Dingo." The Major gave a passing glance to the Stuart tank among the canna lilies. The cannon was impressive, but the broken track betrayed another story. Tanks had been of little use in the New Guinea mud. *Steel coffins.*

Sentries flanked the front doors. They recognized the Aussie and he passed without challenge. Dingo felt sorry for them—overly dressed, in his opinion, in steel helmets, long shirts and trousers. He, by contrast, wore shorts and a light shirt. On his head was the famous "Digger" hat, a wide-brimmed affair with one side hooked up. His nod to etiquette was the white dress socks neatly folded over just under the knee, and leather shoes. Dingo had lived in New Guinea for decades, and like the natives, he was more comfortable in bare feet.

He entered the building, greeted the Sergeant at the desk by name, and strode down a hallway. He knocked on a door, heard a muffled invitation, and came into a corner office with a view of the harbor. A ceiling fan churned the humidity and beneath it, the Commander of the US Garrison, Colonel Henry Chambers, Jr., rose from his desk. He closed the journal in which he'd been writing and came towards the Australian with a crisp "good morning." Wooden sofas faced one another across a coffee table, and Henry waved Dingo to one, while he sat at the other.

"Henry, something unusual came into my possession this morning," Dingo said as he rummaged in his briefcase, "It's been carried by hand a very long way, and it's addressed to you."

"To me?" the Colonel asked in surprise. He saw what the Australian drew into the light and his nose came up like a Carolina bloodhound on the scent.

The office door banged open, interrupting the men. A young native woman backed into the room, carrying a tray with a pitcher and two glasses. She was barefoot, and bare-chested, her breasts with their chocolate tips proudly on display. Her only clothing was a red and yellow grass skirt hung low on her hips. The Colonel looked up abstractedly and sighed. *Now, what was her name? Ah yes.*

"Hala, how many times have I told you to keep your shirt on at work? Now go and put it on."

Dingo barely glanced at her. Every day both men saw native women with exposed breasts. The sight of one more—even though this one was admittedly more attractive than most—was barely cause for a raised eyebrow. Still, the Colonel insisted that the indigenous staff follow rules of decorum. The young Trobriand Islander was a newcomer to the capital. Her ethnicity was evident in the lighter skin of the offshore people. Hala spoke only a little mission-English, but she understood well enough what the boss-man said. Her experience of life, however, was that men appreciated a girl displaying the evidence she would make a good mate, one worthy of a high bride price.

Why have good tits, she thought in her home tongue, *if you do not show them off?* Her response, therefore, was merely to offer the boss-man a fetching smile as she poured, bending so that her breasts bumped together. The men, she saw slyly, could not help noticing. Ice chips rattled into the glasses, followed by the passion fruit juice. Hala departed, hips swinging.

These days, Dingo was meeting with Henry nearly every day. Soon he'd have a new Yank to break in. When Chambers had first arrived, he'd suggested to his Australian liaison that, in private, they forgo formalities. Now Dingo brandished the soiled letter.

"As I say, Henry, it's addressed to you."

"In person?"

"To your rank." He read: *"To the Commander of the American Forces in New Guinea."*

He offered the item and Chambers turned it over in his hands. It was heavily stained, almost worn through at the creases. The Colonel glanced around for the ornate Japanese dagger that served as his letter opener.

Johnny ran along the harbor-side road. There was a crowd of native people of all ages going in one direction, and he remembered it was market day. That would give some an opportunity to earn, and the others, an even greater one to spend. Many carried the shillings minted by Australia for people without pockets. The coins had holes punched through their centers. Some wore the white man's wealth on thongs around neck or wrist.

Johnny heard a babble of languages as he dodged the huddles greeting their *one-talks*—those who shared their tribal tongue. He noticed highlanders with their rugged features, coastal people with narrower ones, and the offshore Melanesians, some of whom reminded Johnny of the Hawaiians. The market was an opportunity to visit friends and kin, and to admire members of the opposite sex. Clutches of young warriors stood together, ogling the girls and making comments. Some females looked away and passed quickly by. Others, Johnny saw, met a man's gaze and smiled boldly back. Saturday was an exuberant mixture of commerce, reunions and romance, rolled into one.

Johnny heard the growl of a jeep, traveling fast. He saw natives jump out of the way. Just then, two boys came running from the crowd, chasing one another across the road. Johnny grabbed them by the necks, ignoring the twinge in his own shoulder.

"Slow down!" he told them as the vehicle barreled by.

"Yes Masta," one smiled. "Thank you, Masta," the other one said.

"Don't call me 'master!'" Johnny said. "You want some gum?" He pulled the sticks out of his pocket and handed them over.

"Thank you Mas… thank you, true!"

"Go on!" Johnny told them, "and watch where you're going."

The road was so congested he had to walk again. Over the heads he saw the marketplace among the warehouses. Once a coffee shed had stood there, but it had been bombed by the Japanese and had burned to the ground. The native market sprang up on the ring of scorched earth.

Today before first light, hundreds of vendors had come in from the villages. The women did the gardening and they came carrying nearly their own weight in *bilums*—woven string bags. These bulged with yams and sweet potatoes called *kaukau,* and a variety of vegetables. Many had a baby tucked in somewhere around her person as well. Others had infants perched on their hips, handy to the nipple, and round-bellied youngsters on their heels. Other folks carried yellow and green papayas, bundles of sugar cane on their heads, tamarillos known locally as "tree tomatoes," and baskets of purple passion fruit.

On impulse, Johnny went into the market. There were only a few Caucasians in the crush—Australian housewives, shopping for their groceries. Johnny passed between rudimentary stalls—four posts in the earth with a grass roof, or simply a mat spread on the dirt.

Many sellers offered pyramids of the green and reddish nuts called *buai*—the betel nut of the Areca palm. The stimulant was hugely popular all over the island. People chewed betel and slaked its acidic burn with quicklime. *Buai* stained their lips and gums red, and eventually, turned their teeth black. A chaw stimulated abundant saliva, which caused much spitting, and every road and public place was splattered scarlet. This disgusted the whites, but the people adored their addiction.

Johnny watched fishermen hawk strings of eels and fish. Other sellers offered chickens, both the quick and dead, and eggs piled on nests of moss. Some brought the denizens of the jungle; marsupial *cuscus* (a cuddly possum), wallabies and tree kangaroos with their extra long tails. Then there were the feathered set, great white cockatoos, green, red and blue parrots, and the flightless cassowaries with their horny crests. Most prized of all, their iridescent plumes desired for headdresses and body decoration, were the Birds of Paradise. These jay-size birds looked like they'd fallen into vats of neon bright paint.

The cacophony in the market was deafening, but above it rose the scream of pigs. All their lives, these had been coddled like children. They shared the family home, and some had suckled at a woman's breast with her infants. But at last their true status in village life had been revealed. They were run down, trussed up, and cheerfully dragged to market. In fact, they were all *kaikai*—food. The hogs did not accept their reversal of fortune quietly. All gave earsplitting voice to their outrage.

As a million flies and mosquitoes swarmed uninvited to the feast, the crowd descended on the vendors. Jeering and joking, alternately trading insults and wheedling for mercy, the people bargained for live and butchered animals, fresh vegetables and not-so-fresh fish.

Johnny cut through the marketplace ripe with body odor and the stench of animals. He approached a group from the Catholic mission. Dozens of teenage native girls were dressed in plaid skirts, and white blouses, with socks and shoes. Overseeing them were several nuns and a white-haired priest, all sweltering in dark woolens. Arranged in a line were their baskets piled with exotic fruit from their compound—guavas, mangoes and melons.

Two of the older girls spotted the approach of the tall American. His dark hair hung on his neck, and they took in the strong arms, chest, and flat stomach under his tight undershirt. They nudged one another and turned dazzling smiles on the dreamy young man.

"Hey handsome!" one sang out, "You see something you like?" She turned her significant caboose and wiggled it.

"You want some mangoes?" the other one called, putting her hands under her breasts and lifting them. There was a collective gasp from the nuns, who ran at the girls and began to slap.

"Naughty! Verra naughty!" Johnny caught an accent thick as porridge. The teenagers were unperturbed. They warded off the blows, beaming all the while. Johnny grinned and winked. He stepped by while the old priest glared at him, jowls aquiver.

"Padre," Johnny said, touching a finger to his head. The gaggle giggled while the scandalized nuns clucked over them.

Johnny turned back and took to the road once more. As he got further away, the crowd thinned and he could run again. His muscles were warm, and he felt a welcome surge of returning energy. He broke into a sprint, jumping the puddles.

Gwyndolyn picked her way towards the hospital, trying not to muddy her shoes. She chatted with Ruthie, her fellow nurse and apartment mate. Even though it was early, it was already ferocious with the kind of heat only the tropics could brew up. Towards the harbor, the sky was blue, but purple-bottomed cumuli were stacking against the inland hills.

It will pour again this afternoon, Gwyn thought, loosening the collar of the uniform she'd ironed last night. This morning, she showered in cool water and slipped it on. Just before leaving the apartment she added the winged cap, bobby-pinned to her chestnut curls.

Gwyn was twenty-three, and a graduate of the Vancouver School of Nursing. A small-town girl from the interior of British Columbia, her life, like millions of others, had been transformed by the second world war in only thirty years. Because of it, all her experience as an RN had been overseas. Gwyn had responded to the

Motherland's call for assistance from her former colonies, the Commonwealth of Nations.

Gwyn had met Ruthie Flynn, an Irish nurse, at the hospital in London. After several months there, both had volunteered to take part in the Allied effort in the South Pacific. At the military hospital in Port Moresby, their patients remained soldiers, but American and Australian instead of British.

At first they had bunked with other nurses on the hospital grounds. They had a common room where they could listen to the news and music on the radio. But soon, as they had done in London, they went in search of private digs. Nearby, they found a flat—the floor of a house owned by an elderly New Zealand couple. It had two small bedrooms, a kitchenette with its own kerosene refrigerator, and a bathroom with a shower bucket.

Most of their time was spent at the hospital. In her spare time, Gwyn made friends with the Australian women. Many were long-time residents who had married men with government jobs or plantations. They set up home and raised their families.

Of course, that was before the Japanese invaded New Guinea. In 1942, the Imperial Navy had steamed around the island toward the capital, and their aircraft had bombed it. The enemy even dared attack Darwin on the north coast of Australia. Thankfully, the American Navy thwarted their incursion, at the Battle of the Coral Sea. Not to be stopped so easily, the enemy then swarmed overland. When it appeared Port Moresby would fall, the women fled with their progeny for "Aus"—Australia.

But here in 1945, in Port Moresby at least, the threat was over. The Aussie womenfolk returned. Once more, they took command of their homes and became the hub around which the men revolved.

The women were earthy and practical, in Gwyn's experience, many with a plainly spoken exterior that masked a pillowy heart. She also struck up friendships with the natives. Contrary to some advice she received—not to get too familiar—she visited them in their humble houses. Gwyn found them to be respectful, generous with whatever they had, and possessors of a lively sense of humor. She enjoyed the frequent laughter.

It was while visiting these native sections of town that she discovered the homeless children. Bands roamed the streets, looking for handouts, sleeping where they could. The balmy temperature made that easy, but Gwyn was troubled that these youngsters had no home, no one to love them. She made inquiries and found they were victims of the war. Some were "half castes," the mixed-race legacy of foreign soldiers. One way or another, they were all orphans.

Gwyn's heart went out to them and her project was born. In it, she found a powerful ally in the Director of the hospital, Doctor Gillis MacClure. The elderly medical man known to everyone as "Doc Mac," went to bat for her with authorities. Recently, Gwyn had been granted possession of a huge house, run down as it was and in need of repair. The Aussie owners had perished in a wartime shipwreck, and no heirs had yet shown up. She would not get ownership papers, she was told, but for the time being, the seedy plantation-style home was hers.

Gywn dubbed it "the Good Shepherd Orphanage," and she raised funds and volunteer work parties from the local churches. Carpenters cut away the worst of the rot, and the place got a coat of Army-green paint, courtesy of the Americans. Gwyn hired a three-person native staff to cook and clean. Soon she had sixteen boys and girls, ages two through nineteen, living in the house.

She set up school in the living room. She cajoled Ruthie and Australian friends to teach. True, it was little more than the alphabet, simple words, and the addition and multiplication tables, but it was better than nothing.

The Orphanage consumed all of Gwyn's spare time. Ever more frequently, her nights were spent sleeping there. She and Ruthie began to talk about what had become increasingly clear. One day soon, Gwyn would move into the Good Shepherd for good.

But on this Saturday morning as she and Ruthie walked to work, Gwyn was unable to focus on the children. Nor was she following the story Ruthie told about last night's dance. Gwyn was thinking about a man she'd agreed to meet later today. She'd noticed the warm gleam in his eye for some time now, and at last he had forced the situation to come to a head.

And that's unfortunate, Gwyn thought. She liked him well enough, but the encounter was going to turn out badly.

For him, that is.

Chapter 3

The Colonel noticed an unpleasant odor wafting off the letter. He brought it gingerly toward his nose. *Stale sweat, smoke—God knows what else!* He picked the Japanese dagger off the table. The men had made a present of it when he'd arrived. He slid the scrolled blade under the flap as Dingo continued talking.

"A patrol brought that in—they'd been out a coupla-hundred miles to the west. They ran across a native runner out there, or vice versa, I suppose. My blokes reckon that *bush kanaka* had spent a month crossing the mountains. *'One-fella moon'*—you know how they talk. The bugger was starved. They had to feed him before he could speak.

"Turns out the *kanaka* had walked all the way from the Catholic mission at the headwaters of the Raub River. Kissim! Know where that is, Henry? Don't blame you if you don't—few do. Other side of the bleedin' mountains. Blimey! The Raub River flows north from there—other way from us, exits on the north coast. Much shorter for our runner to go down the 'Big River,' as the locals call it, but not a good idea. Very bad one. Get to that in a moment. Somehow he managed to cross the range—no small feat in itself. I tell you, Henry, no white man would have made it, not even me." Dingo grinned. "Somehow this *kanaka* managed to avoid his own bloodthirsty countrymen along the way."

The Colonel was well aware Dingo had lived in New Guinea for more than twenty years. It came up regularly in his conversation. The Major called all natives "*kanakas*" unless one was from deep in the jungle, and then he was a *"bush kanaka."* The Australian had grown coconuts at the coast and coffee in the high country. When the Japanese invaded, along with every other able-bodied male, he joined the army. "The wife and sprouts," he shipped back to Aus, to her parents' farm. He'd closed down his plantations for the duration, and turned the Moresby house into bachelor quarters.

The Colonel wanted to get to the letter, but he had his duties as host. He passed a glass of juice to Dingo and took a sip of his own.

"Ta," the Major said. He hung his hat on a knee and drank, while the fan lifted the damp tendrils off his forehead. He drained his glass, wiped his lips with the back of his hand, and continued.

"We haven't had any contact with Kissim since before the war. Between the crocodiles and the cannibals, Henry, the Raub River is the last place you want to be. The priests used to get their supplies by air—the only way in and out. But all that ended with the war. Truth is, with the Japs on their way, we forgot about the poor bastards. Might as well have dropped off the face of the Earth."

"I want to hear more," the Colonel said, "but let's get to the letter."

"Aw yes," Dingo said. "Must admit—got my ears perked up."

— ☆ —

EXCERPT FROM THE JOURNALS OF COLONEL HENRY CHAMBERS, JR.
US ARMY, NEW GUINEA, 1945

The Importance of Teeth

Dear Reader, in order to comprehend New Guinea, you must grasp its size. The island is the second largest in the world, after Greenland, three hundred thousand square miles sprawled across the South Pacific. It is larger than our great State of Texas—more than twice the size of the British Isles.

This impossibly rugged land has perhaps six million inhabitants. This is a rough estimate, as it remains mostly unexplored and extremely dangerous. The Stone Age savages are divided into a thousand tribes that speak a thousand entirely different languages, none of which are written. That makes New Guinea a linguist's paradise, and an administrator's nightmare.

For four hundred years, it was mostly the coastal dwellers who had any interaction with the outside world. These were the ones to meet the sailing ships that brought explorers, adventurers, pirates, whalers, traders, and eventually, colonists and missionaries.

It was the 16th Century Spaniard, Ortiz de Retez, who gave the island its name. Perhaps he was reminded of Guinea in Africa, and he named the exotic place on the far side of the world, "Nueva Guinea."

In the early 19th Century, a vertical line drawn with a ruler down a map in Europe split the island neatly in half. Never mind that it parted rivers, carved tribal lands and even bisected villages. Half a world away, the tiny Netherlands claimed the western portion.

The eastern half was split again with horizontal lines. The British colony of Queensland, in Australia, claimed "Papua," the southern section. ("Papua" is another ancient name for the place, signifying "frizzy hair").

The northern portion was annexed by Germany under the grand title of "Kaiser Whilhelmsland." Deutschland's interest was trade. In order to meet the burgeoning demand for oil, they wanted "copra"—the dried meat of the coconut. As well, they collected exotic pelts, feathers and shells. Many a fraulein had her ensemble set off with an artifact from a headhunter's hand.

As well as literally having to keep their heads while they conducted business here, the challenge for the Germans was how to pay the natives. What would be the coin of the realm with people who placed no value on silver and gold? As with elsewhere in the new worlds, a handful of glass beads went a long way. The gaudy Dutch variety had been popular for centuries. They could barter bolts of cloth, steel knives and axes, and more, but what could they use for currency itself?

They observed that some natives paid one another with teeth—the teeth of crocodiles, the huge fruit bats called "flying foxes," and dogs. Yes, dogs. Some wealthy villagers sported elaborate canine necklaces that made them walking banks.

The 19th Century Deutschlanders hit upon the splendid idea of manufacturing these coveted denticles. Back in the Fatherland once more, their factories began to spit out porcelain. When the traders of the "Neu Guinea Kompanie" sailed again to the "insel der kannibalen" (island of the cannibals), they brought New Guinea money by the caseload. The natives were stunned by the result. These teeth were translucent, absolutely perfect. The pale men must possess the master race of dogs!

For a time, the false teeth did increase Deutschland's bite of New Guinea trade, but they also spread a peculiarly Western malaise; inflation. The factories would churn out far more canine currency than Nature could ever produce.

When the Fatherland fell during World War One (not yet three decades ago at the time of this writing), German New Guinea was erased from the maps. While the Dutch managed to hold the western half, the entire eastern portion came under Australian dominion, now known as the Territories of Papua and New Guinea.

Significantly, even then, it was Japan that laid claim to the other German dominated islands of the South Pacific.

The rest of the world should have been paying closer attention.

Johnny was puffing like a steam engine and his knees were rubbery. The drill of pain in his chest had become a general torment down his left side. Johnny's fingers dug into his shoulder, but he did not slow his pace.

This latest wound was the only one he had not taken in New Guinea. This time, he'd been shot in the ancient Asian city once called "the Jewel of the Orient." Of course, that was before the war knocked Manila down.

Johnny had spent most of the war in New Guinea, then gone with Supreme Commander MacArthur to the Philippines. He'd been there to see the General, with his senior officers and Filipino dignitaries, wade ashore at Leyte Island. He was in the throng of soldiers landed that day. MacArthur had made a rousing speech and then came down the line of men. He recognized Johnny and stopped.

"God's hand is with us, my boy," he said, clapping his shoulder and smiling around his pipe. "The eyes of the world are watching. I have returned, and we will prevail!"

The next time he saw the Commander was on the road to Manila. Johnny was in the back of a truck with other GIs, part of a huge convoy wheeling through the towns. There was a festive feeling in the air. Filipino families lined the roads, cheering their liberators on. Johnny watched the jeep come charging from the rear and recognized the peaked cap, hawk nose, and aviator sunglasses. General MacArthur towered up in his seat.

"Faster men!" he boomed, sweeping his arm. "On to Manila!" A column of tanks rattled by on the embankment. No doubt they would get there first.

But the Philippines turned out to be anything but a cakewalk for MacArthur. Four hundred and thirty thousand seasoned Japanese troops were massed there, and they'd had years to dig in. Every GI who'd faced them on other fronts knew what fighters they were, often choosing death over surrender. And in the Philippines, "the Japs" were made even more determined by their predicament. If they were beaten here, the Yankees' next stop was unthinkable, intolerable; their own sacred homeland.

For his part, Johnny was in good spirits as the convoy swept toward the capital. Every mile brought him one step closer to fulfilling the ardent vow he'd made as a sixteen-year-old boy.

But that was before an enemy bullet almost put the period at the end of his life story.

CHAPTER 4

MANILA, THE PHILIPPINE ISLANDS – February, 1945

The city had been his one-time headquarters and Supreme Commander MacArthur would retake it at any cost. While the tanks were still rolling over the barriers around the city, the General was planning his victory parade. That proved premature by a month.

"The Nips," as MacArthur called them, were fanatical in their defense, and the battle raged street-by-street, foot-by-foot, every advance bought in blood. The enemy gunned down as well the Filipinos who got in their line of fire—men, women and children. By the time it was over, a hundred thousand bodies lay moldering in the ruins, and the Japanese added the Massacre of Manila to the Rape of Nanking, and a sorry list of war atrocities.

In the Philippines, as in New Guinea, Johnny was a sniper. It was a job for which he'd received no training, for the simple reason that the US Army had no sniper program at the time. But Johnny grew up in a military family in which the men were hunters.

When he was seven, his father taught him to stalk rabbits with a .22 rifle. When he was twelve, he shot his first deer, an eight-point buck. At fourteen, Johnny was finally invited along on the men's annual big game trip. At a private reserve in the California Sierra Mountains, he saw his father and grandfather each shoot a Tule Elk bull, the kind with the thick antlers.

That first year, Johnny was permitted only to observe. He was to do what he was told, and stay out of the way. Still, he was in his glory. He slept with the men in the tents and walked the pine-forested trails. He listened to the way Dad and Granddad spoke with the guides and outfitters, and he soaked up their manner of speech. He learned to sit silently for long hours in the blinds, no matter how restless he got, making no complaint.

For his fifteenth birthday, Johnny's parents gave him what at once became his prized possession—a scope-mounted, .30-06 Remington rifle.

In the fall of 1940, the boy killed a seven hundred pound "Tulie" with a huge rack. The last time he'd seen the head, it was on the wall of his grandfather's study in San Diego. Where it was now, he did not know. His grandmother had passed away early in the war, and in December last year, he'd got the cable that told him the retired Rear Admiral had succumbed to a heart attack. The attorney who sent the telegram told Johnny the house would be sold, and his portion of the inheritance would be held in trust, awaiting instructions. So far, Johnny had done nothing about it.

Not long after that hunting trip, Johnny's father received new orders, and the family transferred to Hawaii. A year later, with the world as he knew it torn to shreds, and his country at war, Johnny returned to San Diego. His stay did not last long.

Contrary to his grandparents' wishes, as soon as he turned seventeen, Johnny ran away. He turned into the nearest Army recruitment post, lied about his age and signed up. The officer was content to take his word for it. But even before he hit boot camp, the boy who barely shaved the fuzz off his lip was an expert shot.

Still, it was not until he got to New Guinea that he saw enemy infantry and killed his first man. During his initial day in battle, in fact, he killed five of them. He seemed to have a knack for it. At first it was horrific, overwhelming. But men dying, Japanese, American and Australian, quickly became the everyday norm, almost humdrum. The Army made attack after attack in the equatorial jungles, against an enemy that knew how to fight in this country. The Japanese built nearly impregnable bunkers from local materials, and in the dense foliage, the GIs often did not see them until they were on top of them. The fighting was fierce, often with pistols and knives, and the slaughter was close up and personal.

Most Sad Sacks hated New Guinea, but this was just where Johnny wanted to be. At first, he was just another GI on the front line. But early on, his marksmanship with a rifle brought him to the attention of the brass. Johnny had found his niche. He became a specialist, a shooter reserved for the long-range kill.

From one jungle battle to the next, a routine evolved. First, the regular troops went in. Field command came behind, Johnny with them. When the front line got into trouble, as it usually did, pinned down by enemy riflemen and machine guns, the young sniper was ordered to the front.

Up where the guns were shooting and men dying, the teenager crept alone into the jungle. At first he was as frightened as any boy would be, but he soon learned to do his work. After a while, he found that he looked forward to the times when he was by himself. Then he was the lone wolf, the ambush predator, the anti-sniper sniper.

Without any manual to tell them what to do, he and the other crack shots evolved their own techniques. Some dug a hole and waited under a nest of branches. Others liked to stay on the move, ghosting from one cover to the next. Johnny preferred the high ground with an eagle-eye view of the enemy.

Sometimes he looked down from a hill on a Japanese encampment, but his favorite place was up a tree. These, he learned to pick carefully. They must have sufficient foliage to conceal him, while providing a view of the target. The trunk had to be stout enough to stop a bullet, and the branches spaced for climbing.

After a few close calls, he learned to ensure as well that each perch offered an escape route. After two or three shots, the enemy guns would turn his way. Patrols came at a run. By then, Johnny needed to have slipped down the blind side of the tree. Then he'd either be picking off the Japanese from another location, or gone entirely.

The teenager became a student of enemy behavior. He preferred to shoot officers, and he'd learned the strategy early in life. Johnny recalled the day when he was six and his father took him to the woodpile with a chicken. Dad laid the protesting bird on the chopping stump. Down the axe swung: *whack!* There went the head. Dad set the body on its feet and Johnny was amazed to watch it run in a circle, but it only managed a few steps before it keeled over. The shock of the unexpected death made tears spring to the boy's eyes, but that transformed into startled laughter at the corpse's antics.

"Remember, Johnny," his father told him, "cut off the head, and the body dies. When you take out the leader, the followers don't know what to do." At the time, Johnny had been in a series of fistfights at school, and he'd taken beating after beating from an older boy. Johnny had expected his father to come to his rescue, but the man would not intervene. Instead, he explained there was a pecking order, "on the schoolyard and in life," and Johnny might as well start finding his place in it. But his Old Man did teach him how to use his fists, and his feet.

"Never show them you're afraid, even when you're being beaten," his dad said. "Don't pick fights, but never back down from one. You start running, and you'll never stop." The next lesson had been the one with the chicken and the axe.

"You beat the ringleader," his father said, picking up the dead chicken, "and the others will back off. That applies to the coward at school as well. And remember this: any boy who bullies a smaller one is a coward."

Johnny never backed down from a fistfight. He had some wins and some losses. When he was small, there were always bigger boys. He developed a reputation as a fierce fighter, and he learned to hide his hurts behind a dark scowl. His dad arranged boxing lessons with a military coach, and Johnny's last schoolyard fight happened when he was fourteen. After that, he was on the football team, as big as many and faster than most. The gridiron gave him a place where the venting of aggression was approved.

Years later, alone in the jungle against an enemy who would kill him as soon as look at him, Johnny remembered the headless chicken. Many a Japanese officer paid the price. Of course, picking off the brass was a practice of both sides. Smart commanders quickly learned to remove evidence of their rank. Johnny taught himself to watch body language. The Japanese had a hard time hiding their hierarchical nature. Even across the distance, he saw who took orders, and who gave them.

Johnny had a high rate of success as a hunter of men, and his reputation spread. Still, many of the GIs disdained snipers. They seemed to think there was something unmanly about shooting a man from a distance. But Johnny remembered the stories his grandfather told him about the American frontiersman with his long rifle hiding in the woods, knocking down the British redcoats.

Soon he did not even want to know the names of the new arrivals at the front. Too many of them would soon go down in the mud for good. He tended to stick to himself. Johnny got a name as a loner and a hard case.

But there were times when he did get in another man's face. That was when the fellow did something stupid that got soldiers hurt or killed. Then Johnny couldn't seem to help giving the guilty party a piece of his mind. Unfortunately for his career, he pursued this course of action even when that other man was his superior officer. He was a natural leader in a fight, and he'd often received a field promotion, only to have it ripped away when he shot off his mouth. Johnny didn't care. In fact, he didn't want to get promoted out of the fight.

February of '45 found him still a Private, still practicing his solitary craft, but this time, in an urban jungle. The sniper trailed the line through Manila, Springfield in hand, pockets bulging with rations and shells. Often he was away from base for days at a time, eating his meals cold, sleeping in the ruins. His high ground became the roofs and windows of shattered buildings. From here he picked off the enemy: *every shot a kill.* When the front moved, Johnny drifted behind it like an avenging spirit.

In his three weeks in Manila, he added sixty-three kills to his private count. Only two of those were confirmed. It was rare for other soldiers to witness his marksmanship. But the official tally meant nothing to Johnny. His score was personal.

Eventually, the Americans drove the enemy back into "Intramuros," the ancient walled city-within-a-city. It had been constructed during the five centuries the islands belonged to Spain. Their very name was for King Felipe, the Spanish monarch. Intramuros was their priceless colonial legacy.

When "the Nips" took refuge in Intramuros, General MacArthur had them trapped. Their backs literally to the wall, he knew they would fight to extinction. Unwilling to expend any more of his men against their desperation, MacArthur made the difficult decision to shell them where they stood.

By the time Johnny got there, edifices that had survived the centuries lay strewn about in blocks. Ahead along a rubble-choked street, he saw the GIs were holed up in one building, exchanging fire with the enemy across the way. Worn steps took him up a splinter of wall. He lay on the sun-warmed top and watched. Soon he had pinpointed two enemy snipers in the blown-out windows.

Johnny tugged out a square of velvet, folded it, then again, and laid it on the wall's edge. He rested the barrel of his rifle on it and slid a nickel-clad shell into the chamber. He found his first target in the crosshairs, drew a breath, smoothly released, and fired.

The shot was just one more in the melee. The enemy crumpled. Johnny panned to the second man as his fingers reloaded. He found him kneeling near the edge of broken flooring, his rifle aimed down at the unseen GIs. As Johnny watched, the man fired again and he felt the cold anger rise. He increased slightly the pressure on his right index finger.

This time, the enemy made the long dive to the cobblestones, rifle clattering beside him. Johnny reloaded and continued to watch.

An American tank rumbled into the street, clanked over the bodies and broken stone. As Japanese bullets clanged off the turret, the big gun turned their way. The cannon boomed and walls exploded. Johnny picked off three more defenders when they attempted to escape through a side door.

Fifteen minutes later, the building was another smoking hulk, and the GIs were on the move again. Johnny descended and went after them, hugging the walls. Often he paused to scan ahead, searching for enemy practitioners of his own dark trade.

He heard them before he saw them. In a sunken doorway, two small children stood sobbing. A small boy and girl were beside another Filipina who Johnny guessed was eleven or twelve. She sat silently, legs splayed, staring at him with huge eyes. Her hands clutched her thin stomach, and Johnny noticed the crimson stain spreading across her sundress.

Gut shot—going to die, the soldier commented. Johnny went into a crouch and ran across the road. He spoke quiet words to the little ones and slung his rifle over his shoulder. *I'll find her a medic.*

He bent to pick the girl up, and that's when he was shot.

It was several days before he discovered what had happened. The bullet smashed a rib as it entered his upper left chest, clipped the lung on the way through, broke two more ribs and shattered his scapula on exit. Johnny came to his senses in a hospital bed, swaddled in bandages.

One of the first things he saw was his Springfield standing in the corner. He was relieved. The rifle had been with him so long, it was about as important as one of his own limbs. The scope, he'd brought from home. He'd unscrewed it from his elk rifle the night he ran away to join up.

The middle-aged nurse told him the rifle came in with him. He'd babbled about it in his delirium, and his American doctors decided to leave it with him. The nurse opened the drawer of the bedside table and showed him the Zippo lighter and folding knife that had been in his pockets. Johnny thanked her. These had belonged to his dad and were the only personal things he had left.

He never did meet the medics who brought him in. Nor could he discover what had happened to the children, no matter how many times he asked. In the scope of the devastation of Manila, three more lives hardly seemed to matter.

Johnny's bullet almost killed him, but he had youth on his side and began to heal. But then tropical bacteria invaded. Day by day, the boy grew sicker. Somehow, he clung to life, but he was not improving. March became April, and still he lay suffering.

The papers were full of the action in Europe as American, Russian and British forces raced for Berlin. Late in the month, the newspapers trumpeted shocking news. The bodies of Adolph Hitler and his mistress, Eva Braun, had been found, burned in their Berlin bunker. The Nazi leader's vision of a thousand-year Reich had ended with him eating a bullet from his pistol.

With the architect of their misbegotten dream gone, the whole Nazi house of cards caved in. On May 8th, much of the world went wild, Manila included, with the news that Germany had signed the unconditional surrender.

Johnny Willman was too gravely ill to enjoy the victory party. His physicians decided that the boy needed to be sent Stateside, urgently, on the next available ship.

"It's the end of the war for you," they told the young man. "Back home they've got the newest equipment and latest drugs. You'll do better out of this heat. They'll get you well and give you your old life back. Son, you've done your part."

Problem was, Johnny didn't want his old life back, and unlike many of the men, he wasn't looking for a way out. He hadn't fought from '42 to '45 only to miss out on the invasion of Japan! He did his best to explain this to every doc who came by. They smiled and humored him, and kept his name high on the evacuation list.

It was only the young New Zealand doctor who really seemed to hear him. Johnny latched onto him as his last, best hope. Every chance he got, he told the doc he did not want to be sent Stateside. The Kiwi heard him out, but Johnny sensed he hadn't quite convinced him. He was forced to play his last ace. He told the doc what had happened to his parents.

In all his years of war, Johnny had never recounted this. When other guys asked about his folks, he just said they had passed on and clammed up. He got a few curious looks, but others could tell by his clenched jaw he didn't want to talk. The truth was, this was Johnny's deepest wound, and he did not know how to cope with it, except by doing his job.

But dire circumstances called for desperate measures. This time when the Kiwi doc came by, Johnny asked him to close the door. Then, in blunt phrases, voice raw with emotion, he told him what happened. As the doctor listened, he found he had a lump in his throat. His patient finished up by saying, "That's why I have to keep fighting the Japs until they're finished. Understand? I made a promise." The young American stared into the other man's eyes and knew he'd made an ally.

"I'll help if I can," the Kiwi said, "but whatever we do, you need to stay under medical care. Otherwise you'll die. That's a fact."

"I hear you, doc," Johnny said. Every heartbeat still pulsed in the wound, and he saw the way the physicians' faces looked when they peeled back the bandages.

The newspapers said tens of thousands of American troops were now on the ships, on their way back from Europe. For once, General MacArthur would have all the able-bodied soldiers he needed.

"If they send me Stateside, I'm never coming back. If I could end up in Australia, on the other hand, once I'm better, they'll send me to my unit—right here with the General in the Philippines. You see?"

The Kiwi, Dr. Cowell was his name, did see, but Johnny's scheme was a very long shot. Then, in early July, it looked like he was sunk. In a week's time, a ship would take thousands of Americans to Los Angeles. His doctors had determined John Willman would be on it.

Gloomily, Johnny almost accepted defeat. But then, only two days before he was due to ship out, Doc Cowell came by. A British hospital vessel had just put into Manila harbor with a load of Aussie POWs from the camps in Asia. Some two thousand men, sick and near starvation, were being ferried home. The ship had stopped to take on the Aussies liberated during the Battle of Manila. A few were at this hospital, and they would be transferred aboard this very night. The Kiwi and the Yank put their heads together.

And that was how it happened that just after midnight, a young man on a stretcher was manhandled up a ramp at the Manila docks. At the ship's gangway waited a knot of officers and doctors and Johnny feigned unconsciousness as they checked his papers. His stretcher was transferred from one set of hands to another, and he was carried into a vast hold. He saw hundreds of skeletal men reclining on the rows of beds. His bearers found a vacant one and transferred him onto it. There was a bad moment when they saw the rifle hidden under the sheet. One tried to remove it, but the soldier would not let go. A tug of war ensued. Without speaking, the sick man demonstrated that it was unloaded, then firmly tucked it against his leg once more.

The orderlies had a great deal to do before the ship sailed on the tide. They shrugged and left the fellow alone. These chaps had been through an ordeal most couldn't imagine. Johnny lay back sweating from the exertion. He had not spoken, because he knew that if he did, the jig would be up.

Eventually the banks of lights were switched off and the men fell silent. His wound already suppurating through the dressing, Johnny lay wide-awake as the hours crawled by. Finally, still in pitch darkness, he felt the vibrations that told him the great engines had started up. An hour later, he felt the roll of the ocean. Only then did he drift into an exhausted slumber.

The breakfast trolleys had come and gone and it was late morning before the British doctors came down his row. They finished with the malnourished man beside him and gathered around Johnny's bed. Again, the medical men checked his papers. Apparently there was some discrepancy between the injury described there, and the bandaged chest of the fellow before them. They unwrapped the dressing and exclaimed over what was obviously a badly infected bullet wound.

They peppered the patient with pointed questions, and finally Johnny had to answer. As soon as they heard the marked Californian accent, the doctors knew this was not the Corporal from Woolgoolga his papers claimed him to be. Some terrible mix-up had occurred. They poured over the lesion, disinfected it as best they could, doused it with antibiotic powder and made him swallow some pills. Then they bandaged the boy up and moved to the next case. One of them climbed to the bridge and reported the mistake, but the Captain did not even consider turning the ship around.

The sole Yank on board watched the gulls drifting by the portholes, against the heave of the South China Sea, and even managed a weak smile.

The floating hospital powered down the South Pacific and entered the waters between the New Guinea coast and the Solomon Sea. It rounded the eastern tip of the big island and turned toward Sydney.

Suddenly an underwater explosion rocked the ship. In spite of the crosses painted on her, the floating hospital had come under fire. The hull shuddered along its length and began to sink. Fortunately, it was not the kind of direct hit that would send her plunging in minutes to the bottom, the fate of so many vessels in these waters during the war. The bridge, in fact, never saw what had attacked them. Perhaps it was a submarine, or simply a rogue mine that had slipped its cable.

What mattered was to save the lives on board. Listing to starboard, all her pumps on full, the ship sped for the nearest harbor. That happened to be Port Moresby, on the southern coast of New Guinea. Once in the harbor, the captain deliberately ran his command aground in the shallows so it could not sink. Most of the passengers would be offloaded long enough for the welders to go to work on the old plates at low tide.

The doctors saw to it, however, that the young American was immediately lowered on his stretcher over the side. By then he had been in a coma for two days. His wound, already septic, had turned gangrenous. The medics had observed the stench and the blackening flesh. They pursed their lips, shook their heads and held out scant hope for the poor Yank. Johnny was loaded in an ambulance truck and rushed to the military hospital.

One foot in the grave, far too ill by then to even know where he was, Johnny had returned to the place where he had first gone into battle.

FROM THE JOURNALS OF COLONEL HENRY CHAMBERS, JR.

The Most Warlike Place On Earth

For tens of thousands of years, the New Guineans lived in the Stone Age, and most still do. The people never discovered the wheel, let alone metallurgy. They live in huts with dirt floors, without running water or any civilized amenity. To this day, for most of them, their toilet is the nearest bush. Their enemy is the tribe just over the hill. Yet though their technology is primitive, their societies are complex, infinitely varied, and highly evolved.

At puberty, the warriors initiate the boys into manhood during secret and often violent rites. In many tribes, these include the scarification of the body, and the piercing of the nasal septum. The resulting hole between their nostrils allows for the wearing of many items in the face. Commonly, these are pig tusks, the teeth and bones of animals, and feathers. In Port Moresby, around your Author's office, some of the men find it a convenient way to carry a pencil.

Once the youngsters are recognized as men, they join their elders in the interminable vendetta battles with their traditional enemies. For many tribes, the hostilities go hand-in-hand with a grisly culinary habit abhorred in the civilized world.

Dear Reader, millions of New Guineans are cannibals. Not only do they kill their neighbors—they eat them. Men, women and even children partake of the human repast.

On the maps, New Guinea might appear tame to you, neatly divided by lines. This masks the truth. Most of the ferocious island is unexplored.

More than a million inhabitants of the rugged Highlands never even clapped eyes on a white man until recently. The interior was so mountainous, it was thought to be uninhabited. That was so until the coming of aircraft. Aviators in the late 1920's flew over and saw gardens and villages—evidence of habitation in what had been blank space on the maps. In 1930, rough Australians braved the heights. Armed with guns and guard dogs, they searched for gold.

In the Highlands, they came face-to-face with flourishing Stone Age communities that had no experience of the outside world. The *result was a clash of cultures that reverberates to this day. Some of the villagers fainted dead away at the sight of the white men—the ghosts of their ancestors, or so they believed. Some of the warriors' envy of the goods the foreigners possessed turned to sudden violent acquisitiveness. The Australians were forced to demonstrate just what their firearms could do, at considerable cost of native lives.*

This was a profound event—the very last time Earth would witness such a substantial, isolated tribal community meeting the outside world. The visitors began to trade—a knife for a pig, an axe head for a native girl. It was those young women who first discovered that these were not gods, but men.

Ironically, many New Guineans' introduction to "civilization" was World War. In 1942, the Japanese war machine stormed onto the island. The Asian invaders saw themselves as superior to the natives and ran roughshod over them.

The Australians, and our troops when America arrived, treated the inhabitants more humanely. As a result, the Allies won the support of most Papuans and New Guineans. Thousands of our men owe their lives to the villagers who carried them to medical aid. The natives earned the name given by the Australians: "the Fuzzy Wuzzy Angels."

Yet, while the New Guineans marvel at the modern machines of war and the sheer scale of the slaughter the white and yellow men exacted on one another, they are no strangers themselves to mortal combat.

New Guinea may be the most warlike place on Earth.

The Colonel extracted from the envelope a folded sheet of yellow paper. Moisture had seeped through and blurred the writing that covered both sides. Henry scanned the first lines, turned it over and glanced at the signature, then began to read from the beginning. He looked up only when the Australian cleared his throat.

"Yes Dingo. The writer signs himself 'Father Christopher Bastion' and gives the address as 'The Mission of Our Lady of Perpetual Help, Kissim Village, Raub River.' He says he's an American priest from Kingman in Arizona. 'My dear Commander and my fellow American, I am in need of your mercy and your urgent assistance.'" The Colonel read ahead and paraphrased.

"Bastion and three others arrived to establish the mission in 1937. In all, there were four priests—two Australians, an Italian, and himself. When war broke out, he and his fellow priests were 'guided by God'—his words—'not to return to the outside world.' This was because of the Italian, Father Constanti." The Colonel read the next passage word-for-word:

"'We learned from the rare newspaper carried to us by native traders that Italy was our enemy. This was not so under the loving guidance of Our Lady. Here, we were two Australians (Fathers Sid Brown and Bob Delaney), myself, an American, and our Italian brother, Bruno Constanti. In the greater world, our nations might be at war, but in our lost Eden, we were the true Allies.

"'Here we laid the foundation for 'agape,' brotherly love, far from the reach of international politics. What example would we set for our new brothers and sisters in Christ, we asked ourselves, if we could not live in His love for one another?'"

"An idealist," the Major observed dryly. The Colonel nodded and scanned on.

"The war passed them by. 'No aircraft have arrived since the hostilities began,' Bastion writes, '...but we had everything we needed, provided by our Heavenly Father.' They were even left alone, he says, 'by the savages our people fear above all others—the notorious headhunters of the Valley of the Cannibals.' He says, 'Thanks be to God, those Mambu warriors have not ventured in our time through the wild country that separates us.'" The Colonel read a passage to himself.

"Ah," he said, "now we're getting to the heart of it."

Dingo leaned forward, listening intently.

CHAPTER 5

"'Everything changed at the beginning of May of this year,'" the Colonel read. "'Then the Japanese invaded Kissim. A squad of nine arrived, bringing native guides at gunpoint. Eventually, we learned they had come through the mountain passes from the Sepik. The day they marched in, they surprised our Australian brothers who were, 'by bad luck or God's will'—Bastion's words," the Colonel said, "'working with the faithful in the gardens.

"'The Japanese forced them to kneel and, while Brother Constanti and I watched from the forest, unable to do anything but forfeit our own lives, Sid and Bob were beheaded. Our people panicked at the murder and ran, as did the Sepik guides, and all were shot down. The war had found us at last, and with a vengeance."

"Sodding bastards!" Dingo exploded, rocking forward so his hat fell on the floor. He snatched it up and jammed it on his head.

"Indeed," the Colonel said. "Father Bastion goes on: 'The Japanese have murdered thirty-seven of our people. They have guns, and we have nothing but our faith, and the primitive weapons that are these people's only defense. Still, our men managed to kill two of the enemy. The reprisals have been terrible. They burned down the village, including our home and simple church. They have killed all the pigs and robbed the gardens.

"'We count seven Japanese remaining. As for ourselves, we can barely keep body and soul together. We exist like animals, eating roots and wild fruit, creeping to a new place every night in order to avoid certain death.'

"'My Dear Commander,'" he read on, "'we have long surrendered our fate to God. But now we throw ourselves on your mercy as well. I would not ask only for myself and Father Constanti, but for the lives of our innocent flock. I beg you, if it is within your power, rescue us.'" Colonel Chambers turned the page over.

"There is an airstrip behind the mission—a natural field where they first landed. He says we can put down there.

"He concludes: 'We will continue to hide in the jungle, and we pray that our brave acolyte, Simay, who volunteered to carry this letter across the perilous mountains, will somehow come to you. We pray for your protection, Sir, and your men. We will watch without ceasing for you to come. God willing, you will find us before the enemy does.' And he signs himself, 'Yours in Christ, and Your Fellow American, Father Christopher Bastion.'"

"Called in the heavy artillery there," Dingo grinned. "God, and country. When was the epistle penned?" The Colonel flipped the page again.

"'Sunday, May 27,'" he read, "'in the Year of Our Lord, Nineteen Hundred and Forty-Five.'"

"Two months ago, more or less," the Australian observed. "No doubt the good Fathers have not heard the mad dog Hitler found his 'final solution'..."

"...or that Germany surrendered," the Colonel added. "Peace in Europe! The Italians of course were beaten by then, and Il Duce and his mistress killed by the mob. Father Constanti is no longer an enemy alien. Little do they know."

"Fair dinkum," Dingo agreed.

"There's something else," Chambers said: "a Post Script." He put his finger on the place and puzzled through the words, almost obscured by the stains.

"Something strange here," he said, peering at the Australian over the letter. "He warns me to beware of a 'monstrous crocodile.' He says it arrived in Kissim after the Japs. The people call it, 'the Father of all the Crocodiles. We have a hard time to prevent them from worshiping it,' Bastion writes, 'particularly after it killed five of the faithful.'"

"My word!" Dingo said. "'The Father!' Of course, I've heard of it from the *kanakas*, but I thought it was a myth. But if it is a real animal, I believe I know what the bugger is."

Johnny ran along the Moresby harbor, being jarred in all the places the war had hurt him. An ambulance truck, canvas sides painted with red crosses, came from the direction of the airport, siren howling. Johnny approached a section of the road lined with stores. Across the way, a man was taking the padlock off Burns, Philp & Company.

Johnny's body begged for a breather, but the soldier drove him on. In the western movies he'd grown up with, and in the current batch of war pictures, many a fellow got shot. But then, in the very next scene, there he'd be, maybe with a bandage, but pretty much as good as new. Johnny had learned in the school of war, it didn't work like that. It had taken months to recover from every one of his injuries, and even longer to get back in shape.

As he ran, his fresh scar throbbed, and the older one in his thigh pulled. In order to distract himself, Johnny gazed across the Moresby harbor. There was a freighter at the docks, men unloading it with a crane and net. Further out were two US Navy vessels. One was a gunboat, just getting underway. The other was a destroyer at anchor, sailors over the side on ropes, painting out the rust.

Suddenly Johnny had to stare at the gravel road, trying not to think of his father. His dad had been an officer on a Navy warship. He winced under the barrage of images that came at him, and in spite of his efforts to steer his thoughts another way, he found himself in that other lifetime. *His face, his voice.*

To distract himself, Johnny looked at the PT boat. *What a power launch!* He recited the facts: *"PT" stands for "Patrol Torpedo"*. *Seventy-seven feet long, designed to barrel in on the big ships and let fly its one-ton torpedoes. It has cannons and heavy machine guns. They call the PT's "the plywood fleet," but their hulls are actually mahogany planks. They're powered by Packard—three 12-cylinder engines that push fifty miles-an-hour.*

Johnny watched the launch cut smartly around the hulk of a Japanese-sunk freighter. It turned for the port's mouth and the skipper opened her up. The blat of power reached Johnny across the water.

His heart pounded and the sweat poured down his forehead. He came to an outcropping of rocks and threw himself down. He sat panting for a time, and then pulled out the Camels and lit one up. When he looked out again, the gunboat was a dot in the distance. He was still having trouble keeping his thoughts off his father, so he deliberately turned his mind to another PT he'd run across.

It had been the year before, in the outer islands. There'd been a combined Marine and Army action against an entrenched Japanese camp. Enemy snipers had the men pinned down, and their commander radioed HQ. By then, Johnny was part of an elite core of killers well known to General MacArthur. Johnny had been on the New Guinea coast in the latest action. The first he knew about it, he was given thirty minutes to get his kit together, and then he was aboard a PBY Catalina, heading over the ocean.

The armed Flying Boat took him across the channel of water between the New Guinea islands they called "the Slot." He got a glimpse of the big island of New Britain, and then there were a lot more dotting the Solomon Sea. The aircraft splashed down near one and taxied ashore. It would be back to pick him up in five days.

It was late afternoon. Johnny was just in time for chow and a drink with the men he'd be fighting beside the following day. As another spectacular tropical sunset fired up the west, the men moved to the "cantina." This was no more than a table, a cooler, and a few chairs on the sand, but it had a million-dollar view, and a cold brew from home went down easy.

Johnny was looking at a fellow's pictures of his family when loud engines drowned out the conversation. A PT boat was racing at them. It got close and came on, barreling for the beach. Just when it looked like the skipper was going to park on the sand, he spun it hard around, threw it in reverse, and came to a pretty stop just offshore.

A dozen sailors stripped their shirts off and swarmed over the gunwales. They dove in and swam the few yards, and dripping wet, came up the beach. Their leader was a skinny lieutenant with a shock of dark hair. As he reached the Army men, the "looey" fished a wad of wet greenbacks from a pocket and in what Johnny took for a broad Boston accent, he said he'd buy "every man-jack a be-ah."

Sometimes the Army and Navy guys didn't get along, but a free drink helped. The newcomers mixed with the others, sitting wherever there was a free chair. The skipper ended up beside Johnny. Still standing, he said in a loud voice his name was Jack, and he launched into a joke about a Texan, a Mexican, a Longhorn bull, and a big-chested blonde. Now, Johnny came from a tight-laced family. Early on, his father warned him that swearing was an indication of a poor education and even poorer imagination. He said the only educated men who used foul language were bores who substituted words for fists in order to beat those around them into submission. Language like this was acceptable from his Navy cohorts, but he would not tolerate it in his home.

Johnny's mother took it a step further. She promised her boy that if she heard a 'potty mouth' from him, she'd clean it with soap. Johnny made the mistake only twice of using the words around her that he heard every day at school, even from his football coach. He remembered each occasion with absolute clarity, because both times he'd found himself suddenly going sideways, his usually benign mother dragging him by the ear. At the sink, he'd been ordered to stick out his tongue. She'd lathered her hands and smeared on the suds. Even in the Army, surrounded by men who turned the air blue with their language, Johnny didn't like to cuss. If he did, he tasted Lifebuoy.

A story as graphic as the one the skipper spun would have been beyond the vale. But Johnny had been in the Army for years now. He figured he'd heard it all, and then some, but he hadn't heard this one. The looey built to the punch line and delivered it well. The men roared with laughter, Johnny included.

After that, Jack sat down, turned with an easy smile, and they started talking. First topic was the gunboat, and Jack seemed impressed by how much Johnny knew. Johnny explained he was a Navy brat, and they moved on to various warships. Johnny named a few his forbearers had sailed on. He found himself describing the Pennsylvania-class Super Dreadnought that had been his father's last ship. Jack whistled and asked for his name.

"Johnny Willman." Jack asked if Lieutenant Commander Jeremy Willman was any relation.

"My father," Johnny said shortly, suddenly regretting the tack the conversation had taken. That made retired Rear Admiral Horace Willman his grandfather? Johnny nodded. Jack paused and said he knew what had happened to Johnny's old man, and he was sorry about it. Johnny didn't reply. His throat was too tight.

Jack gave him a look, then got them each another beer. He changed the subject, and Johnny was grateful. The skipper said he'd found an anti-tank cannon that was sitting idle. He planned to "redeploy" it, he grinned. He pointed at his boat, now a dark line on the waves. He would mount the big gun there, near the bow. Then he'd really blow holes in the side of the "Tokyo Express," he enthused. Johnny knew that's what they called the flotilla of enemy ships that delivered troops and supplies through these islands. In order to avoid being sunk by Allied fighters, the Japanese convoys ran at night. And that's where PT boats like Jack's came in.

"We're like those huge crocs out here," the skipper grinned. "We're fast, and we've got big teeth." He went on to talk about racing sailboats in Florida. Johnny described surfing the huge waves at Waimea Bay and Sunset on Oahu's north shore. Somehow, every topic came back to girls. Jack described a drive he'd made around Europe in a sports car, and some of his romantic conquests. Johnny realized that the looey had "known" a lot more women than he had, in the biblical sense.

At 22-hundred, Jack said he had to get back aboard his PT-109. He'd grab some shuteye and at midnight, he and the boys would head "into the slot to find Japs." Johnny said he had his own to hunt in the morning, and explained he was a sniper. He watched his new acquaintance closely, watching for a sign of revulsion, but Jack only nodded. He asked if Johnny would mind if he took a look at his rifle.

Johnny had the Springfield over the back of the chair. He always kept it close at hand, and he generally didn't like anyone to touch it. But somehow, he didn't mind with Jack. He handed it over and was pleased to see the looey took it carefully, in both hands. Jack put his eye to the scope and panned the coconut trees silhouetted against the fading sky.

"If I can ask, how do you look at a man, see his face I mean, and shoot him? I don't know if I could do it." Again, Johnny had his ears tuned for a hint of criticism, but there was none and he thought it through.

"At first it was hard. But you get used to it."

Jack nodded and handed the Springfield back. For a minute, there was silence, then the skipper said it was time to go. He stood and called to his sailors. Grumbling good-naturedly, they got up. Johnny hung his rifle over his shoulder and walked them to the water. The sailors waded in and swam out. Jack stepped into the waves and turned back.

"Let's get together after the war," he said. "Have a few beahs."

"I didn't get your last name," Johnny told him.

"It's Kennedy," the voice came from the darkness. "Jack Kennedy." There was the ghost of that smile and the looey dove and followed the voices of his men.

Sure, we'll get together after the war, Johnny thought. *More likely, neither of us will make it home.*

Now, on the Port Moresby harbor, the PT boat disappeared in the distance. *My number could have come up a thousand times,* Johnny thought. *So far I've made it. I wonder about Jack?* He flicked away the butt and stood, bracing against the pain. *The meeting to decide if I can rejoin my unit is at 9-hundred hours.* He took a few strides and broke into a jog, retracing his route along the harbor.

Keep on point, he told himself. *Do what you need to do to get back in the fight!*

That's the problem with Gwyn, it occurred to him. *I'd like to get to know her, but the Jap invasion is coming right up.* The sun blasted down and he really wanted that shower, as cold as the water could get.

The natives stared as the tall man flew by, undershirt pasted to his chest. *Why do they do it?* they wondered. *Why run in a circle, then stop and walk away?* The white man, as always, was a mystery.

What could I even offer a knockout like Gwyn? Johnny asked himself. The killer-soldier was quick to reply. *Nothing. You've got nothing but heartache to give her. That you've made it this far is sheer blind luck. You're not likely to survive the battle in Japan. And that means, leave her alone. If you care about her at all, that's the best gift you can give her!* His heart hammered like a loose piston and each breath burned.

And while Johnny knew the hard case was right, some part of him still hoped he'd see her today.

Chapter 6

As Gwyn and Ruthie approached the entrance to Acute Care, they paid little attention to the staring men. The medics and natives were stopped in their tracks by the stunning pair. Gwyn was tall, with long legs, her lovely face dominated by wide green eyes, her wavy chestnut curls cut in a bob. Then there was Ruthie with her voluptuous curves and merry blue eyes, her cap barely hanging onto the red riot of hair.

Neither young woman fully realized how, in this male domain of organized death, they shone like beacons of a better world. The men who saw them drank in their passage with admiration, and a pang of something like desperation.

Gwyn found her thoughts racing away—*to him! Get a grip,* she chastised herself. *You're the one who put the boycott on military men. He only cares about more fighting. Most guys have a one-track mind, but his is on the wrong one.* Still, she found herself hoping she'd see him today.

They pushed through the swinging doors of the huge Quonset hut, assailed by the odors of disinfectant and disease. Injured men were laid out on forty beds. The nurses went behind a partition and scrubbed their hands and forearms at the sink. They continued to the nurses' station and exchanged greetings with four Australian counterparts going off duty.

Their eyes roved the ward. Doctors moved among the beds, administering medicine and encouragement. Nurses changed bandages, sheets and bedpans. The kitchen staff of whites and natives wheeled around the breakfast trolleys.

Gwyn was struck, as she often was, by the profound aspect of her work. In spite of everything she did, some of these men would die. Others would recover. And all of them would count on her to get them through the next minutes, hours, and days.

She saw an older physician in a clutch of doctors. This was Doctor MacClure, Director of the Hospital and Head of Surgery, presiding over his realm. "Doc Mac" was a gruff man with a shock of white hair. He was seventy years old, and still a formidable intellect. He did not bear fools or the inept lightly—he bore them not at all. Dressings down by the Chief were legendary, and to be avoided at all cost.

Some feared him, but Gwyn admired Doc Mac. If you did your job competently, you had nothing to fear. Gwyn knew he would always do the sensible thing. When some poor soldier was beyond help, Doc moved out of the fellow's hearing and said so. The patient was given kindness and painkillers and turned over to the chaplain or priest. But if, in Doc's opinion, the man could be saved, he wasted no time getting him to surgery. He was a master of the deft amputation.

In addition to their injuries, he treated his patients for the gamut of tropical ailments. In complex cases—men with infected wounds, and suffering from everything from malaria to dysentery, Doc commenced treatment and ordered tests. If one approach did not work, he tried another, and another, until the man either improved or succumbed.

This morning, Gwyn could tell that once more, Doc had spent the night on the ward. He owned a fine home in the Moresby hills, but as often as not, he slept on a cot right here, behind a curtain.

Now, eyes tired but still sharp, he waited for Gwyn and Ruthie. He launched into a rapid-fire briefing on the night's developments and gave them their instructions. There had been a skirmish somewhere inland, and at first light this morning, aircraft had brought in eleven new wounded Australians. Doc Mac departed to amputate a leg. The nurses went about their duties.

Gwyn brought her mind to bear on her tasks. For the time being, at least, thoughts of the two men were pushed away.

— ☽ —

Doctor MacClure was one of the best medical minds Australia had produced. He had been head of surgery at the Royal Sydney Hospital for decades. In 1940, at the age of sixty-five, he retired. The lifelong bachelor returned to his house on the river in Parramatta, and tended his garden. He concocted homemade tonics for his prize roses, stocked his wine cellar, and went on walking tours in the Blue Mountains and Broken Hill.

When it became clear in 1942 that the Japanese were on their way, sites clearly set on Australia, Doc Mac could not remain on the sidelines. The authorities were only too grateful to have a man of his caliber. He was sent up to Papua and New Guinea. It was there that the military intended to stop the Japanese juggernaut. It was the last line of defense before Australia herself.

In fact, the enemy actually got as close as bombing the Australian city of Darwin. That occurred only two months after the Yanks were hit at Hawaii, and it was known as "the Australian Pearl Harbor." Doc Mac pointed out that more bombs had fallen on Darwin than had on Pearl. In fact, in '42 and '43, "the Japs" made more than a hundred raids against his homeland.

In the same month as the attack on Aus, February of '42, the medical administrator arrived by ship in Port Moresby, accompanied by numerous crates of equipment. He organized and added onto the hodgepodge of edifices that made up the hospital compound. He established surgery tents, installed X-ray machines, and built a lab. This he outfitted in part with captured Japanese microscopes, the only enemy medical equipment up to his standards.

Doc Mac and his staff could now order urine and stool analyses, malaria smears and typhus agglutinations. Experienced as he was, the physician found there was much to learn. The New Guinea ailments were exotic and voracious. He devised a number of breakthrough therapies that saved lives and limbs.

In early 1945, Doc Mac's success rate improved dramatically with the arrival of what he called "one of the highlights of human history." A few years earlier, a Scotsman, Alexander Fleming, discovered that *Penicillium* mold stopped other bacteria in their tracks. But it was an Australian, Doc Mac liked to point out, his old mate Howard Florey, who developed penicillin as a usable treatment for human infections.

By 1944, America was churning out the miracle drug in significant quantities—all derived, Doc Mac heard, from green mold on a single pawpaw. But with the extraordinary demands of war, penicillin remained virtually impossible to come by. Doc Mac took advantage of his connection with Florey. At last, in March of '45, several cases of the precious drug were offloaded in Moresby.

That was how it came to pass, when a dying soldier was rushed off a ship, Doc Mac was ready. With remedies new and old, he prepared to do battle for the young chap's life.

Johnny was comatose when he came in. His wound had been spewing poison into his bloodstream for too long: he was losing the fight. Gwyn took his temperature while he was still on the stretcher and found it 106°F. Doc cut away the soiled bandages and the stench made them gag. The whole chest was red and swollen. Much worse, the tissue surrounding the dark lesion was green and black.

"Necrotic," Doc Mac said. *Dead flesh*. "Gangrene," he continued, and it sounded like the death sentence.

Gwyn helped Doc roll the soldier on his side. They saw the scarred shoulder blade where the bullet had exited. It was purple, but healed over. They lay him on his back again, and Doc probed the wound, while Gwyn wiped the patient's face with a wet towel.

His eyelids fluttered and his lips moved. She brushed a strand of hair from his eyes. His forehead felt like cold clay, in spite of his raging fever. She was worried Doc Mac would pronounce him a hopeless case, but he did not say the words. At least, not yet.

"To surgery!" he ordered. Native orderlies hoisted the stretcher and trotted after Doc Mac and Gwyn to a tent. They transferred the man to the operating table, while Gwyn and the surgeon scrubbed up. The anesthesiologist joined them at the sink. Gwyn knew he could not use ether—it was too volatile in the extreme heat. Instead, he had sodium pentothal and nitrous oxide at his disposal. But as long as the soldier remained unconscious, no drug was needed.

Doc selected his instruments while Gywn prepared the site. She clamped a wad of cotton, dipped it in iodine, and liberally swabbed the entire pectoral muscle. Doc Mac took his scalpel and carved a smooth cone in the flesh, going to the bone. Gwyn and the other physician used clamps to pinch each curl of black flesh and dispose of it.

"Wide edges," Doc murmured, "to lessen the chance of gas gangrene." If that infected the tissue, the man would die. Gwyn applied hemostats to the severed blood vessels until Doc could tie them off. She used a hand suction to remove the blood. The wound looked better, but she saw that the black patches continued deep into the cavity.

"Move him to an isolation tent and put him under a mosquito net," Doc Mac ordered. "Leave the lesion uncovered. Inject him with penicillin. I'll be back in a jiff."

Gwyn followed instructions while Doc drove his car to his house. As he strode through, he greeted the Mount Hagen man who was his caretaker and cook. Doc exited onto the back veranda and crossed the lawn. He came to an odd looking shed. The roof was corrugated metal, but the walls were netting stretched around posts, a screen door in one. A buzzing grew as he approached, and he held his breath against the reek of rotting meat. He unlatched the door, slipped inside, and fastened it.

The place swarmed with green flies. On a rough table rested chunks of well-decayed pork that seemed to move. Doc picked up a glass jar and unscrewed the lid. The meat was smothered in maggots. With a paintbrush, he swept twenty or thirty writhing larvae into the jar. He screwed the lid down and rushed back to the hospital.

Gwyn was at the patient's bedside when he returned. Doc Mac ducked under the netting and took the soldier's pulse. He found it dangerously fast and irregular. He unscrewed his jar and spilled the maggots into the open wound. Even though she'd seen the doctor do this before, Gwyn's stomach lurched. Still, she knew the purpose. These particular fly larvae ate only dead tissue, and left the healthy alone. Doc came back under the netting, picked up the chart, and made a note.

"Maggot debridement begun," he said. "We'll know soon if our patient—what's his name?"

"John Willman," Gwyn answered, having read the report that came with him. "Twenty years old. American."

"We'll soon know if young John Willman will survive the crisis." Doc assigned Gwyn to the boy's care, with her regular duties. As the day went by, she found herself frequently by Willman's side, peering at the writhing grubs. It was both fascinating and disturbing to watch them feed. Encouragingly, the black patches were shrinking. Every three hours, Gwyn administered another shot of penicillin and checked the saline drip. He absorbed three liters of fluid that day.

Finally, at one in the morning, hours after her shift was over, she dragged herself to bed. First thing in the morning, she stuck her head into the tent and saw the soldier was still insensate, but breathing calmly. His pulse had slowed to a hundred and twenty. The swelling was beginning to subside. Best yet, the wound was clean and pink. The maggots were lethargic, but still twitching.

She gave the patient a dose of Penicillin and took his temperature: 104°.

Another day, and it was 101°, his pulse a mere ninety. She and Doc concurred that the man stood a fighting chance. Two mornings later, Gwyn arrived to find a squadron of shiny green flies circling inside the mosquito net. She opened the tent door, lifted the netting, and gave them their freedom. After what they had achieved, it was the least she could do.

When Gwyn turned around, she found the patient's brown eyes open and staring at her.

"I'm John Willman," the soldier rasped. "You call me Johnny." She hastened to give him water from the glass she'd placed by his bedside. He tried to sit up and fell back. She sat beside him, lifted his head and helped him get a drink. It struck her that, shaved and cleaned up, he might be a decent-looking fellow. Of course, he'd have to be fattened up.

"I thought I died. You look like an angel. What's your name?"

"Gwyndolyn," she said. "And you can call me Gwyn."

She beamed at him, and Johnny's pain was suddenly easier to bear.

For the first month, Johnny was too sick to do anything but lay quiet and do what he was told. Doc Mac never said it in so many words, but Gwyn could tell that he was amazed the patient had survived. He took a particular interest in what he called "my miracle man." Often he came by to change the bandages himself, even when other doctors were on rounds. It looked like the gangrene was gone, but the stubborn infection lingered. The survival of "young Johnny" was still touch and go, Doc Mac thought, but he dared now to hope.

Once, when his patient was having a particularly bad night, the doctor asked him a question.

"Do you believe in God?"

The soldier was nauseous and feverish, suffering from a recurrence of malaria on top of everything else. The question caught him off guard.

"I was raised in church," he said. "But after what I've seen..." he tapered off. Doc Mac had seen many a soldier in similar straits. They were fresh from a world where mayhem and sudden death were the norm.

"Young Johnny," he said. "Let me ease your mind. God does not require your belief in order to exist." The soldier gazed without comprehension and the old man patted his arm.

"I hope you won't make the mistake so many do, of thinking we doctors are in the God business. It's a common error, or perhaps a hope, among patients. They dearly want us to tell them we can fix everything.

"Personally, I think of myself more as a gardener. If a limb is badly damaged, or infected, I remove it. If an enemy attacks—like fungal rot on my roses—well, I can treat that. But as for actually making blossoms grow! My! That is an art beyond my few skills.

"Young Johnny, healing happens inside you, through processes we barely understand. You may be shocked to hear this, but when it comes to life itself, science cannot define it. We recognize it, but do not know what it is. In my opinion, life comes from a power greater than mine."

"What are you saying, Doc?" the sufferer grumbled.

"I'm suggesting that you pray for your life, young Johnny," the older man said. "I've seen it have a salubrious effect."

Johnny was too sick to reply. He groaned and turned away. Doc Mac dipped a cloth in water and wiped his forehead.

"You don't need all the answers," the physician said. "I say, just do it. Don't bargain, just ask for your life. And if you can't manage it, don't worry about that either."

Johnny said nothing. The relentless drill of agony had wrung him dry. His mind drifted incoherently for some time, but later that night, the doctor's voice returned. *God does not require your belief in order to exist.* Strangely, it gave him comfort.

In his childhood, Johnny had been secure at the center of the universe. God oversaw everything, then his parents, his grandparents and other adults, then Johnny himself, and the rest of the world. That was the celestial order he'd been taught. But under the ferocious onslaught of war, the construct was torn apart.

Johnny found himself in a living hell, a torment devoid of any loving presence. Human life was a cheap commodity, easily snuffed out. He'd remembered close buddies from the early days before he learned to stop caring. They were complete personalities, with full lives and dreams, turned in an instant into exploded sacks of meat. What was the ultimate meaning? They were no more significant than animals in a slaughterhouse.

Gradually, a cold conviction seeped through Johnny. Their destiny was his. He was not going to make it. Once he accepted that, things actually got easier. He had a new plan. *Before my number comes up, I'll take out as many Japs as I can.*

Now Doc Mac's words lifted a burden he had not realized he was carrying. *God does not require your belief in order to exist.* It was almost as if some part of him worried that losing his faith had killed God.

The night Doc talked to him, sleep continued to elude him. The pulse in his chest tolled through his body like the somber church bells over the San Diego of his youth. *Ask for my life,* Doc said. *What harm can it do?* Awkwardly, he formed the words.

If you're out there, take away this pain. Either that, or kill me. I'm at the end of my rope. That was all he could manage. And then the chant rose from the core of his being.

Fight to live, live to fight! It echoed in his mind, and that was all Johnny knew. He drifted into a fathomless slumber, free for once of the visitations of the living dead.

Next morning, Gwyn found the patient deeply asleep. With a thumb, she smoothed the furrow between his eyebrows. With her thermometer, she confirmed what she already knew. Johnny's fever had broken.

She fetched a basin of warm water, soap, a safety razor, and shaved his face. She studied the clean features and saw how much younger he looked. He was just a boy, whatever ordeal he'd been through. An hour later, Doc Mac sewed up the wound and changed the dressing.

"Young Johnny," he told the sleeping man. "I believe you're on the mend."

Three weeks into his sojourn at the Port Moresby hospital, Johnny was transferred to the general ward. He began talking with the other men, and Gwyn saw the company was doing him some good. Soon all the nurses were introduced to the Yank who had beaten gangrene. Many had a frequent smile for Doc's dashing "miracle Yank."

As for Gwyn, she generally visited in the middle of the night, when the lights were low. Johnny continued to have trouble sleeping. His face invariably brightened as she approached. It was only natural, she thought. Hers was the first friendly face he'd seen after he regained his senses.

The nights were stifling, even under the fans. Gwyn washed the sweat off his face, turned his pillow, and pulled up a chair. They spoke in whispers so as not to wake the surrounding men. By tacit agreement, they steered clear of the war. Johnny loved to hear her tales about fly-fishing with her father in the ice-cold streams of home.

"Where is that?" he asked.

"Peachland," she said, "in British Columbia."

"And where is that?"

"Canada, silly," she said. "You're from California?" Johnny nodded. "You go north through Oregon, then Washington, and there's BC. You've never seen the Peace Arch?"

"Seen it? Never heard of it."

"When you drive from Seattle to Vancouver, you'll find it exactly on the border between the US and Canada. The arch says, 'Children of a Common Mother.' It has an iron gate, locked open forever. Sometimes my friends from nursing school and I picnicked there, on our way to shop in Blaine or Bellingham. Whatever did they teach you at school?" she teased.

"Not much," Johnny grimaced. He loved the outdoors too, he told her, and he was tickled to find a girl who knew how to tie a fly, and land a mountain trout. In turn, he described hunting deer and elk in the California Sierras.

But the times he described riding his surfboard on the enormous Pacific rollers off Oahu, he got really enthused. Gwyn saw his eyes light up. For a few moments, he was able to forget his sweaty bed, and she knew that was as good as medicine.

By his second month at the hospital, it was clear Johnny Willman was on the road to recovery. His bullet wound had knitted into a raised scar. The infection, Doc Mac announced, had been beaten. Johnny's appetite improved.

Gwyn was delighted. But the more Johnny's energy returned, the more he transformed into a different man. And this one, the nurse discovered to her disappointment, she did not care for at all.

Chapter 7

As soon as "the corner was truly turned," as Doc Mac put it, it was a feisty and impatient soldier who emerged. This was the John Willman who'd lost every field promotion he'd been given—and there had been quite a few—by shooting off his mouth. When he saw men killed by ill-informed or just plain lousy orders, Johnny found he had to speak up. Unfortunately, his target often happened to be the very officer who had just elevated him. Every time, Johnny had been busted back to Buck Private.

Luckily for him, his prowess with his rifle was a hot commodity. His field commanders utilized him, but he was regarded with suspicion, something of a loose cannon. General MacArthur was the exception. He admired Willman, and told his officers to ignore what the fellow said. They were to use the sniper like they would a good hunting dog. So Johnny was left alone until they needed him. Then he was sent to sniff out the enemy once more, and show them his teeth.

Now, while Johnny was stuck in hospital, he read "the Stars and Stripes" and every newspaper he could get his hands on. What he saw fed his obsession with getting back to the General. The invasion of Japan was close, that was clear. In Europe they had called it "Operation Overlord." Here, it was going to be "Operation Downfall." He began to berate the medical workers.

"Do more!" he demanded. "Do it faster! Get me out of here."

And it was for this cantankerous soldier that Gwyn developed an aversion. He was impatient and outspoken, and if he was committed to being the squeaky wheel, she was equally determined not to be the grease. Now when she had free time in the middle of the night, she no longer gravitated to the Californian's bedside. Yet, to her annoyance, she found herself thinking about him.

Caring too much for any soldier was against her strict rules. Early in the war, she'd learned that lesson the painful way. Now she threw up her hands. The sooner Johnny Willman did manage to talk himself onto a ship out of here, the better it would be. Or so she told herself.

Johnny continued to make life miserable for those around him. The nurses stopped smiling and coming by to visit. Ministering to the sick and dying was difficult enough, without a hard case riding them.

The fact was, it was not the staff that held Johnny back, but his own infirmity. As soon as he tried to get up and move around, he discovered just how compromised he was.

On one occasion, while wobbling between the beds, leaning heavily on Ruthie's arm, he tripped over his own feet. In spite of her attempt to grab him, he fell hard on the floorboards. Pain seared through his chest, and he let loose some words that made him taste soap.

Johnny grabbed the bed frame and hauled himself back up. Then he gave Ruthie a piece of his mind. As it happened, Doc Mac was in earshot. He strode over, got an arm around the Yank, and marched him back to bed. He made the boy sit, and let him have it.

"Young Johnny, you will curb your tongue! I believe you are intelligent enough to understand that abusing my staff hinders, and does not help, your cause. We have more than enough to do," Doc Mac barked, "without bearing the brunt of your personal war!"

To his credit, Johnny apologized at once to Ruthie, who he genuinely liked, and to his physician.

"I'm sorry, Doc," he said. "It's just that I need to get out of here! I have to be there for the Jap invasion. I'm better Doc, I tell you. Cut me loose!"

"Better!" Doc snorted. "I suppose that is why you cannot walk? If you have medical credentials," he continued, "show me them. Otherwise, accept mine. I will send you packing the minute you are fit. Until then, you *will* pull in your horns."

After that, Johnny redoubled his efforts to walk. He put on a hard face, but inwardly, he was appalled by how wasted he was. He looked at his pale, thin legs, and remembered them tanned and strong, guiding his surfboard through the waves. He demanded a set of crutches and began to get around.

Doc Mac assigned him to a ward where the men were mobile. Here Johnny saw Gwyn less frequently, although he found himself watching for her. But when she did make the effort to look him up, things quickly deteriorated. At first, Gwyn seemed glad to see him, and asked about his progress. But soon as he got on his favorite topic about getting back to the front, her eyes clouded over. She'd make some excuse and hurry off. Johnny, staring at her retreating back, would scowl. *What does she want from me? Why can't she take me as I am?*

Along with his increasing energy came exasperation with being cooped up. Johnny worked through every book he could find, even a couple Gwyn was kind enough to lend him—"Jane Eyre" and "Wuthering Heights" by the Bronte sisters. They were not exactly up his alley, but they gave him something to fill the hours. Then he went looking for other diversions. A highlight of the week was Saturday nights when they showed a movie in the main mess tent. They'd stretch a sheet, set up the projector, and run the reels.

The most recent offering was an action flick, "Raiders of Ghost City." It starred Joe Sawyer in a brimmed hat as "Idaho Jones." Johnny was on the benches with some of his tent mates when he saw Gwyn and Ruthie come in with a group that included a couple of men in civvies. That gave Johnny a shock, one he didn't like.

The lights were turned off and he settled in uneasily to watch the movie. But everything else was quickly forgotten when he saw the lead off. This was a black-and-white newsreel of recent action in Okinawa. The Japanese island was now under American control. The fight had been costly, with fifty thousand US wounded, fully twelve thousand men killed. But it had gone far worse for the enemy. The announcer gave estimates of two hundred thousand troops and civilians slaughtered.

Sitting in the dark, Johnny puzzled it out. *Okinawa—that's where it's going to be. That's where General MacArthur will gather the Army for the invasion. And that's where I have to get to.*

He left while the movie credits were still rolling, before the lights came up. He told himself he'd seen enough, but the truth was, he did not want to watch Gwyn leave with her men friends.

After that, he really went on the warpath. He even hitched a ride to the Army garrison and camped out all day, insisting on a meeting with the American Commander in New Guinea. An aide informed the Colonel that a recovering soldier was waiting to see him. The Commander was up to his ears, and had no time for courtesies. Late in the day, however, an aide reminded him the GI was still outside. In an expansive moment, Chambers had him shown in. He expected to shake the hand of an injured war hero and promise to send him home. Instead, he found himself confronted by an unruly soldier spoiling for a fight.

"A slack rear-guard attitude!" Johnny railed, "that's all that keeps me in Port Moresby! I need to be sent back to the Philippines, and at once, Sir!"

"And just what *are* you doing in New Guinea?" the Colonel bristled. "How did one John Willman, recently of Manila, manage to wind up back in New Guinea? Care to explain, Private?" Johnny had no truthful response to share, so he gave a simple one.

"SNAFU, Sir!" He didn't need to spell out the Army acronym for a career officer. The Colonel did not normally trouble himself with the fate of one man. He was higher up the food chain than that. Now he pulled his face into a mirthless smile and ordered the gung-ho boy back to hospital. He told him he would be released only when Doctor MacClure said so, and then he would get his orders through channels like everyone else "in this man's Army." He warned the Private not to show his face at HQ again without an explicit invitation.

Once Johnny departed, Henry sent someone to fetch Willman's New Guinea record. It took time to locate it, stuffed away in a warehouse. But when at last the Commander came into possession of the dossier, he glanced through it and was both impressed and troubled.

He closed the file and sat back. He was of two minds. He admired a soldier who liked to fight, but he was an old hand at reading "Army-speak." John Willman had the bad habit of criticizing his betters. *Not the Army way. Simply will not do to have any man question command. Still, there's no doubt about his courage, or his marksmanship. So will I send him to General MacArthur—or home for good?*

The Colonel was extremely busy and Private Willman was a minor bother. He had all the preparations for handing over the reins of command to his successor. In addition, there was his research to complete.

Some soldiers, like General MacArthur, were commanders of action. Others, such as the Colonel, were better at administrating the vast machine that was the Army. Certainly, Henry was a gifted bureaucrat. It required special skill to organize the myriad details of personnel, property and operations of the American occupation. Chamber's objective, to be completed by his successor, was to prepare everything for the US withdrawal from New Guinea.

Most of Henry's career had been spent on American soil. He had toiled up the ladder of promotion. The highlight of the 1930's, however, had been the two years he spent as a military attaché at the Embassy in Tokyo. He dutifully put in an appearance at the interminable receptions, but at the same time, he quietly went about his true assignment—the gathering of military intelligence for Washington.

In fact, Henry was fascinated by the bellicose Nipponese Empire. He cultivated the acquaintance of prominent citizens, including members of the Japanese command, and listened to them carefully. As they got to know him, they had much to say about the Empire's rightful place in Asia and the world.

He attended displays of their formidable martial arts, including hand-to-hand combat, and sparring with wooden swords and other weapons. He studied everything he could of their history, heroes, art, and literature. All this gave him special insight into what was to become the enemy Empire. He warned his Washington bosses that war was coming, long before it did.

He was outraged, but not surprised, by the attack on the Pacific fleet and airfields of Oahu. He was back in the States by then, and found himself with new responsibilities for the outfitting and training of the legions of recruits.

In 1944, well beyond the normal age of retirement, still in service due to the war, Henry was offered what he viewed as the feather in the cap of his career. The Army's troops and holdings on the far off island of New Guinea were to be catalogued, and prepared for withdrawal—an orderly handing over of affairs to the Australians.

Henry was well aware it was not his destiny to see the heady days of battle of his legendary predecessor, Douglas MacArthur. He knew he might walk in the great man's footsteps, but he would never fill his shoes. Still, Henry had seized the opportunity. Part of his reason was personal. He had a passion for military history.

Upon arrival in Port Moresby, Chambers was given a tour of his new command. With everything else, he was shown four giant Quonset huts. Each was piled to the roof with file boxes. The Colonel knew he was looking at the raw paper record of the war in this theater.

Most men would have seen only an avalanche of information that would smother them. But Henry, gazing at the mountain of paper, had an epiphany. In these silent storehouses was his motherlode.

Indeed, it was part of his official mandate to sift through all this. He and his staff were to summarize key facts and destroy most of it. Anything still secret, or records that were, in his opinion, of lasting value, he would organize for shipment to the Army archivists.

Like a light illuminating his road through retirement, Henry saw his book. This would be his history of the Army's participation in the war in the South Pacific.

Many a Friday night over drinks at the Officer's Club, the Colonel confided to his inner cadre that his research was the one thing that kept him from going mad in this overheated backwaters. While continuing to fulfill his official capacity, Henry filled journal after journal with his careful notes. Here were the dates, battles, numbers of troops and enemy reported killed, records of conversations, orders given, and much more. All told, he had filled seventeen legal-size ledgers with his longhand. These, he would guard close to his side on the long journey home.

Henry imagined a popular history for the postwar book market. While his material itself was fascinating, in his opinion, he believed he had a sure winner because of the key figure who would loom from its pages. This was no less a personage than Supreme Commander Douglas MacArthur himself. Every time the General opened his mouth, something potent and quotable came out. The newspapers ate it up, and the Colonel had a thick file of clippings.

Chambers even believed that the flamboyant MacArthur would one day run for President. In that case, he predicted the consummate warrior would win the highest seat in the nation. After all, there were few leaders better known, or as popular. As Henry weighed the odds, he concluded that, win or lose, his book would benefit. In addition, it would give him cachet with the leading Charlestown families. He saw himself as a sought-after guest at the better dinner parties. Of course, the royalties would be a welcome addition to a modest military pension.

Now, with his final days in Port Moresby flying away, Henry felt a mounting urgency. No matter how much research he had done, there was always more. And once he departed, there would be no coming back. He called for more and more files, and the boxes climbed his office walls. Every night now, long after everyone else was gone, The Commander could be found writing at his desk.

Shortly after Private Willman left his office, the GI almost faded from the Colonel's thoughts.

But then, against explicit orders, Johnny barged in again. It was the worst thing he could have done.

— O —

FROM THE JOURNALS OF COLONEL HENRY CHAMBERS, JR.

I Shall Return!

When Japan attacked Pearl Harbor and multiple targets in December of 1941, the leader of the American forces in the Philippines was General Douglas MacArthur. This was the warrior who had once been appointed Field Marshall by the Philippine Government. "Field Marshall" is a rank that does not exist in the United States—much, some say, to the General's disappointment. In his days of oriental splendor, he wore a gold-braided uniform of his own design.

Eventually, Douglas MacArthur returned to the khaki uniform and mere title of General of the United States Army. It was no surprise that President Roosevelt would reassign him to our Philippine Islands, to command the 100,000-strong Army of Americans and nationals. The United States, of course, beat the Spanish in the late 19th Century, then purchased the Territory from them, put down a Filipino uprising, and assumed control in 1902.

General MacArthur had believed for many years that war with Japan was inevitable. Your Author has heard the Supreme Commander hold forth on this subject. However, in early December of 1941 when Washington warned him at last and indeed, the Japanese invaders were coming at him, MacArthur was unable to mount a significant defense. It took the enemy a mere two months to rout his Army.

With surrender imminent, the President himself ordered his high profile General to forsake his men and flee. At last, accompanied only by his family and close officers, the Commander boarded a PT boat in the dark of night and slipped away. Of the men he left to the nonexistent mercy of the Japanese, it is known that up to eleven thousand perished. Whatever else, it was a disgraceful defeat for MacArthur.

The General slunk into Australia with his tail between his legs. There, however, he was mollified by the hero's welcome. Australia, he discovered, had been abandoned by Mother Britain. The cream of the nation's fighting men had been sent to aid England. When invasion of Australia by the Asian hordes seemed inevitable, the nation begged Churchill for the return of her legions. It was made clear they would not be sent home. It was a desperate Prime Minister John Curtin who embraced America, in the form of MacArthur, as his nation's only hope.

To the dismay of his own senior officers, Curtin placed them under the thumb of the imperious "Yank." Washington dubbed MacArthur, "Supreme Commander of Allied Forces in the Southwest Pacific Area."

Just who is this military Titan? (Dear Reader, your Author learned the following from Douglas MacArthur's own lips). He was born "under the flag" in an armory in Little Rock, Arkansas. He grew up in frontier Texas where his father was still fighting the Indian Wars. The first sound he claims to remember was the call of the bugle, and he says he could ride and even shoot a rifle before he could walk.

Shortly after the turn of this 20th Century, watched over by his beloved mother "Pinky," MacArthur graduated from West Point Military Academy with Outstanding Honors. He became an aide to President "Teddy" Roosevelt. By the end of the First World War, he was already a Brigadier General, and the most decorated veteran in all America.

How ignominious it was for the consummate warrior to be run out of the Philippines! But while his pride took a drubbing, his legendary ego survived. At his first opportunity in Australia, he announced to the world, "I have come out of the Philippines, and I shall return!"

His words reverberated to the White House. It is said that our recently demised President Franklin Delano Roosevelt took offense and rebuked his General. It was the American nation, not one man, who would liberate the Philippines!

At his very next opportunity, however, the General trumpeted it again: "I shall return!" It was a personal promise, and in spite of an abysmal lack of manpower and equipment and a distance that would be measured not so much in miles, but in years and tens of thousands of lives, MacArthur forged his iron plans.

At one time during the height of the New Guinea campaign, there were many thousands of Allied troops gathered in Port Moresby. During those boomtown days of war, they included the most famous soldier of them all, MacArthur himself.

Still, in every toe-to-toe fight with the enemy, the Japanese continued to teach him hard lessons. They had carefully chosen the territory they would defend, and wherever the Allies attacked, the enemy exacted high casualties. Moreover, tropical diseases like Malaria and Typhoid cut down more troops than enemy bullets.

The General is many things, and for some he has been roundly criticized, but without doubt, he is a gifted tactician. If he was to keep his promise to the Philippines, and then invade the Japanese islands themselves, he could not spend forever grinding out campaigns in obscure areas of New Guinea. This was particularly true when the Navy was carving out much publicized victories across the South Pacific.

It is well known that General MacArthur's archrival is Admiral Chester Nimitz. The General might have the top hand in the Southwest Pacific, but Nimitz is the Commander in Chief of everything else across the ocean.

It was Nimitz who garnered the glory in such pivotal battles as the Coral Sea, Midway, and the Solomon Islands. His Navy took the Marianas, Saipan, Guam and more. After landing MacArthur to fight it out on the Philippines, the Admiral's ships finished the rout of the Nipponese Navy in the battles of the Philippine Sea and Leyte Gulf. It was his Marine and Army unites that made household names of Guadalcanal, Iwo Jima and recently, Okinawa.

Mired in the jungles of New Guinea, General MacArthur worried that his war was forgotten. In order to free himself from the savage island, the Commander devised a strategy he called "leapfrogging." He would bypass the enemy strongholds and go for the prize—the Philippines and then Japan. He would leave the marooned Japanese behind to "wither on the vine."

All US military aircraft belong either to the Army or the Navy. Nimitz commanded his carriers with their fighters, while MacArthur had his land-based Air Force. His bombers had a maximum range of two hundred miles, so that was the measure of each leap his Army would make. The General and his men hopped "up the back of the turkey," as he called New Guinea, a reference to its shape. Late last year, the Supreme Commander was finally done with this island, and was ready to make good his famous promise.

On October 20th 1944, MacArthur waded ashore onto the Philippine Islands, a moment well covered by photographers.

"I have returned," the General thundered on the beach. "By the grace of Almighty God, our forces stand again on Philippine soil—soil consecrated in the blood of our two peoples. Rally to me. Rise and strike! Strike at every favorable opportunity. For your homes

and hearths, strike! For future generations of your sons and daughters, strike! In the name of your sacred dead, strike! Let no heart be faint. Let every arm be steeled. The guidance of divine God points the way. Follow in His Name to the Holy Grail of righteous victory!"

It was vintage MacArthur, and our troops and the Filipinos have indeed rallied to the challenge. At the time of this writing (July, 1945), the United States has won. The latest news says MacArthur's boys are mopping up the last enemy resistance on the wild island of Mindanao.

In my mind's eye, I see the Supreme Commander glare north across the open Pacific. In that direction lies our nation's and his own inexorable destination, the Imperial Empire's heartland.

At Pearl Harbor, the die was cast, and it is certain that this very year, General Douglas MacArthur shall land with force on those shores and lead us to our destiny.

That God-guided destiny is, and always has been, the utter defeat of the enemy, and the absolute victory of the United States of America.

CHAPTER 8

A long line of wrecks edged the Port Moresby runway, the castoffs of MacArthur's Air Force. Every serviceable flying machine had long since departed with the General, ferrying his Army up the north coast of New Guinea.

One of the aged beauties had been dragged out from the rest. This was a Hudson light bomber of pre-war vintage, built for Britain by the American Lockheed Corporation. This Saturday morning, six men swarmed over the battered fuselage.

The Hudson had seen duty with the RAAF (the Royal Australian Air Force). After it had been aerated by shot on several occasions, and had crash-landed twice, it had been stripped of its guns and relegated to reconnaissance. During its last flight, it had been attacked by an enemy fighter. One engine streaming smoke and blown to pieces, it thumped aground a final time. The mechanics declared it beyond repair, and wheeled it to stand with the rest of the relics.

A cursory inspection showed jagged holes all over the body, although the worst of them were covered with metal patches. The entire nose, once a glassed-in turret, was replaced with a metal cone from another wreck.

On each side of the Hudson's fuselage, just below the cockpit windows, was painted a reclining beauty. Scantily clad in a tied-off top and short-shorts, she had flowing yellow hair, long legs, and balloon-like breasts. Beneath her, the artist had rendered in script, "Miss Nippon-These." On the near side, bullet holes stitched across her, and in the tropical sun, she was a faded and peeling rose.

The brains of the salvage operation straddled an engine on the wing. He was Australian of medium height, with freckled skin and sandy hair. He wore filthy shorts and was grease to the elbows. He was a one-time soldier, self-taught pilot and mechanic, and adept jack-of-all-trades.

For the past three months, he'd been at work on the Hudson. It was the centerpiece of his plan—an about-to-be-launched air cargo business. He'd combed the discarded wrecks for one he could save and had settled on the "Miss Nippon-These." He hired mechanics and paid them from his pocket. The repairs they made had been substantial, if primitive.

So far, the pilot had only been able to get one of the aircraft's two engines running. He had dropped the plant the enemy fighter had ruined, and replaced it with one from another wreck. Neither motors nor propellers matched, but the pilot was confident they would serve.

Still, after all his labor, the replacement motor would not start. That was what kept him from getting the craft in the air, but he knew he was close. *Today is the day!* He sat with his legs spread on each side of the engine. The cowling was off and he fished into the innards with his tools. One of his men sat in the cockpit. The side window was open and his hands were up in the tangle of wires. He pulled one strand down, stripped the insulation with his teeth, and touched it to another wire. There was crackling and a puff of smoke behind the instrument panel.

"Bugga!" He jerked the wires apart, pulled down another, and touched again. A light flared in an instrument and he nodded and twisted them together.

"Turn the motor over, would ya?" the pilot yelled.

"Righty-oh!"

The propeller cranked and the pilot pulled his legs away from the blades. The engine caught, ran unevenly as the men cheered, then backfired and stopped. There was a flash of fire, and a gush of oily smoke. The pilot jerked away, frantically slapping at the flames that singed his inner thighs. A cloud enveloped him and he emerged flailing.

"Bloody hell!" he coughed. He spat and kicked the engine with his heels. Muttering darkly, he reached with a screwdriver and twisted again.

Two men with makeshift wooden ladders leaned them against each side of the rear fuselage. They climbed to the jagged hole that had once been the rear gun turret. A jumble of metal and broken glass poked through. One of them peered in, noticed the black crust over everything and scratched his head with a filthy finger.

"Cor blimey! Is that blood?" His friend took a look.

"I reckon so, mate," he said cheerfully. "Let's cover it up." He clambered to earth and fetched an oval of metal snipped from another wreck. The men arranged it over the hole and began to pound it into shape with wooden mallets.

Two more men stood beneath the wings, working on the landing gear. One set of wheels was cocked at a forty-five degree angle, and a brace was broken. The welder tipped the mask over his face while his mate watched through a piece of smoked glass. Sparks flew.

"Go on," the pilot called. "Give 'er another go!" The man in the cockpit complied. The engine sputtered, ground over, and at last roared into life. Gradually it went up in pitch and began to howl, almost blowing the pilot off. He made a frantic slicing motion across his throat and his mate cut the juice.

"Bloody brilliant!" the pilot grinned as his men yelled and whistled. He slipped off the engine and stepped on bare feet to a ladder resting against the wing. He scampered down and noticed the worn leather ball resting on the tarmac. He coaxed it onto a toe, tapped it to his knee, bounced it once, twice, three times, dropped it to a heel, popped it over to the other foot and kicked it up. He knocked it high off his forehead and it spun against the sun. As it fell, he caught it neatly on top of his foot, and rolled it aside.

"I gotta go to town. You blokes carry on," he called. "Now we've got the bloody motor running, she'll be ready to take up later t'day. Whadda ya reckon?"

"Right you are," the man in the cockpit smiled. "I'll watch from down here. And where are you off to, mate?"

"Gotta see a Sheila," the pilot grinned.

"Who's that then?"

"Never you mind. I'll be back in two shakes of a lamb's tail. Ooroo." He tugged on a pair of leather sandals, went to an ancient motorcycle with wide handlebars and climbed on. He kicked it to life and sped away.

"No doubt he's off ta see that nurse—the Canadian," one of the welders said. His partner shrugged.

"Poor old Footy has no luck at all with the Shielas. Here, hand us that spanner."

☆

Colonel Chambers' eyes were fixed on the letter's "P.S."

"Father Bastion warns us to 'beware of the river,'" he told Dingo. "He says a 'monstrous crocodile' has recently arrived. 'It is the biggest one I have ever seen,' he writes. 'Our villagers call it *Ka-him-ka,* which means "Father of the Crocodiles." It is a fearsome creature. "Leviathan, the piercing serpent." It could have crawled up from the fiery pit itself.

"'Our people speak of it as a deity. Brother Constanti and I have barely been able to keep them from worshipping it, especially since it slaughtered five of our flock. This only heightened their desire to placate it. Some of our elders think all the calamities that have befallen us, including the Japanese, are a result of turning from the old ways.'" The Colonel glanced at the Major.

"He calls it 'a test from God.'"

"Or the devil," Dingo retorted. "Leviathan, he says! As I mentioned, I believe I know what it is. One that big is your Estuary or Saltwater crocodile. We call them that because they are at home in the ocean, but they are equally able to negotiate freshwater rivers. Unusual for this one to be so far inland, but not unheard of. 'The Father of all the Crocodiles!' My word! I've heard stories about it all my years here, but I thought it was just another *kanaka* fairy tale.

"The 'saltys' are a plague in the north of Australia. We lose people and livestock to 'em every year. They can drag a full-grown bull into the water and drown it, Henry! Of course, it's worse in New Guinea. What are sticks and stones against such a monster? The people must live on the river, and resign themselves to occasional predation. No wonder they worship the brute!"

"'Beware of the river' is right then," the Colonel said. "I'd like a full briefing on Kissim, and the Raub. It's wise to have all the information—before we go in." He set the letter on the table and looked expectantly at the Major.

"Before we go in?"

"Well, Dingo, I can't very well leave 'my dear fellow American' to the Japs—or the crocodile, for that matter. Part of my mandate is to neutralize or eradicate the enemy where we find him. God knows, the Nips have not surrendered in New Guinea. There are hundreds of thousands of them around."

"Bloody menace," Dingo nodded. "It will take us years to round up all of the Yellow Peril."

"And as you know, these are my last days," the Colonel went on. "In two weeks I leave for the States. But I believe we have time to pull off a rescue before that!"

"Good on ya Henry!"

"Nothing too grand," the Colonel hastened to add. "Let's say, four of my men—commando types."

"A fortnight should be more than enough to get in and out, and bring back your priests," Dingo said.

"We'll call it—oh—'Operation Teeth,'" the Colonel said, displaying his own in a smile. "Show those Japs our bite!"

"That's the spirit Henry! 'Operation Teeth' it is!"

Against Colonel Chamber's explicit instructions, Johnny showed up at Army HQ once more.

He knew he was risking insubordination, but he just couldn't let it go. Again he badgered the Colonel's staff until the Commander decided it was less trouble to see him than not. This time, it was a very frosty officer who had the young man shown into his office. Chambers left him standing at attention while he ignored him for fifteen minutes and went on making notes in a ledger.

Johnny stood rigidly, jaw clenched, until at long last the Colonel closed his book and capped his pen.

"Private Willman," he said coldly, "what in blazes are you doing here?"

"Sir," Johnny blurted, "I am fit for duty, Sir! I request to be returned to my unit, Sir!" The Colonel continued to stare him down.

"I thought I told you, Private, you would be released only on Doctor MacClure's say-so, and not before. Then, like everyone else, you will get your orders through channels, and you will follow them!" Johnny stood with fists balled at his sides, staring straight ahead, and the Colonel sighed. He was inclined to send the boy on to the General. The two deserved each other. But Johnny did not know when to leave well enough alone.

"Sir, some men might be satisfied with being clerks," he blurted, "but a soldier's job is in the fight! That's where I need to be!"

In fairness, Johnny had not intended to insult the Commander, but his haymaker hit a nerve. *Who does he think he's talking to? I'll show this pup a choke chain!*

"Private Willman, you will return to the hospital—at once!" Chambers thundered and slammed his desk. In the next room, his aides shared a nervous look. "There you will remain, bothering no one, until you get your orders! Show up here again, and I'll have you court-martialed for insubordination! Have I made myself clear this time?"

Uh-oh, Johnny thought. He'd heard that tone before. Once again, he'd gone too far.

"Yes Sir!" he said. Crestfallen, he left the office and took himself back to the hospital. Shortly after, Doc Mac came by to add his own rebuke. Johnny was lying on his bed, worn out by his excursion. The old man's blue eyes flashed and his bushy brows were drawn together.

"Young Johnny, neither the world, nor my hospital, revolves around you!" Everyone within earshot turned to stare. "I've just heard from your Colonel. I'm to exert better control over you. Hmmmph! Frankly, I'm fed up with you. But that does not make you well. I do, however, want you out of my sight!"

Johnny was banished to the outskirts of the hospital, to what he and his new roommates called the "the halfway tent." Here they were expected to take care of themselves, make their own beds, and walk to the mess and the showers.

Yet, exasperating as the boy could be, privately, Doc Mac approved of Johnny. There was no medical research he knew of to support it, but he'd observed time and again that patients with a burning desire to live often did so, while others with less grievous injuries succumbed. This young Yank was among those who "swam against the stream."

Doc Mac was disturbed, however, by what it was that motivated the soldier. He suspected his patient clung to life simply in order to kill more of the enemy. On the other hand, who was he to judge? This was war, and perhaps young Johnny was exactly the kind of bloke who was needed.

At any rate, Doc preferred him to the hordes of the callow and cowardly that had slunk through his doors over the years. These were the ones pathetically grateful to their injury because it was their ticket home. Worse yet were the "NPs"—the neuropsychiatric cases—chaps too battle-shocked or terrified to fight. The doctor understood that their predicament was real, but he could not respect the men.

Young Johnny was not of their breed.

— ☾ —

"Let me show you," the Major told Colonel Chambers. The two of them walked to a side table piled with reports and charts. It was dominated by a large colored map, spread open, the corners held down by cannon shells. It displayed the South Pacific, from Australia at the bottom, to the islands of Japan at the top. Across the lower third sprawled the colossal island of New Guinea.

The Major's finger traced up the northern coast and stopped about half way.

"Here's the Raub River," Dingo said, indicating a blue squiggle. His finger followed it until it faded away in the unmarked middle of the island.

"And somewhere here, up at the headwaters, is the village of Kissim, where the Catholic mission is located.

"Here…" his finger moved slightly towards the ocean and he tapped: "is the trouble and strife. This is the notorious 'Valley of the Cannibals.' Home of the Mambu nation—most warlike tribe in all New Guinea. And that's saying something, Henry. No white man's ever gone in there and been seen again."

"Do tell," the Colonel said.

CHAPTER 9

"You know I've kicked around New Guinea a few years?" Dingo asked the Colonel.

"So you've said," Henry murmured. "So you have said."

The door banged and Hala swished in again with a fresh pitcher of juice. She still wore the grass skirt, but she'd pulled on an olive T-shirt stenciled "US Army" across the chest. It was far too tight: *almost worse than naked,* the Colonel thought with a sigh. She replaced the empty jug and departed. The Colonel refilled the glasses.

"Seen some strange things, I have," Dingo went on, eyes absentmindedly following the girl. He looked back at Henry. "You know many New Guineans are cannibals. Most tribes eat their enemies—some even consume their own dead."

"Disgusting," the Colonel grimaced.

"Too right," Dingo said. "But consider this. Our good Catholic priests, like these blokes on the Raub, offer communion to the faithful—the Lord's Supper. The priests teach that the bread and wine literally become the body and blood of Christ.

"It is no less than the eating of God, Henry. Sanctified cannibalism. In some parts of the world I imagine that would be a difficult mystery to communicate. Not in New Guinea! Here they understand what it means to gain a person's power by eating him. They do it all the time."

"What a place!" Henry exclaimed.

"Now, to the Mambu Nation," Dingo went on, "the bush *kanakas* that inhabit the Valley of the Cannibals. Extremely warlike lot, even by New Guinea standards. Worse than the *Kukukuku* tribe, and that's saying something. There are thousands of warriors in the valley, very zealous about defending their territory.

"Nearest I've been, I flew over the place before the war. I swear, some of those *kanakas* were shooting arrows at us! The valley formed a long strip on either side of the Raub River, flanked by sheer mountains, thick with jungle. The entire flat land was under cultivation. I made out four, perhaps five villages on the riverbanks. The only way in and out of the valley appeared to be the river gorges at each end."

"Any way to get through there?"

"Nigh impossible, unless you sent in a coupla-hundred soldiers and modern weaponry. Still, you'd take casualties."

"What, bows and arrows against a full company of armed soldiers?" The Colonel was incredulous.

"Don't underestimate these blighters," Dingo said soberly. "The Mambu are not afraid of the white man, Henry. Many of our patrols learned that the hard way over the years. They will have you for supper, if only to see what you taste like." He sucked his teeth and the Colonel clicked his tongue.

"Then—as your priest mentions—there are the crocs. The Raub is infested with 'em. In fact, the river is named for them."

"For the alligators?" the Colonel asked. "Please explain."

"Crocodiles, Henry. It's named for the crocs."

☼

Johnny came to the road that led to the hospital. He really wanted that shower now. He had the meeting coming up, and hoped he'd see Gwyn there. He hadn't talked to her since Doc Mac banished him to the halfway tent.

She is drop-dead gorgeous, he thought. Finding a beauty like her in New Guinea was a big surprise. Suddenly his imagination took him back to Waikiki Beach, Gwyn beside him, holding his hand! She was wearing a skimpy two-piece bathing suit like Rita Hayworth or Esther Williams. The vision was so real he could almost smell the oil on sun-warmed skin.

He was so dazzled, he stepped in a puddle that sloshed over his shoe. He almost dove headlong in the mud and barely managed to recover. On he staggered, feeling foolish.

His walks had taken him on ever-widening circles through town. To entertain himself, and on the hunt for something half decent to eat, he'd searched out the Moresby restaurants. It was slim pickings. The few he found were in or near the hotels that catered to the expats. Dying for a change from the unremittingly canned and overcooked hospital food, Johnny had tried several.

A week ago on impulse, he'd gone looking for Gwyn. He found her working on the Acute Care ward and noted in her green eyes that glad-to-see-you look, mixed with wariness. He asked her to come out the next night and grab something to eat.

"I don't date patients," she'd said.

"It's not a date," he hissed. "It's just a bite—together." She gave him a level look.

"It's a date," she said, "and I don't go out with patients, or soldiers."

He backed off and bided his time. He set himself the task of finding the very best restaurant in town. It turned out to be a seafood place at the finest hotel, with an Aussie chef. Johnny decided it wasn't up to some of the places he'd gone with his family in Honolulu, but at least the catch-of-the-day was fresh off the grill.

Again he sought Gwyn out, and asked her to dinner. This time he did not even pretend it would not be a date. He spruced up before he went. His fatigues were clean, his hair brushed back, and he wore a buttoned shirt instead of the usual undershirt. He'd even shaved and splashed a little Aqua Velva on. He caught her leaving work, and he did his best to muster his old appeal, the easy smile that had won quite a few hearts back in high school. Gwyn saw him coming, and her tummy gave a funny little jump. Still, Johnny found that the nurse seemed to have no trouble resisting his admittedly rusty charms.

He ended up going for the seafood meal with some of the guys from the halfway tent. They drank too much Australian beer, and while the fish fillets were tasty, he found himself belly-full and heart-empty. For the first time, he began to wonder if he'd been cheated of something. *Like any chance at a normal life.*

Still, he had his promise to keep and he tried to push Gwyn out of his thoughts. Yet she remained an itch that teased the edges of his consciousness. Much of his time in the hospital was lost forever, eaten up by his illness. But now whispers of memory came fading in. Some times, he'd come aware again, to see a beautiful woman with a halo. It was Gwyn by lantern light, seen through the netting. There she'd be by his bed, perched on a chair, often reading a book.

Johnny learned not to show any sign he was awake, or she'd soon be gone. So he'd lay absolutely still, eyelids barely cracked, studying her face in repose. *The soft curls, her lip caught between even teeth.*

She looked younger then, and he could see the girl she'd once been. He traced her features—the lashes, the angle of the cheekbones, the soft lips and the cup of her chin. He followed the line of her neck to the pulse at her throat, then probed the shape within her uniform. *Her breasts against the cloth as she breathed.* He saw the flare of her hips, the molded skirt, the crossed calves.

But Johnny could not hold her there. Shortly after he came to, no matter how still he was, she would glance sharply at him. Then the book would snap shut, and with a quick "sleep well," she'd be gone.

In another time and place, Johnny would have made a serious run at Gwyn. But this was war, and it wasn't over by a long shot. He had no illusions about how dangerous the invasion of the Japanese islands would be. Soldiers who would die to defend a piece of worthless jungle would be much more fanatical fighting for their families. Still, Johnny had to take part in the enemy's ultimate defeat. Only then would he have fulfilled his promise.

That should have put an end to mooning over a nurse. But in spite of his resolve, her image kept getting between him and his war plans.

Then Johnny had a bad dream. In it, he was making love to Gwyn. He was shocked by how vivid the images were, and then he was outraged. This was worse than the usual nightmares. At least, those were populated by dead men. But this fresh torment cut him to the heart because he knew he could not have her. He was pierced through by longing, and there was nothing he could do about it.

Johnny had no other choice but to turn her over to the hard soldier, and the killer did not let him down. *Give her up!* The order came. *This got started because she nursed you. It's normal, but not going further. Let it go!*

But Johnny didn't want to let it go, and he brooded about it. Soon enough, he had to admit it was hopeless. *Even if she liked me, all I can offer is a fling. That would end up hurting her, and that is the last thing I want to do to Gwyn.*

He did not ask her out again. He began to avoid the places he might see her. He redoubled his efforts to get back in shape, because that was his ticket out. But he could not stop his mind filling up with her, and he had no peace.

"Crocodiles—of course," Henry was saying. "'Gators are back where I come from."

"The saltys are far, far bigger," Dingo said, "and unlike your American 'gator, their teeth line the outside of their jaws.

"As for the river: the word 'Raub' is German, named by a Kraut. There was a time when the Hun was all over New Guinea. Still quite a few Lutheran missions hanging on, and so forth.

"The Kraut who named it was famous in his own way. 19th Century bloke, Otto Finsch, who also named the 'Bismarck Sea.' You've heard of Finschhaffen?" The Colonel nodded.

"'Otto Finsch's Harbor.' 'Raub' means 'predator'—something like that. And the place is crawling with the scaly buggers. Lots of the smaller fresh water variety, of course. Grow a mere twelve-foot or so. Still, they are man-eaters—regularly dine on your *kanaka* and his animals.

"But the really enormous brutes are 'saltys.' My guess is this 'Father' is one of them. Long way from his usual haunts, but a bastard that big goes where it wants! Even a fifteen-footer can pull a several hundred pound cow by the nose or leg into the drink. The largest ever killed back home was thirty foot. If this 'Father of the Crocodiles' is in that league, it will weigh about four thousand pounds."

"What? Four thousand pounds!" the Colonel exclaimed. "Imagine that coming at you in the water!"

"Like a submarine—with teeth," Dingo nodded. "And strong swimmers. They can cross the Pacific Ocean. In a scrape with a shark, my money would be on the croc. More intelligent, you see.

"Your male crocodile is extremely territorial. In Queensland, they regularly attack boats. Otto Finsch lost an entire canoe of his *kanakas* at the mouth of the Raub. Overturned their dugout and slaughtered the men in the water as they tried to swim away. Old Otto called it 'Raubfluss'—Predator River—and went on to easier things."

"Well, that's clear enough," the Colonel said. "My men will steer clear of the river! Now let's go over the specifics of Operation Teeth."

"Fire away," Dingo said.

"I'll send four experienced jungle fighters. We'll have to fly them in. I'll need your help there, Dingo. As you know, I have no aircraft at my disposal. I'll pay the charter. The plane can take the men in, and wait for them to finish up. How many days do you think we need?"

"Three days," the Major said decisively. "That should be enough."

"Exactly what I was thinking," the Colonel said. "The plan is simple. Rescue the American priest, Chris Bastion. The secondary objective would be to knock out the enemy, if possible. On the morning of the fourth day, they'll return. Neat and clean."

"And the Eye-tie of course," the Major put in.

"What? Oh yes, they'll rescue..." the Colonel glanced at the letter, "...Father Constanti as well. Naturally."

"And this monster crocodile—and our beloved *kanaka* brothers and sisters?"

"As I said, the men will avoid the river," the Colonel replied. "That simple. Forget the blasted crocodile. As for the natives—I am afraid they are not our concern."

"Not our concern—of course," Dingo said. "Right Henry. Well, I've a coupla-thoughts myself—if you'll allow me."

"Shoot," the Colonel said, taking up his glass and sitting back.

"First—limit the team to two experienced men. More than that will only get in the way. Second, make this a proper Allied operation—one of yours, one of ours."

Henry pursed his lips.

"Sounds good," he said. "Anything else?"

"Yes," Dingo said. "I'll be the 'one of ours.' I'll lead 'Operation Teeth'—with your approval, Henry. I'm the best choice, if I say so myself. I'm the only one with first-hand knowledge of the region. I speak the languages. I know how to handle your *bush kanaka*. And I have conducted many a campaign against the Japs. How does that strike you?"

The Colonel was thrilled, but he allowed himself only a small smile, as befitting his station. Putting "Operation Teeth" under an experienced jungle warrior like Dingo Hawsey was a virtual guarantee of success.

"Dingo, you have my full endorsement," he said. "Glad to have you, Major!" The Colonel offered his hand and the Australian shook it heartily.

"Truth is," Dingo said, "I could use a few days in the bush—get fed up in town. And that means you have only one other bloke to find, Henry."

"Great," the Colonel said. "Now—the clock is ticking. The priest's letter is already dated, and I have two weeks before I go. I want to be here to welcome you back. I'd like you to be on your way by Tuesday."

"Leave Tuesday? Lot's of time, if we find a plane," Dingo grinned. "Puts us back in Port Moresby—let me see, Friday next? We can tear a chop together that night—with the priests, of course. And that still gives you a full week before you have to leave us."

"What about the aircraft?" the Colonel said.

"Leave that to me," the Major replied. "I believe I might know of one. Pilot's a mate of mine." He stood up. "I'll suggest he just touch down, let me and the other bloke out, and come back Friday morning to pick us up. In and out, and Bob's your uncle.

"Tell you what—I'll work out the wrinkles and meet you here first thing Monday. I'll let you know about the plane, and you tell me who's coming along.

"I'll see to it," the Colonel said, walking Dingo to the door.

"One last thing," the Aussie said. "I'd very much appreciate it if your Yank has got experience fighting in the New Guinea bush. There won't be time for me to hold anyone's hand."

"Count on me," the Colonel said. Dingo departed and he closed the door and returned to his desk.

Now who can I send? Something caught his eye.

CHAPTER 10

As the Colonel perused the file, he pulled a handkerchief from his pocket and mopped his face. *Insane heat! I won't miss it—or this primitive place.* Henry's interest was military history, not anthropology! He would continue to write about New Guinea for some time, but as for actually being here, he was fed up. He could hardly wait for the comforts of civilization back in Charleston.

I'd hate to be the one going in-country, he reflected. *But then, that is the privilege of command. But neither can I abandon an American citizen, and it's only a three-day jaunt.* Again, he thought about his book and was encouraged.

Then there's the anecdote for my book! My readers will understand that I, too, have commanded action. And what a tale to tell—a raid to snatch unarmed civilians, priests at that, from the enemy's clutches!

Henry got an image of himself being interviewed by a room full of reporters. In a habitual gesture, he removed the comb from his pocket and slicked back his steel-gray Brylcreemed hair.

But first things first! He returned to the file. The subject of it was as seasoned and decorated a campaigner as he'd come across, but as he knew himself, he was a discipline problem. He'd been promoted an incredible fifteen times, and on an equal number of occasions, demoted again.

The Colonel set the dossier down and walked to the window. Again he stood staring towards the harbor, hands clasped behind his back. *He is the best choice for this mission. He's less than half Dingo's age, but has about as much experience in jungle combat as does the Major. On top of that, the timing's right.* The Colonel had just received a report from the hospital.

Johnny showered for the meeting, and for the first time in days, he shaved. He changed into clean clothes—his other set of fatigue pants and a buttoned shirt. He was keyed up about the outcome, and he warned himself to guard his tongue. Then he made his way to the hospital mess tent and waited in line for breakfast.

A man spooned scrambled eggs onto his metal tray and another slopped on instant mashed potatoes and canned gravy. Johnny grabbed several slices of toast, but bypassed the butter. It had separated in the heat. At least there was fresh coffee. He filled a mug at the urn and topped it up with sweetened condensed milk.

Johnny saw some of the men from his tent and joined them at a long table packed with patients. While he wolfed down his food, he kidded the others about sleeping in all day, while he'd already been to market. He told them about the Catholic girls and they laughed.

Johnny always seemed to be hungry now. Normally his six-foot one-inch frame weighed a hundred and ninety pounds, but when he'd managed to get on a scale here, he'd been dismayed to see the needle settle at one-fifty-something. Since then, he'd packed on a good twenty-five pounds, and he had more to go.

He wiped his tray with a piece of toast, then got another helping. After his third coffee, he still had time before the meeting, so he returned to his tent and took apart his Springfield. Even more than the average GI, he depended on his rifle for his life. He laid the parts out on his cot, oiled and wiped each one, and assembled it again. And at last it was time.

Feeling nervous, ready for an argument but trying to stay calm, Johnny walked to the Acute Care ward. There was frantic activity around the front entrance. A stretcher was being hauled out of an ambulance and a doctor and two nurses were working on the patient, surrounded by a group of men. A jeep stood nearby, engine running, driver behind the wheel. Johnny ducked around the corner where a wooden structure had been built against the rounded side of the Quonset hut.

He knocked and Doc Mac's voice told him to enter. Johnny stepped into the administrator's stark office and found the old man in a bloodstained white jacket, clipboard in hand. Johnny saw it was Ruthie, not Gwyn, who assisted the Chief today, and he suppressed a stab of disappointment. Doc Mac was saying something to him and Johnny forced himself to focus.

"Sorry Doc, what's that?"

"Do you have any pain in the chest?"

"No," Johnny lied. "I'm good." He grinned and rotated the shoulder, ignoring the spasm.

"Well then," Doc Mac said, making a note. The finality in his tone surprised Johnny. He realized the meeting was already wrapping up. It had taken less than a minute.

"I have a busy morning. Young Johnny, we are done with you. It's official. You are no longer a resident of this hospital. You'll have to find another place to stay. I do wish you all the best." Then, wonder-of-wonders, Doc Mac smiled warmly and offered his hand. Johnny took it and shook.

"Keep eating, will you? You need the weight," Doc looked him up and down. "And may I ask you to try not to take the war quite so personally? It seems to interfere with your health."

"I'll try," Johnny said, "And Doc, I owe you my life, I know that. Well—thanks for everything. I'm sorry if I got out of line." The Doctor was still staring at him.

"I'm not sure you know it, young Johnny, but there is more to life than war. Will you try to remember that as well?"

"I'll do my best."

"Good man," the doctor said. "Now, I have a message from your Colonel. He wants to see you, and at once. His jeep is waiting around the front." Johnny's spirits leapt. Maybe there was a ship going north! Doc Mac said goodbye and departed, door banging behind him. Johnny paused to say goodbye to Ruthie.

"I'll see you around," he said. "Sorry if I was a jerk. Say goodbye to Gwyn for me. You heard the Doc. Maybe the Colonel is sending me back to the Philippines."

"Sorry, you'll have to say goodbye to Gwyn for yourself," Ruthie smiled. "Take care, Johnny-me-lad." She stepped up, offered her cheek and he kissed it. Then he was out the door, heading for the jeep. Fifteen minutes later, he was standing in front of the Colonel again, but this time he'd been invited, and that made all the difference.

"At ease," the Colonel said, looking up from the book he was forever writing in. "I understand Doc Mac has given you a clean bill of health." He laid down his pen, rubbed his eyes and leaned back.

"Private, I have an assignment for you. I'm sending you into the New Guinea interior. It's a simple three-day mission I've named 'Operation Teeth.' Show me you can handle this, and I'll send you back to General MacArthur."

"Yes Sir!" Johnny grinned so enthusiastically the Colonel could not help smiling. It was hard not to like the boy, even if he was a pain in the keester.

"I've decided to go out on a limb for you," Chambers said, rising and coming around the desk to face the GI.

"I'm going to give you a promotion. And you will do your best to try and hang on to this one. That is an order."

"Yes Sir!"

— ☽ —

Glen Carmichael leaned the bike against the wall of his house, went in and kicked off his filthy shorts. He stood under the five-gallon bucket on the rope in the stall, twisted the showerhead and cool water cascaded over him. He scrubbed thoroughly, working hard on the blackened arms and fingernails. He lathered the suds into his short, sandy hair, and rinsed off.

He dried himself, decided the short stubble on his face was good enough, and looked through his few clothes. He selected tan shorts and a bright orange shirt. It had been a gift from an auntie—sister of the mother who had passed on when he was a boy. His mum had fallen to consumption, what they now called 'tuberculosis.'

He was dressed in a flash and slid into his sandals. There was a bottle of Old Spice on the dresser and he sprayed some on the armpits of his shirt and slapped a little on his cheeks. On the way out the door he peered into the cracked truck mirror hung on a nail. He licked a finger and smoothed down the one curl that always stuck up.

"Footy me mate, you're God's gift to the Sheilas," he crooned. "She's gotta love ya."

Then he was on the motorbike again, weaving through the Saturday afternoon crowd, on his way to see Gwyn.

— ☼ —

"You'll be under Major Hawsey's authority," the Colonel told Johnny. He waved the GI to the sofas. Once they were seated, he picked a stained letter off the table and handed it over.

"Take this with you. It's a letter from the priest at Kissim.

"'Operation Teeth' will go as follows. You have three days to find Father Chris Bastion. He's an American, and your primary objective. There should be an Italian, Father something-or-other, with him. It's in the letter. Bring them back. Do what you can to kill or capture the enemy troops. That is your secondary mission.

"Stay away from the river. As the letter explains, there's some sort of dangerous gator there.

"Now Son, let me be clear. In spite of anything the priests say, do not bring back any natives! They are not our concern, apart from any relief you can provide by neutralizing the Japs.

"Major Dingo Hawsey will lead. You follow. He's the most able New Guinea hand I've ever met, with a lifetime of experience. Is that clear?"

"Yes Sir."

The Colonel sat forward and stared into the young man's face.

"I've looked through your file, John. You've had more than your share of disciplinary problems. Apart from that, you've got an outstanding record. I'd go so far as to say you're a *bona fide* hero." Johnny stared back and said nothing.

"I'm going to take a chance on you. Your are now Sergeant Willman—I've signed the paperwork. You'll get your stripes in due course. Try to hang on to this one."

"Yes Sir," Johnny said. "Thank you, Sir!"

"Do a good job for me, and I'll send you back to General MacArthur. There's a supply ship scheduled through in nine days, bound for Manila. I'll put you on it before I depart for the States—unless you want to come with me? That's within my power. Are you dead certain you want to return to the war?"

"With all due respect, yes Sir! I want to be there when we take down Japan."

"It's settled then," the Colonel nodded. "What do you need for supplies? One of my aides will take you to the depot and ensure you get what you need.

"Then Sergeant, report here Monday at 0-800-hours for your briefing with Major Hawsey. We have some details to work out, but you two will fly out Tuesday, and the aircraft will pick you up Friday morning. I want you report to me that afternoon. Got it? Good. Dismissed."

Soon Johnny was standing in a storeroom packed to the rafters with equipment.

"Looks like you're well stocked," he said. The Supply Sarg, a middle-aged man with a substantial beer belly, shrugged.

"Most of it's used, if you catch my drift."

Johnny chuckled, then rattled off what he wanted. In short order, he had a box of .30-06 cartridges for his Springfield, a holstered .45 semi-automatic Colt pistol, and ammunition for it. From a pile of knives, he selected a machete in a canvas sheath and a knife-style bayonet that he knew would attach to his Springfield. He chose a webbed belt, and threaded onto it the pistol, knives, two water bottles, and some canvas pockets.

The Sarg brought him a first aid kit. Johnny checked through it; bandages, sulfa powder, iodine, gauze, a roll of tape and cotton balls. There were bottles of water purification tables, which he would use, and anti-malarial pills, Atabrine, which he would leave behind. The bright yellow pills colored his skin and made him feel sick. He preferred the fever.

Johnny asked for syrettes of morphine. The Colonel's aide was watching everything, taking notes, and he approved the requisition. The Supply Sarg said the narcotic was in lockup and went to get it.

Johnny found a used steel M1 helmet with netting and added it to his growing pile. He selected a coil of rope, a mess kit nested together, metal plates and cutlery for two—he didn't know what the Australian was bringing. He grabbed a coffee pot, a one-burner kerosene stove, and a can of fuel. He pulled down a backpack and began to stuff everything in.

The Sarg returned and handed over the morphine—three metal squeeze tubes with their needles under glass caps. Johnny had administered these many times during the fighting—most GIs carried one—and he put them in a pocket.

"Find me a jungle hammock, will you?" he asked, "and a sheet to go with it." In his experience, the ruggedly made hammock with its waterproof roof and mosquito netted sides was the way to go in New Guinea. It kept you out of the mud, away from all the creepy-crawlies.

Johnny turned his attention to food. They needed enough for two men for three, max four days, but he decided to take six days' supply, just to be safe. He sorted through stacks of canned rations and found two cartons to fill.

Into one he put the meat and vegetables. Soon it was stacked with corned beef, stew, potatoes, cooked tomatoes and tomato sauce, mixed vegetables, baked and green beans, and more. He added a pack of hard tack biscuits and C-ration crackers.

The second box, he packed with fruit cocktail, cling peaches, pear halves, applesauce and custard. He added bags of ground coffee, powdered milk and sugar. He decided he'd round up some loaves of fresh bread at the hospital mess Tuesday morning.

"I'll take two cartons of cigarettes," he said. The supply man handed over unfiltered Camels. Johnny almost reached for a box of matches, but decided there was no need. He'd refill his Zippo before they went, and that would be more than enough for this jaunt. "One last thing—a bottle of brandy," he said. The officers stared. "For medicinal purposes," Johnny shrugged. "And that's it."

"Are you sure?" the Colonel's aide asked dryly. "How many days you going for again?" The Sarg fetched a bottle of the amber liquid and Johnny stashed it in his pack.

He tied the hammock roll on top of his bulging backpack, grabbed a shoulder strap and swung it up. Right away, his wound let him know just what a bad idea that was. Pain popped like flash bulbs and he dropped the load. He felt the eyes of the other men on him and he grunted and dropped to a knee. To give himself a moment, he crammed the helmet on his head and breathed deeply. It wouldn't do for the Colonel to hear he couldn't even pick up his pack!

Johnny lit a smoke, grinned through the hurt, and stood. He took all the weight in his right hand, swung the load again and managed to hook his arms through.

"Can I get a ride?"

"Sure thing, Sergeant," the looey told him.

"Give me a hand with that box?" Johnny scooped up one of the cartons of food, careful again to use his right arm, while the Colonel's man hoisted the other.

A short time later, the jeep was pulling up in front of the halfway tent. And this, Johnny saw, was a day for surprises.

She stood in her uniform, surrounded by an admiring cluster of his tent mates. Johnny had his helmet on, knives and the pistol hanging off his belt. He jumped out and sauntered over, feeling suddenly self-conscious under the gaze of those somber sea-green eyes.

Gwyn, it appeared, had been waiting for him.

CHAPTER 11

FROM THE JOURNALS OF COLONEL HENRY CHAMBERS, JR.

The One Punch Fight

Dear Reader, for us to understand our enemy (a key to the art of war), we must first grasp Japan's legendary warrior code, "Bushido." In the 1930's, your Author lived in Tokyo for two years, a Military Attaché to our Embassy. There he had the opportunity to study firsthand this alien and yet refined civilization, its culture and literature, its art and its people.

In Olde England, the knights once conducted their affairs by a code of Chivalry. So, too, did Japan possess a warrior class and Bushido. The Nipponese version of Camelot played out in the Age of the Samurai, one that lasted nearly a millennium.

Technology is the one aspect of industrial civilization that always progresses. And while it provides great boons, it is responsible for more profound alterations in society than war itself.

Bullets and gunpowder transformed the knight in shining armor into a target in a tin suit. So, too, did modern firearms destroy the Samurai as an elite warrior force—for what use is a champion with his sword against a rifleman?

While Chivalry died across Europe and the British Isles, Bushido did not disappear in Japan. The descendants of those fierce old warriors live on. Proud is the military family that can trace its lineage back to the now-outlawed warrior caste!

To the Samurai, a much-admired tactic is the devastating opening strike. As we might put it in the States, "the one-punch fight."

In a story told to me by a military historian over sake and sushi one memorable evening in Tokyo, in this way did a Japanese boy with a stick slaughter a formidable sword master. His secret—the unexpected, fatal blow. That boy, I was told, went on to become Miyamoto Musashi, the most renowned Samurai of the 17th Century. Musashi was both a warrior and an artist, and was undefeated in more than sixty swordfights. His exploits are still recounted to this day in the land of the Rising Sun.

While the Samurai caste system is gone, Japanese strategists continue to admire the ancient code and its tactics. A prime example occurred in the opening years of this 20th Century. Russia, a great world power, craved a warm water harbor. To that end, the Tsar leased Port Arthur on the Chinese mainland. At the time, Japan was just another voice in an Asian chorus, but the fierce island warriors took offense at the Russian Bear's intrusion. Nippon perceived a threat to its dream of destiny as the leader of all Asia, and indeed, for some, even of the world.

In 1904, without any warning (and allow me to emphasize, Dear Reader, without any warning), Japan suddenly attacked the Russians at their port. The action was so unexpected, it earned Nippon a stunning triumph.

Only after the deed was accomplished, did Nippon deliver its declaration of war to Moscow. The Tsar was caught flat-footed. A minor power had bested a great one, and while Russia tried vainly to regroup, Nippon rushed to heap victory upon victory. No doubt this sign of weakness encouraged the revolutionaries, and Tsarist Russia never recovered.

How do we know this? With other world powers of that time, we studied the action closely. The record is readily available. President

"Teddy" Roosevelt himself was an expert in the matter, and won the Nobel Peace Prize for his efforts to broker a resolution between the parties.

Now let us jump forward to Pearl Harbor. The peacetime attack by Japan on our Pacific fleet at Hawaii outraged America, and rallied us to war. It will live forever as the "day of infamy," in the words of our recently demised and greatly missed President, Franklin Delano Roosevelt.

Yet, no one can say the Japanese tactic of preemptive strike prior to declaration of war was unprecedented.

On the contrary. It was entirely in keeping with the mindset and history of Nippon.

Dingo Hawsey drove the jeep to his house and threw his swag together. Truth was, he was tickled by the promised action. *Good on ya Henry!* Dingo was forty-six and as tough as nails. He regularly lifted weights with the lads, and played tennis three times a week.

That said, it was clear his days in the field were numbered. His promotion to Major had meant a jump in pay grade, but it also tied him to a desk. As a man who'd run his own plantations all his adult life, Dingo was a hands-on type of bloke. But as long as the war ground on, he was stuck at HQ in Port Moresby. He knew the younger fellows needed a steadying hand, but the duty often wearied him.

Operation Teeth gave him the increasingly rare chance for a fight in the bush. It was only three days, of course. He'd be back in the office almost before the lads noticed he was gone. And while he'd never come out and say it this way to the Colonel, the outing sounded like a bit of serious fun.

Dingo was alone in the house. Alice, "the wife," was in Australia under the wing of her parents, near Tamworth in New South Wales. The two children, teenage beauties, were boarders at Calrossy School. When things got a bit more settled, Alice had agreed to return to Port Moresby, but not so the girls. They were not little tykes any more, and there were no suitable schools in the Territories. They would stay on in Aus, and come up for the months-long summer holidays over Christmas.

Dingo knocked the dust off his wood framed rucksack, rolled up a blanket, put in a square of mosquito netting for his face, balled up a change of clothes, cooking gear, toilet kit, and the rest of it. It made him feel younger—*reminds me of the months fighting the Japs on the Kokoda Trail!*

The enemy had attempted to invade Port Moresby by sea and failed. After that, the buggers had a go by land. They trekked all the way across the Owen Stanley Range. That took bollocks, you had to give them that.

Capturing Port Moresby would give them control of New Guinea, the ideal staging ground for a rush across the Gulf to take Australia. So they tried to take the Capital from the backside. That plan had worked for them at Singapore, where the Pommies had all their guns pointed out to sea. *Ruddy scandal, that.* But New Guinea was a different kettle of fish. The attack overland had not worked out here.

The hike across New Guinea took a terrible toll on the enemy. Only blokes like Dingo, who knew this formidable, pestilent land, had any idea of what they'd endured. *The blighters ended up sick and starving. Put an end to the myth of the Jap superman,* Dingo grinned to himself. He went to fetch his rifle.

Still, they'd gotten in sight of Port Moresby before they'd been turned around. Me and the boys were there to fight the bastards on the way over, and hound them all the way back. On both legs, I chalked up my share of kills.

That was the Kokoda Trail—"the Track," the Aussies called it. In anyone's book, it was a hellish fight under extreme conditions. But Dingo Hawsey was a man who thrived in the bush. *Helps to walk barefoot like a bloody kanaka—been doing it most of me life. Better than boots that grow jungle rot to strip your toes to the bone. Bare feet let you slip up on a man and pull your knife across his gullet, before he even knows you're there.*

Dingo could sleep anywhere in the bush. Insects and animals didn't put him off. Getting enough to eat was sometimes a problem. He preferred his meat fresh, and included croc on the menu.

Of course, it's best to give the big saltys a wide birth—the brutes like "the Father" this Yank writes about. A bloke must know his limits. Still, I'd like to lay eyes on the bugger the kanakas yammer on about—but from a suitable distance.

Speaking of the natives, Dingo *was* an old New Guinea hand, and he knew how things worked here. *Your kanaka doesn't respect a man unless he shouts and waves his arms a bit.* Both in the bush, and here in town, he insisted they call him "Master Dingo." That was the rule. If some of the bleeding heart Yanks wanted to coddle up to them—let them call you by your Christian name, for example—well, they'd learn that was a mistake. *There are only a few of us here, outnumbered ten thousand to one, and we must keep the upper hand.*

In the Major's experience, if you went soft, the locals were quick to walk all over you. The white man's ways were not *kanaka* ways. *If you want a worker to put in his ten hours a day, you must instill a healthy fear of Yours Truly. Otherwise he'd be off home at his earliest opportunity, and still expect his pay come Friday. No, in order to succeed here, you must have clear rules and a hard hand. That was the only way to bring a bit of civilization to the bush. Anyone who said different,* Dingo snorted to himself, *is blowing air through his arse.*

The Major lifted his .303 Lee Enfield off its pegs and once again admired the fine grain of the English walnut stock. The rifle had a magazine of ten shells, inserted in clips or "chargers" of five shots each. The firearm was loaded, as always, and Dingo dropped some extra chargers in his kit.

He withdrew the Webley pistol from a drawer. It was a six-shooter, made so it opened like a shotgun and automatically ejected the spent cartridges. It, too, was fully loaded, and Dingo dropped in another handful of ammo in a pocket of his rucksack.

From the table beside his bed he picked up his one concession to Yank weaponry, a gigantic hunting knife. This he'd salvaged from a dead GI on the north coast. *Not that the poor lad needed it any more.* The knife had a leather sheath worked in a scene of a deer head against pine trees. He withdrew it and checked the sharpness with his thumb. The blade was a foot long, with a bone handle—*a beaut!* From the first moment he hefted it, it felt like it belonged in his fist.

The Yanks called it a "Bowie knife," he'd been told, although what that meant, he did not know. He had bloodied it in close fighting any number of times, and never went into the bush without it.

Dingo had everything ready in twenty minutes. Then he bellowed for his native cook to bring lunch. He got a plate of cold sliced mutton, a packet of Melba toast, and some pickles fished from a jar. After that, he'd get in three hours of tennis. Tonight at the pub he'd bend his elbow with his mates.

I'll have a chinwag with Footy. He was a Corporal Dingo had chummed with on the Track, and now he was a private pilot. *I wonder how "Footy's Folly" is doing? Perhaps he's got that old bomber ready to fly. If not, he'll know the whereabouts of every available plane.*

Come Monday, the Major would meet whatever Yank the Colonel had selected. Dingo liked Henry, but inwardly, he was scornful of the American's ability to put together a fight. There was no question Henry was good at "admin"—his garrison ran like a clock. But when it came to action in the bush, the Colonel had been forced to rely on Dingo's advice every time.

Whatever Yank he picks had better not be wet behind the ears, or I'll make him sit in camp while I sort things out.

— O —

He was troublesome and bull-headed. And—strike three—he was a soldier. Yet, here Gwyn found herself, waiting for him.

In some ways, she knew Johnny as intimately as he did himself, but in others, he was a stranger. It was his body she knew best. After all, that was her job. She had taken care of his needs while he was comatose, his very life in her hands. She had even peered through his flesh to the bone. On numerous occasions, she had washed his hair, shaved him, and sponged him from head to toe. In that regard, he had no secrets.

But what about the man within? Early on, when he was unconscious, his battle reduced to simply fighting for the next breath, she'd kept watch. When he wasn't out cold or raving, they'd spoken a little and she knew something of his past. Gradually she was forced to admit to herself—he was a manly man, and his looks attracted her.

But as he improved, the soldier came to the forefront, with his cracked-record plan to kill more of the enemy. This bloodthirsty GI drove her away. There was something bent in him, she decided, maybe broken, and she doubted it could be fixed.

But here she found herself, waiting at his tent. After Ruthie told her Doc had discharged the man, Gwyn had come looking for him. She hadn't spoken with Johnny lately, not since he'd returned the books he'd borrowed, but she knew where his tent was.

And now here he came, like a kid with all his gear, looking more like a soldier than ever.

Just what am I doing here? she wondered again, while his buddies helped unload the equipment from the jeep. *I've just come to wish him well,* she told herself. *After all, I nursed him back to health.* Johnny spoke to the driver and the vehicle sped away, and then he came over to Gwyn.

"Will you give us a few minutes?" he asked the other men, and they retreated into the tent.

"Hello Gwyn," Johnny said.

"Hello Johnny. I heard Doc Mac released you. I came to say goodbye. What's your plan?"

"I've been ordered on a three day mission, somewhere in the interior of New Guinea," Johnny said. "There are priests that need rescuing. I leave Tuesday and I'll be back Friday. Then the Colonel promises to get me on a ship the following Monday, back to the Philippines."

"Just what you wanted," Gwyn said.

"What I want," Johnny nodded. She looked away, but then her eyes flashed back at him.

"Is that all you think about, Johnny Willman? More killing?"

He was startled by her vehemence.

"I'm a soldier, Gwyn," was all he could say. *Lame!*

"I know," she said. "I just wondered—when will it be enough?"

Never. It will never be enough for what they did.

"Gwyn, this is war," he replied slowly. "It's over when it's over."

"Funny how some guys seem to find time for other things," Gwyn responded. "But you asked me out. I'd like to know why." Again, Johnny was caught off guard.

"I like you, Gywn," he mumbled. "You're smart—and about the prettiest girl I've seen." *I think about you all the time, even when I don't want to.*

"Well, thank you," she said. *He thinks I'm smart!* Johnny stepped closer and took her hands in his.

"I'd like time with you," he said. "Away from..." he glanced around, "...away from this. But I'm not going to get the chance. I have this job, and then there's the ship back to my unit."

Gwyn looked down and did not reply. He was still clutching her hands. At last she stared into his eyes.

"Johnny, what happened to you?" she asked. "Oh, I know you've been through a lot. I can't even imagine. But all you think about—all you talk about—is killing. Do you have any heart left?"

"I—I…" Johnny trailed off. He thought about what she was asking. *Do I have a heart left? Can I feel—really feel—anything anymore?* Something made him want to be honest with her.

"I guess I don't know," he said. "I'm sorry Gwyn. You're something special. And you deserve—well, you deserve much more than I can give." Chagrinned, he dropped her hands and turned away. He felt a touch on his arm and looked into her face.

"When did you say you'd be back?"

"Friday."

"Then I'll save Friday night for you. We can go for dinner—if you still want to." *What am I saying?* She was scaring herself.

"Yes!" Johnny said. "Dinner, Friday night."

"But…" she added.

"Ok, give it to me."

"But I want you to do something while you're gone. Will you do it?"

"Yes," Johnny said at once.

"Will you try and find what you've done with your heart?" She saw him frown and smiled to take the sting out.

"Not this." She touched a finger to his chest. "I'm talking about the place where you've hidden the best of you."

"Like what?"

"Oh—like hope. And laughter. Enjoying people, life. Being kind. You know—that heart."

Johnny thought hard. *When was the last time I laughed? I mean, really laughed?* He couldn't remember and he shook his head.

"Gwyn, a soldier can't go around *feeling* everything!" he protested. "You're right—you have no idea what I've gone through. The things I've done. But I'll make you a promise. I'll think about what you said. Ok?"

"Friday night," she said. "You'll pick me up?"

"At 6:00," Johnny said. "I'll come by. I know where you live."

He knows where I live? Gwyn felt a flutter of something that might have been excitement, or perhaps fear.

"Ok," she said. "Take care of yourself, Johnny."

She turned to leave and he surprised both of them by leaning forward and planting a kiss on her. She was in mid-turn and his lips landed on the corner of her mouth. He got a glimpse of startled eyes and then she was walking away. It was a sight he'd seen all too often. Johnny watched her go.

You went too far! But if she looks back, it's ok. If she doesn't, she's mad. He stared at her back, willing her to turn around. But she did not. She walked fast around the corner and was gone.

There were whistles and catcalls from the tent. Johnny's buddies had watched the whole exchange through the net windows. Now they spilled out and surrounded him, calling him a lucky son-of-a-gun and worse, while they helped drag his gear inside.

Gwyn walked fast, not even sure where she was going. She could feel the place where he had brushed her lips and cheek. She had been almost overcome by the urge to spin around and stare at him, but she'd fought it off. She knew the reason. Her face was on fire.

What am I doing? she wondered. *What have I done?*

☆

Johnny's mood peaked. *I have a date with the loveliest girl in New Guinea!* That, on top of everything else, made him feel he was floating.

But he might have been deflated if he saw what Gwyn got up to a few hours later. She was strolling arm-in-arm through the marketplace with another man.

After she left Johnny, Gywn returned to her apartment. She changed into a light dress and sunhat, and went out to meet him. As they often had, they wandered through the market so she could buy groceries for the Orphanage. They filled the string *bilum* she carried over her shoulder. The place was still busy, even though some vendors had sold out and left. After that, Gwyn and her companion wandered onto the road along the harbor.

There, Johnny would have seen the fellow take her hand, and it might have disturbed him that she did not pull away. The man, about Gwyn's own age, a little older than Johnny, guided Gwyn out of the stream of traffic to stand beside the water. They were lost in deep conversation. Then, as Johnny had done a few hours previously, the fellow took Gwyn's hands in both of his. He spoke earnestly for several minutes, while she searched his face and did not interrupt.

At last he stopped and she gently retrieved her hands. Then it was her turn to talk, her face serious. When she was done, the man gazed intently at her and then turned to look at the ships.

If Johnny had been watching, he would have seen Gwyn kiss him. True, it was only a peck on the cheek, but she put up a hand and stroked his face as well. It was the kind of affectionate touch a woman only gives someone she cares deeply about.

The couple stood quietly a moment longer, and then Gwyn departed.

The man known to his mates as "Footy" stood lost in thought, a frown on his face. Then his habitual grin surfaced, and he made his way through the crowd in search of his motorbike.

Chapter 12

Tuesday morning, Johnny had an early breakfast with the men from the halfway tent and bought some loaves of bread. The day before, he'd visited the barber. The man got busy with his clippers and the dark curls fell to the floor. *Fighting short.*

He was standing outside his tent with all his gear when the Colonel's jeep pulled up. Johnny was dressed in camo trousers and his undershirt. The belt around his waist bore two canteens of water, the revolver, bayonet and machete. The rope was tied to his pack and he had his helmet on, Springfield over his shoulder. His buddies heaved the food cartons and everything else into the back. Johnny said his goodbyes and climbed in the passenger seat. Soon he'd left the hospital behind for good.

The Colonel's aide raced to the airport and headed across the Macadam. There was a line of wrecks in the distance, but they cut towards an old bomber at the end of the runway. Johnny's first impression was of a piece of junk. It had metal patches all over it and the propellers didn't even match. As they got close, he noticed the pin-up beauty on the side and the name, "Miss Nippon-These." *This can't be our plane!* But it must be, because there was the Aussie Major beside it—the one he'd met yesterday at the Colonel's office.

Major Hawsey. What did he tell me to call him? Some sort of dog. The mission leader stood with his backpack and rifle, dressed in shorts and a shirt with the arms rolled up to display thick biceps. He wore a brimmed hat, the kind the Aussies favored, with the side hooked up. The man was barefoot. A pair of sandals was tied to his pack. *Some of these characters have been here too long!*

The Major was laughing with a smaller man, dressed in white shorts and a light shirt. The jeep stopped and Johnny got out and began to unload. The Major and the other guy came over and lent a hand.

"Morning, Johnny,"

"Morning Major."

"Now, we had that out yesterday," the older man smiled. "I'm in charge, but from here on in, we're just a coupla mates in the bush, awlright? You call me Dingo like I told you." *Ah, that was it.*

"Ok—Dingo." They had Johnny's gear out and the jeep sped away.

The Major put a hand on the shoulder of the man beside him. "This here's a good mate of mine, our pilot—Glen Carmichael."

"G'day mate," the fellow grinned, extending a hand. "I hear you're a Yank, but we'll try not to hold that against you."

"Thanks Glen," Johnny said dryly as he shook. He must have gripped a little harder than he meant to, because the pilot grimaced and squeezed back.

"Call me 'Footy,'" the man said.

"Footy? As in—foot?"

"Footy," the pilot said, "as in 'football.'"

"Soccer to you Yanks," Dingo nodded. "Footy's quite the boy on the field."

Johnny turned toward the aircraft.

"Tell me we're not flying in that!"

"She might look a bit rough, but she's sound," the pilot said defensively. "Miss Nippon-These will get you there, and pick you up come Friday, no worries, mate."

"You guarantee that?" Johnny asked.

"Bloody right!" Footy sputtered.

"Johnny, if Footy says so, you can count on it. Come on lads, stop the pissing and let's get this mission in the air!" Dingo grabbed a food carton and headed for the aircraft. Footy shrugged and picked up the other box.

"Let's not get off on the wrong foot," the pilot smiled. By the time they reached the wooden ladder leaning against the door into the bomber, the Major was aboard. "Up you go. We'll be hunky dory, you'll see."

"Ok," Johnny muttered as he climbed, "but I don't like it. I don't like it at all."

He stepped into the Hudson and saw it was all open space, the metal interior and wiring on display. In the middle sat a bench seat bolted to the floor that looked like it had come from a truck. The men deposited their gear and the pilot went to the cockpit.

"Tie everything down," Dingo said, "in case of turbulence."

Johnny uncoiled his rope and lashed his gear to the ribs using slipknots. Dingo watched approvingly, then took the end of the rope and did the same, not quite as expertly. Johnny wedged his helmet and rifle under the strands. The men sat down and realized there were no seatbelts.

One engine roared to life, and then the other, blowing smoke. Soon they were yowling and the aircraft began to creak forward. A hairy spider as big as a hand climbed out of the fuselage over the men and dropped fast, legs spread. Dingo whipped off his hat and swatted it away. It scuttled across the floor and ducked into a hole.

The Hudson went bounding down the runway, motors roaring. On and on they rumbled and Johnny thought they'd never lift off. But then the shuddering stopped and the aircraft tilted up. They watched the treetops fall away.

Footy put the craft into a steep climb. The altimeter, he saw, wasn't working, but he figured they were at about seven thousand feet and leveled off. There followed a long stretch with only the vibration of the engines and the whistle around the patches. The air felt cold and thin. Dingo gave Johnny a wink, pulled his hat over his eyes, and fell asleep.

From time to time, Johnny went to the windows and stared down. He saw only the interminable green jungle, occasionally parted by the coils of a brown river. After some hours, Johnny felt the plane's engines labor as they climbed over the mountain range. He glimpsed snow on the tallest peaks.

He was hungry and he tore off the end of a loaf and ate. It occurred to him that he was getting into the supplies for the trip, but he wasn't concerned. He'd brought double what they needed for three days, and Friday's breakfast, before the flight back.

The Hudson shot into a cloudbank and the windows went dazzling white. After a time they exploded into brilliant blue again. Dingo dozed on and Johnny wandered back and forth to the windows. Now below them was a rumpled cloud blanket as far as he could see.

As he watched, the bomber threaded between enormous cumulous towers. They boiled up a thousand feet above them and Johnny suddenly felt tiny. As the Hudson passed between the thunderheads, he saw bursts of light within and guessed it was lightning. Crouched at the windows, he watched for some time.

Once more the bomber banked around a cloud and he realized they were going in circles. When the floor leveled out, he worked his way to the cockpit and stuck his head in.

"How're you doing?" he yelled over the thrum. The pilot turned towards him and Johnny saw worry on the man's face.

"Not good," Footy said. "I can't see the bloody ground." There was a hand-drawn map spread on the copilot's chair and Footy squinted at it. "Look," he called. "We're in the vicinity of the Raub, but I can't see. Get Dingo up, would you? I need his help."

Johnny woke up the Major and they returned. Dingo waved Johnny into the co-pilot's seat while he stood in the doorway, holding on.

"I reckon the Raub's below us," Footy said over his shoulder, "but it's socked in. No landmarks. The usual in New Guinea, I'm afraid. Why they call the blasted place 'the pilot killer.'"

"What now?" Johnny asked.

"We need a break in the clouds—a way through," Dingo said. Footy ran a hand over his face.

"I'll circle for a bit—but I need enough petrol for the return flight. We must find a way in the next fifteen minutes, or we have to call it off."

"Abort the mission?" Dingo yelled.

"If we must, mate," Footy called back. "Now put your eyeballs out there." The men stared in every direction but saw only clouds. At last Footy tapped the fuel gauge.

"That's it I'm afraid…"

"There!" Johnny yelled. He'd seen a flash of green through the side window. "A hole!"

Footy stood the Hudson on a wing and dropped the nose. The bomber screamed down, an arrow against the thunderheads. The gap was there, a patch of jungle in the white, disappearing fast. Just in time, Footy brought the Hudson through. At once the light dimmed and rain splattered against the patched windows, blurring the view. Footy saw the band of water to one side and wrestled the craft that way.

On the ground, the drone of engines had been noticed for some time. Hostile eyes watched the black shape drop suddenly out of the rain. The roar was loud as the enemy aircraft careened at them along the river. The patrol turned with guns ready and ran for the only place an aircraft could land.

The bomber shot low over the river's surface. The men stared at the jungle rushing by. It was Dingo who saw the open bank.

"There!" he shouted. "A village!"

"Right mate," Footy called. He squinted through the drops that quivered across the windows. The clearing came up fast and then was below. Johnny made out blackened circles, the remnants of huts. Behind that was a strip of grass surrounded by jungle, and then a mountain that climbed into the clouds. They were over dense jungle again. Footy banked hard over the river, leaving Johnny's stomach behind.

"Gotta be Kissim!" Dingo yelled, hanging onto the doorway.

"And the airstrip!" Footy called. *The landing site the priest wrote about,* Johnny realized.

They were back over the village. Johnny stared, but saw no one, no movement at all. The bomber turned inland and there was the field. The pilot made a pass over it while he worked the controls. The landing gear clunked into place. They could see nothing but rain, mist and the waist-high *kunai* grass.

"Look ok?" Johnny asked.

"It'll have to do," Footy said grimly.

The mountain flank came up fast. Again the pilot spun the Hudson and they were headed back at the field. A crosswind shoved them sideways and rain rattled like pebbles along the fuselage. Footy nudged the nose into the wind and the plane crabbed on, dropping lower.

Then, with a stutter of rupturing metal, bright shafts of light poured into the cockpit. A new set of holes opened as Johnny stared. Footy fought the stick and the bomber yawed wildly.

"Machine gun!" Dingo bellowed. There were clangs to Johnny's right and he glanced along the wing and saw chunks of the engine flying off. The propeller froze, black smoke billowing behind it, and there was the stench of gasoline. The aircraft dropped hard again and Footy fought it.

"Bloody hell!" he gritted. The ruined engine exploded in an orange fireball and Johnny saw the grass rushing at them.

Then three men burst from the jungle into the waist-*high kunai*. The leader had a machine gun and the other two, rifles. They turned and aimed at the aircraft. Johnny saw tracers come from the machine gun. The windshield exploded and bullets whined overhead and punctured the bulkhead. Dingo dropped to the floor.

"Bloody, bloody hell," Footy snarled. "Hang on!"

The plane fell like a stone, hit dirt and bounced. They struck again, hopped up, fell back, and stayed down. The landing gear collapsed with a scream of rending metal and the bomber slammed down on its belly. Now it was no more than a mass of twisted, burning metal, hurtling down the field.

Johnny couldn't take his eyes off the soldiers. They were close enough now that he could see they were Japanese. The guns kept firing and shot clanged around them. Pieces flying off, the Hudson bore down on the men. Suddenly the shooters perceived their danger. They stood frozen for long seconds, then broke and ran for their lives.

The Hudson slewed so Johnny's side window gave him a ringside view. The machine gunner ran first, another on his heels. The third man stumbled and fell. The wing on Johnny's side dipped down and mowed the grass. A rain of stalks flew into the smoke and fire. The first two Japanese managed to clear the wingtip. The third man was on his feet again, but too late. The wing plowed him under.

The bomber continued in a din of shrieking metal. The jungle was coming at them fast now, and then the wing smashed into a giant boulder. The fuselage drew a circle around it and at last it ground to a stop. In the comparative silence, there was only the pinging of metal and the whoosh of the fire consuming the engine. Johnny glanced back: Dingo sat on the floor, bleeding from a cut on his cheek, but apparently ok.

"Get out!" Footy screamed, fumbling with his harness. "She's gonna blow!"

Johnny threw himself back at his equipment, pulled his slipknots and his stuff tumbled loose. He jammed on his helmet, got his Springfield over his shoulder, and bent to help Dingo with his knots. Everything was taking too long.

Footy dashed up, scooped up a box, threw open the door and bailed out. Dingo, rifle in hand and pack on his back, followed. Johnny had his pack in one hand and a food box in the other. He tossed the things out and, holding his Springfield, he jumped. He hit hard, rolled and felt the jolt in his shoulder, but protected his rifle. He gathered the spilled cans and bread back in the box, got his pack on and ran after the others.

The machine gun opened up again and they dove onto their

bellies. The *kunai* provided cover, but no protection, and the bullets cut through the grass, searching them out.

FROM THE JOURNALS OF COLONEL HENRY CHAMBERS, JR.

The Samurai and the Cowboy

Dear Reader, in order to illuminate the profound difference between West and East, America and Japan, I beg your indulgence in a metaphor.

If Japan is the Samurai, then America is the Cowboy.

Just as the Asians have their traditions, so too do we have our unique mythology. America has the legendary Cowboy who tamed the Wild West. He is the frontiersman who rode the range and brought order to a hostile land. Somehow he managed this without organized law enforcement, and none of the niceties of civilization.

As to his character: the Cowboy is self-sufficient and a man of few words, but when he does speak, you do well to listen. He has hard fists and six-shooters on his belt, and he is not afraid to use either set. He is slow to anger, but when push comes to shove, he comes out blazing.

In the face of bullies, bandits, gunslingers and mercenaries, he is the ordinary folks' only hope. He is the champion of a woman's honor, even when it is somewhat tarnished, as it might be on the frontier. He is the defender of the innocent and the helpless. Circumstances at times force him to become both judge and executioner, and then it is his bullet fired through a black heart.

The Cowboy is part outlaw, part marshal, and all man. In this regard, America is unique. No nation loves a good-hearted rogue quite like we do. We admire the principled man who finds himself on the wrong side of the law. Our Cowboy-hero demonstrates the deep truth on which, in part, our nation was founded. Corrupt institutions and men will bend righteous laws to evil purposes.

It is not words in a law book, but the Cowboy's conscience, under God, that dictates right from wrong. Eventually he must take the high road, even if that results in his own destruction.

So where do we find our hero of the Wild World in the mid-20th Century? Where was he when the Samurai swung his sword, and our boys died by the thousands at Pearl?

For Nippon, that strike was born of an ancient, honorable tradition. Our Cowboy, however, had no knowledge of that oriental code. In fact, our Western hero's ultimate contempt was reserved for the kind of lowlife who would sneak his gun out and shoot a man in the back.

Therefore, when Japanese warplanes fell from peacetime skies onto Pearl Harbor, the Cowboy Nation perceived the heinous act of a despicable coward.

On December 7th, 1941, the Samurai committed the worst error in its two-and-a-half thousand years of Empire. Nippon imagined a bold blow that would cripple its enemy. America would be forced to sue for peace on Nippon's terms. Instead, it merely thrust a needle into the eye of a giant.

Most certainly, America felt the sting. With a roar of outrage that rocked the world, the Cowboy climbed to his feet, drowning out the cooing of the Doves and Isolationists.

Through a sheen of blood, the Cowboy glowered across the oceans. He intoned the names of his enemies and called down righteous war upon them. Both the Samurai Warrior and the jackbooted Nazi must have felt the icy winds of destiny change at that moment!

America would rush first to England's side and do battle against

Hitler's hordes, but the Cowboy's special fury would be reserved for Japan. The slaughter of the two thousand, three hundred in Hawaii, the destruction of our Pacific fleet, the invasion of our Philippines and the egregious assault on our sons there: these affronts would burn hot in the mind and heart of America.

Now, in mid-1945, the Japanese Empire has paid dearly, and will continue to pay, for its actions. It does not matter how long it takes or how steep the price. America has determined that the future of Nippon has been reduced to two ineluctable words: "unconditional surrender."

Indeed, at the time of this writing, America and its Allies have bested the Nazi beast. Now we batter on the very doors of Japan. The Samurai Warrior fights on, but he is grievously wounded, and already he must feel his imminent doom.

And it is here, Dear Reader, that our metaphor ends. For as Japan is not merely the Samurai, America is much more than the Cowboy. Both nations are composed of thousands, if not millions, of competing and divergent voices. Your Author has attempted only to establish what the 18th Century German philosophers called "Zeitgeist"—the spirit of the age.

In reality, America is a sophisticated and complex society composed of more than one hundred and thirty-three million citizens. These are the product of every ethnic group and nation on Earth. Together we form one great Republic. America is our world's most potent and prolific industrial force. Our love of freedom, our power, influence, and business interests, cover the globe.

America is renowned for its warmth and generosity. Our nation makes the best of friends, and the worst of enemies. As we continue to teach Nippon in the crucible of war, those who ignore this fact do so at their mortal peril.

At the time of this writing in mid-1945, only the second global war in history is entering its final chapter. Both occurred in the first half of this 20th Century. The cost, already inconceivable, will be much greater before we are done. It is estimated that between fifty- and seventy-five million people have perished in this handful of years, most of them civilians. Much of the old world lies in ruins.

But rising tall from the rubble, towers the United States of America. Only one other world power remains on its feet—our uneasy Ally, the Soviet Union. Of that brutal and repressive society under "the Butcher" Joseph Stalin, we will say little here.

Where have the others gone? Germany's star burned briefly and flared out. Hitler's dream of the Third Reich and a thousand-year reign did not even last a decade. And while the once great European nations will no doubt attempt to regroup, the world has changed forever. Their former colonies have sipped the heady nectar of freedom.

Even the glory that was once the British Empire continues to fade towards darkness. Vestiges can be seen here and there, in trains that run on schedule, a body of Common Law, and that greatest of legacies, the English language.

The United States of America remains the champion of democracy, freedom and justice for all. As a nation and a society, Americans know best how often, and how far, we fall short of our high ideals. Yet we will continue to fight, until we bring them to fruition.

This much is clear. America is the last great hope of the world.

Part 2
The River

☽

"Can you pull in leviathan with a fishhook
or tie down his tongue with a rope? ...
Who dares open the doors of his mouth
ringed about with his fearsome teeth? ...
Strength resides in his neck; dismay goes before him...
He makes the depths churn like a boiling caldron...
Nothing on earth is his equal—a creature without fear."
– Job 41

☆

"I had a vision...the phantom-bearers, the wild crowd of obedient worshipers, the gloom of the forests, the glitter of the reach between the murky bends, the beat of the drum, regular and muffled like the beating of a heart —
the heart of a conquering darkness."
– Joseph Conrad, Heart of Darkness

☼

"A good plan, violently executed now,
is better than a perfect plan next week."
– General George Patton

CHAPTER 1

The three men crawled away from the wreck as fast as they could, while machine gun bullets whined overhead. Then the explosion came, flattening the grass. It was followed almost immediately by an even louder boom. There was a roar of flame and Johnny felt the fierce heat on his back. *Both wing tanks.* A shower of twisted metal crashed down around him.

Footy wiggled into a shallow depression, pushing the box. Dingo slid in after him, while the machine gun chopped the grass over their heads. Johnny left his pack and the box and, rifle in his hands, crawled to the others. When he was close, he motioned for them to stay put. He wagged a finger at the machine gun, then to himself: *I'll take care of them!* He slithered away.

Good on ya Johnny! Dingo thought, flat on his belly. Perhaps the Colonel had done right by him after all. He and Footy tucked their heads down as slugs struck just in front of their hole and showered them with dirt.

The land sloped away. Still in the *kunai*, Johnny stood, bent double and ran. The enemy rifleman saw the undulating grass and tapped the machine gunner's shoulder. A line of slugs chased Johnny across the field. He heard them biting at his heels and began to zigzag like the football pass receiver he'd once been. Finally to the tree line, he threw himself behind a trunk. Bullets tore into it and a splinter nicked his face. He kept the tree between himself and the enemy and climbed. The gunner lost sight of him and went back to probing the field with lead.

Full of adrenaline, Johnny hauled himself up. *Take the high ground!* Fifteen feet in the air, he paused on a limb and peered through the leaves. What he saw chilled him. The enemy soldiers had fanned out and were walking fast through the grass. They were almost on the Australian's hiding place—Johnny could see his trail coming away from them.

He grabbed the bark with his left hand and rested his rifle on it. He had both eyes open. One absorbed the whole scene—*the Japs walking in the rain, the burning hulk behind them.* With his other, he had a close view of the machine gunner. He aimed at the chest and shot. The man slammed over.

The third enemy threw himself down in the grass. Johnny watched the place while he reloaded by feel—a much-practiced move. He fired, hit his target, and the wounded soldier staggered up and tried to run.

Dingo's head came into view. The Major leapt across the short distance, his big knife raised. The combatants locked together and fell. The blade flashed above the grass and down. Dingo stood, looked toward the jungle and beckoned with the bloodstained blade. Johnny climbed out of the tree.

By the time he got to them, Dingo and Footy had checked the enemy corpses and found they were almost out of ammunition. There was no point hanging onto their machine gun or rifle, but they wouldn't leave them for others to find. They heaved them into the burning bomber.

They headed for the jungle. Johnny glanced back. The Miss Nippon-These flamed fiercely, smoke churning into the rain.

☆

Soaked through, Johnny, Dingo and Footy sat under a lean-to hidden in the trees. They had tied a sapling across two trunks, propped more against it, then overlapped elephant ear leaves to make a roof. The rain fell steadily and night came fast. They ate a cold meal out of the cans, not willing to risk the stove without knowing where the enemy was. The group was grim: they were grateful no one of them had been hurt or killed, but all too aware of their predicament.

Footy was particularly downcast. He'd lost his aircraft and everything he'd poured into it. Here he was, deep in the unknown wilderness, with only the clothes on his back. It was chilly in the rain, but not cold, and Dingo offered to spread his blanket as a bed for both himself and the pilot. Johnny unrolled his hammock, took out the sheet, and offered it to them. He figured they needed it more than he did.

It was almost dark by the time Johnny got his hammock tied between two trees. He sharpened four sticks and wedged them through the grommets at each end of the hammock bed, and the waterproof roof. The water sluiced off. Stout mosquito netting formed the walls, and the part he would sleep on was a double layer of sturdy cloth. Johnny undid the brass zipper and slid in, then leaned around and shoved his muddy boots upside down through the web of strings at one end. He knew the Aussies were watching, although neither said a word. Dingo was faintly contemptuous of the need for anything but a bit of cover and a place to stretch out. *Bloody Yanks and their bloody equipment!* Footy thought.

Dingo made the bed with the Yank's sheet and told his mate to lie down. He was concerned about their bad start, and he felt sorry for Footy, losing his aircraft like that, but otherwise, he was content to be here. Killing three of the enemy right off the bat boded well.

As he lay snug beneath the drumming rain, Johnny's thoughts went to Gwyn and their last conversation. *What did she mean, find your heart? Ok, I don't feel things like I did when I was young,* he was forced to admit to himself. *Not even like I did when I first got to New Guinea.* The soldier had something to say: *that's a good thing. Feelings! They're worse than useless—they'll turn you stupid, and stupid gets shot. You turn weepy every time a buddy gets his, and you'll be next on the hit list.*

Johnny thought about the enemy soldiers they'd taken out today and the familiar hatred welled up in him. *See?* the killer told him. *You do have feelings—just not the kind a girl understands.*

Dingo had said they must take turns on watch. He volunteered for the first shift. Johnny fell asleep quickly. He woke in deep blackness, his bed shaking. He remembered where he was, unzipped the hammock, fumbled for his boots and slid in his feet. He got up and felt the light rain on his buzzed scalp. It was letting up.

Johnny sat under the lean-to with his rifle ready while the others slept. When Footy started snoring, Johnny nudged him. The pilot rolled over and fell silent. Three hours later, Johnny shook him awake and crawled back to his hammock.

When he woke next, it was to dismal gray light. The rain had stopped, but water continued to run off the glistening leaves. Johnny got up again and rotated his shoulder. It felt pretty good, considering the workout he'd put it through. He nodded at Footy who was sitting red-eyed on the edge of the blanket, hair every which way. Dingo was still sleeping.

Johnny stepped behind a tree and relieved himself. *A cup of hot coffee sure would go down good. Can we light the stove? No,* he answered himself. *Not with the Japs out there. I wonder where the Kissim natives are?*

He realized with a jolt that he was staring at one of them. A black man—no, it was only a boy—had materialized in the foliage. Johnny's fist shot out and seized the kid by the throat. His other hand pulled the bayonet-knife with its sixteen-inch blade from his belt. The boy trembled but did not make a sound.

Good. I don't have to hurt him. Johnny kept a hand on the boy and urged him around the tree. Dingo was just sitting up, twigs in his hair. Johnny forced the native down on his knees beside him. He appeared to be in his early teens. He wore only a faded red loincloth around his hips, a shell the size of a silver dollar tied on his forehead, and another bark string around his neck with a carving on it. In the center of his chest were four wavy lines of raised scar tissue.

"Can you ask him where the priests are?" Johnny said.

Dingo tried two of three different languages and at last the boy answered. After a minute, Dingo reported that he could not get any information about the priests. Whenever he asked, the kid clammed up. Johnny studied the carving on the boy's necklace. He reached out a hand and touched it.

"Crocodile," he said to the boy.

"*Pookpook*," Dingo said in the trade language.

"*Ka-him-ka*," the boy whispered.

"Father of the crocodiles," Dingo translated.

"*Ka*," the boy said, holding up the wood.

"The Father," Dingo said.

"Is it near?" Johnny asked. Dingo spoke, and the boy peered anxiously around the clearing, but said nothing. He turned to Dingo and whispered some words.

"We're to go with him," the Major told the others. "He'll take us to his people."

The men broke camp and hid any sign they'd been there. Dingo handed his rifle to Footy, and pulled out his pistol. He ordered the boy forward and walked behind him, one big hand on his shoulder.

Footy came next, Lee Enfield in hand, hefting a box of food. Johnny came at the rear, pack on, other carton under his arm.

The boy took them on a circuitous route that broke out at last among the burned huts. The men walked silently through the village and notice the remains of two larger edifices. The Major and the boy exchanged words.

"The priests' house and church," Dingo said over his shoulder. *So much for the brave new world of brotherly love,* Johnny thought. New Guinea could look like Eden, but to soldiers like him who'd fought here, it was more like hell.

The native boy was edgy out in the open, his eyes darting everywhere, and the men walked with their fingers on the triggers. Then they were in the rainforest again, going single file between the towering trunks. Johnny found he admired the way Dingo moved on bare feet. He had a confidence about him. Footy, too, looked like he had experience, Johnny had to admit. The pilot carried the rifle ready, watching the jungle.

The boy stopped abruptly and the men halted behind him. Native warriors stepped from behind the trees and surrounded them. They were armed with longbows, arrows on the strings. The white men aimed their firearms back at them.

"Easy!" Dingo told his companions. The natives wore the same red loincloths as the boy, shells on their foreheads, and similarly scarred chests.

The teenager talked fast, Dingo occasionally adding a phrase. An old man with a frizz of white hair stepped from the circle. He spoke, and the men let the tension off their bows. The white men cautiously lowered their guns as well. The old one said another word, and the warriors returned to the forest. The boy stayed by the old man's side. The elder motioned the newcomers to follow and limped away.

Ten minutes later, they came to a clearing. Weak light filtered from the clouded sky. The men saw two mounds of fresh earth. In the gloom behind were two more hummocks, overgrown with creepers. Each one had a cross of peeled sticks lashed with vines at one end. The old man paused at the nearest one and turned, his face pulled down by sadness.

"Papa Chris," he said. He pointed to the next. "Papa Bruno." He moved to the overgrown sites.

“Papa Sid. Papa Bob.” The white men stared at one another.

“The four priests,” Dingo said.

“Bloody hell,” Footy put in.

The elder was moving again and they followed. They broke onto the open riverbank. The area was covered in graves, thirty to forty of them, Johnny guessed. About a third had crosses, and the rest, branches strung with bones and amulets. The old man spoke in his language to Dingo.

“These are the Kissim people, most killed by the Japs. We got here too late,” the Major said sourly. He sat on a rock and stared at the river.

“Ok,” Johnny told him. “But we’ve still got work to do.”

“Let’s get the bastards who did this,” Footy said in a strangled voice.

“Right,” Johnny nodded at him. *Maybe I can learn to like the pilot after all.*

“There’s that, of course,” Dingo said. “Let’s have a chinwag.” Johnny and Footy went down on their haunches. Johnny extracted and passed around a box of cigarettes.

“We can risk it out here in the open,” he said.

“Right you are,” Dingo agreed. He and Footy each took one and passed the box back. Johnny saw the old man watching and handed him the pack. He gave a toothless smile, took two and gave one to the boy. He went to hand the box back and thought better of it. He pulled out two more and stuck one behind each ear. Johnny flicked his Zippo and lit them. When they were all puffing, including the boy, Dingo spoke.

“Operation Teeth is buggered beyond all recognition. There’ll be no aircraft to pick us up on Friday, because here’s Footy, sitting with us.”

“More’s the shame,” Footy said dejectedly.

“By now they’ll know in Moresby you didn’t make it back mate,” Dingo told him. “They’ll have sent word to my office—and to you Yanks as well,” he nodded at Johnny.

“They won’t forget us,” Dingo said. “They’ll stir up an aircraft and come looking.” He paused. “Of course,” he went on thoughtfully, “I’m the only one who really knows where Kissim is. The Colonel has only a vague idea, I’m afraid.”

“Then there’s the weather,” Footy added, glancing up. “We’re socked in—for who knows how long?"

"Ok," Johnny said. "They're going to look for us. We can't do anything about that. We're too late for the priests. So why don't we get on with the rest of our mission? Let's take out the Japs." He withdrew Father Bastion's letter from his pocket and unfolded it.

"The priest said there were seven enemy soldiers when he wrote this. Assuming they were still alive when we got here, we knocked off three yesterday. That means four left."

"Four, Johnny—that's what I reckon as well," Dingo said.

"How do we find them?" Footy asked.

"That's the easy part, mate," Dingo replied. "We get a *kanaka* to show us."

As it turned out, the natives knew exactly where the Japanese camp was. The boy led the white men as close as he dared to a bald hill. The men saw the low profile of logs at the top. The enemy had dug a bunker three-quarters underground. Through his scope, Johnny saw the gun slits that covered every approach.

"They've picked the place well," Dingo said. "You can count on your Jap for that."

"We could try sneaking up on them at night, but that's risky. There's a better way," Johnny said.

"What do you reckon?"

"Ask the boy where they go for water," he replied. Dingo did. The native led them to a trail that went to the river. Johnny suggested a plan. After all, he was the expert at this particular kind of warfare. Dingo approved.

It was the afternoon of their third day of waiting. Johnny was fifty feet up a tree with a view of the path. Dingo and Footy were hidden in the jungle below. The three of them had waited like this through the long days. It rained frequently and the cloud cover stayed dark and heavy. There had been no sight or even a sound of any aircraft.

This is Friday, Johnny thought. *Tonight I've got a date with Gwyn! Does she even know I'm not back? And maybe,* he thought, *I won't be, for a long time to come.* In his mind's eye he saw Gwyn in a pretty dress, wearing jewelry. They were in a fine restaurant, facing one another across a linen tablecloth. He got a pang of regret and forced his thoughts in another direction.

The prior afternoon, Johnny had glimpsed the Japanese patrolling a distant trail. He'd confirmed there were four of them, each carrying a rifle. He could have shot at least one of them—he tracked the man through his scope. But he did not want to take out just the one, and give away their ambush site. *No. Get them all!*

The previous evening, his group ate another cold meal at a new camp close by. They had slices of bread spread with canned spaghetti. Footy voiced his impatience with this waiting game. It was pointless, he said.

"Let's get on with it! Let's go after the buggers."

But Johnny's expertise as a hunter of men made him disagree.

"Keep your britches on," he told Footy. "They must be running low on water. If we go looking for them, we could just as easily get bushwhacked. They know this terrain better than we do."

"Johnny's right," Dingo said. "Men and animals, they all have to drink."

"Another thing," Johnny said. "When the Japs show up, and they will, let me get first shot. Then join in."

"And why is that?" Footy snapped.

"Because I'm the best shot," Johnny said evenly. The pilot began to protest, but Dingo put a hand on his arm.

"Johnny is the best with a rifle, mate. I've seen his record. We'll give him first go. Then see what you can do."

Early that morning, the three had taken up their stakeout again, and remained there all day. High in his tree, Johnny took in breaths that felt like rain waiting to happen. A bead of sweat trickled down his forehead and tickled his nose, but he did not move. Like other jungle animals and insects of prey, he knew to stay absolutely still. *Movement attracts the eye—that's the telltale.* Many of his victims had made that fatal error.

Johnny had sprigs of leaves woven through his clothing and in the netting of his helmet. The barrel of his rifle was wrapped in vines. He'd smeared mud on his face. The day dragged on, and the hissing of the cicadas lulled him, but he would not drift off. He was wedged in the tree so he would not fall, but he knew sleep was every soldier's Achilles' heel. Then even the most seasoned commando was as vulnerable as a baby.

Through years of practice, Johnny could slow his breathing and sit completely still for hours on end. In fact, this was his element. Still, he couldn't quite believe that he was back in the New Guinea jungle. He thought he'd left this place behind him for good! He remembered that Saturday, less than a week ago, when he'd learned he'd been released. Then it had looked like his scheme to get back to his unit had fallen into place.

How did it all go so wrong? He sighed, and his mind buzzed back to Gwyn. *What a knockout! She's as pretty as a movie star. But why is it, every time I talk to her, I hem and haw like a moron?*

He thought about that day at the tent, when she promised to save tonight for him. *Our first date!* Three hours from now, he should be on his way to pick her up. *And after dinner at the Islander, would she let me kiss her goodnight?* He could almost feel those full lips, and a prickle went up his back.

The swelling and ebbing of the cicadas tapered off. In the direction of the river, ducks exploded up. All of Johnny's awareness sharpened. Then he saw it—motion in the jungle along the edge of the unseen river. *That's no breeze. Something moves there!*

The hunter put his eye to his scope and his finger curled around the trigger.

CHAPTER 2

Only Johnny's eyes moved in his impassive face. Through the crosshairs, he watched the foliage shudder. He made out brown flashes in the greenery, and these resolved into skin that became four men slinking among the trees.

They approached parallel to the river, along a faint side trail that joined the one Johnny watched. Adrenaline went through him like an itch, and he wondered if Dingo and Footy were aware.

One by one, gazing warily around, the enemy soldiers stepped onto the broader path. Johnny had his Springfield up, and through the scope, he watched them come, willing them all into the open. The soldiers were emaciated, he noticed, their uniforms in shreds and their feet bare. The two in the middle carried canvas buckets in the crooks of their arms.

Johnny's scope revealed their faces in profile. The leader was short and squat, and appeared to be in his late forties. He wore a helmet, and his face was fixed in a frown. The helmet itself was the usual kind they wore, but blackened. *He's been cooking in it.* The hard soldier grinned inwardly. Fire made a helmet brittle, useless to deflect a bullet.

The second man had a conical "coolie" hat of woven reeds. The third wore an old cloth cap, and the last one had a strip of cloth knotted around his scalp. Each man carried a rifle, and Johnny saw the one at the back had a sword dangling from his waist.

Johnny was studying this one when he whirled and seemed to stare right back. *He feels me looking at him.* Johnny had observed this phenomenon before, as if sight was not passive, but rather something that probed the world. Johnny looked into his face and dubbed him "Headband." The cloth was soiled and had a faint image of the red sun on it. *The "meatball,"* Johnny thought. He felt the hatred again, strong as the morning he'd first seen the circle on the aircraft. Through the crosshairs, he saw the black stubble on the scalp, the dark triangles of the eyes, the weathered skin.

The others continued to move away. In seconds, they would be over the riverbank, out of sight. Johnny decided to shoot them in order, front to back, so they'd block the trail. *Helmet, Coolie, Cap then Headband.*

The three were on the lip of land that went to the river. Headband jogged to catch up. Johnny aimed at the first man. He centered the cross hairs below the rim of the helmet, tilted down between the shoulders and squeezed. The Springfield kicked and Helmet dropped. *Spine shot.*

Johnny's eye was already on his next target while his fingers reloaded. Coolie flinched when the first man collapsed, the clap just reaching him. Johnny squeezed again. *Heart shot.*

The last two were suddenly hyperactive. Cap leapt off the trail and tore through the undergrowth. Headband jumped the corpses and raced for the river. Johnny heard a rifle cough below—*a miss.* He stayed on his plan. Again his fingers inserted a shell in the chamber as he panned the undulating shrubs. He could picture the runner clearly, even though he could not see him—another sniper skill. He fired, and a bush shook and went still.

Then there was one. Reloading, Johnny whip-panned to Headband, and found him on top of the bank. There was another clap from the Aussie rifle—*another miss.* Johnny's lip curled. He had the enemy in his crosshairs, but before he could slam the bolt home and squeeze, the target went over the top, out of sight.

Johnny hitched his rifle over his shoulder and slid down the tree. He saw Dingo go tearing by, revolver in hand. At his heels raced Footy with the Lee Enfield. Johnny had to look where he was landing. When he glanced again, the trail was empty. He sprinted after the others. He heard shots—*four, five of them.* He scrambled up the bank, reached the top, and froze.

Nothing in his life had prepared him for what he saw on the other side.

Scientists say the saltwater crocodile has been around for two hundred million years and shared the planet with the dinosaurs. But "dinos" and all the other "saurs" disappeared *en masse* sixty-five million years ago, with two exceptions. One is the bird, the "living dinosaur." The other is the crocodile, the closest relative to the ancient ones of all the so-called reptiles.

The crocodilians not only survived, they went forth and multiplied. ***Crocodylus porosus,*** the giant ocean-going kind, voyaged from Africa to India, infested South East Asia, colonized the subtropical areas of Australia and ventured as far north as the frigid Sea of Japan.

They invaded the island of New Guinea as well. Here they found an ideal home. There were no other large animals with which to compete. They were the apex predator of the entire place, and included all animals—including man when he arrived—in their diet.

The massive bull was forty-four years old and in its prime, the dominant crocodile of the river and the surrounding ocean. Except when it indulged the occasional urge to copulate, it was too aggressive to tolerate company. It even killed the odd female that came too close when it was not in the mood.

Alone as it preferred, the reptile spent much of its day basking on the riverbank. It luxuriated in the warmth seeping into its vast body. It spread its six-foot jaws, gaping at the sun. This normally revealed its sixty-eight teeth, but recently it had cracked one off on the skull of a pig. The replacement was just beginning to bulge under the gum.

During most its long years, the bull relaxed completely as it basked, for nothing dared disturb it. But things had changed. Always now, the crocodile was uneasy, even here in the heart of its territory at the mouth of the river.

The reptilian brain had no way to make sense of the ships and aircraft, bombs, artillery, and soldiers with firearms, which invaded its realm. But it did observe them, and it reacted with territorial fury. Yet its anger was impotent—the invaders remained far off. At times its unrequited aggression was so strong, all the muscles in its four thousand pound body tightened like cables. Even when the interlopers were not in sight, the beast fretted.

On several occasions, soldiers saw the monster in the distance. Invariably, some shot at it. They did this instinctively, without knowing why. If pressed, they would have said it was sport.

The bull knew it was being attacked only when it felt blows against its scales, and then heard the claps of sound. Sometimes it felt merely the thumps against its thick hide, but other times, there were stabs of pain. Infuriated and alarmed, the reptile rushed into the river.

Once, when the sting was particularly sharp, it whirled with jaws agape, but found no tormenter to confront. The giant raised its head and roared, to the horrified delight of the far off soldiers.

The changes in its territory tormented the beast. It grew ever more agitated, and at last, could not remain. It swam into the South Pacific and navigated the huge rollers to distant islands. There it lolled in a lagoon formed by a coral reef, consoling itself on the plentiful fish.

On shore, it discovered another herd of the two-legged animals. When these were foolish enough to venture onto the lagoon in a hollow log, the crocodile went to meet them. One swipe of its tail knocked them into the water with it. It was easy to pluck the toothsome morsels as they thrashed and screamed.

Occasionally, one of the creatures made the mistake of sleeping on the beach. Then the great predator eased out of the waves and came for it. The foolish one would awake in the embrace of the mighty teeth. When the herd discovered what had happened to its missing member, what cries and carrying on there were then!

The predator might have doubled its span of years in that place, but its instincts drove it back to its river. While returning across the ocean once more, a furious buzzing came from above. The irritated reptile shifted course and swam on.

A Zero fighter flashed over, returning from a mission. The pilot saw the monstrous black shadow weaving below, and swooped down for a closer look. He absorbed the unbelievable length, as long as his aircraft. He imagined himself in the water with it, as one day he might very well be. At once, he threw his aircraft in a loop, screamed back and opened up with his 7.7mm machine guns.

The crocodile heard the thunder, saw the spurting water, and dove. Through its transparent eyelids, it watched white spears drill for it and went deeper. The danger passed, and it felt a patter like rocks that rolled off its back.

The pilot cut another tight circle, but there was only the dancing Pacific, and he gave up his diversion and continued to base.

The reptile swam submerged, fear and ire pumping through it. Only when it must, did it come up for air, suck in a breath, and sink again.

A day later, the crocodile tasted mud in the stream. Following the trail, it came in sight of familiar land and navigated to its channel. As it coursed between the banks, its kin saw the return of their violent patriarch. Many had witnessed it maim and even slaughter other bulls that had dared mount a challenge, and they bolted for their lives.

The crocodile cruised through the murk and lay among the reeds. It had hatched near this place, and it knew every hole where the big fish finned. But even now, it could find no rest.

Ever stronger, an impulse rose within it. At last the crocodile lifted off the bottom and turned into the current. It swung the great tail and surged against the stream. On it went, while the bright light crossed from one horizon to the other. Then, in the dark, guided by the flow, it continued. Eventually, the light returned, and on it swam as the rows of triangular scutes along its back transferred heat into its body.

During its lifetime, the predator had made several excursions up the river. All this was its territory, and every other crocodile that saw it coming froze where it was, or flailed rapidly away.

The bull continued, and it remembered the places of the two-legged herds. Long before it saw their nests along the shores, it scented the body odor and the tang of smoke. It drew closer and saw the animals themselves, and heard their plaintive cries. It would have been natural for the reptile to stay for a time and feed, but now, driven by something stronger than hunger, it swept by.

The villagers clustered along the banks to witness the passage of the fearsome spirit of the river. Each tribe identified it in its tongue as the Father of the Crocodiles, and even the fingers of brave warriors trembled as they pointed out its passage to their young. Since birth, the little ones had heard frightening tales of the giant, but they had not seen the manifestation of the dark deity until now.

As the crocodile surged towards them, the people were appalled. Surely, some of them would die. But when it voyaged on, their knees went weak with relief, then wonder. Why had they been spared this time? Should the incarnation of the river's anger have chosen them, or their children, they would have been powerless. They must live on the river—there was nowhere else to go. Their sorcerers could perform all their incantations, but the giant *pook-pook* was a force far greater than that.

The reptile traversed the low country and swam into the highlands. Eventually it penetrated the foothills of the central mountain range. Now the country was so remote and wild, it no longer saw the two-legged prey. At last the mountains pressed in, the banks drew close together, and water ran swift and clear. At times it roared in rapids the crocodile must climb, dragging itself over the stones, until it came to deeper pools and glided on.

It entered territory it had never seen. It explored the new realm and discovered another herd of the two-legged prey. It was quiet here, and the impetus that had driven it so relentlessly began to ease. Its natural hunger returned.

From the waterweeds, only its eye knobs showing, the crocodile watched the movements of the prey. It noted each individual that came to the river, and at what light of day. It chose its target, eased by night into its chosen place, and crouched absolutely still, covered by water.

Soon it sank its teeth into the good flesh once more. Its belly ceased to complain, and its nerves calmed.

The reptile had killed one of the females a few days before. It carried the carcass to a solitary place on the river, ate its fill, and hid the rest under a deadfall. This morning, it nosed the remains out and bit into flesh redolent with rot.

Content, it drifted along the bank and crawled out to bask. It lay enjoying the blaze of heat on its back, and the warmth that seeped into its belly from the soft mud.

Then all at once, the Father was attacked. The explosions it feared rang in its ears, while pain pierced its head and body. The reptile whirled, and this time, it found its tormenters right beside it, within easy reach.

Johnny scrambled up the bank and froze. The slope fell away into the river, and lying along it was an enormous crocodile. It was so massive, it dwarfed the three men along its flank. In the presence of their far more ancient foe, these had forgotten one another.

Johnny saw the enemy beside the tail, firing his rifle. Footy was in front of him, shooting into the flank. Dingo was near the head, firing his pistol into it.

The Father!

Even as the knowledge thrilled through Johnny, the crocodile looked at him. He saw the thick neck, the folds in the skin as the head turned. He watched the jaws fly open and saw all the long teeth, wet with saliva. But it was the yellow-green eyes that drew him with their predatory malevolence. Johnny noticed the dark malformed scales shaped like a crescent moon over one of them.

He was bringing up his rifle when his peripheral vision caught the ridged tail swinging inland. His attention remained on Dingo, who was in extreme danger. The Major fired repeatedly while his feet backpedaled.

But the crocodile was too fast. The wide head went sideways, the jaws slid around Dingo, covering him from chest to knees, and it bit him. Johnny heard bones crack and the grunt that squeezed out of the Major. The crocodile lifted him like a feather as hat, pistol and knife fell away.

Johnny was still getting his rifle to his shoulder when the tail hit the enemy. Instantly, man and rifle parted company. The firearm tumbled into the water, while the Japanese flew over the bank in a crash of branches.

The Father, Dingo drooping from its jaws, turned to the river. Its flank struck Footy and bowled him onto his back. It had only been seconds since Johnny arrived, and he had the crosshairs on the huge speckled eye with the vertical iris. He squeezed the trigger as the tail came to the end of its swing and bumped his legs. It was like being tapped by a steel beam. Johnny flew sideways as the bullet exploded from the muzzle at 2,900 feet-per-second. Instead of the eye, the shot hit the crocodile's foreleg.

It was a high velocity 150-grain slug in a metal jacket and it ripped through scales and flesh, shattered bone, and tumbled on. The end of the Father's foot blew off, a mass of toes and claws that fell in the river.

The crocodile hissed in agony and swung its head to its injury. It saw the shredded foreleg and the creature behind it. A blast of pain slammed through it as it stared at the helmeted man.

That image would remain vivid as long as it lived—the ruined limb, the smooth-headed man, and the overwhelming agony. It sucked in a breath, and drew in the unique body scent of its adversary.

Johnny reloaded. The crocodile heard the clicks and fear welled with the pain and fury. For a moment it vacillated, caught in the equal urges to attack and escape. The man between the teeth heaved and groaned. *Dingo is still alive!* Johnny realized.

The Father threw itself into the river, landing in a wide splash. Again the armored tail swung, and Johnny barely managed to hop over it. Footy rolled frantically to avoid being crushed under the belly. A back leg thudded down and the claws just missed his head.

Johnny regained his balance and fired from the hip. The bullet carved a groove up the scaled back, and then the beast was submerged, a wavering darkness, moving off.

Footy sat blinking in the mud. Again Johnny reloaded, but there was nothing left to shoot. The Father and Dingo were gone.

"Bloody, bleedin', ruddy hell!" Footy babbled. Johnny was the first to come to his senses.

"It's over! Get Dingo's things. Let's go."

He spun and went in search of the enemy.

CHAPTER 3

Johnny climbed the riverbank and found the enemy soldier sprawled on his back. He'd banged his head and was just coming to. Johnny loomed over him and put the barrel of his Springfield hard against the man's chest.

"Get up, Jap!"

The man climbed shakily to his feet. He was skinny, Johnny noted again, about starved. His shirt had no buttons, his trousers were rags and he was barefoot. He'd lost his rifle, thanks to the croc, but he did have the sword in its wooden scabbard on his rope belt. Footy came up behind Johnny, Dingo's hat on his head, the Bowie knife and revolver through his belt, the Lee Enfield in his hands.

"Put your hands up!" Johnny told the enemy, not knowing if he'd understand. He indicated what he wanted with his free hand and Headband slowly raised his arms.

"Go get that sword," Johnny told Footy. He aimed at the foe while Footy sidled towards him. "Don't get between us," Johnny warned. The pilot nodded, pulled the loop on the man's rope belt and drew the sword off, and stepped away.

Footy slid out the blade and held it to the sun. It was a long curve of gleaming steel, free of rust. They saw the silver hilt and pommel, the ornate wrapping of the handle. A wavy line ran behind the cutting edge the length of the blade.

"I'll be a wombat's second sister," Footy said admiringly. "This looks like an old one! Proper samurai sword—not the usual factory rubbish. I claim it—it's mine."

"You can have it," Johnny said. "Ok," he continued to Headband, who he was now thinking of as "the Jap." "You can put your hands down."

The man's pants were sliding off his hips and he grabbed them and retied the rope while he kept watching the helmeted soldier. He could tell by the accent the man was a Yankee. He observed those cold eyes and he somehow knew, this was the one who had slaughtered his countrymen—and that his own life still hung by a thread.

Yes! The thought rushed through him then. *Kill me!*

The shame of being captured was unbearable. *After all these terrible years—this!* He felt the urge to rush the man and as he did so, he would find himself in the next life.

But my religion forbids suicide! Hard as it is, I must continue to live. So if I must endure the humiliation, I will do it for my country, and only for a time. I will watch, and when the opportunity comes, I will kill these enemies, even if I die trying.

"You speak English?" Johnny asked. The captive stared back and said nothing.

"Jap, you want to try to run, do it now. Otherwise, you're my prisoner. Even twitch the wrong way," Johnny told him, "and I'll kill you." He nodded at Footy. "He will too—you count on it. So what's it going to be?"

"The bloody heathen doesn't understand!" Footy said. "Why waste your breath?" Johnny shrugged and he and the enemy continued to stare at one another, but the man made no move.

"Let's go." Johnny motioned with his rifle and "the Jap" rose shakily to his feet and pushed through the foliage. He put a hand to his head on the angry knot rising there. Johnny came behind, barrel in his back. Footy followed, Dingo's rifle in one hand, sword in the other.

They approached the two bodies in the trail. The Japanese glanced down at the older man whose helmet had rolled off, and the other one with the reed hat. His face betrayed nothing as he stepped over. They went by the place where the third corpse sprawled in the undergrowth. Johnny drove the prisoner on, but Footy ducked into the bush and assured himself the enemy was dead. He saw the bullet hole through the body and realized Johnny had made the shot blind. He was impressed with the Yank, in spite of himself.

Back at camp, Johnny cut a length of rope and tied the prisoner's hands behind his back. He forced the man to sit against a tree and lashed him to it. Johnny was the son of a Navy man, and he'd been taught his knots from an early age. He could tie twenty varieties before most boys could tie their shoelaces. In short order, he had the prisoner trussed so escape was impossible.

For the first time since they'd come to Kissim, Johnny and Footy cooked a hot meal and brewed a pot of coffee. They tucked into plates piled with beef stew, mopped up with slices of bread.

Johnny felt a tremor in his arms and legs, the aftermath of the unaccustomed exercise and the adrenalin. He was disturbed by Dingo's demise, but he'd seen too much during the war to allow it to affect his judgment. He was encouraged by their triumph against the enemy, and preoccupied by the ferocious crocodile.

He and Footy talked about the Major's death. The pilot was distraught over the loss. Both knew that Dingo's death might spell their own doom. The Major was the only one who knew the river, and had seen it to the coast. He had been the single member of the expedition who spoke a smattering of the languages.

Johnny saw Footy's hands trembling and recalled the bottle of brandy. *Like I said, for medicinal purposes.* He got it from his pack, poured a generous slug into two mugs, and topped them up with the coffee. He handed one to Footy and raised the other.

"Here's to the Major," Johnny said.

"Dingo! A good bloke and the best of mates," Footy said. "Blast that bloody croc to hell! Here's to him."

"To Dingo."

The men touched cups and drank, while the captive watched. They lit cigarettes and hunkered down for another powwow. Operation Teeth had taken another bizarre twist. Their expedition leader, the most seasoned of New Guinea hands, was dead in the river. They were on their own, short of supplies, deep in the savage and unexplored interior of New Guinea.

"The priest warned about that croc" Johnny said. "Even then, I didn't imagine it was so big!"

"Struth! That's gotta be the bloody Father," Footy said.

"For sure," Johnny said. "There can't be two that size! Did you see the scar on its head?"

"Yes mate! I've seen saltys in Queensland all me life," Footy said, "but never one like that! Blimey! The biggest I saw was one half his size!"

"So much for staying away from the river," Johnny grimaced. Footy saw the prisoner looking at them.

"You, Jap!" he called. "What the hell you staring at?" He turned to Johnny. "Think the bugger understands English?"

"Maybe," Johnny said. "Some of the ones we captured learned it at school. A lot more than we learned Jap, that's for sure! But what does it matter if he does?" he shrugged. "We're all in the same boat."

They continued to mull over their options. The upshot was, they would wait in Kissim for three days. If no aircraft showed up, they'd move on. Thanks to Johnny's foresight, they had food for that time and a little longer, but they both agreed, they would not sit in Kissim and starve to death.

"This is Friday," Johnny said. "If no rescue comes by Monday, we move. Our only hope is to follow the river to the coast. Can't be more than a few hundred miles. At least we'll have a fighting chance. At the ocean, we'll be able to signal a plane or ship."

"I see your point," Footy said, "but you've forgotten something. What about the bloody 'Valley of the Cannibals' poor old Dingo went on about?"

"What did he call them? The 'Mambu headhunters,'" Johnny nodded. "Yeh, well, they're right in our path."

"We could try another way," Footy said. "Didn't the priest say the Japs came through the mountains further up?"

"It won't work," Johnny said. "They had guides from the Sepik. And another thing. No rescuers will even think to look for us that way."

"I agree mate. And the Sepik has its own bloody savages."

"Ok," Johnny said. "Our best chance is the Raub. No rescue by Monday, and we follow it to the coast. We'll just have to take our chances in the Valley of the Cannibals."

"Right mate, bloody Mambu, here we come. At least, following the river, we can't get lost."

The men left the prisoner tied to the tree and went to see if they could find anything at all in the native gardens. As soon as they were out of sight, the captive struggled frantically in his bonds, but made no headway. *The Yankee is good with a rope.*

Johnny and Footy went carefully through the dug-over vegetable mounds, but did not turn up even one bug-eaten yam. They were surprised not to see a single native.

After that, Footy wanted to take another look at the airstrip. He was preoccupied by the fact that the wreck compromised any rescuers' ability to land. They passed through the destroyed village and came to the grassy strip. They paused and gazed at the burned out hulk of the Hudson. As they remembered, it sat square in the middle of the field.

"No good," Footy said. "No aircraft can land, even if they do find us."

"Even worse," Johnny said. "If they see that, they will probably think we died in the crash."

"Crikey! Hadn't thought of that," Footy said. "If we're here, of course, we can wave."

The rain had let up and the dark cloud cover had lifted a little. Johnny was staring up the mountain when he saw movement.

"Look! That's where the people went." There were about forty men, women and children, strung along the high trail.

"They're leaving the place," Footy said. At the end of the line were the old man and the boy. "Cooeeee!" the pilot called through cupped hands. The pair turned and the boy pointed down. The old man raised a hand, and then they resumed toiling behind the others. Johnny and Footy watched until they were lost in the clouds.

"Nothing left for them here, I suppose," Footy said.

"Just the Father," Johnny said, "and more death."

The men returned to camp and found the prisoner where they'd left him. Johnny noticed again how starved he looked. He opened a can of baked beans, wiped his spoon on his shirt, and fed it all to the man. "The Jap" gulped it down, and Johnny gave him a drink from his canteen.

Meanwhile, Footy sorted through the Major's pack. *All I have is what Dingo brought. It has to do until we're rescued, or we make it to the coast. If we make it to the coast*. The knife's sheath and pistol holster had gone with the Major to his death, but at least he had the knife itself, and the revolver and rifle. In addition, there was Dingo's rucksack, bedroll, some clothing that would be too big, and the hat, which would be a blessing in the sun. His eyes misted up, holding his mate's things, and he turned away so the others would not see.

The mood in camp was somber. Neither man said what they were thinking. In all likelihood, there was a perilous journey to come that they were unlikely to survive. And now they had an added burden—the prisoner. Neither said it, but both thought about simply doing away with him. No one would ever know, and in many battles here, captives on both sides had died that way.

That night, Johnny and Footy divided up the watch. It looked like they were alone in a deserted village, but they could not take the chance. Johnny adjusted the prisoner's rope so he could lie on the ground, hands lashed behind his back to the tree. It was not the most comfortable arrangement, but as it turned out, he was the only one to get a full night's sleep.

The next three days were long and dreary as the men waited. It rained most of the time, a chill deluge that soaked everything and dampened their spirits. There was no sign of an aircraft.

The following morning—Johnny reminded himself that it was Tuesday—they broke camp and prepared to hike. He was already fed up spoon-feeding "the Jap." Footy made it scornfully clear that he would not help. Johnny untied the prisoner's hands and told him to feed himself. He gave the man the same thing they had for breakfast, a plate of warm hash and the crust of their last loaf of bread. Footy glared daggers at the captive with every bite he took.

"We don't have enough food to go around, Johnny," he complained. "Now we've got to trek all the way down the Raub with a prisoner? You must be bloody joking! I think we should shoot him and be done with it. No one will know. He died in the battle, that's all we say, if we say anything."

"I hear you," Johnny said. "But I've never executed a man who's surrendered."

"You don't mind shooting them in the back," Footy jeered. "I saw you do it."

"That's different," Johnny said. "That's battle. But like it or not, he's our prisoner of war."

"If you can't do it, I will," Footy said. "Are you going to stop me?" He pulled Dingo's revolver, aimed it at the man's head, and cocked the hammer. The Japanese stared back at him.

"That's not right," Johnny said. "But I won't stop you, or report it. Do it now—or this is the last time we talk about it."

He returned to roping his hammock onto his pack. Footy's arm was straight out, finger on the trigger. The Japanese stared into the barrel of the gun and Footy got the strange feeling the crazy bastard was hoping for the end. After a long moment, the Aussie scowled and let his gun arm drop.

"Bloody hell," he snarled. "I can't shoot an unarmed man! Blast it to hell!"

"We'll take him with us," Johnny said. "Let's get out of here."

"And when we get to the bleedin' cannibals?" Footy asked. "No man's ever gone in there and—well, you know. And here we come, with a prisoner in tow!"

"We've got guns," Johnny shrugged, "and surprise on our side. Dingo said they've never even seen a white man. We'll just march in like we own the place, and bluff our way through."

"Against a thousand bloody cannibals?" Footy asked. "Sounds more than iffy." Something occurred to him and he brightened a little. "If it comes to it, we can trade the bleedin' Jap to the bloody *kanakas.* Our lives for his."

"Might work," Johnny said.

"Alright mate," Footy said. "But I don't like it. I don't like it at all."

Footy's mates gave it until Wednesday morning, but when there was still no sign of the Hudson, they took the news to Australian HQ. They, in turn, sent word around to the US Garrison.

When Colonel Chambers heard about it, he got a sinking feeling. But he resolved to wait at least another day or two before he did anything precipitous. *These things have a way of working themselves out. Dingo Hawsey and Johnny Willman are some of the best fighters in New Guinea. And the pilot too—the Major had vouched for him. What was his nickname, Booty?* The three knew the jungles far better than the Colonel ever would.

Furthermore, New Guinea was notorious for abrupt weather changes. Many a pilot had been forced to put down somewhere and sit it out. Henry would lay dollars to doughnuts the men would show up, with the priests in tow.

But then, come Friday afternoon with no sign of Operation Teeth, Henry's alarm ballooned. His main concern was the safety of the men, but he had not bothered to mention the little action he and Dingo had dreamed up to his superiors in Australia. The Colonel did not want to have to explain an unapproved operation gone wrong. Much better to bring it up once the thing had resolved itself, which he fully expected it would.

The problem was, he had no aircraft to send looking for them. The only planes that showed up in Port Moresby these days were under other orders.

It dawned on the Colonel that he had a very sketchy idea of where Kissim might be. Dingo had shown him on the map, but where the Major's finger had touched down could cover hundreds of miles.

Why did I talk myself into this escapade at the eleventh hour? I didn't get this far in the Army by showboating!

Friday afternoon, Gwyn showered, slipped into a sage green summer frock she'd purchased in London, pulled on the single pair of stockings she possessed—they were hard to come by with the war on—and slipped on shoes. She dabbed "Evening in Paris" perfume behind her ears and at the base of her throat. Ruthie came home, changed, and headed out with her boyfriend. 6:00 o'clock turned into 8:00 and still no Johnny. By then Gwyn knew in her heart he wasn't coming. But still she waited. By 11:00 as she stripped off her dress and washed her face, she found she was furious—with Johnny, of course, but even more so with herself.

Once again, she'd climbed out on a limb for a military man. Gwyn blew out the lantern and lay on her bed, but sleep would not come. She was still awake when she heard her friend let herself in after 2 a.m.

At 8 o'clock Saturday morning, Gwyn roused a sleepy Ruthie, cajoled her into throwing on some clothes, made her a cup of strong tea, and dragged her along for moral support. Together, they walked the thirty minutes to US Army Headquarters. Gwyn demanded of the Sergeant at the desk that she be allowed to see the Colonel, and at once.

An hour later, they were shown into the Commander's office. They found the Colonel behind a stack of paper on his desk, file boxes open all around. He came over, greeted them cordially enough, and sat with them on the sofas.

Yes, "Operation Teeth" was overdue, there was no question, but the men were more than competent. Did anything in New Guinea happen on time? He allowed himself a chuckle. The Colonel assured the women he was monitoring everything closely. As soon as he could arrange it, he would send an aircraft to check on the mission. In the meantime, he fully expected them to show up at any time. The women were not to trouble themselves. His aides came in carrying more piles of papers requiring the Commander's signature.

"The burdens of command," he sighed and stood up. He personally walked the nurses to the front entrance and called his driver to take them home.

"It will all turn out," he told them. "Then we'll wonder what the fuss was about. I don't depart for Australia for another week. I am sure we'll have our happy ending long before that."

Still unhappy, Gwyn and Ruthie departed. Henry Chambers watched them go, and only then admitted to himself how deeply worried he was. The minute his vehicle returned, he had it take him to Australian HQ. There he corralled Dingo's Number Two and went over the situation. They agreed they would both do everything they could to find another aircraft to reconnoiter the Raub.

"But don't fret yet Colonel," the Australian said. "No one's better in the bush than the Major. If Dingo can't handle it, no one can."

With all he had to do, the intervening days passed in a whirlwind. The Colonel had his feelers out, but it wasn't until the following Wednesday that a DC-3 arrived at the Port Moresby airport. It was a private craft on a freight run from Cairns.

By then, the Colonel knew something was very wrong. He personally drove to the airport, and then stuck his neck out and commandeered the craft. As it turned out, the pilot was sympathetic. He was good mates with Footy Carmichael. He did say he would need a requisition form, and a formal letter to his principals from the American Colonel.

"There will be an account to pay, of course," he warned. "But then, you Yanks are made of money." The Colonel snorted. This was a common misconception among the Australians. They had no idea of the sharp-pencil boys who picked apart his expenses. But he agreed to everything. What choice did he have?

At first light the following morning, the DC-3 lifted off. On board were three of Dingo's most experienced Patrol Officers. None of them had ever been up the Raub River on the ground—who had? But as it developed, it was moot. The entire region was smothered in clouds. The aircraft circled for some time, and then returned to Port Moresby.

Colonel Chambers had a truck standing by to bring the rescued men to his office, but it was only the pilot and the Australian officers who turned up. Henry told the aviator he would not force him to stay, but the US Army would count it a great favor if he would try.

"Please, talk to your owners and tell them this is a life-and-death situation." The Colonel would give him the run of his own radio room.

The pilot was able to get through and get his answer. He could stay on for two more days, but that was the limit. After that, contracts would be broken and the cost would become prohibitive. He quoted a figure that gave Henry heartburn.

Still, The Colonel cabled the US Army superiors and requested authorization for the unusual expenditure. Within the hour, the General was on the radio demanding a conversation. The price for two additional days of aircraft charter would be covered, Henry was informed, but that was it. As it was, he would be called on the carpet to explain when he touched down in Australia. The General would expect a full account of what he was already calling "the incident," before the Colonel could continue to the States.

What's the worst they can do, Henry snorted to himself, *fire me?* Of course, he would do everything he could for the men of Operation Teeth, and take the consequences. Still, on Saturday, come hell or high water, he and his aides would be on that flight to Australia. If he was anything, he was Army to the core, and orders were orders.

Friday morning, the American Commander himself joined the others onboard the DC-3 for its final run. Operation Teeth was now a full-week overdue. This time, at least, the weather cooperated. The pilot was able to thread through the clouds and locate the Raub River. Flying visual, the aviator followed it upstream. At last, running close to the halfway mark on fuel, they passed over the burned and abandoned village. The Patrol Officers agreed, this had to be Kissim.

Then, their enthusiasm at locating the site was dashed. They saw the burned wreck on the airstrip. The pilot came back lower and personally confirmed it.

"That's 'Footy's Folly,' for shore," he shouted. "No shred of a doubt."

The bomber appeared to have crashed on landing. The observers knew that the chances of anyone surviving that violent impact were slim. One wing was bent around a bolder, and everything else was twisted and burned out.

The DC-3 could not land—the wreck blocked the way. The pilot made a few more passes while the observers craned through the windows, but they saw not a soul, not even a native or an animal. At last, the pilot shook his head, climbed through the clouds, and set a course for Port Moresby. It was a long and somber flight home.

It was Friday afternoon when the Colonel got back in his office. At his house, his suitcases stood lined up beside a number of boxes, ready to go. In his office, he put his last few private pictures in his briefcase, and the room looked entirely anonymous once more. In an hour, Henry would leave Army HQ for the final time.

He and his aides had one last task. They went through the stacks of papers the Colonel had prepared for his successor. Henry took a sheet off the top, his report on Operation Teeth, and added a few sentences summarizing the day's events. He replaced it and was done. He asked his men to allow him a minute alone. One more time, he went to the window and gazed across the Port Moresby harbor. Then he exited the office and closed the door.

It took another half hour to make the rounds and say goodbye to the staff. By now, he should be in his quarters. Although he had little interest in anthropology, he had some final packing of artifacts. He had to nail the lids down on crates containing longbows and assorted arrows. He had some fine stone-headed axes, an adze, and a collection of spirit masks. He had an hourglass-shaped drum, and his most exotic item, acquired from a Patrol Officer—a real human skull from a headhunter's lodge.

This evening, there was to have been a farewell drink with his officers at the club. Dingo should have been there, Henry thought, but there was no use dwelling on that. But instead of being able to enjoy his last night, Henry had a distasteful task he must handle himself. He drove himself to the hospital, asked for directions to the Canadian nurse's house, and proceeded. As it happened, he caught both Gywn and Ruthie at home. The Colonel accepted the seat at the kitchen table, declined the offer of refreshments, took a breath and launched in.

"I'm sorry to be the one to have to tell you," he said, and Gwyn got a bad feeling of déjà vu, "but I have listed Major Dingo Hawsey, Sergeant John Willman with their pilot, Glen Carmichael, as Missing in Action."

"Officially missing?" Gwyn's hand went to her throat.

"Is it true?" Ruthie chimed in.

"Unfortunately, yes," the Colonel said. "Today I flew over their destination and personally saw the wreck of their aircraft. There was no sign of survivors, I regret to tell you." The women's faces blanched and he soldiered on.

"I must leave New Guinea first thing tomorrow. But this is not the end of the trail! No, no, not at all. Dingo, Johnny and—ahh—Booty, could very well have survived..."

"Footy," Gwyn interrupted.

"Footy, yes," the Colonel said. "I believe it is very likely they are alive," he hastened on. "If anyone can survive on this island, it is those three.

"The efforts to locate them will continue. I have prepared a full report for the incoming Commander. I have left your name, Gwyn, and asked him to contact you the minute we have news." The Colonel glanced at his watch and stood.

"I'm afraid I must go—I still have much to do." He shook hands with each woman and departed. In fact, his suitcases had been packed for several days. His clothes for the trip were in one small bag, and Henry could hammer down those crate lids in fifteen minutes. *There's even time for that drink at the club – I owe that much to my men.*

Sharp at 7:30 the following morning, the Colonel and his aides boarded their military transport, and within minutes were airborne, on the first leg of the long journey home.

That same morning, Gwyn packed the last of her things in her shipping trunk and moved to the Orphanage. The day had come at last. Before she was even out the door, Ruthie's boyfriend arrived. He cheerfully helped load the trunk into the "boot" of Doc Mac's sedan. Gwyn's staunch ally in her orphanage project had volunteered to drive her over.

Gwyn gave Ruthie a hug and both wiped away a tear. They would see each other nearly every day at the hospital, of course, and they would visit, but it was the end of something that had begun two years ago in London.

Doc turned into the hibiscus-lined driveway of the newly painted plantation house. As the car crunched up the gravel drive, the children who had been anxiously waiting, scampered alongside. This time, "Auntie Gwyn" had come to stay!

Once her trunk was in her room, she left the orphans under Doc Mac's care in the living room. He took the opportunity to check their teeth, peer into their ears, and dress minor scrapes and cuts. Gwyn placed her things in the drawers and closet.

Doc Mac stayed for a lunch of sandwiches and lemonade, served on the lawn. Then he departed, and Gwyn found herself with all of Saturday afternoon before her. She had nervous energy to burn, and she threw herself into a few of the endless tasks required to care for a vast house and sixteen children. They spent the afternoon together, tidying the place, and there was time for a game of "rounders" in the yard, played with a tennis racquet and five bases.

Two women of the native staff had been busy all day in the laundry house, working the gasoline-engine powered washing machine. Now there were rows of sheets and children's clothing billowing on the lines. The young ones' best set of clothes would be laid out for church tomorrow. After that, Gwyn had promised them an afternoon at the beach, and a rare treat—ice-cream cones for all.

Come Monday morning, she would be back at the hospital—and on it would go. She could fill every minute of every day, and still have more to do. But as the hours grew into days, many times she felt herself being swept away by anxiety. Where was Johnny? Were he, Footy and Dingo even alive?

Monday morning at the US Garrison, Hala entered the corner office. Soon there would be a new boss-man! She carried a broom to make the final sweep she'd been ordered to do. The Colonel with all the rules was *gone-finish,* and the other officers did not seem to mind when she forgot to put on her one and only T-shirt. She despised the constriction, and could not begin to comprehend the terrible harnesses with which the white women bound their chests. It was natural, she thought, that a woman's *soosoo* should be left as Papa-God made them—loose and uncovered.

Hala had been taught how to turn on the overhead fan, and then told to leave it alone. When she came in, she found the room stifling. She turned on the control, as far as it would go. A breeze began to stir the air and she hummed an island song and whisked her broom. But then the overhead contraption began to whiz faster and faster. Soon there was a wind howling. Hala watched in dismay as it peeled the stacks of papers off the desk and scattered them across the floor. It was a disaster! She might lose her job, and there would be no precious pounds to send home.

Worse, Hala had a terror of being yelled at by the white men. Her heart was pounding like a drum! She rushed to the control knob and spun it off. Thankfully, the tornado subsided, but the room was a mess. Hala froze in panic.

A brilliant question occurred to her. *What would a white man do?* The answer came, and a smile spread over her pretty tattooed face. She dropped her broom and gathered the errant papers, clutching them to her chest. She went to the filing cabinets where she had seen the men put these things. She yanked open drawer after drawer, but they were full. Finally, at the bottom of the end row, she found one half empty. She stuffed everything in and closed it up.

There, she thought. The room was tidy again. *Hala, you are one smart girl!* She continued to sweep, singing her happy tune. And then another thrilling thought occurred to her.

I wonder if the new boss-man is married?

CHAPTER 4

Johnny, the prisoner, then Footy, walked along the path beside the river. Johnny had his Springfield over his shoulder, helmet on, and his pack on his back. The Japanese came next, his hands bound behind him. Then there was Footy, Dingo's Digger hat and wood-framed pack on, the samurai sword sticking from the top. He carried the Lee Enfield over a shoulder, and had the Webley revolver and the big knife stuck through his belt.

The first half-day's walk south of Kissim took them along a well-worn trail, but by mid-afternoon, they entered less traveled territory. The jungle had reclaimed entire stretches, and Johnny had to shoulder through vines or slash with his machete. Insects fell on the men, mosquitoes drifted in clouds, and they had to be alert for thorny branches and stinging nettles.

Johnny remembered Father Bastion's letter had said the Mambu headhunters had not been seen this far up the river during the years the priests had been in Kissim. Still, Johnny's war experience told him not to take anything for granted. Warriors could be only feet away in the dense vegetation and he wouldn't see them. In addition, there might be more of the enemy around—this was unknown territory, and anything could happen.

On top of that, there were all the dangers inherent in the rainforest. *Snakes, for instance.* Stepping on a Death Adder would be fatal. The serpent was another ambush hunter. It hid under leaves, and that made an overgrown jungle trail a perfect place. The end of its tail was an appendage that resembled a grub. The predator hid itself and raised the twitching tail. When a hapless animal or bird investigated, it found itself suddenly confronted by the poisonous head of the serpent.

When a man stepped on a Death Adder, even as the fangs went through the skin, it was over. Like its relative the Cobra, the Death Adder's venom was a potent neurotoxin. The exquisite torture of it was that a man lived long enough to know what had killed him. Rapidly, he was paralyzed, stopped breathing and died. And that was just one of the thousand of fascinating and terrifying ways life was snuffed out in the jungle.

To his growing resentment, Footy's view was mostly the prisoner's back. With hands bound behind him, "the Jap" could not ward off the canes that whipped him, and the Aussie took a little satisfaction in that. At one point, a writhing centipede dropped onto the prisoner's head. The man cried out and twitched it off, and Footy crunched it under his sandal. *The bugger was lucky that time.* The sting of the jungle centipede would put a man in agony.

Footy's shoulders hurt from the pack and he hitched it up. The sword standing in it clattered. He resented the weight—*but it's a beaut, a real Jap samurai souvenir, and I will have it!*

At midday, the men came to an open place in the forest. In it stood a betel-nut palm, branches loaded with the lime-size nuts. There was the sound of trickling water and they saw a puddle near the roots.

"Watch the Jap," Johnny told Footy. He knelt, washed his face in the clear water, brought a handful up and tasted it. It was sweet and he drank his fill. He took the two canteens off his belt, spilled out the metallic dregs and refilled them. Then he made way for Footy, who drank deeply and replenished the bottle that had been Dingo's. He soaked the Digger hat in the water and put it back on, and stood up. Johnny spoke to the Japanese.

"Drink." The prisoner sank by the pool. He extended his bound hands behind his back and looked at Johnny. Johnny just stared back so the man put his face to the water and sucked some up. He choked and didn't get much. Again, he stared at the Yankee and thrust out his hands. Johnny sighed.

"Untie him," he told Footy, "I'll cover you." Footy sniffed: *who does the bleedin' Yank think he's giving orders to?* But he did as asked. The Japanese nodded thanks, rubbed his chafed wrists, and cupped his hands and drank. He splashed water over his face, pulled the soiled headband off, rinsed it and tied it back on. Then, with a quick glance at the others, he stripped off his ragged shirt and splashed water on his chest and underarms. Footy grew impatient.

"Here!" he called. "We haven't got all day!" The Japanese held up his shirt in one hand and pinched his nose with the other. Johnny laughed and even Footy chuckled.

"True," the Aussie said, "you are number one stinky!" Johnny dug the bar of soap out of his pack and handed it over. The prisoner soaped up his head and body, scrubbed and rinsed his shirt and struggled back into it.

"Tie his hands," Johnny told Footy.

"You do it, mate," Footy replied, picking up his rifle and pointing it at the captive. "You're better with knots."

"My dad was a sailor," Johnny grinned. The Japanese put his wrists together and held them out in front, not behind.

"Half a mo' you bugga! Behind your back!" Footy called, but the captive was staring at the American.

"Why not," Johnny gave in. He wrapped and knotted one of the prisoner's wrists, and lashed it to the other. "You won't get out of that," he said.

"What are you doing?" Footy protested.

"If he tries anything, you know what to do," Johnny said. "Let's march."

"Who made you bloody king of the bush?" Footy muttered to his back as the Yank strode off.

Late in the afternoon, the pilot called a break.

"Oy, hold up, Johnny. Give us a ciggy, would you?" Johnny leaned on his pack against a tree, took the box from his pocket, handed a smoke to Footy, took one himself, and lit them. When he was done, Johnny threw the butt on the ground and went to stamp it out with his boot. But before he could do that, the captive scooped it up and took a few quick drags.

Johnny chuckled. He took a slug from his canteen, and offered it to "the Jap," who held it in his bound hands and drank.

"Ok," Johnny told him. "If you're going to drink, you're going to carry." He hooked one of his bottles onto the man's rope belt, and they hiked on.

Sunset came and the trail grew dim. The river had been running beside them through a series of roaring rapids, a mist in the air. As night fell, they made camp. With the Father possibly nearby, Johnny picked a place a good fifty yards from the river. He made the prisoner lie down by a tree and once again, tied his hands, his ankles, and roped him to the trunk. He hung his hammock while Footy spread his blanket. Over dinner of canned franks, green beans and potatoes, the pilot said they must already have descended a thousand feet in altitude.

Again, the two took turns on watch while the captive slept. In the morning, Johnny opened two cans of stew and warmed them on the kerosene stove. He opened a can of peach slices, and distributed the food on three plates. Afterwards Footy gathered the dirty plates and cutlery and went to the river. He studied it suspiciously as he approached. When he was reasonably sure no big predator lay in wait, he washed the things, glancing nervously around.

They hit the trail again. Sometimes now, the path disappeared entirely, so Johnny had to cut a way with his machete.

☆

Two more days went by as the men trekked out of the mountains. The Raub River alternated between boiling rapids and smoother stretches of fast water that tumbled from the high country toward the plains.

Somewhat to his surprise, Johnny found he was enjoying the journey. Each day his legs grew thicker with muscle, and the wound site in his chest hurt less. The nagging discomfort was that he was always hungry, craving fresh meat and greens. But it was sweet relief to be out of the hospital and the endless days in bed. Sometimes the pack strap cut into his scar and got it aching. Then he bore the weight in his hands, and distracted himself by looking at the countryside.

In this pristine wilderness, there were abundant Birds of Paradise, flocks of parrots, and many feathered species he did not know. Gorgeous orchids hung from branches, tree ferns towered overhead, and there was a profusion of fragrant blossoms. On the rainforest floor, strange toadstools and fungi grew. The insects were legion. There were butterflies in rainbow colors, giant moths that flapped through the gloom, and beetles with horned heads. There were some two or more feet long that looked like sticks, complete with leaves and bark, but had six legs.

On the afternoon of the third day out of Kissim, the men's spirits soared when they heard the unmistakable hum of engines.

"A plane!" Johnny shouted.

"A DC-3, I reckon," Footy called.

They charged for the river and burst onto the rocky bank. Longingly, they stared in the direction of the sound. Each strained to see the silver flash that would be their rescue. But the rumble became a drone, and then faded away. Long after it was gone, the men waited. At last they were forced to admit it was hopeless.

Footy strung together a flamboyant string of words. He threw himself down and put his head in his hands. Even the Japanese slumped on a rock. The lost opportunity was harder to bear than nothing at all.

"Let's just sleep here tonight," Footy muttered. Johnny picked up a rock and hurled it into the water.

"And what about the Father?"

The Aussie's head flew up and he stared at the river.

"Aww yeh," he said. "Got me head on crook. Let's move off—much farther off." And they did.

They heated more cans for dinner. After, they smoked. When he had a half-inch of unfiltered Camel left, Johnny handed it to the prisoner. The man sucked it down so far, he scorched his fingers and muttered.

"You're going soft," Footy scoffed at Johnny.

The two did an inventory of their remaining food. The bread was long gone, and they had enough hardtack for one more day. There was half a bag of coffee, but no powdered milk, and only a twist of sugar. There was only one more can of corned beef, another of baked beans and two more stews. There were two cans of fruit cocktail, and that was it.

"It's enough for one more day—two if we stretch it and go hungry," Johnny said.

"I'm already starved. We have to find some gardens," Footy said.

"Sure," Johnny agreed. "But gardens mean natives—and you know the rest."

"Bleedin' Valley of the ruddy Cannibals, mate," Footy nodded. "Bloody problem."

Johnny tied the Japanese for the night, then wandered back to the river for some time on his own. He sat on a boulder staring at the flow of water. Again, he thought about Gwyn. *She probably thinks I'm dead*. He pictured himself surprising her—*I'm back!* He'd pick her up in his arms and kiss her full on the mouth. The intensity of the image shocked him.

Where did that come from? And what a crock, his killer mind mocked. *Have you got malaria? You need to be thinking about getting off this river and on to Japan! Besides, she doesn't even like you.*

Oh yeah? a voice answered in his head. *Then why did she say she'd have dinner with me?* Johnny knew he had a crush on Gwyn, he might as well admit it. But once again, he lectured himself, there was no future in it. *Not here, not now.* For years, his plans had been brutally simple. *Find the enemy—make him pay.* But now, wherever his thoughts turned, there she was.

Johnny steered away from her and turned to General MacArthur and the Philippines. *I think it's the 1st of August today. August! Has my unit left for Okinawa without me?* He was flooded again with the sense of urgency. *I need to be there! If this "three day mission" had gone right, I'd be on a ship to Manila by now!*

Johnny saw a movement on the river and his heart jumped. A shadow ghosted along. A whirlpool spun out there, and something huge slid into it. He stared until a branch came up, shaking leaves, and he knew it was only a waterlogged tree caught in the spiral.

Where's that monster croc? Johnny remembered Dingo bloodied between those cruel teeth, and the way he had struggled before the brute took him into the river. During the war, Johnny had seen men die in all kinds of ways. He'd even witnessed death by crocodile. He and a platoon of GIs had been fording a river. They were wading through chest-deep water when the man beside Johnny let out a scream and went under. There was nothing but a bloodstain on the surface, and the rest of them ran. It was over that fast. But the Father had taken Dingo on land, and he knew the Major had realized exactly what was happening.

To be eaten alive! Johnny shivered. *To know you were no more in the end than a croc's meal!* Again, Johnny saw the glower the crocodile had given him after he shot its foot off. *I hope the thing bled to death! But don't count on it,* he warned himself. *Do not count on that!*

It was almost dark. He went back to camp, made sure the prisoner's bonds were secure, and strung his hammock. In pitch black now, he sat on a fallen log for the first watch. Footy rolled in his blanket and soon was snoring. The prisoner snuffled deeply as well. Soon they had a duet going. At least it was company, Johnny thought.

On the fifth morning since they departed Kissim, the men found themselves hiking beside a much wider Raub. Since early this morning, they'd seen increasing evidence of humans. Most obviously, there were crimson blobs beside the path. *Betel spit, from the mouths of cannibals*. No longer did Johnny have to swing his machete. Now he and Footy walked on high alert, their rifles ready. By early afternoon, the terrain changed. They entered a deepening gorge. The banks were jungle-covered cliffs that towered higher and higher on each side.

Late in the afternoon, their trail dead-ended into a wider path. Johnny held up a hand and the other two stopped. The new trail was more than a yard across, packed hard by the passage of hundreds of feet. Now the foliage on each side was uniformly stained red.

His rifle at his shoulder, Johnny stepped onto the wide path and whirled in each direction. There was no one to be seen. He waved the others out.

"*Kanaka* highway!" Footy mouthed. Johnny nodded and continued in the downriver direction. The rosy light of sunset was spilling through the woods. He quickened his pace. Danger was all around, and they had to find a hiding place to wait out the night.

The gloom deepened. Then, ahead, Johnny saw the trees thin out. Again he held up a hand. He put a finger to his lips and motioned for the others to get down. He crept forward alone, got on his belly and crawled the last few feet. He parted the undergrowth and gazed out.

He was looking down a grassy slope to the river a hundred and fifty yards off. Stretching away was a wide, long valley, between sheer mountain slopes. The river wound like a fat brown snake down the center.

Back in Kissim, Johnny had been certain that following the Raub was their best hope for survival. But now they were here, he was overwhelmed with uncertainty. And his heart was in his throat, because he was staring at hundreds of living, breathing Mambu savages.

Spread out before him was the Valley of the Cannibals.

CHAPTER 5

Johnny crept back and brought Footy and the Japanese forward. They crawled to the vantage place in the undergrowth. In the fading sunset, the trio saw the broad Raub meandering through the valley. The land on either side was garden-plots in shades of green. Steep mountains thick with jungle flanked each side. *What did Dingo say? He'd seen it from the air. "Impossible to pass that way."* In the far distance, mountains pinched into another gorge.

Dotted all across the landscape were Mambu people. Women toiled in the gardens. Men talked in groups. Some on the river stood upright and paddled their dugout canoes. Crowds were congregating on the trails, returning to the villages for the night.

There are thousands of them! Johnny counted five villages, beginning with the nearest one about two miles away. Each had a perimeter fence and lay beneath a pall of smoke, no doubt from the cooking fires. The largest one was in the far distance, near the end of the valley. *Maybe a six-hour walk, maybe more*.

He heard something and glanced that way. He froze when he saw a squad of warriors coming. He gave Footy and the prisoner a warning touch. Nine Mambu came single-file along the path. They were armed with bows, axes, spears and clubs, and were naked except for the long yellow gourds hiding their penises. Johnny did not think it was a war party. *Border patrol,* he guessed.

The warriors gazed all around with keen eyes. They passed within thirty feet of the watchers, and continued towards the river. Johnny's group waited behind cover as the last sunlight climbed the eastern slopes and exploded into the clouds, dying them crimson, then dusky rose, then charcoal. The first stars flickered over the peaks.

In the near darkness, the three crawled back into the forest. They pushed away from the trail into dense forest. Fifty yards in, encircled by trees, they stopped.

"We sleep here. No stove," Johnny whispered.

"Not even a ciggy," Footy agreed. Johnny untied the prisoner's hands. Footy opened a can of beans and another of stew and the two men ate this cold, leaving a portion in the bottom for the prisoner. They remained hungry, but all they had left was fruit cocktail, and that was their breakfast. *Not only do we have to get through this deadly place, but we're going to have to beg or steal food from the cannibals,* Johnny thought grimly. It seemed an impossible task, and he pushed it out of his mind.

Johnny tied the prisoner for the night. He did not bother to hang his hammock: he'd sleep on the ground. *We may have to be up and fighting for our lives in a heartbeat*. It was Footy's turn to take the first watch.

"The valley is huge," Johnny whispered as he lay down. "It's going to take all day to cross."

"*If* we get across," Footy said. "Dingo says no one's ever gone in there..."

"Yeh, yeh," Johnny interrupted. "At least we've got surprise going for us. We'll march straight through. If we have to, we'll shoot their ringleaders and run."

"And that's your plan?" Footy hissed.

Johnny spread his hammock on the leaves and stretched out on it. Footy sat with his rifle. The captive seemed to fall asleep at once, and Johnny envied him. He just couldn't get there. He knew he needed rest and a clear head for the perilous day tomorrow, and he squeezed his eyes closed, but the minutes lumbered by. He heard every sound in the jungle, and each time Footy shifted.

At long last he drifted off—only to be shaken awake. It was his watch.

Two miles away, a Mambu sentry stared at the river. Every night, the warriors guarded the gorges at each end of the valley. These were the vulnerable points through which any enemy must enter. Once more tonight, he did his duty, even though no foe had been foolish enough to attack the Mambu in their territory during his lifetime. The *Mambu-ato,* their war chief, had issued his orders, and his elite guard came by regularly to ensure they were followed, on pain of death.

The clan the sentry belonged to must obey. Twice a day, he and his kinsmen patrolled the perimeter. Every night, they watched the gorge and the river. If a sentry fell asleep, his own relatives would beat him senseless, for if it was the *Mambu-ato's* guards who found him instead of them, he would pay with his head. In addition, there would be a fine of women, pigs and weapons laid upon the entire village.

The warrior watched the river and kept himself awake with *buai.* His brothers and cousins slept beside him. It was shaping up to be another long and eventless night.

Suddenly he leapt to his feet. Something moved on the face of the deep! It was hard to see in the starlight, but it might be an enemy canoe, a crocodile, or a piece of driftwood. He saw it again. The thing was huge! Add that to all the supernatural events of recent days, and there was reason for his consternation.

One moon ago, an elder-woman renowned for her trances had seen the river god in her dreams. Her familiar spirits awakened her and guided her through the sleeping nation. There, under the cold face of the full moon, she witnessed a portentous event.

When it was over, she scurried to the war chief's men's house and roused the guards. While she waited outside, they woke the *Mambu-ato*. Respected as she was, if she had dared to enter the realm of the warriors, she would have been cut down. As it was, her life was on the line. The chief was notoriously cranky when his sleep was disturbed.

Within minutes, his close advisors spilled out like angry ants. They brought the wooden chair from which he held court. Its back was carved in a high arch, a totem crocodile on each side, snouts meeting overhead. They placed this ready for the *Mambu-ato,* while shamen and warriors arranged themselves by rank around the native throne.

At last Bumay, the *Mambu-ato* himself, came out yawning and threw himself into his seat. He was a powerfully built young man, sulky and half awake. He adjusted the hastily tied gourd that pinched his testicles, raised a leg and scratched a fleabite on his hind end. He called for *buai,* a nut was given to him, and he began to chew. A sorcerer commanded the crone to speak. How dare she disturb the chief, and the leaders? Bumay squirted spittle on the ground and stared at her.

The woman spoke. The Papa of the *pookpook* had come to the nation once more. It had been many years, but he had returned. She described her dream and the way the spirits led her to the river. There she saw the deity—the giant *pookpook* with the moon on its head. Watched by its sister in the sky, the *Mambu-matu* went by. Although the incarnation of the river's power had not been observed within the lifetime of many of those gathered, she had seen it in her youth, and there was no doubt. The Chief was wide-awake now, his petulance forgotten in the face of this stupendous news.

"What must we do?" he asked his sorcerers. The deity must be propitiated, they replied. If not, the dark power would consume the Mambu people. It would feed on them until they divined what had brought it here. Ultimately, they would have to perform all the correct rituals, and make human sacrifices. How much better, the elders argued, to do what must be done at once!

Bumay responded decisively. By first light, a war party composed of scores of his best fighters was milling in front of his spirit house. While the shamen beat drums and cast spells to guarantee success in the manhunt, the warriors got ready. They rubbed their bodies with black grease and painted one another. They donned towering white egret headdresses, chose their weapons, and followed the *Mambu-ato* out. They streamed through the fence and took to the trail through the downriver gorge. The war chief broke into a trot as they went towards their neighbors, their favorite enemies.

Two days later they returned, dragging four live captives. Often the marauders were only able to bring back dead meat, but the rituals to appease the Father required living sacrifices. This time, they had been fortunate. Three of their prisoners were the usual Uhuli men. But the fourth was an exotic addition. This was a foreigner with yellow skin. The fact that he was emaciated to the point of starvation did not detract from his value as a rare specimen.

In a costumed ceremony attended by the entire nation, the victims were sacrificed on the river's edge. While the crocodile did not deign to make an appearance, the river, of course, was watching.

The men's heads were severed from their bodies. The *Mambu-ato* himself took the yellow man's head off with a blow of his axe.

The skulls were mounted on spears set in the riverbank. The priests carved prize pieces of the meat, and then the carcasses were floated on banana log rafts into the stream, intended for the Father. The dead heads oversaw their bodies drift away.

Bumay had the testicles roasted on sticks, and ate several of the succulent morsels that were so good for absorbing a man's power. He distributed the rest to his favorites. Other cuts were passed among the people, so all could have a taste. There was considerable interest in sampling the foreigner by those with a penchant for the exotic. They pronounced the taste spicy, but not as good as the usual Uhuli flesh.

As the days passed, the shamen informed the *Mambu-ato* that the slaughter and the gifts to the river had worked their magic. The Father refrained from preying on the nation. In fact, the great *pook-pook* was gone.

Now the sentry who saw the movement on the river roused his kinsmen. Together, they gazed at the ghostly scene. And then, all of them saw it. A giant shape slid along the surface. There was no doubt. It was the *Mambu-matu*. Strong magic and great events were afoot, and the men were frightened. It was one thing to face a human enemy in a fight, but this was a spiritual force, and when the great ones appeared, the people were bound to suffer.

The warriors muttered anxiously to one another and stared until the moon went down. Come tomorrow, they must report all this to the war chief.

Johnny was surfing. He stood on the ocean, the foam swirling around his ankles, the arc of the wave over his head. There was a roar of water and he felt the surge of power through his feet. He glanced down and there was his long wooden surfboard. He was glad to see it! He'd lost it years ago. Now here it was again!

He looked at the translucent rising water and tried to turn into it, but the board had become sluggish and would not respond. He glanced down and saw with horror that his feet rode the back of the enormous crocodile.

The head as big as his body turned back over its shoulder and Johnny saw the moon scar, but it was red, and blood dripped from it and ran like tears around the yellow eye. They fell into the ocean and stained it crimson. He was transfixed by the huge teeth along the rough mouth, and the way it curved in a knowing grin.

The crocodile opened its jaws and it lunged back at him. He tried to leap away, but could not move, and the teeth bit into his wounded shoulder.

Johnny grunted and Footy's hand went from shaking him to

covering his mouth. Then Johnny remembered. This was the day they must walk through the Valley of the Cannibals. There they would confront the most feared warriors in New Guinea, and somehow get across. He looked around and saw first light filtering down through the forest giants.

There's a good chance we won't see sunset, the soldier spoke up. *But let's get on with it. This is as good a day as any to die.* Johnny crawled to the prisoner and untied him.

Footy opened the can of fruit and ate the first third. Johnny went next, then handed it with the spoon to "the Jap," who finished it and drank every drop of syrup. Johnny tied his hands in front again.

Johnny and Footy double-checked the load in their firearms. When they had their packs and headgear on, rifles in hand, Johnny pulled out the cigarettes. He put one between his lips, gave another to Footy, and on impulse, handed one to the captive. Looking surprised, the man took it in bound hands and dipped his head. Johnny lit them all with his Zippo.

"It might be our last smoke," he said and grinned as he led off. All three puffing, the men strode from the forest into the open. Johnny walked fast, trying not to be quiet.

"Whatever happens, act confident," he said over his shoulder. "Keep moving—don't stop for anything."

They came to the edge of the trees and went down, scanning the valley. It was daybreak and quiet, only a few women in the distance moving toward the gardens. He lengthened his stride, the other two following.

The trail took them into a grove of banana trees. Johnny rounded a corner and bumped into an ancient couple. The man was cutting down a bunch of red bananas with a bamboo knife while the woman held open a string *bilum*. The two of them were bickering as they attempted the insertion. Johnny took in the homely faces, sparse teeth, and white hair.

The Mambu couple saw the strangers. Their mouths fell open and everything tumbled from their hands. The old man clutched his chest and fell back while the woman fetched up against a tree. Babbling, the man lurched for Johnny and grabbed his arm.

"The stories are true," he gasped in his language. *"Our ancestors can return from the land of the dead!"* He reached a quaking hand and rubbed Johnny's cheek, then looked to see if the white

came off. *"They are spirits!"* he cried to his wife. The old woman crept forward, lips pulled back over her stumps of teeth. Tears sprang from her eyes and ran down her wrinkled cheeks as she stared into Footy's face.

"Do you see?" she said, *"Here is my uncle Fumayma!"* Her fingers stroked the blonde hair on the Aussie's arm and he grinned at her.

"What are you saying, Mum?"

"They have forgotten how to talk," the old man observed. The woman reached for Footy's sandy hair that stuck out under his hat and tugged.

"Ouch!" he said, pulling back.

"The hair has burned in the spirit world," she nodded. Footy took a pinch of her own stiff curls and gave a playful twist. The woman jerked back rubbing the place and squinted at him. Footy laughed and his attention went to the fallen bananas.

"I'm bloody starving—may I?" He tore one off, peeled it and shoved it all in his mouth. Johnny leaned his rifle against his leg and broke off a few, stripped the skin from one, and ate it in a few bites. He tossed the peel and attacked another. The couple stared as the two men wolfed down a hand each.

"Good!" Footy said to the old folks, rubbing his stomach.

"Our relatives still like our bananas," the woman observed.

Johnny remembered the Japanese. He peeled one for him and put it in his hands. The man shoved it in. Johnny fed him four in a row. The elders came close, the native man shorter than the prisoner. He touched the Japanese skin and stared into the slanted eyes.

"This one is different," he said. *"He is like the foreigners they killed downriver. You remember the taste?"* He put a gnarled finger on the rope that tied the Japanese's wrists.

"I do not think this one is a ghost," he said doubtfully. "Perhaps our ancestors brought him for food?"

"Struth!" Footy exclaimed. "Their eyeballs are going to pop out!"

"They must think we're from Mars," Johnny smiled. He dropped his pack and began to stuff it with the fruit while Footy did the same.

"I reckon the stories about these bloody Mambu are exaggerated," Footy said hopefully. "If the buggers are all like this, we just might survive. "

"Don't count on it," Johnny warned. "Let's go!"

The trio moved off and the old ones hurried to keep up. The man hung off Johnny's arm while the woman hobbled beside Footy, grinning at him while she recounted everything that had happened since he, her mother's brother, had gone to the spirit world.

"What are you on about, Mum?" Footy grinned at her. "Are you completely daft?"

The men strode along the path among the gardens and a clutch of women carrying digging sticks saw them coming. At once they broke into shrill cries and came running to the strangers, heavy bark skirts swinging, breasts bouncing on rounded bellies. Soon there were some twenty women surrounding the travelers, all trying to touch their skin and hair. Johnny forged through them, batting away the hands that kept reaching into his clothes and touching his pockets.

"Smile!" he called. Footy pasted on a grin and even the Japanese bobbed his head and stretched back his lips. The crowd swelled with each step and now Johnny was shoving to get through. The smell of ripe bodies rose.

"We're friends!" Johnny called, smiling. Natives pressed from all sides. The Japanese in particular seemed not to like that. He came close behind Johnny and ducked his head.

"Friends!" Footy took Johnny's example and shouted in a jovial voice. "Bloody good mates!" He smirked at a young man, then had to shoulder aside a heavy woman in his path.

"Good morning, you great bloody cow! A lovely morning, isn't it? Yes, we are all best mates here, you bloody, horrible savages!" The noise grew deafening as more Mambu came running, every one of them hollering at the top of his lungs.

The path led them to the fence made of saplings around the first village. The path continued beside it, and as they went by, natives spilled from the huts and rushed to the commotion. Johnny gazed at the crowd and saw the dark skin, broad faces and rugged features.

Increasingly, it was warriors who snatched up their weapons and came at a run. These included the sentries who had witnessed the marvelous events of the night. *This might be what the deity's visitation signified,* they thought—*the coming of foreign invaders!*

They bulled through the throng. There was sure to be some killing!

Every man was naked, Johnny saw, except for the outlandish genital coverings. He'd heard about penis gourds in New Guinea, but he'd never seen them until the Mambu valley. They were the color of yellow squash, but from man to man the shapes varied. Some were short and simple—others, long and twisted. They were held around the waist by a string. Hanging at the back was a single long leaf that more or less covered the crack of their buttocks.

Most men wore a circlet of bound pig tusks through their noses. Some had great shells hanging on their chests. They carried arrows and spears with fire-hardened points, axes and knives of stone. The throng increasingly hampered Johnny. More and more, those confronting him were agitated men. At last, facing a bristling wall of points, he was forced to pull up.

The Mambu harangued the strangers, shouting in their faces. Johnny's group did not understand a word, but they saw the violent body language. Still, the old couple remained at their sides, clinging to their arms. They talked continuously until warriors pulled them off.

This is it, the soldier voice told Johnny. *We're surrounded and outnumbered. There's no escape. We can't shoot them all, but we can die fighting.*

"Get ready to fire!" he called to Footy.

The Mambu headhunters confronted the strangers, whipping themselves into a murderous frenzy.

CHAPTER 6

The Mambu warriors were hopping up and down in their fervor to attack. Johnny thrust his rifle into the air and fired. The shot cracked across the valley and echoed back. Those nearest fell, pricking themselves on the weapons behind them. A few in the crowd fainted and fell down. The whole group cowered, and some turned uneasily to the mountains that had answered the invaders' loud challenge. Johnny reloaded. A native grabbed the spent cartridge that flew out and singed his fingers.

But then the warriors pressed forward even closer, infuriated by their fear. Their razor points hovered inches from the strangers' skin. Johnny reloaded and said the first desperate thing that came to him.

"We go to the chief!" he yelled.

"Big chief!" Footy picked it up and tried it in the trade language. *"Luluai!"* He, too, shot his rifle in the air. In the deafened silence, he called again: *"Luluai!"*

Johnny knew that word and he took it up.

"Loo-loo-eye! Loo-loo-eye!" This was the common term for village leader, but it meant nothing in Mambu. However, one of the more widely traveled headhunters had heard it downriver. He was a thick, older man, and a brother of Chief Bumay. This was the first thing the strangers had said that made sense.

"Luluai!" he repeated in his hoarse voice and then said it in his language.

"Mambu-ato!" The War Chief!

"Mambu-ato," other voices joined in. The hoarse warrior continued.

"*Bumay!*" He shook his spear and repeated his brother's name, stamping his feet. *"Mambu-ato—Bumay!"*

The people took up the chant. *"Bumay, Bumay, Bumay!"*

"The dog-strangers call for my brother, the Mambu-ato! We will take them to him!" the warrior cried. But the head of another clan disagreed.

"No! Kill them now," he screamed. *"They have broken taboo! The strangers invaded our valley and you know the penalty!"*

"They are the spirits of our family!" the old couple shrieked. *"Do not offend them!"* A hundred voices joined in, each with an opinion.

"Hear me!" The hoarse warrior gained dominance by sheer volume. *"The dog-strangers must die, all of us know this. But they call for my brother, and this is the law. Their lives are forfeit to the Mambu-ato—to him alone!"* The assembly considered this—out loud, and all at once.

Johnny, Footy and the Japanese watched the debate without comprehension. At last it seemed the warriors reached a consensus. All pointed to the village in the far distance. The crowd surged that way, pressing Johnny's group forward. The Mambu danced as they walked, shaking their weapons and chanting.

"*Bumay! Bumay! Bumay!*"

"We're in for it now mate," Footy called.

"We bought ourselves some time," Johnny replied. "Stay ready!"

It was a long trek, pressed in by their escort of warriors, dragging a tail of hundreds. They passed village after village, and at each one, the throng increased. After seven long hours, at last they approached the final and biggest village. The crowd pressed them against the fence. A half-mile further was the end of the valley.

Faint with hunger, already awash in body odor, the strangers were assaulted by a reek of garbage and excrement. In order to enter the village, each person must go through a gap in the fence, one at a time. In the opening stood a stump. Each one must step onto it, then down on the far side. It was an ingenious way to prevent any attack in numbers.

The squad led by the chief's brother went first and waited for the foreigners. Johnny was next, and stepped down among people, yapping dogs, pigs, chickens and screeching children. It was bedlam.

Once the three strangers were over, the procession surged into the Mambu town, while those behind continued through the bottleneck. Johnny's group was forced between the huts and the crush grew worse. Hundreds of residents swelled the crowd. To their consternation, Johnny and Footy found themselves being forced apart. They used the stocks of their rifles to push back together, on each side of the prisoner.

They saw two types of native habitations—long rectangular houses with peaked roofs from which men spilled, and round huts for the women and children. Through each doorway they could see fires burning. There were no chimneys, and the smoke seeped up through the thatch.

For the Mambu, the arrival of the outlandish strangers was a once-in-a-lifetime event. That three foreigners would invade their valley was beyond belief! Every member of the nation came rushing to take part in the momentous occasion. There would be a satisfying slaughter, no doubt, and then, exotic meat.

As the three men moved within their phalanx, they were frequently pricked by spear points at their backs. After a particularly painful jab, Johnny spun and caught the young warrior in the act. He used his Springfield to knock the spear aside and hit the offender in the jaw with the stock. The fellow, about Johnny's age, staggered back and fell hard on his butt. At once he jumped up and screamed in fury.

"Bumay!" Johnny yelled in his face. The crowd took up the chant again, and they surged on. Shortly, they burst into an open space on the riverbank. Surrounded on three sides by huts, it was spacious enough to accommodate maybe a thousand people. It offered a sweeping view of the Raub, and there were canoes all over it, driving at them.

Johnny's attention went to the grandest edifice in the entire town. It was one of the rectangular men's houses, but twice as high and several times as large as any other.

"*House Tambaran*," Footy nodded. "Likely to be this Bumay's roost." The roof of the A-frame soared to a high point at their end. Like all the other buildings, it had an open entrance, but no door. The men could see the fire flickering on the hearth. The triangular wall was covered in flattened bark. On it were elaborate paintings of animals and mythical figures. At the top was a rendering of a giant crocodile. Above the curled body were toothy jaws that went into the peak.

On each side of the doorframe stood a pyramid seven or eight feet tall. Johnny thought they were stacks of white rocks, but something about them made him take a closer look. He raised his scope, and his stomach turned over. He was looking at empty eyes and nose holes over rows of white and black teeth. They were human skulls. The upper ones were white, some with patches of kinky hair still attached. Those at the bottom were yellowed ivory.

"Human heads!" Johnny said.

"Bloody cannibals!" Footy spat. He and the prisoner stared as well. Elderly men surrounded the big house. Some sat cross-legged, scraping at skulls cradled in their laps. When they saw the strangers, the elders put aside their work and hobbled over to gawk. Again, a multi-voiced exchange took place. Mambu continued to press into the meeting area, and now the place was packed shoulder-to-shoulder with men, women and children.

The ancient couple the men had first met wormed their way forward. They came weeping, and embraced Johnny and Footy. They shouted to the crowd, and some nodded, while others seemed to scoff.

"Bloody drama, eh mate?" Footy called to Johnny. "Whadda ya reckon they're on about?"

"No idea," Johnny said. "Let's try to get some food."

"Right mate!" Footy said. *"Kaukau,"* he yelled, using a hand to mimic putting food in his mouth.

"Kaukau," Johnny called. Hundreds of heads spun their way and mouths dropped open.

"Kaukau!" said Mambu voices. Others repeated the word in their own tongue, and a roar erupted. *"They want sweet potatoes!"* Women reached into their *bilums* and pulled out roasted tubers, and passed them hand-to-hand to the strangers.

Johnny and Footy ate one-handed, holding their rifles. Mouths full, they grinned at the natives. A startled laugh went up. An animated discussion took place, and women scurried to the huts. The Japanese nudged Johnny.

"Ok, ok," Johnny said. He gave the man a potato and he ate fast. More food kept coming, and soon there were piles on the ground.

A chunk of cooked pork was thrust into Johnny's hands. He felt his juices run and bit in. A roasted chicken was handed to Footy, burnt bits of feathers and all. He tore a leg and chewed. Another pork roast was handed to the prisoner. He ate ravenously.

"Save some," Johnny said. He went on a knee beside his pack, rifle against his side, and put his hands out. The natives passed him more *kaukau* and meat. He shoved these on top of the bananas. Footy filled the other pack from the piles. The Japanese ate like there was no tomorrow. *And he may be right,* Johnny thought.

With some provision made for a future that did not include the taking of their heads, the men ate at a more leisurely pace. The food continued to flow.

While he chewed, Johnny studied the far side of the village for an escape route. Beyond the chief's house was another row of huts, and over those he saw the end of the valley. He was craning at the paths between the huts when another chunk of meat was put in his hand. He lifted it to bite, and the Japanese hit him with his fists.

The meat fell to the dirt, and Johnny glared at the prisoner. The man pointed down and the horror in his face got Johnny's attention. He looked and saw only a fire-blackened joint on the bone. *A pork hock,* he thought, and then stared harder. He recoiled and felt the urge to vomit. How could he have missed it! He was looking at a human forearm, elbow to wrist, crisp skin with veins below.

"Dear God!" Johnny gasped. Footy's eyes went wide as well.

"Bloody cannibals," he choked. "May they rot in hell!" The Mambu warriors were watching the strangers closely and they grinned and laughed. They knew revulsion when they saw it. Some of their neighbors did not consume human flesh, and they interpreted the reaction as weakness.

A village mutt rushed forward and snatched up the meat. But before it could run, the hoarse warrior raised his spear and stabbed, skewering it to the earth. He bent down, pulled the joint from the teeth, and waved it to the crowd. The people roared their approval. The chief's brother displayed his *buai*-stained grin, brought the meat to his mouth, and tore off a strip. This he chewed heartily, reveling in the outrage on the invaders' faces. The crowd cawed at the show.

"Let's get out of here!" Johnny growled. While the people's attention was on the warrior, Johnny and Footy slung on their packs. They took the prisoner's arms and muscled forward. They came up against the warriors, who whirled to face them. Like a cloud coming over the sun, the mob's mood turned. Mirth became sneering cruelty, and the blood lust rose.

The brother tossed the gnawed arm into the crowd. A woman caught it and began to eat. He put a foot on the dog twitching in its death throws, jerked out his spear, and leveled the bloody point at Johnny.

A shout erupted from the old men who remained near the big

house. All eyes turned to see a new group of about thirty warriors come into the clearing from the far side. Their bodies shone black, decorated in whirls of red, white and yellow. Each wore a soaring white headdress, and had pig tusks through the nose, points up. They, too, wore penis gourds. Each of the sturdy young men carried one or more weapons whose points and blades were wet with blood. Some at the back dragged burdens the watchers could not make out.

War party, the soldier in Johnny observed. The warriors came by the big house talking exuberantly, but broke off when they saw the vast gathering and the three light-skinned aliens.

Even though he'd never seen him, Johnny knew Bumay at once. The heavily muscled man led the group. His headdress was the most magnificent, his penis gourd, the most intricately curled. He wore a shell the size of a dinner plate on his chest, and in one hand carried a huge spear, in the other, a stone axe, both crimson. The warriors around Johnny formed an aisle.

"Bumay, Bumay, Bumay!" a thousand voices called. The *Mambu-ato* stretched his scarlet lips back to expose the ebony teeth of the *buai*-addict. He strutted along the riverbank and stopped fifteen feet from Johnny's group. His men formed an armed wall around their leader.

"We asked for the chief, now we've got him," Johnny said out of the side of his mouth.

"Yes mate," Footy agreed. "We're in the deep poo now."

CHAPTER 7

Johnny's group faced the arrogant chief. Bumay made a comment to his warriors and guffawed. It was a barking laugh that irritated Johnny. The war chief passed his axe to another man, grasped his huge spear in both hands, and leveled it at Johnny's chest. *Do something or else!* the hard voice said.

"Bumay!" he yelled in his deepest voice. He had the satisfaction of seeing the chief's eyes widen at hearing his name. Johnny stepped towards him.

"Greetings from Harry Truman, President of the United States of America!" he shouted. "And it's not important what I say, just so long as it's loud!" he bellowed. Out of the corner of his eye he saw Footy staring at him strangely.

Chief Bumay let loose a string of words Johnny didn't understand. He accompanied this with stabbing motions of his spear, which Johnny did get. His warriors scowled, and menaced the intruders with axes and clubs, while bowmen put arrows on the strings and drew them taut.

The hoarse warrior stepped to Johnny's side and spoke to his brother, but in a voice intended for the assembly. Bumay cocked his head, nodding sharply while his eyes went from Johnny, to Footy, to the prisoner, and back again. When the brother's oration was done, the old couple pushed between Bumay and their spirit-ancestors. They raised their hands and told their tale.

After only a few sentences, the chief's lip curled and he interrupted. His warriors grabbed them and shoved them into the crowd. Deliberately, his eyes on Johnny, Bumay threw back his head and laughed again. He swaggered toward the tall man and this time, pressed the point of his spear to the white man's chest. Johnny was wearing his undershirt, and the point went through and drew blood. It was all he could do to stop himself from shooting the chief right there.

While he was preoccupied, the young man he'd knocked down earlier snuck up behind him and flipped the helmet off his head. It hit the dirt and rolled towards Bumay. The chief trapped it under his bare foot and picked it up. He turned it this way and that, studying the lining and straps. He spoke, and a warrior stepped to each side. They unpinned the egret headdress and removed it.

The chief sneered at Johnny and pulled the steel helmet down on his curls. He struck the butt of his spear on the ground, held it at arm's length, and struck a regal pose. The crowd shrieked with delight. What a splendid man was their *Mambu-ato!* Johnny knew he was being ridiculed, and he glowered at the chief.

Bumay thumped his spear on the ground and shouted over his shoulder. The men at the back came dragging their loads. At the last moment, Bumay stepped aside and his warriors dumped three corpses on the clay.

They were native men, Johnny saw, but outfitted very differently than the Mambu. They wore cloth *laplaps* knotted around their waists, and each had a feather protruding from the tip of his nose. They wore headdresses of bamboo circlets with springy stalks, topped with strips of painted bark. Their torsos were painted with broad bands of yellow and white around their pectoral muscles, and they were marked all over with raised scar tissue.

It was clear the three had been killed in battle. One had an arm hacked off. A Mambu dragged it nonchalantly by the hand. The other two were spiked with arrows.

Bumay watched the visitors intently for their reaction. Johnny heard a hiss of breath from Footy, but kept his own face hard, staring at the chief with his chin stuck out.

Again Bumay thumped his spear and warriors came dragging two more carcasses. Johnny saw uniforms and thought for a second they were GIs. But then he made out the black hair and realized they were Japanese. The bearers dropped them with the others. These, too, had arrows in them and deep slashes in the flesh. Johnny glanced at the prisoner and saw him fixated on his countrymen. Johnny's gaze went back to Bumay and saw the insufferable grin. Now the cold fighting rage rose within him.

Bumay pointed with his spear at the Japanese and said something. His warriors chortled. Johnny almost shot Bumay then, but got a grip on himself. He could kill the chief, but his warriors would certainly avenge his death at once. They needed an escape plan.

Show them what rifles can do! Johnny aimed over their heads and pulled the trigger. The report cracked like a whip and sizzled across the river, and the crowd jerked back. Johnny watched Bumay while his hands reloaded and was pleased to see the native flinch.

The chief, however, was not thrown for long. He had witnessed the foreigner's magic sticks in action down the river, and while he feared them, that had not stopped him from slaughtering their bearers.

Bumay had not been born *Mambu-ato.* He had earned the position in single-handed combat with the most formidable warriors of his nation. Two of the men, his closest rivals, he had killed and eaten. Other times, he had spared the loser's life, while taking his youngest wives and his choice of their lands and possessions.

In the previous year, he had at last challenged and defeated the reigning war chief. It was expected the victor would put the vanquished to death, but this Bumay had not done. He had made the man his slave. After that, the clans gathered for the lavish feast to confirm Bumay as leader. He accepted their tributes of virgins, pigs and prime gardens, including a fine grove of betel trees, and then demanded more.

Bumay was his nation's finest warrior. He was beside his own spirit house, at the center of Mambu heartland, surrounded by hundreds of the fiercest fighters on the entire river. No outsider had ever entered the Mambu valley and lived to tell about it. The intruders confronting him, Bumay thought, were already dead men.

There were only two of them. The third was obviously their captive and of no consequence. Yes, these were the hairy, reddish foreigners with killing sticks. But two men against his entire nation? It was no contest!

Johnny saw the emotions play over Bumay's face and knew he was getting ready to kill them. Urgently, he spoke to Footy. "Aim at a pile of skulls. Wait for my word!"

"Right!" The muzzle of the Lee Enfield swung around.

"Bumay!" Johnny called again. He raised his arm and dropped it. "Fire!"

There was the crash of Footy's shot and a skull pyramid exploded. Skulls bounced down with a sound like dry wood. A gasp went up from the crowd. Nearby warriors picked up orbs of shattered bone and stared.

Bumay was livid. Now the invaders had committed sacrilege. He fixed his scowl on the tall one and allowed the urge to kill him swell. He felt fear as well in the face of their strong magic, and because of that, again he made a show of laughing. *I will spear that one and drink his heart-blood while he watches*, he promised himself. His muscles bunched for the killing ecstasy, and he stepped to the corpse of one of the foreigners and put his foot on it.

"Look at this one!" he called. *"Dead! Now these will die as well!*

"Get ready to run!" Johnny said to Footy. "I'll take Bumay. You shoot the brother, and as many as you can. Go for the far side!"

"Roger," Footy said, lining up his shot only a foot away.

Bumay saw a skull near his feet and he kicked it in fury. It spun away, spewing teeth. He shook his spear and screamed.

"Are we dead men?"

"No!" the warriors shouted.

"We are Mambu, the only true people! These invaders have broken our law and they die now!"

Johnny was in his killer mind, and it no longer mattered if he lived or died. His eyes flashed to the pilot. *Rifle up, good man.* He glanced at the Japanese and saw he was calm and alert, even with his hands tied. Johnny felt a flash of respect. *He is not afraid.*

Johnny flexed his knees and took a breath as his gaze returned to Bumay. His helmet was still on the chief's head, and his eyes went to it, then back to the black eyes. Bumay saw the anger on the strange face and felt satisfaction, sweet as wild honey.

"The tall one is mine!" he thundered. *"Kill the others!"*

What happened next took the space of heartbeats. Bumay jerked his spear back to stab Johnny through the chest. Johnny aimed his rifle at the chief's head, but as he fired, a club glanced off his arm. The bullet shattered Bumay's left shoulder and he spun and went down, dropping his spear.

Footy shot the hoarse warrior so close, the powder scorched the curls on his chest. The bullet tore apart the heart and went on through the two men behind. All three sprawled, knocking others over. Footy fired fast, working through the magazine, and more warriors found themselves hugging dirt. Johnny was only a little slower, having to reload between shots. Mambu closest to the strangers lurched back, those further away pressed to attack.

Abruptly the Japanese moved. His bound hands flew to Footy's pack. He grabbed his sword and jerked up. There was a flash of steel, and it was in his hands once more. He felt a rush of elation. *If this is the time to die, let it come!*

He swept the blade almost upright in a semicircle. The tips of arrows and spears clattered to earth in a rain of fingers. Mambu brought stumps before incredulous eyes.

The warriors were too close! Johnny swung the butt of his rifle again, breaking a man's jaw and driving them back. Again, the sword flashed across the sun, and a warrior's head leapt off his shoulders. There was a gasp from the crowd. Johnny put his rifle against a man's jaw and shot, feeling the spray of hot blood. Footy's rifle spat again and again, and warriors with arrows on the string spun and shot their fellows.

Two Mambu grabbed Johnny's rifle. He kept a grip on it while his other hand drew his pistol, thumbed the hammer, and shot as fast as he could. His rifle came free. The Japanese helped carve some elbowroom. A warrior swung his axe at the prisoner's head. Johnny shot the Mambu through the ear and the stone blade whistled overhead and struck another headhunter across the eyes. The victim screamed and staggered away, trying to tug the stone from his face.

A hefty warrior rushed Footy, took him in a bear hug and began to squeeze the life out of him.

"Help!" he gasped. Johnny put the pistol to the Mambu's temple and scrambled his brains for him. Suddenly, the three men found space around them. Warriors recoiled from the ring of death, leaving the ground thick with the writhing and the dead.

Their departure revealed Bumay on his knees. It had been only a space of breaths since the chief launched the attack. One arm hung bleeding and useless, but the strong right arm was sound. Bumay grabbed his great spear and sprang up. He raised his chin and howled his famous war cry. At once, his men felt their courage flow into them. They rallied to their leader, as they had so many times in battle.

Four hundred cannibal warriors turned to face the invaders. They would overwhelm them in a single rush.

CHAPTER 8

The Father dove away from the sharp noises and pain with the man in its teeth. It swam underwater and the prey stopped twitching. The reptile was too overwrought to be hungry. It opened its jaws and the current took the carcass. Then it rushed downstream, overwhelmed by the agony of its ripped leg and the puncture wounds along its head and body.

After some distance, it came to a place where the water was shallow and boiled over rocks. As the creature bumped over them, the foot was battered and the suffering was terrible. It grunted and hissed and writhed its way down.

The Father continued day and night, trying to outrun its torment. It swam with its throbbing limb held stiffly to the side. Bacteria invaded the flayed flesh and infection set in. The leg swelled so the scaled skin was too tight. The Father's misery was relentless, and it grew more desperate by the hour.

In its fevered brain, the distress was one with the image of the smooth-headed man. Each beat of its enormous heart pulsed with the desire to hurt its tormenter. The predator began to swim on the surface, uncaring if it was seen. It swung its head back and forth, back and forth, endlessly searching along the bank for the source of its affliction. At last the rapids were behind it, and it had relief from the stones. The river grew wider, thick with silt.

In the light of yet another dawn, the Father snuffled the stench of the two-legged pack. The odor enraged the reptile. Its teeth clattered together, and it felt the shudder all through its skull.

In mounting fury, the crocodile raised its head and observed an enormous herd of the creatures. At once it rushed to attack, but then heard the sharp explosions that made it prickle all over with anxiety. The extreme emotions, magnified by the unbearable days of suffering and the poisons pumping through it, unhinged the reptile.

It threw itself from the river and up the slope. Fiery pain shot up each time its weight fell on the raw leg. The Father burst over the bank and stopped, tail twitching, facing the greatest gathering of the animals it had ever encountered.

Hundreds of Mambu heard the splash and turned from the fight with the foreigners. They were thunderstruck. The enormous supernatural crocodile had materialized by magic. It crouched on the bank in all its monstrous glory, water pouring off ten thousand scales. Here, in the flesh, was the calamity they both worshiped and abhorred. They even forgot the strangers as they stared into the malevolent eyes of the Father of all the Crocodiles. In awe, they took in the moon on the head, and the bloody stump of its leg. They believed the Father could not be harmed, and they wondered what this manifestation meant.

The river's anger grunted, rushed among them, struck with its tail, and six people died. Then the beast stood up, stared across the herd and froze. There, of all things, was its single-hearted desire—the smooth-headed man. The predator opened its jaws and let out a bellow that filled the village. Then it charged, rage overwhelming its pain.

The old woman who saw it in her dreams watched the deity bear down. When it was close, she raised her arms and screamed.

"Mambu-matu!"

The god ran down its handmaiden, and a clawed foot tore out her throat. The Mambu scattered before it, trampling their neighbors.

Fighting for their lives, none in Johnny's group noticed the crocodile come from the river. Johnny and Footy each shot again, pistols hot in their hands. But when the beast roared, the hair stood up on their necks. A warrior menacing them glanced over his shoulder at the commotion, and the sword unzipped his belly.

The sea of natives parted, and Johnny saw the Father come at a lurching gallop.

Bumay, too, witnessed the appearance of the deity. This time, he could not deny his fear. He might be *Mambu-ato,* War Chief of the People, but here came the *Mambu-matu,* the very Chief of Chiefs.

The prisoner saw his chance. He ran to his fallen countrymen. Standing near them were the warriors who had dragged the bodies up. His sword swung, and another man lost his head. The corpse tottered while the man beside it tried to jump away. But the blade flew like a hawk. It parted the soft flesh under the rib cage and separated the spine. Two bodies went down in a shambles.

A warrior sprang at the Japanese from behind, stabbing spear raised. Johnny shot, and he tumbled across the prisoner's feet. Across the space, "the Jap" met Johnny's eyes and he nodded.

"It's the great bloody croc!" Footy shouted and Johnny turned back. The predator's eyes were fixed on its enemy as it plowed through the herd. A few men tried to defend themselves, but points that could penetrate wooden shields simply bounced off thick scales. Many Mambu died between flashing teeth.

"Run!" Johnny shouted.

With the stock of his rifle, he bashed a path and bolted, Footy close behind. Bumay, still wearing the stranger's helmet, saw the tall one run and turned to spear him through the back. That was his fatal error.

The Father saw the smooth head just before him. It spread its jaws and took its tormenter in. It put all the pent up torture into bringing its jaws together. Long teeth carved through Chief Bumay, crushed his pelvis and cracked the spine off like a twig. The spear dropped from his hand and fell under the Father's foreleg. The great weight fell on it, the shaft splintered, and two feet of iron-wood jammed up the injured limb.

The Father hissed in horror and ground its teeth. A death scream squeezed through Bumay's throat. Savagely, the crocodile shook its head, and the man flung to and fro. The upper body detached and sailed through the air. It slammed to earth, the helmet popped off the head, and rattled away.

Johnny had taken only a few steps when he heard the mortal cry. He turned in time to see the torso fall, and then somehow, his helmet was tumbling at him. He caught it, jammed it on and—now behind Footy—ran for his life.

The fresh assault on it made the Father gag. It spat the chief's legs. Then it bellowed its anguish once more. When it closed its jaws, it blinked in sudden confusion. The blood of its enemy was still in its mouth, but there, running into the distance, was the smooth-headed man.

Johnny ran like he never had before. He was just behind Footy pumping by the chief's house, neck-and-neck between the huts. He passed the smaller man as they came into the open, and there, coming up fast, was the perimeter fence. Johnny turned for the gap.

The Father tried to chase its enemy down, but each step was searing. It reached the chief's house and could go no further. It rumbled its frustration and lashed its tail. Four elders were crushed like flies against the wall, and the appendage kept going. It crashed through the woven reeds and battered the tree trunks that held up the house. With a great cracking, the edifice trembled, and then imploded. Thatching, splintered poles and reeds tumbled onto the central hearth.

The Father turned and limped back to the river. The clearing had emptied. The herd cowered among the nests. The crocodile came upon the upper portion of the truncated chief. Bumay was barely alive. The crocodile scooped him up. It tossed its head and the huge throat opened.

The people watched the *Mambu-ato's* hands embrace the snout of the god. The chief's chest went between the jaws, and his head followed. Bumay's eyes were open, fixed on his people. Again, the scaled neck rippled, a hand traced the moon scar like a caress, and the teeth came together. The skull popped like a grape. The reptile continued to the river. At the top of the bank, it fell on its belly, slid into the water, and was covered up.

The *Mambu-matu* and *Mambu-ato* were gone, but the wrath of the river was not done with the nation.

The chief's mansion had been lofty and spacious. Outside, Bumay had sat in judgment over tribal disputes. Inside, with his sorcerers and elders, he organized festivals, many of which involved the consumption of their human victims. The edifice had been home to some fifty of his clan warriors. Long chains of woven rattan, formed over generations, looped from the ceilings. Each link represented a head taken.

It was here that every Mambu boy was brought for initiation into the violent life of men.

The floor above was an even more rarefied domain. To this feared realm, only the *Mambu-ato*, the shamen and most trusted elders, could ascend. It was up here that rituals were performed over fresh heads to deliver their owners to the dark forces. This was the resting place of the Mambu fetishes, idols and spirit masks. This was where they kept the sacred instruments—the bull-roarers, drums and flutes.

When the Father of the Crocodiles knocked down the *Mambuato's* house, all the artifacts rained down as well. Eager flames embraced them, smoke billowed up, and the inferno consumed it all. As the people watched, the seat of political and religious power of the Mambu nation burned to bitter ash. Their terror knew no bounds.

Then, on the face of the water where the deity and the chief had lately disappeared, a gust of wind rose up. It rippled across the surface to the land. It became a dust devil that danced into the conflagration. Faster and faster it spun, feeding on the heat.

A column now, it caught up bundles of flaming grass, fanned them red hot, and flung them across the surrounding roofs.

Johnny jumped through the fence and sprinted for the gorge. He did not have to look back to know Footy followed. He heard the footfalls and ragged breaths.

He pelted on until there were three hundred yards between them and the village. Just ahead, the river poured into the jungle and they could hear the thunder of falling water. Johnny's heart tripped like a jackhammer, and he doubled over. Footy dove beside him.

"Hell's bells," the Aussie gasped. He dropped his rifle and rolled on his pack. Johnny collapsed to one knee. He glanced at the village and was alarmed to see someone racing after them. He raised his rifle and recognized the man through the scope.

The Jap!

He came at them with his bloodstained sword in his bound hands. Johnny waited until he was close.

"Stop there!" The man panted like his heart would burst. He shot a look back, saw no one coming, and sank on both knees.

"Put down the sword!" Johnny ordered. The man stared.

"Put—it—down!" Johnny said.

And then the Japanese spoke.

"Must crean first!"

Footy sat straight up.

"Bloody hell!" he crowed. "He speaks 'Engrish!'"

CHAPTER 9

The Japanese kept his eyes on Johnny while he wedged the handle of the sword between his bare feet. With his roped hands, he pulled up grass, wrapped it around the blade and wiped, hilt to tip. Johnny alternated between watching him and darting glances back at the village. His attention went to the cloud of smoke that billowed suddenly over the roofs. The Japanese discarded the grass and repeated the process, then wiped the blade with the tail of his shirt. He knelt, placed the sword across the path and backed away.

"Footy," Johnny said, "go get it."

"Crikey!" Footy said. "Shoot him if he moves!" The Aussie, clutching his side, went toward the Japanese. He snatched up the sword and moved behind Johnny.

"What the bugger can do with this thing!" he exclaimed, a hand touching his own neck. "Struth, mate!"

"And with his hands tied," Johnny said. Footy slung his pack down and slid the sword into its scabbard once more.

Now there were shouts from the village. A group of warriors clustered at the fence and men were coming over. Behind them, a thick column of smoke churned into the sky.

"There's a fire in the village," Johnny said. "And here comes the posse. We've got to run some more. You—get behind me," he told the Japanese. The prisoner trotted to stand with Footy.

"All this time, you speak the King's English," Footy confronted him. The man shrugged.

Johnny lay on the path and rested his elbows. He held his rifle steady and put the scope on the lead runner. The man came at a good clip, spear held high. Six or seven were strung out behind him. Johnny shot the leader. He tossed up his arms and tumbled.

The next runner faltered, but then jumped over his comrade and ran on. Johnny jacked in another shell and tracked him. This one waved an axe. Johnny shot again and watched him somersault into the grass. Suddenly the entire string pulled up, rethought their ill-conceived plan, and bolted. They virtually flew through the fence and stood muttering on the far side, staring out. Johnny smiled without mirth and put another bullet into the bunch. That did it. The warriors scuttled for the village, but halted again as a wall of flame gushed from the whole row of huts.

Johnny watched the smoke boil against the blue sky and it came to him this was a glorious day. His wound ached, his lungs were raw, but it was sweet to be alive. He grinned at Footy and the prisoner.

"Hey!" he said, "it was touch-and-go there, but we made it. Good fighting—both of you!" He got to his feet.

"You," he said to the prisoner, "go first! Then you, Footy. They're stopped for now, but who knows for how long? Let's go, go, go!"

The three men charged into the jungle. They ran while the mountain flanks drew together, and they were sprinting down the gorge. They heard the river cascading beside them as the forest closed over their heads.

The path took them to the brink of a drop off. They stared down a steep rock scree. The trail zigzagged across it. The jungle canopy formed again a hundred feet below. The Japanese headed off and Footy fell in.

Johnny decided to take the short cut, straight down. Half running, half falling, he went fast in a slide of rocks. The other two paused as he rumbled by, then came after him, the Japanese having to scamper on his bare feet. Johnny slammed to earth and stood aside while the others landed in a rattle of rocks. They jogged off again.

And so, alternately running and walking, the trio left the Valley of the Cannibals behind.

The rapids had roiled through the gorge, but now the land was flatter, and the river flowed swift and silent beside them. The mountains spread apart again, and the path dropped into the rainforest. The men clambered over rocks slick with water. The dank smell of mushrooms filled the air, and orange fungal shelves grew on the trees and deadwood. The river entered fresh sets of rapids that flooded toward the lowlands, and water music echoed all around them.

At last they came to a meadow and took a break. Johnny and

Footy were anxious to take stock of their ammunition. The pilot found he had two chargers left for the Lee Enfield and he inserted them in the magazine. Johnny had only five cartridges for his Springfield. Back in the Mambu village, he'd burned through shells as fast as he could shoot. He reloaded his .45 and had a pocketful left. Footy broke open the Webley revolver, which ejected the casings, and put in six more. He had a few more, and that was it.

"We're a little low on ammo for a tour of the New Guinea bush," Footy observed.

"Right," Johnny said. "We can't do any hunting. We have to reserve every shell for defense. "

Each man ate a Mambu sweet potato and they departed. They walked until nightfall and camped by a stream. As usual, Johnny and Footy took turns on watch. The Mambu might have given chase after all, and who knew whose lands they trespassed on now? In the morning, they breakfasted on the old folks' bananas.

"For shore they'd never clapped their peepers on a white man," Footy said. "Crikey, I thought they'd have a heart attack."

"But they acted like they knew us," Johnny said. "I wonder what was going through their heads?"

The men walked all day, pausing to fill their bottles when they found fresh water. They walked over hills, the mountains behind them, and the path alternated between wooded and grassy land. The river continued to the side. From time to time, they startled crocodiles that went thrashing through the reeds into the water, but these were all of the smaller freshwater variety.

The jungle gave way entirely to *kunai*. This provided respite from the mosquitoes, but the sun beat relentlessly. Johnny thought his brain would fry under the helmet, and for a while, he walked with his shirt draped over his head. All of them were grateful when the jungle came again, even though the shade was hot as a sauna.

At mid-afternoon, they came to a pretty place of low grass and spread out trees. A clear spring burbled over stones. The bushes were smothered in fragrant yellow flowers, and hundreds of pale blue butterflies clustered over them. The men sat to drink and wash. Johnny broke out the cigarettes and passed them around, with one to the prisoner. Footy humphed, but said nothing.

The Asian smoked it down to an ember, then put it out in the dirt. When he looked up again, his eyes went wide. He pointed over the other men's shoulders. The two whirled to find a line of native warriors. There were eight of them with longbows, arrows on the string.

Johnny knew at once these were not Mambu, but somehow they looked familiar. And then he recalled the corpses in Bumay's valley. They had worn the same *laplaps,* bamboo headdresses, and hawk feathers in their noses. Their chest muscles were marked in yellow and white as well.

Johnny slid his hand towards his Springfield, but a huge newcomer stepped his way with his barbed arrow aimed at Johnny's chest.

"I wouldn't touch your rifle," he said in a broad Australian accent. "Me boys are a bit nervous. You don't want an arra in ya, do ya?" Johnny retrieved his hand.

"That's betta," the man nodded. "You lot just sit easy and we'll talk a bit."

"Blimey!" Footy exclaimed, "Where in hell did you come from?"

"Well, not hell, mate," the warrior said, letting the tension off his bow, although his men remained poised. He smiled, displaying ruby inner lips and blackened teeth, and picked between the front ones with a sharp fingernail.

"Where did you learn to speak such perfect English?" Footy crowed.

"In Australia, mate. At school in Adelaide," the native said.

"Adelaide?" Footy repeated, dumfounded.

"Adelaide."

"Who are you?" Johnny asked.

"My name is Mulakuwapatawny."

"Wow," Johnny said.

"Strike me pink!" Footy chimed in.

"And where are you from?" Johnny went on.

"The Uhuli village—the Lighthouse Mission, mate," he said. "This here is Uhuli land. Fo'give me, but the betta question is—who are *you*, and where are *you* from? I need an ansa, b'cause as you can see," he glanced at his war party, "me *one-talks* need ta know."

Johnny stood up slowly, showing empty hands.

"I'm Johnny Willman," he said, "Sergeant, US Army. This is Glen Carmichael—Australian."

"Ahh, I like the Aussies," the warrior grinned. "And you Yanks too, a course. Allies, we are!"

"Call me 'Footy,'" the Australian said. "What do they call you again?"

"Mula-kuwapa-tawny," the man said slowly.

"Hold on!" Footy said. "What?"

"That's a jawbreaker," Johnny added.

"Aww—call me Mula," the warrior grinned, enjoying their discomfiture. His face went serious again and he scowled at the Japanese. "And this bugga?"

"Our prisoner," Johnny said. Mula narrowed his eyes at the man.

"And how do you come to be on our land?" he asked.

"We've come from Mambu territory," Footy said. "Bloody Valley of the Cannibals, mate."

"Do you know a chief called 'Bumay'?" Johnny asked.

Mula couldn't have looked more surprised if he'd been slapped. He spun and spat a string of betel juice.

"That fella's the brutha of satan," he said, licking the red off his lips. "Wot about Bumay?"

"Glad you think that..." Footy said.

"...because Bumay is dead," Johnny went on. "And maybe thirty of his men."

"Or more," Footy added. "Maybe fifty. We didn't stop to count."

"And when did this bloody miracle take place?" Mula asked.

"Yesterday," Footy said. Mula spoke rapid-fire over his shoulder to his men. The Uhuli crowded around, all talking at once. They unbent their bows, but kept their circle intact, arrows on the string.

"Nothin' personal," Mula said at last, "but we find this ratha hard to believe. No one comes outta the Mambu valley, not evva! I've lived here all me life and I've nevva seen it! You go in there, the only way you come out is *pekpek*." This tickled him and he roared with laughter. He retold his joke to his men and they all howled.

"*Pekpek* is..." Footy explained.

"I know—crap," Johnny said. "Well, we did it," he went on to Mula, "and we're not *pekpek* yet, as you can see."

"This fella Bumay," Mula went on. "He's killed a lot of me people, mate. You lot couldn't fight 'im yestaday, b'cause, you see, he was here. He killed three of me *one-talks*. We hunting them sons-a-satan t'day."

"We're telling the truth," Johnny said. "I shot Bumay—but that's not what killed him. A crocodile got the chief."

Mula stared at Johnny in absolute disbelief.

"And this Jap here," Johnny pressed on, realizing how strange it all sounded. "We captured him at Kissim, up the river."

"Kissim—aww yeh? Nevva been that far," Mula said. He stepped to the Japanese, put his broad face close and smiled in an unfriendly way.

"We don't like these yella fellas," he said. "We hunt 'em. Bad fellas. They killed Masta Billy—our missionary. An' Missis Sarah, they carry her off."

"When was this?" Johnny asked. Mula scratched his head and spat *buai*. Again, he conversed with his men.

"Two Christmases," he said.

"That's two years," Footy explained.

"You men got quite a yarn," Mula said. "Masta Billy, he had some yarns. But yours—it's a good 'un.

"Now. We need ta find out if wot you say is true. You come with us. You stay in my village." Johnny and Footy glanced at each other.

"Look," Johnny said, "we need to keep going."

"We've got to get to the coast, mate," Footy put in.

"The way I see it," Mula said, "you lot are on my land. You *say* you been in the Mambu valley. I've lived here all me life, and I've nevva done that. But you two—and 'im…" he nodded at the prisoner, "... you go through. You fight Bumay an' his boys—on Mambu land! You get help from a *pookpook*! You kill a lotta Mambu and you come outta the valley! That is a lot for us to eat, mates."

"A lot to swallow?" Footy asked.

"Yeh," Mula agreed, "a lot ta eat—and swalla. I gotta tell you, some of me boys, they think you're pulling our foots. They say we kill you now—you and the Jap."

Johnny and Footy had been sitting while Mula talked, but now they rose and gripped their rifles. Mula grinned.

"Aw, yes, you got rifles," he said. He shouted a command and his men bent back their bows, arrows steady. Mula smiled his black smile.

"Now—if wot you say is true, you got no worries," he said. "I hope wot you say is true, as the one-God is my witness!" Mula looked up and clasped his hands around his bow. He stared back at the white men.

"But if you lyin'," he said, "well, ya gotta die. You see that?" He looked solemn for a moment but then his smile flashed again.

"If wot you say is true, then we'll have a *singsing*—bloody big party, mates. We'll kill some of me pigs, have a dance. We hate them Mambu! So ya see, you really our guests of honna. That's how to look at it." Johnny and Footy shared another glance.

"Ok," Johnny said, "but you say you can't go into the Mambu valley. How are you going to verify the facts?"

"Berryfry dee fek," Mula repeated. "That's good, I like that one." He thought for a moment. "What does it mean?"

"Verify the facts," Footy repeated slowly. "It means, how will you find out what we say is true mate?"

Mula conferred with his men. While he was doing that, Footy dug in his backpack and extracted a hand of bananas. He passed some to Johnny, who shared with the captive, and they began to eat. Mula's warriors began to mutter unhappily. The Uhuli chief looked back and saw what the strangers were doing.

"Aw, that's bad form, mates!" he hissed. "Don't eat without sharin'! The boys don't like that!"

"Sorry," Johnny said.

"We didn't know," Footy added. They dug in their packs and passed out the bananas and *kaukau*. These went hand-to-hand around the group. The warriors went down on their haunches to eat, weapons nearby. Johnny drew a chunk of meat from his pack and looked at it suspiciously.

"We took this from the Mambu," he said to Mula. "Know what it is?" He gave it to the native who sniffed, then bit in. "This is pig, mate," he said with his mouth full, "bloody good pig!" Mula ripped the meat in two and offered half back.

"No, that's okay," Johnny said hastily. "You go right ahead."

Mula grinned and passed the portion to his men. Johnny and Footy dug out all the meat and handed it over. There was a good deal of smacking of lips and grunts of pleasure. When it was done, Mula wiped the grease from his fingers on his chest.

"Nothing as good as the food of your enemies," he sighed as he stood up. "Awlright then, here's what we're gonna do. Anda here," he pointed to a young warrior with stringy hair, "he got himself a sweetheart near the Mambu valley. I tell him he's *longlong*—crazy, I mean. He's gonna get himself killed—but he's a young bloke." Mula said a few words in his language and the men grinned at Anda.

"I'll send him to talk with his sweetheart. Tonight he'll find out wot's wot. You blokes stay with me in the Uhuli village. You fellas can hang onta your rifles, your pistols, your knives—bloke's gotta keep his weapons. But you havta stay with us till we find out wot's wot. Right by you?" Johnny and Footy knew they must go through the Uhuli lands. And now they'd given away all their food and had to get more, no doubt from Mula's people. They really had no choice.

"Okay," Johnny said.

"Right by me," Footy said. Mula looked at the prisoner.

"One more thing. Can me boys have your Jap?" Johnny saw the prisoner's eyes tighten.

"When you say *have him*," Footy asked, "you mean...?" he drew his thumb across his neck.

"Could be," Mula nodded. "That could very well be, mate. The boys came out for blood t'day, didn't they? It would do them good. You consida it a fava to me."

"Well mate," Footy said thoughtfully, "I reckon we can work something out."

CHAPTER 10

Johnny mulled over Mula's request to turn the Japanese over to him, and Footy's willingness to go along. He looked at the prisoner and found him staring back. He turned his attention to the native.

"I'm sorry, no can do," he said politely. "He's our prisoner. And remember, he did fight your enemy yesterday."

"Fair dinkum," Footy admitted. Mula considered this and slapped his thighs.

"Awlright," he said. "My boys'll listen to me. But you watch him," he warned, wagging a finger at the prisoner. "We have a score to settle with them Japs! The blood of our families and our missionary is on 'em." He grasped his bow and arrows and stood, his greased body catching the sun.

"Let's be off, shall we?" He had a last word with Anda, who waited while the others departed downriver. Then the young warrior turned and loped toward the Valley of the Cannibals.

The three travelers and their entourage followed the river into the lower country. As they walked, Mula peppered them with questions—the purpose of their journey, their experiences in Kissim, and with the Mambu. Every time he said the name of the enemy, the chief spat red. Johnny and Footy recounted their journey. The Uhuli chief was keenly interested in everything to do with the headhunter valley, and the confrontation with Bumay.

When they came to the part about the dead natives, Mula exclaimed, and insisted they describe the corpses in detail. He identified the men by name and looked grave.

"Those are me scouts," he said. "I sent 'em ahead yestaday. Them sons-a-satan Mambu musta surprised 'em. All we found was blood on the grass." Mula spoke to his men and a discussion ensued, accompanied by groaning and even some tears.

Late in the day, the forest opened onto a broad *kunai* plain. Beyond this was a field of gardens, laden with all kinds of vegetables.

Mula explained that these were the Uhuli's.

His men cut stalks of purple-skinned sugar cane. The chief handed two-foot lengths to Johnny, Footy and even the Japanese. They copied the natives by stripping the tough outer skin with their teeth. They bit chunks of the white, fibrous interior and crunched them between their molars. Their mouths flooded with sweet juice. When they'd sucked the liquid out, they spat the pulp. Chewing and spitting, their flagging energy renewed, the party continued. Eventually they made out the Uhuli village in the distance, a town of huts among trees along the riverbank.

"Home!" Mula sang. The usual ragged village mongrels came to bark. Running behind them were scores of warriors. From far off, they recognized their kin and shouts echoed across the distance. By the time Mula's war party reached the others, women and children had joined them. There was a grand reunion. The chief turned to his guests.

"Now I gotta tell them about me dead bruthas," he said sadly. He began to shout in his language and the people grew quiet. Then a woman screamed, others began to wail, and all the people gave in to their grief. The newcomers were surprised to see Mula and his warriors sobbing freely, tears spilling down their cheeks. Slowly the procession moved on, arms around one another's shoulders.

They came to a wall of piled dirt, with logs across the gaps. They climbed these and were absorbed into an even larger crowd on the other side. They paraded by the Uhuli houses. These were different than any the travelers had seen so far. They were built on stilts of poles, sunk in the clay. There were eighty or ninety of them, Johnny guessed, ranged along the mudflat. Simple staircases, tree trunks with notches for steps, leaned against holes in the floors. The natives ran nimbly up and down them. A woman with a bundle of firewood her own size carried it on her head into her home.

Mula led the way beyond the huts to a low hill. On it was what must be the mission. It had a cross of white-painted boards nailed to a peak of the metal roof. It was a huge, square edifice, with a steel water tank on one side, and an outhouse. The walls were gray panels, inset with wood-framed windows and doors. They drew close and stopped.

"This a happy time," Mula said, "we like visitas like you! But this a sad time as well. We gotta say goodbye to our dead bruthas. T'morra—if Anda fartyfry your freaks, we gonna feel much betta!

But tonight, I gotta send me poor *one-talks* to heaven. The people gotta get ready."

The crowd ground to a halt and Mula spoke to them. Again, the women set up a high pitched keening. Then the Uhuli dispersed, heading for their homes. Many of the warriors, including the war party, continued on around a corner of the building. Mula led his guests to the door. He swung it open on rusty hinges.

"Welcome to the Lighthouse Mission," he said proudly. Johnny led the way into the gloom. It took a few seconds for their eyes to adjust, and then they made out a combined kitchen and living room. Afternoon sun filtered through windows of louvered glass thick with dust, several panes broken. Mosquitoes and flies droned in the shafts of light. Mula came in last and set his bow and arrows with a collection of weapons against a wall. These included two rifles, Johnny noticed—an ancient muzzleloader and a Japanese model. Mula saw where he looked.

"Yes mate, I got rifles, but no bullits. I need bullits," he added hopefully.

"Sorry mate," Footy replied. "We don't have ammo to fit those guns."

"We're low ourselves," Johnny added. Mula sighed.

"I need bullits," he repeated, "and many utha things."

The kitchen was dominated by a cast iron stove. Beside it was a rough counter made of two-by-fours and planks. A metal sink emptied through a short pipe over a hole in the floorboards. Dirty plates and cutlery were piled up. A metal bucket of water stood nearby. The kitchen table was a sheet of plywood nailed to posts. Six store-bought wooden chairs were arranged around it. Deep in the gloom was a soiled and sagging sofa and chair, with an old packing case for a coffee table.

Along one side of the main room was a wall with two doorways in it. Through the first, the door itself hanging by one hinge, the men saw a mattress on the floor. A half-naked native girl was in the process of rising from the jumble of sheets. She cradled a baby, while another child sprawled beside her.

"'Ello love," Mula called. He turned to the men. "This is where Masta Billy and the Missis lived. I keep it good, till we get a new missionary. Have a seat." He gestured toward the chairs.

Johnny and Footy took off their packs and leaned them and their rifles against the wall. They sat at the table with Mula and the

Japanese. The woman approached. She wore a cloth skirt in a floral pattern gone gray with dirt. The baby suckled her breast and another boy, naked except for a string around his waist, trailed her, knuckling his eyes.

"This is me wife, Makamalingatopa," the chief said. He saw the consternation on his guests' faces again and grinned. "The Masta and Missis, they called her 'Miriam,'" he went on. "You call her Miriam. They called me 'Mark,' but well—now I'm Mula again. These here are me sons. Luke, he's got six Christmas—and the baby, he's Billy—one Christmas. I named him after me missionary."

"Welcome to de Lit Hass Missin," Miriam said. She offered what might have been a pretty smile, if not for the black teeth. "Would you like some tea?"

"Oooo, tea? Right! Good on ya, Miriam," Footy enthused.

"We gotta problem," Mula shook his head. "No tea. Not for a long time now." He said something to his wife, who looked crestfallen.

"Aw, no worries, mate," Footy said, sounding heartbroken.

"We got water!" Mula perked up.

"Right, water it is," the pilot sighed. Miriam dipped an assortment of chipped glasses and cups into the bucket and passed them around. Mula spoke rapid-fire in his language as she worked, apparently telling her about his trip. He began to cry again, and she sobbed as well. Soon he cheered up, and then was laughing between his sentences, pointing to the white men. They heard the words, "Bumay" and "Mambu." Miriam giggled along.

"I tell her about our dead bruthas," he said. "And your good yarn—killing Bumay and them sons-a-satan!" He lobbed a gob of *buai* and almost hit the hole under the sink. It splashed down among similar stains.

"Sorry," he said shamefacedly. "We don't spit in the house." Suddenly he scowled at the prisoner.

"Now I tell you why I don't like these yella fellas! When his lot come to me village—many times—we hide in the bush. The Masta and Missis, they hide with us. But one morning them Japs come early—in a motorboat. There's alotta guns.

"They come into the mission and grab Masta Billy outa bed." Mula pointed towards the bedroom. "They drag 'im outside—and shoot him. Wickid bloody Japs!" he yelled at the prisoner. The man dropped his eyes and stared at his bound hands on the table.

"Me an' me boys—we watch—but they got the guns. Masta Billy an' the Missis—they good people. They sent me to Australia, ya know, before the war."

"Yes," Footy murmured, "Adelaide."

"Adelaide," Mula agreed. "The Lighthouse Church. I learn bloody good English at the school.

"But them Japs—they keep Missis Sarah inside the house. She scream a long time. They bring her out. She got blood on her legs. She see poor Masta Billy—*dead-finish!"* Mula shook his head and tears splashed again. Miriam cried, and the boy, Luke sobbed with her. At last the chief wiped his nose on his arm, careful not to soil the feather protruding from the end.

"The Japs, they drag her to the boat. Then, you sons-a-satan buggas!" Mula shouted at the Japanese, who flinched back. "You grab our women—eight women! You find our pigs! Seventeen pigs!" The prisoner stared away while Mula glared into his face. At last the chief turned back to Johnny and Footy.

"They rob our gardens—take all we got! Then they go."

"What happened to Missis Sarah?" Footy asked.

"No idea, mate," Mula said sadly. "We plant Masta Billy in the ground. Then we went afta them Japs—the Uhuli way—quiet-like. We look for Missis Sarah a long time—the Missis, and our women, and our pigs. But the Japs, they gone." He shrugged.

"We know some Japs still around. They hide inna jungle. A lotta them, they go downriver, long-time finish. And Missis Sarah—she *gone-finish*." Mula went from anger to deep sadness again, and began to bawl loudly. Miriam, Luke and even the baby began to howl as well. Not knowing what to do, the three newcomers looked uneasily away. At last Mula pinched his eyes with his thumbs and spoke.

"Now you tell me why we don't kill this fella?" he asked, pointing at the Japanese.

"I hate the Japs as well," Johnny told him. "But this man surrendered. You know what that means?"

"Yeh shore," Mula said. "He give up to you. You kill him if you want."

"No," Johnny said. "That's not how it goes. He's a prisoner of war. We have to take him back. The Aussies will lock him up until the war is over."

"Bloody right," Footy said.

Mula worked his fingernail between his teeth and noticed the horizontal slant of the sunlight.

"Time for the news," he announced, scraping back his chair.

"The news?" Johnny repeated.

"What are you on about?" Footy asked.

"I got a wireless!" Mula said, grinning broadly. "I get all the news from Sydney. That's Australia, mates! I know them Germans finished in Eeew-rope. They say the Japs finished *quick-time* now. Come along, let's have a listen!"

The men stood, and Johnny motioned for the Japanese to come. Mula led them to the second door in the wall. The chief went into the dark room, struck a match from a box, raised the glass and lit a hurricane lantern.

"Masta Billy's office," he explained as the yellow glow revealed the interior. The men saw a wooden desk and office chair, with four more like the ones in the kitchen against a wall. A Royal portable typewriter sat on the desk, although there was no paper to be seen. Beside it stood a radio in a carved wooden cabinet. Johnny whistled.

"All this, Masta Billy hide in the jungle from them Japs," Mula said. "But now—no Japs." He shrugged, and raised the lantern to display a curious contraption. It was a bicycle mounted on two sawhorses, the front wheel removed. The rear wheel had no tire, but a rubber belt went around it. This stretched to a metal cylinder with a pulley, attached to the wall. From that, alligator clipped wires ran to the radio.

"This how we gen-rate the juice. You want a go?" Mula asked Johnny.

"Sure," he said. He climbed on and began to pedal.

Mula set the lantern on the desk and turned a knob. It clicked, and light faded up behind the radio glass. A wave of static rose, and Mula fine-tuned it. Suddenly, music burst out—the strains of an orchestra. He made a fine adjustment and the whistling lessened. There was a crescendo of horns and rolling timpani, and it faded away. The dispassionate voice of an Australian announcer came on.

"Good evening. This is the World News from Sydney, New South Wales. It is Monday, August the 6th, 1945.

"The world leaders who attended the historic Potsdam Conference near Berlin in Allied-occupied Germany, are returning home.

"One of those in attendance, President of the United States, Harry Truman, met with King George the Sixth at Plymouth in England. President Truman is reported to be *en route* to America by sea.

"As announced by the Potsdam Declaration, Germany will lose every nation it took by force since the Nazis came to power. In addition, the nation will be stripped of a further twenty-five percent of all the land it possessed back in 1937.

"Efforts have begun to carry out the Potsdam provision for the demilitarization and 'denazification' of Germany, and for the prosecution of hundreds of war criminals.

"The Potsam Declaration has also demanded the, quote, 'immediate and unconditional surrender of Japan,' end-quote. We have a response from Tokyo. Premier Suzuki has repudiated the demand, in an official statement to the effect that the enemy nation will, quote, 'take no notice,' end-quote, of the demands of the Allied leaders.

"In that case, the Potsdam declaration promises, and I quote, 'the prompt and utter destruction' end-quote, of Japan.

"The United States announces it has escalated the bombing of the Japanese homeland. In the last two weeks alone, tens of thousands of tons of bombs have been dropped on more than thirty cities. This is reported to have resulted in widespread destruction and presumed loss of life. Furthermore, the Americans claim that mines have been now been dropped in every port, sealing off the enemy Empire.

"From Supreme Allied Commander General Douglas MacArthur in the Philippines: the mop-up of Japanese troops on Mindanao is almost complete. General MacArthur's authority has been expanded by the President to the Japanese 'Ryukyu' Islands, which include Okinawa.

"From Burma: the rout of the enemy by the Allied forces continues. It is estimated that more than twenty thousand Japanese troops were killed in this last week alone.

"From New Guinea: the remnants of the Japanese Eighteenth Army are surrounded at Numbogua, with the report of heavy casualties."

The broadcast continued as the audience in the Lighthouse Mission hung off every word. When the news concluded, and music once again warbled into the room, Johnny quit pedaling and

Mula clicked off the radio. Footy turned to the Japanese.

"See? You're about to lose," he gloated. The prisoner stared at him for a long minute and then shrugged.

"It is impossible," he said. Even though the others knew he could speak English, it was a shock to hear it.

"What?" Johnny retorted. "You heard the news!"

"That is one man. We know these tricks. It is impossible," the Japanese repeated slowly. "The Empire of Nippon has never been defeated."

"Well, get ready for it," Johnny said in a steely voice. "You're going down—and I'm going to be there to see it happen!"

"It will not happen," the prisoner insisted. "My people will fight to the death. No foreigners will ever conquer us."

"Who's this 'we' and 'us' you talk about?" Footy asked. "You don't mean *you*, do you? You won't be there," he sneered. "You, mate, will be rotting in one of our prisons!"

The Japanese stared at the other men, then looked down and went silent.

"But I *will* be there—in Japan," Johnny told him. He turned to Mula. "You heard what they said! My unit will soon be on its way for the invasion. We have to go, Mula!"

"No worries," the chief told him. "Anda will be back sometime t'night. We'll have our *singsing* tomorra—and you'll be off. If what you say is true," he added.

"Ok," Johnny said. "It's been a long couple of days. I'm beat. Where can we put him," he nodded at the prisoner, "for the night?"

"This way," Mula said. He led them through the living room to a door in the back wall, opened it, and they went into what was clearly the building's largest room.

"This the Mission church and school," Mula explained. His face fell again. "No church—no school—for long time now. Not since Masta Billy go to heaven, and Missis Sarah taken by them Japs." Along the far wall were a series of tall, narrow windows, all with the glass broken out. To their right was the main entrance, two heavy doors standing open in the weeds. The floor of the room was hard-packed clay, and on it stood the pews—benches made of planks nailed to posts. Lounging on these were the Uhuli warriors, some they recognized from the trail. These were stripping off their fighting gear, while other groups sat plucking one another's sparse facial and chest hair with bamboo tweezers.

At the other end of the room was the modest pulpit—a pole with a square of wood nailed on. On the wall they had come through, sheets of black painted plywood were nailed up, a faded alphabet and English words scrawled on them in chalk.

Through the windows, Johnny noticed a tall tree alive with the giant fruit bats they called "flying foxes." These hung upside down, bickering noisily, and jostling one another as they came awake for the evening's feed. They began to drop off and flap away, in search of bananas. They ate some of the local produce, and in turn, the natives ate them. Mula spoke to his men and turned to his guests.

"Your Jap can sleep here," he said. "I've told me *one-talks* not to hurt 'im—unless, a course, he makes a run for it. Then they can have him. Awlright?"

"You hear?" Johnny asked the prisoner and the man nodded.

"Now," Mula said. "Time for suppa. We got a special treat for you—come see!"

His smile was back.

CHAPTER 11

It had been a week since her last frustrating visit to US Army HQ and Gwyn had kept herself busy. The Colonel was gone, and the word was, his replacement was here, but in spite of Chambers' promise, Gwyn had received no news. She could bear it no longer. She searched out Doc Mac and told him everything.

Soon it was the doctor's car that pulled up at the US Garrison. Gwyn and the hospital administrator were ushered in to see the new Commander, a Colonel Waters. He invited them into what had been Chamber's office and asked how he could be of service.

"What has become of the rescue of the men of 'Operation Teeth?'" Gwyn asked. Colonel Waters looked mystified.

"I'm sorry," he said. "You know I'm new here. I've just returned from a tour of our bases. 'Operation Teeth?' Please explain." By the time it was all sorted out, it had been nearly three weeks since Johnny, Dingo and Footy had left Port Moresby.

That night after the orphans were asleep, Gwyn lay in bed and wondered about all the responsibilities she had taken on. She mulled over the round about way she had wound up in New Guinea, and the vow she'd made in England never to get involved with a military man.

Gwyn had graduated from nursing school in Vancouver, British Columbia, in the spring of 1942. With the coming of war, the Motherland's dire need of medical personnel had been in all the news, and Gwyn had volunteered.

It had been years since her mother had passed away, and her father had died the year before while she'd been at college. She'd gone inland for the funeral, held in the church in which she'd once attended Sunday School. She was surprised by how small and dowdy it looked. Of course, in Vancouver, she'd split her time between Christchurch Cathedral and the grand Baptist edifice downtown.

She visited old friends and discovered to her dismay that she'd outgrown many of them. Most were married and some had babies. Gwyn instructed the family solicitor to put the house for sale, and returned to her studies in the city.

She had her inheritance deposited in her account at the Royal Bank, and put much of it in Victory Bonds to assist the war effort. Now she met with the banker to arrange for funds to be transferred overseas, if and when she so instructed. She purchased a new wardrobe at the Timothy Eaton's Store and bought a sturdy steamer trunk from the Hudson Bay Company.

The day came when it was time for her to board the train at the False Creek terminal. From here, the western terminus of the Canadian Pacific Railway, it would take the better part of a week to cross the continent. She was soon grateful she'd treated herself to the luxury of a private sleeper, where she could retreat.

They left in the evening, and the following day, after crossing the dry sagebrush interior, they made the stunning climb into the Rocky Mountains. Gywn marveled at the soaring peaks, but the plunging depths scared her. The train thundered across rickety looking wooden trestles and she drew back from the windows that hung over thousand foot drop-offs. Another night, and they descended to the prairies. There were endless farms and cattle ranches, and the towns where passengers came and went, many of them men in uniform.

Gwyn enjoyed the dining car with its real linen and china, and decent meals, in spite of the war shortages. Other times, she wandered the aisles and conversed with fellow travelers, or sat in her berth and wrote in her new diary. This was a leather-bound book with a strap she could lock. She strung the tiny key on her necklace.

In the vast Province of Ontario, the train rolled through forested hills inset with gorgeous lakes. They chuffed on, and at last arrived at the eastern Maritimes. The journey had taken her from the Pacific to the Atlantic Ocean.

In Halifax, she met the other nurses on the same journey. Together, the nine of them boarded the twenty thousand ton liner-cum-troopship, the SS Duchess of Bedford. There they found thousands of Canadian soldiers also bound for the UK.

Smoke churned from the checkered stacks, the hawsers were thrown off, and the ship drifted from the quay. As the mournful horn shook the harbor, Gwyn stood in the crush at the back rail and waved madly to well-wishers she did not know on the dock. She remained there, bemused, as North America itself receded into the past, and they were on the blustery Atlantic.

The nurses shared adjoining cabins and spent much of their time there. It was a rough crossing, and many were seasick, but not Gwyn. Sometimes she buttoned herself into her tweed coat against the biting wind and paced the deck. But the eager soldiers were more bother than a plague of Okanagan mosquitoes. No matter how many she swatted down, they just kept coming. No doubt, the odds were to blame. The men outnumbered the women, three hundred to one.

Many of these Canucks were raw-faced prairie boys who'd never before been fifty miles off the farm. And so far their war had been no more than a romp across Canada, and a voyage on a one-time luxury liner. They were generally a good-hearted bunch, but Gwyn thought they could have hosed down the decks with testosterone. Their boisterous energy was quickly too much for her to bear.

At the time, reveling in her own adventure, Gwyn had no interest in a romantic entanglement. When her countrymen's overtures got to be too much, which they quickly did, she retreated to her cabin. There she passed the hours with her fellow nurses playing "hearts" and "euchre," writing letters home, and making entries in her diary. (Months later, she wished she remembered more of the men when the news reported the slaughter. More than half of them were summarily captured or killed by the Germans at an obscure French port named 'Dieppe').

Then she saw England for the first time, a landmass in a nimbus of dark clouds. "The Duchess" docked at industrial looking Liverpool. There the nurses and the soldiers went their separate ways. With a last round of shouts and waves for the women, the Canucks marched off.

The women boarded a train to London. Staring at tall buildings through sooty windows, Gwyn could hardly believe she was truly in the homeland her parents had reminisced about all those years. In mere hours, she stepped down into the one-time capital of the British Empire, and still the hub of the United Kingdom. She felt like she was in a storybook. It hardly dampened her spirits that clouds hung low over the buildings, and a steady drizzle fell. After all, she had brought her umbrella. She was to discover she needed it as often as she had in Vancouver.

At a government office, she and her fellow nurses were given their postings. They would be dispersed across the British Isles, to Europe and even Africa. Gwyn discovered she was to remain in London.

Gwyn checked into a rooming house one of her nursing teachers had recommended, and reported to the hospital. The hulking edifice overwhelmed her. Gwyn was frightened, and suddenly felt that coming here might have been the biggest mistake of her life. Inside, she kept getting lost, and was forced to ask repeatedly for the office of the Matron of Nursing.

There, in the waiting room, was another young nurse. Gwyn first noticed the curly red hair that the woman was attempting to wrestle under control with bobby pins. She soon discovered this was Ruthie, from Ireland, a newcomer like herself. The two chatted up a storm, relieved to find a friendly face.

Shortly they were welcomed together by the no-nonsense Head of Nursing and given their duties.

Over the next days, whenever they got a break, the young women sought each another out. They were kindred spirits, they decided, and while they put on a brave front, they felt like colonial hicks in the grand and gloomy city.

A week or two later, they decided they would room together. They searched out a flat not far from the hospital, and felt very grown up negotiating the rent. It had only one bedroom, for which they flipped a shilling. Gwyn ended up in the sitting room. She would sleep on the sofa, her clothes split between her trunk and a box. The arrangement offered no privacy, but had the advantage of being close to the coal burner. But even when they found fuel to buy, or collected lumps along the railroad tracks, it was always frigid. Gwyn's home might be in the far-off colonies, but at least Canada knew about central heating, an amenity the Mother Country had not embraced.

When they both happened to be home, and awake at the same time, the girls bundled in blankets, put their feet to the brazier, and got to know each other. Gwyn described her hometown, Peachland, on a huge lake in the interior of British Columbia. Lake Okanagan, she told Ruthie, even had its own monster, like Loch Ness. It was no lie, she swore. "Ogopogo" was a gigantic but shy creature.

"Get on with you! I think you're having me on. And I suppose you've seen this 'Ogopogo' with your own eyes?"

"Yes," Gwyn said, "I saw it once, near evening, a huge thing moving below the surface."

Many had seen it much more clearly, she hastened to add. There were photos and films. Ogopogo had an enormous body, flippers, a long neck, and a smallish head. The creature's existence had been confirmed by the big city newspaper, the Vancouver Sun.

Gwyn talked about ice cream and sodas with girlfriends as they watched the boys romp on the beach. Those were the summer days that stayed light well past 9:00 at night. And in the winter, it was home with her parents in front of a snapping fire, while the deep snow piled up.

Gywn had a lot of stories about fly-fishing with her father for trout in the mountain streams, but Ruthie had little interest in such "tomboy" things.

"Your turn then," Gwyn said, "where are you from?" The Irish lass flashed an impish grin, her hair a halo in the fire's glow.

"Me?" she said, "Well darlin', I'm from nowheres—a wee farm with one milk cow, an hour's walk from Pallas Grean."

"And where's that?"

"Along the road from Limerick to Tipperary," Ruthie smiled. "Blink, and you'll miss it."

Ruthie's stories revolved around boys. She'd met them in town, and at school, and crept off for trysts around the farm. Gwyn heard all about Paddy, Pete and Rolly. And then, Ruthie said with a wink, she'd really spread her wings when she'd gone to nursing school in Belfast.

In spite of the ongoing bombing of London, Gwyn and Ruthie managed outings, dodging the ruins and cratered streets. Together they stared through the gates of Buckingham Palace, disappointed not to catch even a glimpse of the King. Gwyn did take pictures with the Brownie box camera that had been her father's. Other trips took them to the Tower of London, Westminster Abbey, and Trafalgar Square.

Afterwards, they searched out pubs where they might get a meat pie—or Ruthie's favorite, steaming fish and chips in cones of newspaper, sprinkled with malt vinegar and eaten with the fingers.

Wherever they went, as usual, they had to ward off the men, most in uniform. Gwyn was more diligent at this than was Ruthie, and they might let the eager lads treat them to a glass of beer. In this way, Gwyn learned the differences between lager, ale, bitter, porter and stout. The girls enjoyed a laugh and sank a pint or two. They never, however, brought boys back to the flat. This was a pact Gwyn had insisted on from the beginning. And so it was that sometimes she returned alone, while Ruthie disappeared for a day or two.

But then, in spite of herself, Gwyn fell totally, hopelessly, dangerously in love.

"Arse over teakettle," as Ruthie put it.

☼

Anda, spear in hand, loped through the jungle, retracing the route the strangers had traveled earlier that day. Rapidly, he climbed into the high country. It grew too dark to see anything but the faintest outlines, and still he pressed on. When the moon rose, he was able to go faster again. He traveled silently, alert for enemy warriors, but saw no one.

In the early hours of the morning, he slowed and searched the path for a particular rock. He found it, got down on all fours, and crawled through dense foliage. Soon he was able to stand again and jog along a thin trail for another hour. He came to the flank of a mountain and climbed straight up over a ridge, and dropped into a hidden canyon. At last he heard the trickle of a stream, and made out the silhouette of huts against the stars.

Six armed men surrounded him. Anda spoke a greeting and they said his name. The men squatted together and passed a thin cigar, as long as an arm.

These people were Mambu, but only distantly related to the inhabitants of the great valley. Even their language was a dialect. The intermarried clan that inhabited the five huts had small gardens scattered in the jungle. They maintained an uneasy truce with both the Mambu nation and Anda's Uhuli, based on a complex set of favors done and debts owed.

Anda met one of their teenage women by chance, while hunting wild boar in the hills. His courtship of her was at first tolerated, then encouraged, because it strengthened the clan's ties to Mula's Uhuli. At the same time, Anda was warned, the relationship must be kept secret from the Mambu of the valley, or the people would suffer deadly reprisals.

Yesterday, two of their men had trekked to the big valley to barter Bird of Paradise feathers and *buai* for *kaukau* and other food. But they returned early, without making the trade. Instead, they carried a burden of frightening news. They related it all to Anda, while the galaxies wheeled across the heavens.

When the men finished their story, they disappeared into the darkness. Anda waited alone. The girl emerged from a doorway. With quickening pulse, Anda saw the starlight outlining her shoulders and plump breasts. She carried a *bilum* of food she had cooked especially for him.

Anda took her by the hand and led her to a place among the roots of a forest grandfather. In anticipation of his visit, she had swept away the insects, and lined it with dry moss. Anda laid her down, parted her skirt and mounted her. She thrust up to meet him, watching his head move against the leaves and stars.

Eventually the girl stole back to her hut. Her parents, who slept on skins spread on the dirt floor, watched her enter. The young woman spooned into the warmth of her siblings, and the family slept again.

Anda carried the bag of cold *kaukau* across a shoulder, spear in hand as he retraced the path in the ghostly light. He ate while he traveled, careful not to drop anything that would betray that he had passed this way. After what he had learned in the night, he did not expect to encounter the Mambu, but a man's life depended on eternal vigilance.

On the main path at last, Anda ran hour after hour, anxious to share the astounding news.

Mula led his guests to the kitchen table and they sat. Johnny untied the captive's wrists. The man was preoccupied, *by the news,* Johnny thought. Miriam brought plates piled with baked sweet potatoes. These she'd cut open and smothered in tomatoes and green beans. Also on each plate were chunks of meat, swimming in their juices. Johnny poked suspiciously with his fork.

"What's this?"

"Me *one-talks* dragged this outta the rivva," Mula grinned. Seeing the incomprehension on the other faces, he laughed. "This is *pookpook*, mates—croc! You evva try it? *Pookpook* is good eating—you give it a go!"

"Are you sure?" Johnny asked, "That it's croc I mean?" It was Mula's turn to look perplexed.

"Look, I don't want to be eating any person," Johnny told him bluntly. "I don't eat humans, Mula."

The Uhuli chief took offense.

"We don't eat no 'ooman beans here! We are not bloody cannibal, mate! I'm hurt, I am, that you think that."

"Don't take it wrong," Johnny said, "but in the Mambu valley they gave us human flesh."

"Bloody cannibals," Mula shouted and banged his fork on the table. "Them sons-a-satan! They eat us Uhuli, why do you think we hate 'em? But we, the Uhuli, the only real people—we do not eat no 'ooman beans."

"Aw yeh," Footy said, "that's what they all say in New Guinea, mate! That's the old story here. 'It's them, not us!' Till you find yourself chewing on some bloody arm or leg."

Footy, too, was eyeballing his plate. The prisoner would not touch his helping. Mula speared a piece, popped it in his mouth, chewed with relish and swallowed it down.

"Aw, eating 'ooman beans, that's bloody primitive, that is!" he said as he loaded another forkful. "We Uhuli, we not eat people. Nevva did, even in the old days." He filled his mouth again.

"Naw. We headhunters!" he went on proudly as he chewed. "That's what Masta Billy say. Headhunters—not cannibals."

"What's the bloody difference?" Footy asked.

"Big bloody difference," Mula insisted. "Headhunters—we take enemy heads. Cannibals—they eat you mate. See?"

"Mula, you swear this is croc?" Johnny asked, studying the meat on the prongs of his fork. His stomach growled.

"I swear onna Bible," Mula said. Johnny decided to trust him. He put the meat in his mouth and it was tasty. Footy watched the Yank, then forked up a bit, sniffed, and ate. The Japanese studied the other men. When he saw them swallow, he decided to brave it.

"'Course I've eaten *pookpook* before—back in Aus," Footy said. "But in this country, you want to bloody well make sure what's on your plate."

The meat was firm, Johnny found, whiter than beef, more like pork. There was nothing fishy about it.

"This is *pookpook* like I told ya!" Mula insisted as he took more.

"We Uhuli gotta fight, same as you blokes, to protect ourselves. Sometime we kill Mambu to even the score. 'An eye for an eye, a tooth for a tooth,' Masta Billy tell us the Good Book say. That the Uhuli way! We like that. But we add one: 'a head for a head.'" The chief laughed loud and pounded the table with a fist.

"A head for a head!" He enjoyed himself so much, Footy and Johnny had to chuckle, and even the Japanese smiled.

"That's a good 'un," Mula said, wiping his eyes. "We usta take Mambu heads—put 'em in our *House Tambaran*. But since Masta Billy, mate, we don't bring no 'ooman heads inta this village no more.

"We all good Christian now. Masta Billy took us in the rivva. He bap-tide us. We burn down the spirit houses and all them heads. And we had some good 'uns—even one *Mambu-ato* from before.

"Now, with Masta Billy gone, some of me *one-talks*, they go back to the old ways. Some take heads, hide 'em in a jungle. But I don't allow heads in a village. Things not easy with me missionary gone. But..." he banged the fork on the table again, "...we Uhuli are *not* cannibal mate! The real people are Christian!"

"Well, good to know," Johnny said, scraping his plate.

Miriam had taken a chair at the table and was eating as well, baby asleep in one arm. Luke climbed on her knee and ate from her plate.

"Good dinner, Miriam," Johnny said. "Thank you." She dazzled him with a dark smile. The men all had seconds. When they were done at last, nothing left in the pots, Miriam took the plates and scraped them out the door. There were squeals, yips and excited clucking.

"Now sleep," Mula said, standing and stretching. He took a lantern and led them to the bedroom door. "You can have me own room," he offered. The men peered at the stained mattress and the pile of grubby sheets.

"No, no," Johnny said, "that's ok, we'll bunk in the living room."

"Couldn't take your bed, mate," Footy chimed in. Mula seemed pleased. The Aussie spread his blanket on the sofa while Johnny and Mula walked the Japanese to the church. They got the prisoner settled on a bench, and Johnny brought out a rope to tie him.

"No need," Mula told him. "You," he spoke directly to the Japanese, "you run—if you like." He looked around at his men, said a few words that caused a laugh, and grinned at the captive.

In the living room, Johnny roped his hammock from the poles. Footy stretched out on the couch. He could feel every spring in it, but it was better than the hard ground he'd been lying on. Mosquitoes whined around his ears and he spread the square of mosquito netting over his head.

Johnny lay in his hammock and heard Footy snore. He was exhausted, and it seemed more than physical. He pondered it, and slowly he realized he was weary of all the killing. After three years of war, he had entered strange new territory. It wasn't just about the Japanese anymore. In the Valley of the Cannibals, he had slaughtered natives for the first time.

Complicating everything, his sworn enemy, "the Jap," had fought at his side. It had never even occurred to him that something like this could happen.

Killing the Mambu was in self-defense, he reminded himself, but he remained uneasy. *Sure, they're cannibals, but this is their country. What beef do I have with them?*

In mid-thought, Johnny fell asleep. Neither he nor Footy saw the moonlight that spilled through the windows. In the church, the Japanese slept like the dead, and did not hear the warriors' voices, or the sounds they made as they moved about.

Mula assigned the guard, and the others accompanied him, Miriam and the children, back to the gathering place in the village. Here they found the people already gathered. The fires flared, and the Uhuli prepared to mourn their dead.

The five wives of the three fallen men sat together with ashes smeared on hair and skin. They began to keen, and their mothers, sisters, and all the women took up the ritualized wailing.

Two of the wives worked themselves into such a frenzy of grief they called for hatchets. Helped by the others, they each chopped off a finger at the first knuckle, and stanched the blood flow in more ashes.

When the first wave of grief ebbed, Mula addressed them. He sketched the story of each man's life, and described their relationship to dozens of those present. These connections, a man's "line," were of paramount significance in village life. When that was done, he said a prayer asking Papa God to take the souls of the dead into heaven, repeating as much as he could recall of what the missionary had said on these occasions.

Then, feeling guilty because "Masta Billy" had tried to stop the practice, Mula called for the dead men's possessions. The wives came prepared with these—weapons they had left behind, and other items of dress. These were placed before the chief, and then he and others each picked one up.

They lit torches, and the entire community walked upriver. At last they approached the secret and sacred place, a grove of trees with an enormous one at the center. This was the Uhuli Tree of the Dead.

None of them had talked about this, let alone showed it to the missionary. They knew that if they did so, they would lose it. So even though they had embraced the new faith in Papa God, and the loving son, Jesus, they continued to revere the remains and relics of the ancestors.

The people surrounded the enormous trunk and Mula sent the dead men's clan brothers up the tree with baskets of food and gourds of water. Putting on a brave front, but in truth quivering with terror, the warriors climbed among the hanging bones and possessions of the departed. For all time, this had been the Uhuli way of preparing the fallen for the journey into the spirit world. If the rituals were not done right, the ghosts would not be appeased, and would not embark on the final journey. They would turn malevolent, and come back to haunt their own families. The result would be disease and calamity.

Many times the missionary, firmly but with compassion, had explained to Mula the old and new ways did not mix. But without "Masta Billy" to guide him, Mula found many complex situations where he was torn between two worlds. Now, in order to relieve his unease about what they did at the Tree of the Dead, he told himself that his brothers could use their weapons, food and water, to help them on the journey to Papa's heaven.

The Uhuli returned to the bonfires. For several hours, one after another, they rose to reminisce about their dear kinsman. They recalled acts of kindness, unusual prowess, and exploits in battle. Already, the tales were taking on mythic proportions.

The fond recollections were interrupted more and more frequently by outbursts from the warriors. These worked themselves from grief to fits of anger. A man would leap up and swear by all his ancestors, that he would not rest again until he had avenged his lost comrades. The loathsome Mambu would pay with their heads! On and on the outpouring went, until everyone had a chance to speak. Their grief spent at last, the people stumbled to bed.

Mula led his family to the mission bedroom, got them settled, and padded into the church to be with his men. They kept an eye on the sleeping prisoner while they talked through the momentous events of the last days. They discussed the white men's fabulous yarn from every angle, and voiced the impassioned hope that it was all true—the demon *Mambu-ato* and his hated cannibals had been destroyed.

A particularly intense discussion centered on the *pookpook*, the legendary Father of the Crocodiles. Before the missionaries came, the Uhuli had worshipped the beast. They had grown up hearing that it had lived since the dawn of time, and several of the elders argued that the old rituals of appeasement must be revived. If not, they warned, the Papa would descend on them once more, and feed on the Uhuli.

But on this point, Mula was insistent. There would be no revival of the former ways. The days when they feared every illness and accident as the work of a malevolent spirit were done. "Masta Billy" and "Missis Sarah" had shown them the way, he said. They were children of Papa God, and they were in charge of the world, not victims of it. Mula made his point: they would pray to Papa God to save them, not to the crocodile.

At last the chief crept through the living room where his guests slumbered, crawled into the sheets beside his wife and sons, and passed out.

The sky was flaring on the horizon when Anda entered the village. The dogs scented him and barked, but only a little. The sentries, in turn, heard this, and knew who approached.

Cocks had been prematurely announcing the dawn for several hours. All the animals were up now, and vying for scraps that had been tossed from the huts. Anda passed by and approached the mission. The guards watched him come, and an elder stole into Mula's bedroom and roused the chief. As he rose, Miriam and the boys stirred, but fell back asleep. The Uhuli went to the church and joined the other warriors. The prisoner turned on his bench, cracked an eye to peer at the men, then slumbered again.

Mula handed Anda a cold *pookpook* leg. The young man had to hold the limb in two hands. He ripped off bites as he recounted his tale. The chief plucked a betel nut from the branch being passed around and stripped the skin with his teeth. He took the nutmeat in his mouth and felt the familiar burn. A gourd of white lime powder was passed and he dipped the stick in and sucked. He chewed, his spittle increased, and he squirted a jet onto the ground. Immediately he felt guilty. "Masta Billy" had been very strict about that—no *buai* in the church! But now, sadly, Mula was one of the worst sinners, and the floor was heavily stained.

Anda talked for more than an hour, the tale stretched due to continual interruptions, but at last it was told. Mula took some minutes to think it through, then gave a series of orders. Warriors departed for the village.

In the living room, Johnny awoke to the shaking of his hammock.

"Time to get up and shine," Mula grinned through the netting. "I got big news, mate!"

Chapter 12

Johnny had slept in his pants and he unzipped the hammock and slipped out. Mula wore his broad, black smile.

"Anda's back! I wish me ol' dad was alive ta hear wot he say!" Johnny smelled coffee and saw Footy in the kitchen with Miriam.

He went to the church. The prisoner was awake and Johnny told him to come and eat. On the way, he smiled to the warriors, Anda among them, and said good morning. They beamed and repeated, *"good-fella mornin'!"*

Footy was with Mula and the family at the table. Johnny and the prisoner sat. Breakfast was sweet potato mixed with crocodile stew. Mula was cutting slices of yellow "pawpaw." Footy passed around mugs of strong coffee. The sugar was gone. Mula spoke between bites.

"You'll be glad ta know, mate—Anda done fortify da feet."

"Verify the facts," Johnny murmured.

"Wot I said," Mula nodded. "Bumay village is burn down—*gone-finish!*" The chief could not contain his glee. He threw back his head, held his belly, and laughed. Miriam and Luke giggled and even the baby cooed.

"Anda, he hear a lotta white fellas come outta the sky and fight the Mambu. These white men got big magic—they kill plenty a Mambu! Anda's mates, they seen a lotta dead men. Meebe fifty, meebe a hundred—all dead! Dead!" Again, Mula laughed and slapped the table.

"They say a big yella man..." Mula looked doubtfully at the prisoner, "...he gotta magic knife and he cut a lotta Mambu head.

"They say one bloody *big-pella pookpook* spirit come outta the river and fight along-side the white men. This what they call the *Mambu-matu*, mates! This the Papa of them sons-a-satan! The *pookpook* eat Bumay, their numba one *pekpek*-head." Again, Mula guffawed, delight transforming his broad features.

"They say the *Mambu-matu* burn down the bloody village.

"Ahhh, wotta day, wotta day! These magic fellas," Mula looked doubtfully at the unwashed men at his table: "This you lot—for shore?"

"That's us," Johnny grinned, pretending to hold a rifle. "Big magic men from out of the sky."

"Bloody right," Footy said. *"Bigfella fight true!"* Mula shook his head indulgently at them.

"The Mambu—they got a lot to do now," Mula went on. "First, they gotta make magic to find out why they been punish. Find out why Papa *pookpook* fight them—kill them—eat that bloody Bumay.

"Then—for shore, mates—them Mambu, they gonna find someone ta blame. Oh yes! That the Mambu way! And who they gonna blame?" He slapped his chest.

"The Uhuli! That's who! Why? They always do! Then they gonna come this way—in four, five days, I reckon. An' we gonna wait for 'em—back in the bush. I got me *one-talks* watchin' the track outta the valley now. When they come—with no Bumay, a lotta the men gone—we gonna get 'em. We gonna cut us some Mambu head!"

Johnny and the others had finished eating and sat back, drinking coffee.

"Tell me more about this croc," Mula went on. "He the *pookpook* with this mark..." he cupped a hand and placed it over his eye, "...like this?"

"That's him!" Footy said.

"You know the Father?" Johnny asked.

"Aw yeh, mate," Mula said. "Everybody on the Big River know the Father! He the Papa of the *pookpook,* that for shore. He got strong magic. Masta Billy, he not like us to call 'im 'the Father.' He say, we got only one spirit Father, up in Heaven. But I say, this *pookpook*, he a demon Papa, come ta eat the people. And pigs. And dogs." Mula paused and thought again.

"What I wanna know—what the Papa *pookpook* do, helpin' you blokes fight the Mambu? Why the Papa eat that *pekpek*-head? Tell me this, Masta Johnny."

"Don't call me 'Master!'" Johnny said. "I'm Johnny—call me Johnny."

"Awlright—Joe-nee," Mula said smiling. "I like that!"

"The Father's a crocodile," Johnny said. "Just a crocodile. It's a big one, for sure. But I shot its foot off. It's flesh and blood, like any animal."

"Not magic mate," Footy added, "though that is the biggest

bloody croc I've ever clapped eyes on. And believe you me, I've seen big ones back in Aus. Johnny here bloody well did blow its foot off," he continued. "The Father's no devil—but I do believe it is hunting this Yank." Johnny shrugged and laughed it off.

"Naw, naw, don't laugh," Mula told him, face serious. "It could be, could very well be. That the *pookpook* way. A croc want a fella, it watch him. Once a *pookpook* pick a fella, it get him by-n-by.

"If the Papa want you Mas… if this *pookpook* hunt you, Joe-nee, you watch out. Mebee you gotta big problem, going down his rivva."

"Ok," Johnny nodded.

"Now," Mula said, "your yarn, it prove true. This a big day! To-night we gonna make one big *singsing*. We gonna eat, we gonna dance! Our enemy Bumay *die-finish!* Many Mambu *die-finish!* I say thankya—all Uhuli say thankya!" Mula looked at the prisoner.

"You, Jap—you my enemy," Mula said, "But you kill a lotta Mambu! For that, we not gonna kill you, awlright? Now you a friend of the Uhuli." Mula grinned at the man and the prisoner gave him a genuine smile and nodded.

"Tonight we dance. Tomorrow, you go your way along the rivva. Me—I'm bloody happy!"

Mula leapt to his feet and performed an impromptu dance, singing at the top of his lungs. From outside the door, warriors joined in. The chief grabbed a battle-axe and shook it in the air. The boy, Luke, a finger in his mouth, gazed wide-eyed at his father. Miriam looked on smiling, the baby asleep on her shoulder.

☆

After breakfast Johnny told Mula they needed to wash both themselves and their clothes. Mula said he'd show them where. Johnny, Footy and the prisoner gathered all the dirty things, including their grubby towels and the bar of soap. Mula escorted them to the riverbank. Miriam and other villagers came to watch.

"Hold on," Footy said uneasily as he stared at the opaque, muddy water.

"What about the Father—or any croc?" Johnny asked.

"We *washwash* in the rivva all-a-time, mate," Mula told him. "We look for *pookpook*—but..." he shrugged and grinned, "…most times, no croc."

"How about someplace else," Johnny said, "somewhere with clean water? Back in the forest maybe?"

"I know a spot," Mula nodded. "Masta Billy, he *washwash* like us, inna rivva. But Missis Sarah, she no like it. She like the place I gonna take you."

Mula spoke to the villagers and it became clear there was an outing in the making. He posted guards around the village, and led off. Johnny had not tied the prisoner's hands this morning. They walked in a crowd of Uhuli warriors, Miriam and the other women, and a gaggle of children. There were fifty or more who streamed through the gardens and into the jungle.

After about an hour, they broke onto a grassy bank where a brook gurgled over smooth rocks. Tiny orange and pink butterflies flew everywhere, and a flock of neon green parrots chattered in the trees. Dragonflies darted across the stream, touching their tails. The prisoner, Johnny noticed, watched them with a look of delight.

Miriam and the women encouraged the travelers to hand over the things they brought in a pack. Johnny and Footy stripped down to their underpants and the Japanese took off his shirt. These items were passed to the women as well. The prisoner kept his pants on, as he had nothing beneath. The women soaped each item, beat it on the rocks, then wrung it and spread it to dry.

The men eased into the wonderfully chilly water. They waded upstream to a deeper pool and sank down, out of the steamy heat into silent bliss. The current washed away the sweat and grime, and the men came up gasping. Standing, they scooped water in their hands and drank.

Johnny called for the soap and little Luke came running with it, chased by his friends. Johnny lathered his hair and body, then passed the bar to Footy, who did the same, and it was the prisoner's turn.

The Uhuli watched the show, pointing and laughing. The children scampered and splashed around the foreigners, but few of the adults showed an inclination to come in. Johnny called to Mula to join them, but the chief just grinned and crossed his arms.

"I already *washwash* this moon," he replied.

Eventually the trio hobbled out and sat in the sun. Vapor steamed from their clothing. A few warriors remained watching the forest, while most lay down and dozed in the shade, Mula among them. It struck Johnny that, except for their own presence, this could have been a scene from a thousand years ago.

Eventually the crowd meandered back to the mission. Mula said he had things to do, and left with Miriam and the children. The prisoner sat at the kitchen table while Johnny and Footy emptied their packs and reorganized. Johnny checked his first aid kit. The supplies were dry in watertight cans. After that, Footy stretched on the couch and napped. The Japanese lay on the floor, head on his hands, and did the same.

Johnny had noticed there were photos on the living room wall. Now with daylight at its brightest, he took a closer look. The frames were thick with dust and fingerprints, and the photographs were faded and damaged by mildew. In the first one, Johnny made out a young couple in white, she in a wedding dress and he in shorts and a shirt. *The missionaries—Billy and Sarah.*

He moved to the next frame. There was the same man in a patterned shirt, his arm around a gray-haired couple, two young women beside them. *Family portrait.* The following photo featured Sarah as a teenager, with long fair hair and kind eyes. *She's pretty.* The young woman held hands with an aboriginal girl who smiled shyly.

The final photograph showed a group of young men and women in front of a building that looked like a school. Johnny studied the rows and picked out the missionary couple. Written in ink across the bottom was: "Bible School, December 1938."

Why would Billy and Sarah leave their homes and come to this place? Why pick New Guinea? The soldiers Johnny had known couldn't wait to get out of here. *Why the Uhuli village?*

All at once, Johnny got a strong sense of the Australians in this very room. He imagined them sharing a meal at the kitchen table, the place clean and tidy, curtains on the windows. Here the two had lived, with music from the radio and news from Aus to ease their homesickness. The couple had spent months, even years, in this place, helping one another face the alien world that waited on the other side of the door.

Then Johnny thought about their bad end, when the man lay shot and dying. *Did he know his wife was being raped? Had he wished then that they had never heard of New Guinea? Did he believe God had deserted them—or did he see himself as a martyr, rushing to his reward?*

Once more Johnny found his thoughts going to Gwyn. *What*

would she say? He wished she was here. He'd have more to talk about than going to Japan. But wishing that was like wishing his parents were alive. *Pointless and stupid,* the soldier observed. He slipped into his hammock and drifted off for an hour.

When Mula returned sometime later, he found his guests seated at the table. Johnny and Footy were cleaning their firearms and had them disassembled and spread out.

The chief made an impressive entrance. On his hair perched a spectacular headdress of springy bark decorations, so tall he had to duck to enter the room. His forehead featured a white cross with rays of red around it. In the tip of his nose was a fresh and magnificent hawk plume. Bold lines of white and yellow were drawn across his face, and others outlined his prominent pectoral muscles. His chest had been plucked of hair, and his whole skin glistened with pig fat. He wore a *laplap* of brilliant yellow cloth tied around his waist, and he turned to display his back, painted in crocodile scales.

Johnny was drawn in particular to the necklace of big conical teeth Mula wore around his neck. The chief sat down and Johnny examined it.

"*Pookpook* teeth," Mula explained. "I killed the crocs meself. You blokes wanna see the place for the *singsing*?" He and his guests strolled through the village. Everywhere, Uhuli were painting one another and putting on their *bilas,* their tribal decorations.

Mula led to the clearing between the houses, almost as spacious as the one in Bumay's village. To the side was a pit about ten feet long and four feet wide, the dirt piled beside it. The men walked over and looked in on a row of hog carcasses. These were packed all round with *kaukau* and leaf-wrapped vegetables.

"This the *mumu*," Mula grinned. Five pigs had been slaughtered that day, a significant event in village life. Early in the afternoon, a great fire had been built in the pit. As it burned, special stones were laid on. When the wood was gone, the rocks radiated heat. On these, a layer of banana leaves was arranged, and then the butchered pigs and all the rest placed on top.

As they watched, men worked hollow bamboo tubes through the food packages and wedged them between stones. Women covered everything with another blanket of banana leaves. The watchers stood back while men scraped the dirt over and made a mound.

Other men came with bamboo containers of clear water from the stream, and poured this into the hollow standing poles. There was a hiss within the earth as the water splashed onto the super-heated rocks. It was the steam, Mula explained, that would do the cooking.

"You wait," he grinned. "The Uhuli *mumu* the best you evva tasted!" He glanced at the sunset.

"Time for the news."

"Right!" Johnny said. He'd almost forgotten. The men returned to the Mission office, and this time it was Footy who climbed on the bicycle-generator. A song Johnny had never heard filled the room, although the women's voices were familiar. It ended, and a cheerful Aussie spoke.

"That's the latest from the Yank Andrew Sisters," he said. "It's called 'Along the Navajo Trail.'" He pronounced it "Nava-joe," and Johnny grinned.

"And now, time for the news." There came the clacking of a machine, and the serious voice from yesterday spoke.

"Good evening. It's six o'clock. This is the World News from Sydney, New South Wales. It is Tuesday, August the 7th, 1945.

"American President Harry Truman has announced the first atomic bomb has been dropped by a United States aircraft on the Japanese City of Hiroshima." The prisoner sucked in his breath.

"What?" Footy said.

"Shhh!" Johnny responded and every ear strained to hear.

"President Truman announced the news from the mid-Atlantic, aboard the USS Augusta. The American leader is returning to the United States following the Potsdam Conference.

"President Truman said the atomic bomb was more than two thousand times more powerful than the largest bomb ever used to date.

"An assessment of the damage caused to the City of Hiroshima has been impossible, due to the huge cloud of impenetrable dust over the target.

"The atom bomb was dropped from an American B-29 Super-fortress, known as Enola Gay, at 8:15 a.m. local time. The plane's crew reported a column of smoke rising and intense fires springing up.

"President Truman said the atomic bomb heralded the, quote, 'harnessing of the basic power of the universe,' end-quote. The

President went on to say that this marked a victory over the Germans in the race to be first to develop a weapon using atomic energy.

"President Truman then warned the Japanese that the Allies will now completely destroy their ability to make war. Quote, 'This is the last chance for Japan to avoid utter destruction,' end-quote.

"President Truman said, and I quote, 'If they do not now accept our terms, they may expect a rain of ruin from the air the like of which has never been seen on Earth. Behind this air attack will follow, by sea and land, forces in such number and power as they have not yet seen, but with fighting skill of which they are already aware.' End-quote.

"In other news..." the announcer continued with lesser action of the day. Johnny urgently reached over and lowered the volume.

"Have you ever heard of an 'atom bomb?'" he asked Footy.

"No mate," Footy said. "What is it? It must be a bloody big bomb."

"Can one bomb destroy a whole city?" the Japanese broke in, startling the other men. "Is this a trick?"

"This is no bloody trick!" Footy shouted. "This is real, mate!"

"You heard what they said," Johnny joined in. "President Truman said it! It's true." Something occurred to him.

"Is that where you're from?" he asked. "What was the city?"

"I am not from Hiroshima," the Japanese said shortly.

"Is it possible one bomb can wipe out a city?" Johnny echoed the prisoner's question. No one had an answer. Mula's eyes were going from face to face. He was especially impressed that the white men were so shocked.

"Mula, we've got to leave!" Johnny said. "First thing tomorrow! You heard what they said—the invasion of Japan is coming. I've got to be there!"

"Shore, mate," Mula said. "You're free ta go. This big news—this Adam bomb?"

"Atom, atom," Footy corrected him. "And it's bloody big news."

"Who is this 'Atom'?" Mula asked.

"It's not a person—it's a tiny thing," Johnny said, "so small you can't see it. That's what I've heard."

"And this tiny thing makes a big bomb?" Mula asked.

"I don't know," Johnny told him. "I never heard about this." He looked at the Japanese. "But it's the end for Japan."

"Why so important for you to be there, for the end of Japan?" the prisoner asked Johnny, his voice raw with emotion. "Why?" Johnny didn't answer. He stared hard at the captive until the man lowered his gaze. In the silence, they heard the announcer:

"This has been the news." The other fellow with the light-hearted voice came on.

"The very best news! They've turned up the heat on the Japs! And now we continue with our musical entertainment of the evening. Sit back, relax, and hoist a cold one to the blessed Yanks!" The strains of a big band gushed from the speaker. Mula turned the radio off and Footy dismounted the bike.

"What does it mean?" the pilot asked in wonder.

"Beats me." Johnny shook his head.

"Well mate, nothin' we can do about any bloody big atta-bomb," Mula said. "We gotta *singsing!* This a cel-bration over them sons-a-satan Mambu.

"You blokes come along now. You the guests of honna!"

CHAPTER 13

At Mula's urging, Johnny and Footy left their rifles behind. His warriors would guard the mission. They did keep their pistols and knifes on their belts.

The prisoner spoke to Johnny: he did not want to go to the *singsing*. He looked so distraught, Johnny felt sorry for him and spoke to Mula. They agreed the captive could be left with the warriors in the church. Mula, Johnny and Footy departed for the party.

Night had come and torches lit the village. Mula carried his longbow and a prize man-killing arrow. His guests admired the hardwood head, fully thirty inches long and bound into the shaft. The point bristled with barbs and was adorned with rings of bright paint and tassels of thread. The chief carried a huge battleaxe with a head of polished green stone.

As they went, more and more villagers in their best *bilas* joined them. It was a large group that streamed into the central clearing. Bonfires burned around the perimeter and cast yellow light over hundreds of Uhuli. The chief led his guests to the cooking pit. There they encountered Miriam. She, too, was dolled up. Her skin shone, and intricate designs were painted on her breasts, back and legs. She wore a flouncing grass skirt, multiple strands of bright beads around her neck, and flowers woven through her hair. Baby Billy slept in a *bilum* on her back and Luke, the older boy, was painted as well. He had the yellow and white lines on his cheeks and chest, just like his dad, and he clutched a small spear.

Mula and his men shouted greetings to each another over the crowd. The people fell silent as their leader walked into the firelight. He launched into a speech in Uhuli that carried to everyone. At times, he made the people roar with laughter. Alternately, he was solemn and the crowd hung on his words. He made frequent gestures towards Johnny and Footy.

He called, and men with hourglass-shaped drums came forward, beating on the skin heads. The unmarried younger women formed lines facing one another. Spirals of paint focused attention on their pert breasts, and they had enhanced the much-desired appearance of broad hips by layering on grass skirts. With wide smiles, the teenagers sang, swaying and clapping their hands. The lines gyrated through one another, turned and crossed again.

The boys took their place, Luke with them. The drums beat faster and the little men shouted and waved their spears. They were followed by the younger girls, their waists encircled by strings of flowers, blossoms in their hair. Then the married women, including Miriam, gathered. They danced in a circle, following one another, each holding the waist of the woman in front.

It was the teenage warriors' turn. Each wore a white feather in the end of his nose. Mula explained that at the time the boys' voices changed, he and the mature warriors held the ceremonies that transformed them into men. It was at this time that their noses were pierced. A boy was made to bite into a chunk of pork. At all cost, he was not to cry out or show fear as the awl went in. Immediately, the stork feather was inserted into the bloody tip to keep the wound open until it healed.

Each man-boy would wear the white feather until he either attacked an enemy in battle, or killed a crocodile. That was how he earned his hawk feather. They were only for full warriors who had proven themselves. Mula had earned his "two Christmas after I became a man." That would have been when he was fourteen or fifteen, near as Johnny could figure.

Then, accompanied by the men of his clan, Mula had gone by dugout to a tributary where a river crocodile lived. This had been carefully selected for him. It was bigger than he was, but not by much. Some men paddled, while others held up flaming torches.

When they saw the red reflection of the *pookpook's* eyes, they glided in, and Mula flung himself on the crocodile's back. It was serious business. Some boys were mangled, even killed, during their ordeal. Mula wrapped his legs around the croc and pinched its jaws together with his fists so it could not bite him.

Only then could his father and uncles help. They jumped in and dragged the furiously twisting reptile onto the bank. There, Mula slit its throat. That earned him his first hawk feather. The chief held up his necklace and pointed to the four teeth from that first kill.

Another Christmas, he said, and a raiding party brought back a captive Mambu. The Uhuli warriors rounded up Mula and the other young men and suggested everyone fire an arrow into the hated cannibal. That way, each would get credit for the kill. Some moons later, Mula killed his first Mambu in battle and harvested his head. That had been his favorite skull, he said, "til Masta Billy show me the erra of my ways."

While Mula regaled Johnny and Footy, two flute players joined the drummers. Their instruments were bamboo tubes thick as a man's arm, two or three feet long. The inner wall had been left intact at one end, and a hole burned near it. The men held the instruments sideways to their lips and blew across the opening. The first man sounded two notes, and the second echoed this in a higher pitch. Back and forth it went, while the drums beat along.

Now the white-feathered warriors danced, each leaping high in the air to outdo his friends. They jabbed at one another with sharp bamboo spears, the thrusts coming increasingly close. The crowd shouted encouragement, and the dancing grew frenzied. Then a razor edge touched flesh and blood flowed. Mula and the other men chortled and called comments to each other.

As a boy was injured, he dashed to the sidelines where elders slapped pig fat mixed with soot into his cut. Mula pointed out the multiple raised scars on his own legs and torso. The young warriors' incisions would heal this way.

"They scars a honna," he grinned. The treated boys were soon back threatening their friends once more. Mula told his guests that next, he and "me bruthas" would act out Uhuli history, their triumphs in war and the hunt.

When it was time, he strode to the dance area, his bow and arrow in hand, his great axe through his belt. He called to his warriors, and the hawk-feathered men gathered around, each with a bark headdress.

Big drums, hollowed out trees with slits in them, were rolled up and new drummers beat them with cudgels, resounding bass thumps. The hand drums joined in, and warriors stamped in time, facing their people. Mula shouted phrases, each one repeated and embellished by his companions. Every so often, they punctuated the singing by twanging the bowstrings, shaking their weapons and shouting their battle cries. Mula finished his recitation, and another warrior continued, and then another.

At last they were done, and Mula called them to the *mumu*. The women had been busy while the men danced, and Johnny and

Footy came to the pit and watched. The dirt and top layer of banana leaves had been stripped. The steam carried a mouth-watering aroma. Women jumped down and sliced up the pigs. Others waited with stacks of cut banana leaves, their plates. On each square, the servers piled juicy pork, sweet potatoes, and a variety of vegetables. A contingent of elderly men crowded around and provided much advice, ignored by the women.

At last Mula called out in a loud voice. Silence descended and all eyes turned his way. The chief handed his bow to a warrior, glanced at Johnny and Footy and grinned.

"Let's pray, mates." He pressed his hands together and the gathering followed suit. Even the women busy in the pit paused and bowed their heads.

"Thank you true, Papa-God, for bringin' us togetha!" Mula shouted. "Thanks for killing them bloody Mambu—for new friends and good food." He added some phrases in Uhuli and bawled, "let's eat!"

Women went into the crowd, passing out the laden leaves. Miriam brought the first serving to Mula. On her heels came two of the most fetching unmarried girls, who giggled and handed huge helpings to Johnny and Footy. On his square of banana leaf, each man had a generous slab of pork, soft bamboo shoots, yellow and orange sweet potatoes and yams, beans in edible pods, and whole cooked tomatoes. The men sat on stones, balanced the leaves on their knees and ate with their fingers in the firelight, while the sky blazed with a million stars. When every one had eaten, and many, including Johnny and Footy, had second and then third helpings, the *singsing* continued.

A group of dancers came out from between the huts. They wore fantastic costumes made of light bamboo frames, over which were stretched painted and feathered bark paper and animal skins. Several men carried each assembly. There were crocodiles with flapping jaws, undulating snakes, flamboyant birds and more. The drums built to a furious crescendo, stopped, and the animal-dancers went still.

A humpback "boar" emerged into the firelight. The actor's mimicry was superb. Oinking and snorting, the pig dipped his snout to root in the dirt. But now the "crocodiles" crept at it. It wandered blithely on, unaware of its danger. Some in the crowd screamed warning, while others laughed excitedly, caught in the spectacle.

On the boar came, tossing it tusks, and the crocs slid up.

At once, a crocodile rushed it and enclosed the pig in long jaws. The boar let out a series of uncannily lifelike squeals as it was dragged off. Mula and his warriors rushed into the act. They ran at the *pookpook* and mock-stabbed it, as other "crocodiles" threatened the men. But the Uhuli fighters, joined by the white-feathered novices, finally prevailed. They drove the *pookpooks* out of sight among the huts.

Dance followed dance. The white men's eyes stung from the smoke and their heads began to nod. Johnny asked Mula for permission to leave, and for food for the prisoner. He and Footy walked back to the mission. Johnny took the leaf-plate to the captive, found him asleep, and woke him up. The man looked at the Yankee with dull eyes and muttered he was not hungry. Johnny shrugged, set the food beside him, and went to the living room. Footy was already on the couch. Johnny stepped outside, used his toothbrush and powder under the stars, and climbed into his hammock.

Within minutes, he and Footy were out like lights. In the clearing, the *singsing* went on and the hours wore away. From time to time, parents carried their offspring to their huts. Eventually, the elderly climbed the ladders as well. Some of the dancers simply dropped where they were and passed out, while feet continued to pound beside their heads.

None of the Uhuli saw the disturbance across the river, in the darkest shadows beneath the bank. A *cuscus* possum was the only witness. It was asleep on a branch over the water when it was blasted awake by an exhalation through huge nostrils. Terrified, its nocturnal eyes bulging more than usual, it stared down and saw something massive move. It squeaked in fright and scampered to the very highest twigs. There it curled again, complaining into its soft belly fur, and covered its eyes with its paws.

The Father stared across the river, saw the light flickering on the prey animals, and felt the tickle of smoke. But it was not hungry, its leg throbbed, its bones ached and its head hurt. It breathed deeply, submerged, and swam downstream. Carried by the current, aided by occasional sweeps of its great tail, the Father passed through lands that, unbeknownst to it, the Uhuli called their own.

Mula and his warriors stimulated themselves with fresh *buai* and kept on dancing. Only when fingers of light probed the eastern sky did the last diehards reel away.

The chief returned with his men to the church. He changed the guard, he and his *one-talks* stripped off their headdresses, and they lay on the benches and conked out.

Johnny awoke with the morning streaming through the windows. He saw Footy, up early again, but alone in the kitchen. The Aussie bent over, lighting the stove. Through the bedroom door, Johnny made out the recumbent sleepers. He slid out of his hammock, took it down and rolled it. He greeted Footy and said they'd be on their way in a few minutes.

Johnny went to the church and woke the prisoner. He saw Mula nearby, out cold among his comrades, and did not disturb him. The guards nodded to Johnny where they crouched chewing *buai* at the doors.

Johnny and the Japanese went to the kitchen. The coffee was percolating on the stove by then, but Footy was not to be seen. They were at the table, sipping from their mugs, when the Aussie came back with his hands full of eggs.

"I've been watching where the chooks were laying," the pilot winked. There was a cast iron skillet on the stove, and Footy threw in a pork rind he found on the counter. When it was sizzling, he cracked in the eggs. He chopped cooked *kaukau* from a pile and dropped this in as well. Shortly, he was sliding plates in front of the men and they ate.

When breakfast was done, Johnny told the prisoner he would tie his hands again. The man listlessly held out his arms. Johnny and Footy were putting the last things in their packs when Mula came in, yawning and scratching under his *laplap*.

"Top o' the mornin' mates," he said, his voice a rasp. "Time to be off, is it?"

"Yes," Johnny said. "That was quite the party."

"Yes, ta. Looks like you went all night, mate," Footy added.

"Right," Mula agreed, pinching red eyes. "Gotta stay with me *one-talks* at a *singsing*."

Uhuli warriors followed Mula in, arms loaded with rolled leaf packages they piled on the table.

"Food for you lot," Mula said. Johnny and Footy stuffed the cooked pork and vegetables in the top of their packs. They arranged their weapons on their belts, slung up their loads and picked up their rifles. Johnny put his helmet on, and Footy, the Digger hat.

Miriam shuffled out of the bedroom, the children still asleep. Johnny and Footy thanked her, and Johnny gave her a kiss on the cheek. Then, to the other men's surprise, the Japanese went to her, said thank you in English, and made a bow.

Outside they found an escort of ten warriors. The group set off, Mula and his men yawning hugely. They passed the rows of dugout canoes along the downriver path. They went through gardens and came to the perimeter wall. Sentries stood around an opening and Mula exchanged greetings as they passed by.

It was a fine morning, the breeze off the river having a hint of coolness. Johnny gazed across the swirling surface. *Where is the Father? Well, one thing's for sure,* the soldier said, *it's out there, and it's looking for you.*

The sun rose and cast long shadows. Vapor rose from the reed beds. The men walked for an hour and came to a sapling fence along the jungle.

"The end of our land," Mula said. "Me *one-talks* will stop here, but I'll come with you blokes—*a long-way likilik*."

"'A little bit of a long way,'" Footy grinned.

"Yes mate," Mula said. "We go into Taifora land. They strange ones, the Taifora. They friends of the Uhuli, and prob'ly wouldn't hurt you, but best if I'm with you. Got their own ideas, this lot. I'll guide you 'round 'em."

Johnny's group shook hands with the line of warriors. Then the Uhuli men watched the foreigners who had killed Bumay and his Mambu, disappear with their chief into the forest.

CHAPTER 14

"What did you call the next tribe?" Footy asked.

"'Taifora,' mate," Mula said. "Had their own missionary one time, but the Mambu got him, early on. That was before the Masta and Missis come to the Uhuli. The Taifora, they got some Christian, some of they own ideas. 'Misguide,' that's what Masta Billy call 'em."

"Misguided? How?" Johnny asked.

"You see for yourself," Mula shrugged, "soon enough."

They hiked the morning away and ate a cold lunch. They began to hear drums echoing through the forest.

"Awlright," Mula said, "no talk now." A few minutes later, he ducked around a tree and the others followed. They found themselves going up a jungle-covered hill. From the top, Johnny paused to look back, and there was the Raub winding into the distance. The men continued along the spine of the ridge as the drumming grew louder.

Mula motioned for the men to get down. They slid on their bellies to the edge of a cliff. Johnny found he was looking onto a field thirty yards below. Behind it in the trees was a village, but it was the activity on the grass that commanded attention.

A line of twenty drummers stood along the far side, facing his way. Each of them beat on the now-familiar hourglass drums. They wore headdresses of brilliant green feathers, and were painted from head to toe in the same color, interspersed with bands of yellow. Around their hips were short skirts made of the same glossy feathers.

On the near side of the field was a tower built of four tall poles. Perched on top, just below the watchers, was an open-sided hut. Two men stood under the grass roof, staring up and away. They had hands cupped around their eyes, and they appeared to be looking for something.

A pole stood beside the field. From it, a long strip of cloth fluttered. On the opposite side, midway down the line of drummers, was a homemade table of saplings and vines. Behind it stood six men, the most outlandishly outfitted of the lot. They had bleached white crocodile skulls tied on their heads. Their bodies were painted green like the others, but they had pieces of skin tied around biceps, chests and thighs, from which sprouted iridescent Bird of Paradise plumes.

"Taifora priests!" Mula whispered.

The six were busy with a small box on the table, also made of sticks. A vine ran from it to a woven ball one held. He spoke some words and passed it to the next shaman, who did likewise. The ball went along the line.

The drums beat faster, and the warriors began to hum in deep voices. Johnny realized something was moving in the forest. A shape emerged from the shadows, and it looked like an airplane. The effigy was cleverly made of long saplings bent into a frame, covered with painted bark cloth. Six native men walked inside it, heads poking through appropriately placed holes. The "aircraft" was complete with wings and a tail, and had a propeller of bark that spun on the nose.

The contraption drifted down the field. The drummers were humming louder now, a sound like engines. The thing stopped by the priests' table and, as the drums beat faster, the men inside lifted it off and laid it on the grass. Each of them had a stick box in his hands. The six walked to the table and put their offerings there.

The drums were at fever pitch and the warriors broke into frenzied vocals and looked up. Johnny thought they'd been spotted, but then realized the Taifora were staring beyond them, into the sky. The priests were gyrating and shrieking like men possessed, and Johnny felt a touch on his arm. Mula motioned to leave.

The group backed into the forest and descended the other side of the hill. Half an hour later, they emerged on the riverbank.

"What in the world was that?" Johnny asked in a low voice.

"Masta Billy call it the 'Cargo Cult,'" Mula said.

"Aw, yeh," Footy said. "I've heard of that, but first time I've seen it. It's all over New Guinea they say, sprung up here and there on its own."

"What's the Cargo Cult?" Johnny asked.

"Right mate," Mula said. "Let me try. Some people believe you lot—you whites—are their dead family come back to life."

"Ok," Johnny said, and thought about the old Mambu.

"I saw a plane," Footy said.

"Yes mate," Mula said. "It go like this. God have a son, who die for everyone, that's wot they say, right? The son go to heaven and make big houses, plenty big houses for us, right?"

"I guess so," Johnny said. "Something like that."

"We see you white blokes. You come along, cut a path in the bush. You talk to a magic box. I know it's wireless like me own, but some of these fellas, they bloody primitive! Then a *baloose*—a plane—it come! And the cargo come out. These fellas here, they want that cargo! Right mate?"

"Right mate," Footy said.

"So what does that have to do with God?" Johnny asked.

"Ahh," Mula said. "Where does the cargo come from? From big houses far away, the white men say. Some people think Jesus go to heaven and make the cargo for his children. But the white man, he get it first. Then he want it all himself. He don't share with God's children!"

"Whoa!" Johnny said. "Now that's what I call a good yarn!"

"These Taifora, they make the magic, but the goods don't come. How do they explain that?" Footy asked.

"Ahh, they just don't get the magic right," Mula grinned. "One day, soon enough, they gonna get it. Then the *baloose* come!"

"That is so nuts, it almost makes sense," Johnny said.

"More like, the most buggered story ever told," Footy added. Johnny was reminded of a family at the church back in San Diego. They told everyone that if they just tithed right, prayed right, did it all right, there was a fortune coming their way.

"Watch out for anyone who thinks God Almighty is their personal slot machine," Johnny's father warned.

"Mula, if the Taifora put half that effort into real work, they could buy the cargo!"

Mula stared at Johnny intently.

"Is that right, Mas…is that right, Joe-nee?" he asked. "What you mean, 'work?'"

'Oh—let's see," Johnny said. "Like growing coffee, tea and coconuts. Or…" he snapped his fingers, "…how about croc skins? They're worth a lot of money."

"Is that true, Joe-nee?" Mula asked. "I don't know nothin' 'bout those utha things, but *pookpook* skins, I can get. We trade 'em for cargo?"

"Sure,'" Johnny said. "Right Footy?"

"Bloody right mate," Footy chimed in. "Take the skins and rub 'em in salt. Dry 'em in the sun. You sell 'em for money, and money buys cargo. That's the Australian way."

"Japanese way too," the prisoner spoke. The others stared at him. He'd hardly opened his mouth all day.

"I think 'bout that," Mula nodded. "Thank you to verify the facts. Now this is where I stop. You got *a long way likilik* to the big water. Maybe five days, maybe ten. I don't know, mate—nevva been there, but that's wot I hear." The travelers turned to leave.

"You tell 'em when you get back," Mula went on, "the Uhuli need anotha missionary! We need guns and bullits, clothes, knives, axes. We like them motors for our canoes—an' petrol! I keep the Lighthouse Mission nice n' ready for the next missionary," he added, "you be shore an tell 'em that!"

"Yes, yes," Footy said, impatient to be off.

"You save your croc skins," Johnny smiled. He offered his hand and Mula pumped it vigorously. "And thanks, Mula. You're one of the good guys."

"One of the good guys," Mula smiled broadly. "I like that! Thank you for killin' that *pekpek*-head and those sons-a-satan. Joe-nee, you watch out for the demon Father! Don't let him eat ya!" Johnny waved and headed into the forest.

"Nice guy, that Mula," he said.

"Yes mate," Footy said, "but crikey, he can talk!"

— ☾ —

The party walked for several hours. They finished the water in their canteens and stopped at a spring. Johnny tasted it and found it funky, but that was normal. They'd had to make do with all kinds of sources on this trek, and he'd run out of purification tablets days ago. They drank their fill, topped up their bottles, and moved on.

The day grew darker, which did not help their mood. Rain clouds gathered in the north, and they heard the boom of thunder. All three were subdued. They'd left the friendly Uhuli behind and were in unknown territory again. They toiled through the forest, and emerged beside more gardens. Women were digging in the distance, but when they saw the strangers, they fled into the jungle.

Whenever the path drew close to the river, the men paused and scanned the banks for crocodiles, one in particular. Several times they passed a mudslide, and fresh dung. They saw eyes watching from the reeds, but none with the great span of the Father.

At midday, they slumped on rocks to eat. The day was close, and they were all sweat soaked. Johnny untied the prisoner's hands as Footy dug cold *mumu* food out of the packs. The Japanese ate mechanically and Johnny did the same. He wasn't hungry. He had a dull headache and his stomach was queasy. He hoped it wasn't a malaria attack coming on. Johnny retied the captive's hands and asked how he was doing, and got no response but a twitch of eyebrows.

As they took to the trail, the last patch of sunlight disappeared and the whole sky went dark. The trio pressed on while thunderheads piled overhead. Then, over the river, a shaft of lightning flashed and thunder ripped the sky. Another blinding arc zapped to earth ahead on the trail, accompanied by an explosion like artillery, and at once, they smelled rain.

The first fat drops splashed on them and Johnny pulled his helmet lower over his eyes and walked into the oncoming storm. The trail approached another clump of jungle and the men ducked under the branches. All the forest creatures had gone silent and the only sound was drops spattering the leaves.

There was a roar of approaching rain, and then it struck in earnest. The forest canopy absorbed the first barrage, but the water licked over branches and soon everything was running. The men were soaked and the path turned into a ditch of melted mud. Johnny and Footy's footgear pulled up clods and for once, the captive's bare feet gave him an advantage.

Eventually they emerged from the trees and slogged in torrential rain through a cane field. The sullen river ran forty yards off, the surface pocked by drops. The rain drummed on Johnny's helmet and gushed down his collar. A sheet sluiced in front of his eyes and he could barely see his feet splash through deepening puddles. The flashes and booms were constant.

Johnny's head hurt and for some reason, he became fixated on the crocodile. He was peering ahead when his heart turned over. There it was! It rushed at him through the blinding rain, more massive than he remembered it that first time, when it killed Dingo. Somehow he knew it was not real, but the monster kept coming in the lurid lightning. Its mouth was open and he smelled putrid decay that made him want to heave. It was the reek of death he'd lived with for much of the war.

The beast opened its jaws and thunder erupted from its belly. The sound vibrated in Johnny's gut, and something turned in there. Lightning shot from the yellow eyes and blinded him. He shivered from head to foot, spots of light danced, and all his skin rose in gooseflesh.

Desperately, he conjured a trick from the war in an attempt to drive the apparition away. When the horror of the endless days of killing threatened to overwhelm him—when Johnny woke in the morning knowing all he could look forward to was shooting more men—the only way he could keep going was to escape within his mind. Perhaps it was only for a minute or two, but if he could get respite, he could go on. That was how he fought the impulse to just stand up and take his final bullet.

One of his best distractions was a memory of his mother. Not that he'd ever tell this to a fellow soldier, even under threat of torture. But in the private place in his mind, it was Saturday morning, and Mom was in her kitchen. She baked pies from scratch for Sunday dinner, whether his dad was ashore or not. That world—her world—was so safe and clean, contrasted to the stinking gore-soaked one in which he existed.

Her Betty Crocker cookbook is open to the page, even though she knows each recipe by heart. She makes lemon meringue pie with golden peaks. Or maybe it's cherry pie with a crust on top, pricked with a fork, pinched around the edges. She has her apron tied on, the flour sifter and rolling pin ready. She hums a tune, "Somewhere Over the Rainbow."

But now as Johnny forced himself into the thunderstorm, Mother flashed in and out of view, crackling with electricity. Then something twisted inside him again, and Mom was overrun in a rush of gruesome dead men.

The living dead came at him, riding on the rain. Here were his brothers in arms the instant they were shot and dying, stabbed and dying, blown up and dying. And here, too, were the ones he had chosen with his scope before he touched them with his killer finger. They came with the others, heads and bodies ripped apart, but somehow alive again.

It's my nightmare, he realized, but this was all wrong. The dead only haunted his sleep, and here he was awake on the river.

And then it was Bumay who drifted across the flooded plain. But it was only half the chief—the upper torso, with its guts looped down, dragging through the puddles. Johnny stared at the cannibal, unable to turn away.

Bumay cocked his arm back, the one holding the black spear, and he grinned his black grin and aimed at Johnny's heart.

CHAPTER 15

With all his will, Johnny braced himself against the rain that cut into him like broken glass and tried to make Bumay disappear. He looked down between flying splinters to the place far below, where boots splashed through dirty water.

An angry buzz swelled in his ears and an animal jumped in his gut. Bumay floated at Johnny, grinning his dark grin, his spear back. He came to Johnny, who ducked, and the chief drifted right through him. He felt the tug of the guts as they passed. And now, running in exaggerated slow motion, came the Mambu warriors.

Johnny found his rifle in one hand, pistol in the other, and he fired again and again without reloading. He shot the men point blank and flesh roses bloomed on them. He saw each bullet go in—into the chest, the neck, the skull—and explode out in showers of bone. A man with a fierce and noble face raced up and Johnny put his pistol to his jaw and fired. The chin shifted and bullet and teeth blew through.

There was a pounding of village drums in the rain, and behind it rose whistling radio static. Johnny heard a cheerful Aussie say, an atom bomb went off this morning, an atom bomb, a bloody big bomb went off.

A long way down, far too far to control, boots knocked together. Fear shot up from his feet and he shuddered like a tree under the bite of the axe. He struggled for balance, scraped up the poor shreds of his will, and staggered on, into whatever hell awaited him.

Footy was thoroughly wretched. When the rain began, he unhooked the brim of the hat, but the water poured off it and ran under his clothes. The mud squelched and his feet slid inside his sandals. The storm beat him down, and his world shrunk to the back of the prisoner's head. He saw the bristles and the knotted cloth, all running with rain.

When he glanced beyond the enemy, he made out the Yank, still grinding on. He glanced around and noted they were in a cane field. He skidded through the mud as they came down onto a low stretch close to the river. Alarm spiked as he watched the floodwaters breach the riverbank and spill across the field. It drowned the path, and swirled between grassy hummocks.

Then he saw the Yank stumble. Johnny almost fell, and swayed to a stop. The prisoner, head down, ran into his back, and that set the Yank lurching off like a drunk.

"Johnny!" Footy called, "hold up, mate!"

The face came around like a moon against the darkening day. Footy took in the slack lips and rolling eyes. The prisoner froze as well, and his head spun back.

"You, Jap!" the Aussie snapped, "go by! Then wait." The man sidled around Johnny and turned. Footy splashed to the Yank's side and grasped his bicep, but it was wrong, all slack.

"Mate," Footy said urgently, "you're ill!" The American's lips moved, but nothing came out. Johnny felt the fist pinch his arm while another reached into his guts and twisted. The rumble was so loud, Footy heard it over the downpour.

"Sick!" Johnny said, and the word banged around his head but did not find his mouth.

We've got to seek shelter! Footy thought, and he stared wildly for a place. There in the field was a small hill, turned into an island by the flood. It had a tree that would provide some cover.

"There!" the Aussie barked at the Japanese, pointing with his rifle, "go!" The man led off while Footy dragged Johnny through the knee-deep water. They reached the slope and climbed.

"Sit!" Footy ordered the prisoner, motioning to the tree. The man put his back to the trunk and slid down, bound hands on his knees.

Johnny groaned and thrust his rifle to Footy. Urgently, he began to undo his pants. There was a boulder in the rain and he stumbled to it and dropped, pack still on. His body began to convulse and he moaned in distress. The sound and the smell were atrocious and Footy, standing beneath the tree, felt a wave of nausea—*from the stink*, he told himself. He stood fretting, feeling hot and anxious. *Of all the times, Yank!*

The thunderstorm bellowed and crashed, and the sky ran with water. One second it was garishly lit, then dark twilight. The flood expanded until it seemed to fill the world.

Johnny forgot where he was. He turned his head to see what

was hitting him, and drops fell out of the eggplant sky and struck his eyeballs like pebbles. He dropped his chin on his chest and sat panting while the spasms wracked his body.

Footy suddenly felt leaden with fatigue. A rifle in each hand, he sat on a buttress root. He felt the prickle of heightened danger as he gazed from Johnny to the prisoner. He found the Japanese staring back, black eyes unreadable. And then the pilot felt the first cramp tear his own belly.

Johnny felt as if his life force was draining out and his eyelids came crashing down. Outwardly, he seemed to be unconscious, but within, the nightmare raged. Again, the cannibal chief floated across the flooded field, yelling unintelligible words that were too loud. *His face is proud and cruel. Everything is black except my green helmet on his head. His skin is black, his teeth shine black, his spear is black against the night.*

Johnny raised his rifle and shot the horror in the face, but the bullet boomeranged in flight and slammed into the shoulder. *Bumay spins—and there is the Father! It leaps up below to take him. There is the moon cut on the head, and it bites the hanging guts and drags him down. He comes down like a balloon, and the Father bites the chest. Bumay screams, how he screams! My helmet pops off his head and flies away. The scream never ends, but now it is laughter, crazy laughter. Bumay laughs while the Father eats him and it is the best joke! The crocodile bites and swallows, bites and swallows.*

Johnny tasted what he knew were raw human brains and he leaned forward and vomited. Thunder rattled his bones. Another blast of lighting lit up the inside of his skull. It was white hot and he felt his brain begin to bubble. His skull cracked open, and his awareness shot up into the blaze of light.

The prisoner sat with his back to the bark and knew the Yankee was finished. He had been laid low with the belly sickness many times, and had seen countrymen die this way, with nothing to expel but black water. He felt a wave of pity, and rejected it.

Pity is weakness—his Father's voice. Katsu made his thoughts stern and considered his duty. He must throw off the disgrace of being a prisoner. *I am a soldier, and I will kill my enemies and escape. Yes,* he thought, *but not quite yet. The Australian is watching.*

The man had the rifle pointed at him, very close. He saw what looked like a snarl on the white face, and knew it was a mask over fear, and was encouraged.

The storm raved on, and the Japanese made his muscles relax and thought about the atom bomb. The news had set off a profound conflict inside him. Part of him thought it was possible such a gruesome thing existed. *The destruction of Hiroshima is true.* His captors, he could see, believed it totally, and this was hard to refute. If it was so, the Empire of Nippon was finished, for who could fight such a hideous thing? It left him sad and desperate.

But there was another possibility and it rose like anger, a core of steel within his disgrace. This part rejected the poisoned words of the radio. *It is a trick—the enemy is a master liar. Nippon has beaten them all. All we have done is take the living space my people need so desperately. And we have taken control of weaker, lesser people who lack discipline. We will be their firm but benevolent leaders. We will have a better life, and we will share it with all those in Asia!*

Now, in spite of setbacks, in spite of being cut off from High Command and any word from home, I believe in our Empire! I give my life to the Emperor. I serve him, and the sacred Empire of Nippon. If my poor contribution means anything, we will prevail!

There is no such thing as a single bomb that wipes into oblivion hundreds of thousands, perhaps millions of humans. Humanity has not sunk so low that it will wipe entire cities from existence at a single blow!

These feelings were so strong, they made him nauseous, like the sickness on the ships coming here. He wished with all his being for a truth to cling to in this flood of confusion. *True news from home!* His eyes had closed and he returned his gaze to the Australian. Again, he stared down the dark hole of the rifle. It was still not time and he closed his eyes and waited.

Katsu had come to New Guinea under the inspired, if somewhat fanatical, General Yazawa. In spite of the Commander's aura of invincibility, and the white stallion he rode, he was soon proven to be mortal. Katsu had seen the Commander shot out of the saddle by an enemy sniper. What an absolutely irresistible target he must have made! Since then, Katsu had served under a string of officers.

At last he had joined the tens of thousands of his countrymen near the town of Wewak. It was in this general region, further northeast on the coast. The Raub River would deliver him within hiking distance of the stronghold.

Katsu was a Captain, *Rikugun Taii*, in the *Dai Nippon Teikoku Rikugun,* the Imperial Army of Japan. Under his superior officer, *Rikugun Chūsa* (Lieutenant Colonel) Yuudai Matsui, he and three hundred troops were assigned to capture and hold an area of the Sepik River that encompassed five villages.

Katsu and the Colonel did not get along well. More accurately, it was the Colonel who found reason to bait Katsu. It was all because of the sword. Katsu had been born into a samurai family. The ancient warrior caste had remained Nippon's elite for the better part of a thousand years, until gunpowder and modern weaponry had rendered them obsolete. In the 1870s, the samurai were stripped of their privileges, and outlawed.

Still, Katsu's family was the very flesh and blood of the old warriors. The Takano had been samurai for more than five hundred years. On the day before Katsu departed with the Army for the New Guinea islands, his father had honored him by presenting to him the ancient *katana*, the samurai sword, to carry into battle.

The Lieutenant Colonel, on the other hand, came from a wealthy family, but of lowly merchant lineage. He made it clear in a thousand small ways that he despised his junior samurai officer and his precious sword! Katsu believed the man was envious, but for whatever reason, his superior seized every opportunity to belittle Katsu and brutally exert his authority.

Their occupation of the Sepik had been successful, but as the months dragged on, neither food, supplies nor relief came. In fact, there was no contact with higher command. What could the troops do but wait? What little rice they had left, damp, rancid and full of weevils, the Colonel reserved for himself and the officers. Katsu found this offensive and would not partake. With the men, he scavenged for sweet potatoes in the native gardens. There was never enough.

The fetid place by the river swarmed with mosquitoes and vermin so at times, Katsu thought he might go mad. Once every last vegetable, pig, chicken and even the dogs had been eaten, the troops began to die. Starvation was abetted by malaria, dysentery and a host of fevers, and men fell like flies.

Then, when it seemed things could not possibly get worse, the enemy found them. The fighters screamed out of the sky and strafed the men, who scattered into the jungle. They heard motors on the river. Gunboats sped into view, machine guns blazing.

Colonel Matsui seized his samurai underling and ordered him to round up what men he could. They would run for their lives. Katsu was able to collar only seven soldiers. The Commander leveled his rifle at the native men still in the village and ordered them to guide him upriver. They were unwilling to venture into other tribal land, so Matsui shot one. The other four fell into line.

The party trekked away, robbing gardens where they could. Each night, they must stand guard over the natives, or they would run off. But the enemy gunboats followed and more of the fighters thundered over. Numerous times, Katsu and his group were forced to throw themselves down in the jungle and hope they would not be seen. From time to time, they heard the machine guns hammering, and knew others of their countrymen had met their end.

The enemy was all over the river. The Colonel ordered the guides to lead them away. They struck out overland, and eventually found themselves climbing the forbidding mountains. By the river, they had been too hot. Now they were too cold. Finally, all of them sick and near death, they encountered a stream that turned out to be the headwaters of the Raub River. They followed it down and came upon the village.

Their urgent priority was food, and they went in search of the gardens. There they stumbled across the *gaijin*, two white men, surrounded by natives. The Colonel knew Katsu spoke some English and ordered him to interrogate the enemy.

They were Australian, the white men explained, but Christian priests, men of peace. Katsu translated and Matsui listened with his face pulled into his usual sour frown. The Colonel replied he did not believe them. They were spies, like all the hairy ogres, and they would be executed—at once. Katsu began to speak, and the Captain called him a fool and told him not to translate this. He barked orders, and the troops seized the white men and made them kneel. Protesting anxiously, the priests were forced on their knees and made to look at the dirt, which stretched their necks.

"Now you, my precious Samurai," the Colonel said in a venomous voice, "withdraw that *katana*! Let us discover if it is useful for anything besides digging me a toilet!" One of the soldiers, a homely man with buckteeth, guffawed. Katsu shot him such a furious look that the man ducked his head and was quiet.

Katsu did not like to draw the sword unless he intended to use it. It was certainly not for showing off. Yes, he had killed enemy soldiers with it in hand-to-hand combat, but when this group invaded the Sepik, he did not require anything other than a rifle.

Now, under a direct order from his Commander, he reluctantly withdrew the blade from the scabbard. The eyes of the men widened as the shining steel came out. Katsu kept it clean, oiled and free of rust. While none of the others had personal experience with a priceless antique such as this, they knew enough to recognize the genuine article.

"How beautiful!" one of them sighed.

"Yes, beautiful," the Colonel sneered. "A beautiful relic from an outlawed caste. Where was it made?"

"Bizen," Katsu said. The name of the place was also one of the names of the blade.

"And you, Takano. I expect you know *kendo*?"

Katsu had trained faithfully in the martial art, two hours or more a day, six days a week, since he was a boy.

"Yes, honored Lieutenant Colonel Matsui," he replied with exaggerated courtesy.

"What *dan* are you?"

"I have been fortunate enough to achieve the fifth level."

"Impressive, Captain," the Commander said, while his tone implied the opposite. "And no doubt you are also a master of *iaido*?"

This was the martial dedicated exclusively to swordsmanship. While *kendo* involved sparring, the exchange of blows with body parts and wooden swords, in *iaido* there was solitary practice only. *Katana* were far too deadly for sparring.

"I am third *dan*."

"Again, impressive." The Colonel struggled to curl his downward-cast lips in a smile. "Well, Takano. Let us find out if that *katana* has some value. Use it now—behead these men! I command you!"

When the sword had slid from its scabbard with an audible ring, the white men glanced at Katsu in terror. The younger was the short one, his head bald on top. The elder had shaggy gray hair in need of a cut. Both men wore well-washed shorts and shirts, and sandals on their feet.

The bald one began to pray in a panicked voice, begging God to spare their lives. The older man told him to be calm. Then he, too, began to pray, but in a quiet, firm voice.

"Our Father, who art in heaven..." The younger priest joined in, his voice steadying as he continued.

Katsu had existed in distress for a long time, but now he found himself in an impossible dilemma. He was a career military man with a renowned father. He was accustomed to submitting himself to the absolute hierarchy of the Army. Orders were to be obeyed at once, without question. Yet it was clear these *gaijin* were exactly what they said they were, Catholic missionaries. He had never even imagined that one day he would be ordered to kill a priest, whether Christian, Shinto, Taoist or Buddhist.

"I am sorry, honored Lieutenant Colonel Matsui. These men are civilians, and priests at that. I cannot see any reason..."

"Silence, Takano!" the Commander bellowed. "Do not be insubordinate, or reveal yourself a coward before the men! There will be immediate consequences!" The Commander held his rifle at his waist, aimed at the Captain.

"Do as I command at once—or give me the sword!"

"...lead us not into temptation but deliver us from evil," the priests intoned.

Katsu saw the entire fate of his career, and the honor of his family, hang on these seconds. Abruptly he reversed the sword, holding it by the blade, the handle toward his superior. The Commander grew even more furious.

"Just as I thought Takano! You are a coward, and absolutely useless!" The Commander shoved his rifle to a soldier and marched over. He grabbed the handle and jerked so that Katsu would have lost fingers if he had not released it fast enough. The Colonel clutched the weapon and raised it in the air. Katsu saw immediately that he was a clumsy amateur.

The Colonel spun and slashed at the younger priest's neck. The blade chopped into the flesh like butter, but it was a bad cut that did not reach the spine. The man screamed and his companion shouted in horror. The soldiers held the struggling priest in place as he tried to clamp a hand to his neck, which poured blood.

The Colonel raised the sword and hacked again. It was another inept blow that did not even strike in the same place. The victim began sobbing, while the older man tried to struggle up, yelling at the men to be human! Katsu's heart was moved, but he betrayed nothing on his face.

Twice more, Matsui struck. None of the blows were terminal.

The priest struggled weakly until at last he choked on his blood and died.

Katsu felt a strong new emotion sweep through him—pure contempt. The Lieutenant Colonel went around and stood beside the older priest.

"Lord help me!" the Australian cried, and Katsu realized he was about to intervene. He ran at Matsui and, as the Commander raised the sword to strike again, he put his hand over the other man's and squeezed. The Colonel tried to jerk away, but Katsu's grip was like iron.

"Please step aside, honored Lieutenant Commander Matsui," he said. The older man felt his fingers being crushed, and now he noticed the blood splashed all over him. He nodded and let the Captain take the sword.

"Your turn then," he said. He stepped away to watch. Katsu raised the blade and the old priest looked up at him.

"One blow, son," he said, "Please! One blow!"

"Yes Father," Katsu said. "Forgive me."

"May God forgive you."

Katsu raised the blade, all his force focused, and down it flashed. The priest's gray head tumbled from his shoulders and rolled away.

"Good job, Captain," the Commander said in a smug tone. The troops let go of the bodies and stood.

"Perhaps you are not entirely obsolete, after all."

Katsu faced the older man, the bloody *katana* comfortable in his grip.

"Please do not speak to me just now, honored Lieutenant Colonel Matsui!" he said. For the first time, the Commander realized the mortal danger he was in, and felt fear. He gazed at the warrior standing before him. The man's shirt was a rag that hung open, and his trousers were a disgrace. But he also saw the bunched muscles in the arms, shoulders and stomach. Most clearly, he saw his own death shining in those dark eyes. At once, he bit off the insulting retort he'd been about to make.

"Yes, well...." Hastily he took a few steps and turned as if to admire the view. Katsu gasped for air and regained control of himself.

The natives, including the Sepik guides, saw the slaughter of the white men in mounting alarm. Someone shouted, and they all panicked and scattered.

"Shoot them!" the Commander called. The solders raised their rifles and brought the runners down. Minutes after they had arrived in Kissim, twelve bodies lay scattered on the ground.

The squad of nine took control of a nearby hill. They excavated a pit at the top and built a bunker of logs. Here, they lived and kept watch. Here, they were reasonably safe. But still, they must go for water, and scrounge for food, and then they were vulnerable.

Indeed, a patrol was ambushed. Two of Katsu's soldiers were killed with arrows. It was a terrible way to die, he thought, as he observed the spiked bodies. He ordered his men to set an ambush. They captured a native man and brought him before the Colonel. As it turned out, the prisoner knew some of the trade language.

The Colonel revealed a hidden talent. He sharpened some bamboo slivers and went to work on the captive. He slid them slowly under the man's fingernails. Within five minutes, the native had divulged that there were two more white men hidden with the villagers. The Commander ordered the man to take them there, at once. He balked.

Matsui had his men untie the native's loincloth and continued to work his spikes into sensitive areas. Within minutes, the fellow was hobbling through the jungle on his way to betray his people.

This time, although Katsu did not like the Colonel's methods of interrogation, he was in agreement with his leader. If they allowed the slaughter of their men to go unpunished, they would all die. They were outnumbered, running short of ammunition, and they must respond with strength. They hunted down and shot the white men, and every villager they saw. Peace returned to Kissim.

But then the enemy aircraft brought more soldiers. The Commander and all the Japanese were slaughtered, except one. Katsu was the last of the squad.

But what a disgrace! At least the men had not lived to see this—their Captain, a prisoner. And the thing that ate at Katsu's mind all the time since, was that he had been disarmed by a brute animal. Certainly, it was a fearsome monster. But it was a crocodile that had delivered him to the enemy.

And then, at the pivotal moment when he had the choice of death or surrender, he had succumbed. He let himself be taken prisoner. *Of course, the situation was always temporary,* he reminded himself now. *My escape was only a matter of when.*

Do not think so much, it is a mistake, his father's voice said in his mind. *Take rest when you cannot act, act the instant you can. This is the way of the warrior.*

The storm continued to rage. Katsu opened his eyes. He saw the enemy and knew he was fading like the day itself.

All that stands between me and freedom is this pitiful ogre. And he, too, is sick, I can see it. Still, I will not act. He points his rifle at me, but this is sure. In minutes, I will take him, and regain my katana. Again, he closed his eyes and breathed deeply.

The sword "Bizen," known to the men of my family as "Katsu-mushi-maru," has sung in battle in my hands, and the hands of my father, and his father, and all our forefathers, for three hundred years. I will regain the blade I was named for, and I will take my enemies' lives. Then I will go down the river and rejoin my country-men. I hope we will be shipped north to defend our homes and families when the gaijin invade. But if we must stay here and fight to the death, so be it.

The Australian grunted when the cramps squeezed his belly, and again Katsu opened his eyes. He watched the man as a snake studies an injured bird.

Footy knew he was in terrible trouble, and he glanced at Johnny, still slumped in the rain. *No help there.* He flashed another look at the enemy and saw him staring coldly back.

"You move, Jap, and I'll shoot!" The pilot kept him covered, while his other hand undid his shorts. Footy jerked them down and sat back on the root as the first stream spewed out. On and on it went, wave after wave, until he grew faint and panicked.

Shoot him now! He ordered his finger to pull the trigger, but somehow the rifle barrel was in the mud. With enormous effort, he hauled it up.

Katsu looked into the metal hole and was fascinated, wonder-ing which beat of his heart would be the last. But suddenly the Australian doubled over.

Footy's vision seared white, and static deafened his ears. He was aware as if from a long way off that he was falling.

Katsu watched the enemy topple into the mud, the rifle drop-ping from his hands.

Now act!

He stood and went to kill the man.

CHAPTER 16

It was during Gwyn's second month in London that she fell for the English pilot. Reginald flew fighters and had come out on the losing end of a clash with the Luftwaffe. She'd assisted in the surgery where most of the shrapnel was removed from his side. A few shards were too tangled in nerves and blood vessels, and these he would have to live with.

The pilot's friend and squadron leader, a man not much older than the patient, came by when he could. He told Gwyn the aviator was from northern England, somewhere near the border with Scotland, and had only his infirm mother left alive. The pilot was alone, and Gwyn came by to visit on her own time. The flyer, who insisted she call him Reggie, was obviously grateful.

Professionally, Gwyn nursed Reggie back to health, while privately, she tumbled for him. He had a rakish look—a flop of auburn hair and sleepy, knowing eyes. He had the dry, self-deprecating humor she'd learned to appreciate in her father. But beneath his sardonic exterior, Gwyn perceived that he was kind, intelligent, and mature beyond his nineteen years.

It developed that many nights, her shift done, Gwyn sat with him for several hours. On one occasion, while the rest of the ward slept, Reggie reached for her hand and she did not pull away. At first ironically, and then more seriously when she did not make fun of him, he began to draw word pictures of a life they might share after the war.

They would find a cottage in the countryside near Bowness-on-Solway, where he was from. He said he'd raise sheep and do some fishing. He told her it was the most beautiful country in God's world, but he also was anxious to hear about her home. Gwyn described the wild mountains and orchard country of British Columbia. Reggie said maybe he was wrong: they'd live there instead. He had read as well about skiing and the hot springs in Banff, in Alberta's Rocky Mountains, and was keen for a visit.

A few nights later, he put his hand behind her head, drew her to him, and kissed her on the mouth. Gwyn found her heart beating like a humming bird's wings.

Another week, and Reggie dared slip his hand under her blouse. Aroused and alarmed, Gwyn permitted some exploration, and then pulled away. By training, she was a modern woman—by her morals, an old fashion one. Both aspects warned against rushing into a sexual encounter. In addition, there was the sobering reality of the men in the other beds who were sleeping—or worse, pretending to.

Gwyn was determined that, as far as consummating a relationship was concerned, she would wait for marriage. It might be quaint, but she was a virgin. She intended to find the love of her life and live with him forever. During high school in Peachland, one of her teenage friends had gotten "in the family way," as it was whispered. She vanished for a year. The girl's parents put it about that, on account of her asthma, she was staying with relatives. But as some wag said, the infection had entered somewhat lower than the lungs. In fact, as in all small communities, the truth was known to all.

Then, at the nursing school in the city, three students were forced to drop out due to pregnancies. She made a solemn vow that such ruinous behavior would not sabotage her.

Gwyn's weeks with Reggie became two months, and the doctors told him he could return to duty. His squadron leader had been his only regular visitor. At first Gwyn thought his visits did Reggie good, but when she realized that all the man talked about was the desperate need for pilots, she developed an aversion.

The night before he was to be released, Gwyn stayed with Reggie all night on the ward. He was quite mobile again by then, if a little weak. At midnight, he took her by the hand and led her down the stairs. They skirted the bombed out wing and entered the courtyard. For much of the day, it was crammed with staff and patients smoking, but at this hour, it was deserted.

Reggie went on a knee and proposed marriage. Her emotions awhirl, she barely heard him say he had no proper ring to give her. He swore there was a diamond coming, but in the meantime, he begged her to accept his signet ring. He also offered a photograph. Gwyn asked for more time, but she accepted his gifts, and in her heart she had already said yes. He rose, took her in a passionate embrace, and kissed her.

Early next morning, Reggie departed for his base. He left with a promise to see Gwyn the coming weekend. The car drove off, and it came to her that she'd never even been with him away from the hospital.

Saturday morning, however, it was not Reggie but his commander who showed up. Gwyn was at work on the ward when he took her by the elbow and guided her into a hallway.

Bluntly, he told her Reggie's Spitfire had been shot down. They were returning across the Channel from a successful mission, when the Messerschmitt came out of the blue. It opened up on Reggie from behind, and the attack was over in seconds. The squadron leader had been flying right beside him. He dove his own plane down, all the way to the water, even breaking radio silence to beg the pilot to bail out. But Reggie had not.

"Was there any chance...?" Gwyn rushed to ask, but the tears that formed in the man's eyes gave her the answer, and all her own hopes crashed and burned.

In the crucible of her suffering, Gwyn vowed never to get involved with a military man again. Through no fault of their own, they were untrustworthy. All she had left of Reggie were the pitiful gifts from the night he proposed. There was the ring, and the picture of him in the cockpit of his fighter, one hand raised, that ironic half-smile. Over Ruthie's protests, she shoved it into the coals and watched him bubble and flame away. She posted the signet ring back to his squadron leader with a note to return it to Reggie's mother.

Since meeting the flyer, she had written page after page in her diary. Now as she read it, she found it unbearable, the mawkish gushing of a schoolgirl. She locked the book, stuffed it in the bottom of her trunk, and did not touch it again.

Her anguish, Gwyn discovered, made her work far more difficult. It was hard to muster a kind word for a patient when she, herself, was in torment. Yet every day there came a new batch of patients who deserved nothing less than her best.

From then on, Gwyn put her calling first. She continued to treat everyone with compassion, while keeping a hard rein on how involved she let herself get with any individual.

But after her flyboy was gone, Gwyn found it difficult to remain at the hospital. The halls were haunted by more than the usual ghosts. She decided she must leave. She had read the news about the shortage of medical personnel in the South Pacific conflict, and made a decision she announced to Ruthie. To her surprise, her friend said she wanted to come along. She hadn't left Ireland, had she, only to meet more Englishmen! Could they not go together? And so the two applied for reassignment.

A month later, they were on a ship for Australia. They went north to the Territory of Papua on New Guinea Island, a place Gwyn had barely heard of. At the military hospital in Port Moresby, at last Gwyn had more than enough to distract her from her painful memories.

When the young women did get a day off at the same time, they ventured to the beach. Under a layer of coconut oil, Gwyn browned like a hazelnut. Ruthie, however, had to stay under her parasol, or her peaches-and-cream complexion would soon rival her hair. The young women enjoyed the outings, but would not swim. They were given dire warnings of the sharks and crocodiles that patrolled these waters. Nor were they to venture down here at night, the Australians told them, because the crocs came out. The nurses shuddered and stayed well away from the waves.

As for nightlife, there were some very rough taverns they would not even walk by. But they did go to dances at the better hotels. The entrances and public rooms were segregated between "men" and "ladies and escorts."

Of course, Port Moresby was still a military town. Again, the ratio of men to women was daunting. A girl could be danced off her feet all night, and still have a string of would-be suitors competing for her company, sometimes violently.

Both women preferred the invitation-only soirees at the plantations outside of town. The nurses became regular guests at the rather grand homes where the Aussie owners lived like rough royalty of the bush.

Sunday mornings, if they were not working, they went to church. Only the most hardened reprobates among the "expats" did not attend services. Ruthie went to mass at 8:00, while Gwyn attended the Methodist service at 10:00. She especially enjoyed the familiar old hymns, played by the minister's wife on her prized pump organ. Sunday afternoons, Gwyn was always at the Orphanage.

In fact, it was because of this project that the young women found themselves spending more time apart. Ruthie was happy to help out with the children now and then, but she did not share Gwyn's passion. As well, she now had a steady boyfriend.

He was nice enough, Gwyn thought, but she had her suspicions. He was an older man—all of twenty-seven, to Ruthie's twenty-three, and Gwyn worried that he had a wife and kiddies back in Aus. It would not be the first time a fellow conveniently forgot to mention his obligations. And then there was the matter of his name.

"Never trust a man who starts right off by telling you he's a 'Dick,'" Gwyn cautioned her friend, only half teasing. She could see Ruthie was crazy about the government clerk, but she did not want her friend to get hurt again. Since she'd known her, she'd watched her Irish friend go through a number of painful dissolutions. Whatever Dick's real intentions, they both knew it would soon come to a head. The man was due back in Aus in a few weeks, and then they would discover if Ruthie was part of his future, or once more, was left in the dust.

There was always something for Gwyn to do. She had a new child to settle in. Only yesterday, a friend of hers, old "Trader Ben," had returned from another expedition through the far-off villages. He brought with him a seven-year-old girl whose entire clan had been killed in a mudslide. The rest of the village considered her taboo, and she had been abandoned. Gwyn did her best to calm the terrified youngster, introduced her to roommates her own age, got her bathed, treated her head lice, and talked her into wearing new clothes.

When Gwyn had volunteered for overseas service, she had planned to be gone from Canada for two years. After that, she expected to return and pursue her career in Vancouver. But already she'd already been gone longer than that, and her commitment to the children of the "Good Shepherd" grew deeper each day. Still, she had not acknowledged even to herself that she was going to stay on in New Guinea.

She did wonder what a life here had to offer. In this far outpost of the civilized world, could she find a good man to love? Would she ever have a family of her own? She decided that if and when she gave her heart to a man, there would be no half-measures. Therefore, she would not do it lightly.

Her solitary state was not for a lack of suitors. One in particular was a former soldier. When Gwyn first met him, he was a Corporal in the Australian Army. He first encountered the nurse at a party at a friend's plantation. Immediately, he'd been smitten by the girl with the lovely green eyes. They danced together, and went out in a group of friends, and he soon let her know he was "dead keen" on her. But Gwyn gave the spirited rejoinder that she had zero interest in military men.

She'd offered friendship instead, and the man had settled for that. When he had Gwyn on his arm, he was the envy of all his mates. Then, a few months back, he told her his time in the service was over. He was a natural mechanic, and a mate had taught him to fly a plane, although he never had a formal lesson. Still, he got up in every crate he could, and boasted there was nothing men had made with wings that he could not fly. He announced to Gwyn that he intended to establish an air cargo service between Aus and the New Guinea Territories.

Glen, better known as "Footy," let her know he had never given up on her. He even went so far as to say that he'd traded in the uniform for a chance with her. In return, all he wanted was an opportunity to prove himself.

In fact, Gwyn was very fond of Footy. He was colorful, cheerful, an interesting companion at a dinner or dance, and his prospects looked good. But Gwyn had not yet felt her heart move on his behalf.

Now, how bizarre it was that he should be lost in the wilds of the island with the one man to whom Gwyn truly was attracted! Johnny touched her somewhere beyond her intellect. She felt that, under other than the circumstances of war, he might be a fun guy. They both loved the outdoors, and had read a lot of the same books. When he described hiking in the California mountains, or surfing off Oahu, she'd seen the joy come alive in him. On top of that, he was determined and persistent, two admirable qualities. She observed how hard he worked to get mobile again, and how he'd lobbied for his dream, no matter how misbegotten she thought it was.

More than that, Gwyn knew he was attracted to her. She'd have to be blind not to see it. She probably knew it better than he did. She caught herself wishing she'd met him before the war, before the years of turmoil and death had changed him. If they'd met on a beach in Honolulu when they were both teenagers, would they have liked one another?

But there was no getting around it, he was a professional killer. More than that, he liked his work. He seemed to live only in order to kill again. When she'd discovered that, she had been extremely disappointed. *And why was that?* she asked herself. *He was just one more soldier, one more patient.* She barely knew the man.

When Gwyn contrasted the reality of Johnny with the love she desired, the differences were obvious. She wanted someone full of life and joy. Someone who could face the knocks that were sure to come, with resilience and enthusiasm. She desired someone who approved of her being the strong woman she was, but would be there to lean on when she needed him.

In her heart-of-hearts, she wanted a lover with whom she could be her true self. She longed for someone who would forgive her faults, and love her just as she was, and she would give the same in return. She waited for the man on whom she could lavish all she had to give, for as long as she lived.

It was a tall order, she knew. She was idealistic, maybe naive, compared with modern girls like Ruthie. In fact, although Gwyn told her friend most things, she did not reveal these deep secrets of her heart for that very reason.

All her ruminating came down to this question: was Johnny Willman for her? The fact was, she did not know. At times, she doubted it severely. Yet, when Ruthie told her Doc Mac had turned the soldier loose, it was she who'd gone looking for him! Then, face-to-face with the soldier, in spite of the defenses she'd built, she'd offered to have a date with him. *What was I thinking?*

He'd stood her up, but that did not change the fact that she had compromised her promise to eschew military men. Night after night, she lay in her solitary bed, pondering these things in her heart. But what was the point? Johnny was lost in the New Guinea wilderness. She wondered then, *does he think about me? Does he care?* And she was forced to lecture herself, she did not even know if he lived. Her intuition said yes, but she felt he was in terrible danger.

Protect him—she loosed it like an arrow into the night. *I know he is damaged goods, but whether he's for me or not, keep him safe!* Gwyn strained to hear some sort of answer, anything at all, but the vast darkness brooded in silence. She lay aching until she was overcome by exhaustion.

The next day, all of Port Moresby was in an uproar. The news traveled like wildfire. The Americans had dropped some devastating new bomb on Japan, and it promised to be the end of the war. Gwyn joined in the general celebration.

But she worried that in all the commotion, Johnny and the others would be forgotten.

The Father drifted in the darkness. It held its torn leg stiffly and let the current carry it. Only when it had to breathe did it rise. Its head broke the surface, it unsealed ears, eyes and nostrils, and sipped the air. It observed a dull gray day and felt the beat of raindrops on its skull.

Forked lighting struck a tree beside the river and it exploded in a fireball. The Father experienced a gush of fear at the sound, very like the attacks that had hurt it. At once it sank into liquid silence. It drifted deep with the scent of the rain in its lungs.

When the crocodile rose again, there were no more explosions, but the shower continued. It navigated close to the bank and found it flooded. The current was swirling into wide new territory. On impulse, the great predator let the water push it along. As it slid over the lip, it brushed its flayed leg and hissed. Then it was coursing through the shallows.

Ever since its injury, its body had attempted to heal. But recently, the leg had been brutally damaged again. Now something was deep inside it, worrying the joint. A cyst had formed around the alien object. The bullet damage to its foreleg had been severe, but in the reptilian way, it was regenerating a foot. It would never re-grow the toes and claws, but skin and scales were forming a clubfoot.

The energy to cope with the agony, and the process of healing, consumed its stores of energy. The infection that made it nauseous came in waves, but at this time, the Father was hungry. Across the muddy shallows it saw a hump of land with a tree on it. Suddenly its senses were on high alert. Its eyes tracked prey there. One of the two-legged animals stood near the water. The crocodile submerged and sped that way.

The man looked across the flood, wondering when he could leave. The flashflood had turned the mudflat into a lake covered with torn vegetation.

Alarm spiked. Lines of ripples were coming at him. It might be driftwood, but that was wrong. This cut across the current!

The wake stopped at his feet. A gigantic head, bigger than he was, burst from the water. He barely glimpsed the scarred eye as the jaws flew open. The teeth embraced him before he could scream. All his flesh quivered and came apart.

The other men marooned on the island woke with hideous death stalking among them.

CHAPTER 17

The Japanese stood up on the island created by the flood. His time had come. His enemies had been conquered by the belly sickness and it would be easy to kill them. The American was unconscious and the other, the rude one, had just fallen in the mud. These two had treated him well enough, the prisoner thought. In return, Katsu would give them the gift of a swift death—his sword across their necks.

He took a step, his tied hands reaching for his *katana* in the Australian's pack, but suddenly he felt carved in two. The intense agony knocked him on his knees and he vomited, while filth blasted into his trousers. *I am sick as well!* But he was samurai, and an officer of the Empire. He forced his body to crawl to the Australian. But again, weakness betrayed him, and he fell on his side while the inner storm rattled his limbs.

After a time, the intestinal tumult eased, if only a little. Again, he ordered his limbs to move, but they were wooden and belonged to someone else. The Australian was almost within reach, yet the distance was interminable. He lay hyperventilating, mustering his strength. He stared at the enemy and saw the vacant eyes, the loose neck.

With supreme effort, Katsu raised himself to seize his *katana*, but as his hands came up, they seemed to draw a sword through his own entrails. The affliction knocked him flat on his back once more. Again, he soiled himself as his body tumbled uncontrollably down the slope and into the water.

Rise! Take our katana and do your duty! It was his father's furious voice. Katsu tried to obey, but his body jackknifed repeatedly and his eyes stopped displaying the world.

I will do it soon, I promise, Father. He lay half submerged in the flood. Now he was unconscious, with only the merest flutter of his chest to betray that any life remained.

Above him, a man sat slumped on a rock, also senseless. The rain continued to fall, and gradually this one toppled sideways and fell. A third man curled in the mud beneath the tree.

All were oblivious, exposed to the elements and whatever else would come their way.

—●—

By degrees, Johnny returned to his senses. He was aware of a wretched smell, but could do nothing except breathe through his mouth. Rain continued to fall on him, but it had eased a little. It came to him it was late afternoon, night was coming on, and he had been lying on the rock for a very long time. His whole side was numb. He stretched out his legs and felt the painful prickle of returning sensation. At last he was able to sit up. His pack lay in the sludge, but he did not remember taking it off. He stared up at black tree limbs against a bruised sky, and then at the reddish lake all around.

Slowly, Johnny recalled what had happened. He saw Footy in a fetal position among the tree roots. The pilot still had his pack on, the two rifles beside him.

The Jap! A wave of distress shot through Johnny and he stared around the knoll, but there were only two of them on the island. The day grew darker and Johnny saw the Aussie fight for consciousness. Eventually Footy's eyes flickered open, and he groaned and struggled to rise. His lower body was exposed and he got his shorts up. He managed to shrug out of his pack and then keeled over and passed out.

Johnny forced himself to stand. His legs quaked as he reeled to the water, crouched, and rinsed himself and his trousers. He stood, got his sodden pants done up, wobbled to Footy, and slumped against the tree. He fumbled for the rifles and propped them upright. He sat stunned while night came on. Eventually the Aussie cracked a bloodshot eye and squinted at him.

"Bleedin' hell. Reckon I blew me arse off." He wrinkled his nose. "What a pong! Who died—was it me?" He got on all fours, crawled to the water, sluiced out his shorts and scrubbed his bum, then crawled back and lay shivering under the tree.

"That was ghastly," he muttered. "I'd rather have Christmas with the nuns than do that again." His eyes fluttered shut and he began to snore.

Johnny forced himself to crawl to his pack. He dragged it back and stood it against the trunk, then propped Footy's beside it.

There was something clamoring in his fevered mind for attention, and he tried to grasp it, but it would not come. He slumped lower as the rain marched in sheets across the black lagoon.

Johnny found he was famished. His belly felt caved in, but the prospect of digging out something to eat was too much. His head felt huge and he thought he would remove his helmet, but his hands would not rise.

The night crept over him and stole his mind.

Johnny awoke in a dull and dismal morning and gazed across a field of mud. *Where am I?* He was only vaguely interested. After some minutes, it came back—the dysentery, the rain, the island. He turned and saw Footy asleep on the dirt.

At last Johnny remembered—*the Jap is gone!* His eyes darted over the island that had become a hill again, but there was no enemy. Panic jolted him and he checked the rifles—*both against the tree.* He pushed himself to stand and gazed around.

He was on a hill of dirty grass in a sea of mud. Fifty yards off, the surly river flowed between its banks once more, under a leaden sky. Johnny forced himself to walk in a full circle. *No Jap.* He was anxious and his still-tender stomach did flip-flops. He knelt and went through his things—*pistol and knives on my belt. Everything is in my pack.* He checked Footy and the man seemed to have his gear as well.

The sword! Johnny saw it standing in Footy's backpack, and relief flooded him. *But the prisoner wouldn't leave without his sword—or our guns! And why are we alive?* He pondered that every which way, but could not explain it.

Johnny shook the other man. "Come on buddy! Wake up!" At last Footy opened his crusted eyes.

"Bloody hell! Are you still here?"

"Listen!" Johnny said. "The Jap is gone."

"Ooo, I've been through the wringer," the pilot groaned, propping himself on an elbow. "What do you mean—gone?" He pulled his hat off and knocked the clods of mud against the tree.

"Gone. As in scrammed, vamoosed, skedaddled."

Footy grunted, worked his way to his feet and tottered to the edge of the mudflat. "Why didn't he kill us? Why didn't he take his bleedin' sword—or our guns?"

"Or the food?" Johnny asked. "But he didn't." Footy scratched a bite in his whiskers and suddenly sucked in his breath.

"Crikey! Company!" He pointed and Johnny looked, but saw nothing. Then the mud shifted, and he made out the crocodile. It rushed in their direction and froze again, and Johnny saw the alien eyes staring at him. He noticed motion in another direction—another croc.

"Look!"

"Struth!" Footy was pointing as well. There were at least a dozen predators coming from all sides, intent on the men.

"Let's get out of here!" Johnny said.

"How? Where?"

Johnny pointed to the ribbon of puddles that had been the path, and the place it climbed into the jungle.

"There!"

He stepped to his pack and hauled it on, noticing that the illness had stolen his strength. Footy grunted into his own load, and the men snatched up their rifles.

"River crocs," the Aussie wheezed. "Not giants like the Father, but bad enough. Any one of these bastards can take us."

"We can shoot our way out," Johnny said. "But there are too many."

"No good," Footy agreed. "And we're short on ammo. You want to wander New Guinea without a gun?" The men went to the edge of the knoll, ready to leap off and run. But they'd have to negotiate deep mud and flooded sections. And now there were four crocs between themselves and the path.

"They'll be on us faster 'n a dingo on a duck," Footy said.

Johnny strode to the top to stare down the other side of the hill. He stopped when he saw the ring of predators approaching. The first was a big brute that had just reached the hill. It rushed up at Johnny. He jumped back and whirled to look at the tree. The attacker hissed and waddled closer.

"Climb!" Johnny yelled. He slung his rifle over his shoulder, sprang to the tree and swung up. Footy turned to do the same. Johnny got his hands around the lowest branch as the big male arrived below. It was ten feet long and thick as a barrel. Johnny pulled up just as the croc lunged. Its jaw ground his boot against the trunk. He got his butt on the branch, but his pack jammed under the next limb, and his legs dangled down.

The croc fell and immediately jumped again, jaws open. Johnny jerked his legs up in the nick of time, and the croc's teeth crunched into the branch he was sitting on. It hung for a second and belly-flopped to earth. Johnny tugged his pack free and stood up. *Where's Footy?*

The Aussie had skidded to a stop when the bull came between him and the tree. Now another slipped up behind him.

"Come on!" Johnny yelled, trying to balance himself and get his rifle ready, but it tangled in the branches.

The big one faced Footy and roared. More crocs climbed the knoll on all sides. The Aussie was surrounded and he froze.

"For your life, get up!" Johnny yelled.

The Aussie stared around, the crocs slid closer, and Johnny could not get his rifle free.

Then Footy did something that looked like suicide.

Chapter 18

Footy slung down his pack as five scaled brutes came at him. He reached inside and pulled out a leaf package. He opened it and bamboo shoots spilled out.

"Bloody hell!" He shoved his arm back in. More vegetables, which he threw away. Finally he came up with a slab of pork.

"Take this, you rotten bastards!" He lobbed the meat between two crocs and they hissed and turned for it. Johnny was still trying to get his rifle loose from the twigs so he could shoot. Footy dug in his pack again, and came up with more pig. This he tossed in another direction, and three more predators jostled away. But in the meantime, six of them had come up the grass.

Footy probed deep and came up with his last roast. He bounced it in his hand as he looked at the big male between him and the tree. Its head went up and down, following the bouncing pork. Footy dropped it and kicked hard. The meat struck the croc between the eyes, zoomed off and splashed into the pile he'd made in his illness.

The croc didn't seem to mind. Its head went sideways and it scooped up the meat and the muck. Footy grabbed his pack in one hand, rifle in the other, and ran directly at it. The bull grunted and spread brown-stained jaws to welcome him. The Aussie made a desperate leap, cleared the snout, landed between the croc's eyes, and used it as a springboard.

A croc ran from each side and launched at him. Footy got his arm through a pack strap and wrapped it over the branch. He shoved his rifle at the Yank.

"Help!"

Johnny grabbed the firearm and pulled, dragging the Aussie behind it. The leaping crocs missed his legs and, jaws wide, slammed together. Teeth clashed like hammers and they tumbled down on the big one.

Footy let go of the rifle, grabbed the tree and clung there. With the weight suddenly gone, a rifle in each hand, Johnny lurched backward along the branch. He would have fallen if he had not thudded against the trunk. The big croc snapped at the two on top of it, and they hissed and backed off.

Johnny regained his balance and found his Springfield had come free. Footy stood up beside him and took his rifle back. The quarters were close, and Johnny got out of his pack. With one hand, he shoved it up and set it on the next branch. He climbed after it, and continued until he found a good place to perch. Footy came up as well and stopped on the limb below. The two stared down at the scaly reception party.

"Strike me pink!" Footy panted. "I was nearly a *pookpook* sandwich."

"I guess we know what happened to the Jap," Johnny said.

"Struth! One of those buggers got him!"

"Only way he'd go without his sword, or our stuff," Johnny said. "But now what?"

"Yes mate—now what?"

The men considered this while fifteen crocodiles milled below. The big male nipped each one that came too close. They, in turn, edged away, pushing others. The cluster maneuvered until they lay around the trunk like spokes in a wheel.

Footy looked down and hooted like a monkey. The reptiles cocked their heads. Johnny drank from his canteen. Footy took a swig from his own.

Johnny remembered the brandy and, feeling weak from the sickness and now jittery, it struck him as a fine idea. *We're stuck up here for who knows how long?* He pulled it out, uncorked it, and took a swallow. It went down like sweet fire. He tapped Footy with the bottle. The Aussie looked at what he was being offered.

"A little early in the day, isn't it mate?"

The absurdity of that, here in a mud patch a million miles from anywhere, made Johnny laugh. Footy got the joke and neighed as well. He grabbed the brandy from the Yank and took a long pull.

The men drank until it was a third gone, and their heads were spinning. Johnny put the cork in the bottle and returned it to his pack. He pulled out some wrapped pork.

"Lunch," he grinned at Footy. "You don't mind if I dig in?" The Aussie suddenly realized he had no food left. Johnny let the leaf wrapper flutter down while he bit in. The reptiles fought over the scrap and tore it to shreds.

"Mula was right, their *mumu* is the best!" Johnny said with his mouth full. "Too bad you decided to feed the lizards."

"Not the time to play 'silly buggers,'" Footy said anxiously. "Give us a bite, would you?"

Johnny took another mouthful and chewed. "Mmmmm!"

"Stop taking the piss out of me!" Footy said. "Now, be a mate!"

"Sure—if you say 'please Johnny,'" he laughed with his mouth full.

"Up yours with barbed wire—sideways!" Footy whined. "Don't make me shoot you!" Johnny finished the meat and extracted some beans he forked in with his fingers.

"Bloody hell!" Footy snapped. "You're a right bugga, you know that? Alright Johnny, stop being a bloody wanker and give me a bloody bite to eat. Please."

"Now was that so hard?" Johnny asked. "Here you go!" He extracted another piece of pork, held it out and let it tumble.

"Crikey!" Footy lunged for it. He swayed alarmingly, but caught it, and the crocs craned up. He had to stuff the meat in his mouth and use both hands to clutch the branch. The big bull clawed up the tree trunk, snout just below his dangling feet.

Johnny chuckled and dropped a pack of veggies. One hand free, the meat between his teeth, Footy just managed to grab it. Eyes bulging, he glared up at the Yank.

Johnny stared down at the filthy face, the hat back and the hair every which way, a slab of meat protruding from the mouth. He chortled wildly and was forced to grab the tree for balance. Footy watched the Yank snorting, helmet jiggling, and the sheer silliness cut through his exasperation. He launched into spasms of high-pitched laughter.

The crocodiles watched carefully, and understood nothing.

Finally, the men chuffed to a ragged stop. They wiped their eyes and ate in silence. The crocodiles smelled the meat, and this they did comprehend.

"You know about crocs," Johnny said. "Do they eat their own kind?"

"Shore," Footy said. "Bloody cannibals, the lot of them."

"Nice bunch," Johnny observed. "Right at home in New Guinea. There are more than twenty now. We can't shoot them all. How 'bout this?" He told Footy his idea.

"Hardly counts as a plan at all," the Aussie complained.

"Got a better one?"

"No."

"Want to do it?"

"Right then. I'm with you."

Johnny swung down beside Footy. They helped one another get their packs on. The crocodiles saw the movement and stirred hopefully.

Johnny and Footy aimed their rifles at the hind end of the big male.

"Ready?" Johnny asked.

"Ready mate."

"Fire!" Two rifles clapped almost simultaneously. On each side of the bull's tail, just behind its back legs, a chunk blew out. Blood misted the air and the wounded croc shuddered and whipped around to nose its injuries. Its kin flinched away at the noise, then came instantly back on the tang of fresh blood. Eagerly, they snuffled for the source.

The injured croc bolted for the river, dragging its broken tail. At once the others were on the blood trail. The gang slid down the slope on their bellies and ran across the mud flat. Johnny and Footy reloaded and prepared to jump.

The bull was slowed by the weight of its tail. Its nearest pursuer caught up and bit the gaping wound. In its agony, the male shot for the sky, crashed down and bit its attacker. The two rolled across the field. They came to a stop with the big male belly up. It struggled to roll over, but more crocs rushed in and one bit the neck. The wounded bull's jaws flapped impotently while others chomped into its body. Scales ruptured and blood gushed.

The men could no longer see the injured animal because of the pile-on. But then it heaved from the scrum and rushed for the river, the rest close behind. It reached the bank, dove in, and tried to lash away, but went nowhere. The tail canted uselessly to the side, and only the stump swung. A free-for-all erupted in the shallows. The next bite tore the tail clean off, and then teeth slammed in from all sides.

The bull's head sank and its last breath burbled up. Tan water turned to burgundy.

"Go!" Johnny yelled. He and Footy jumped together. They skidded down the muddy bank, splashed through a pool, and dashed for the trail.

They went by the carnivore picnic, and at last they were seen. A twelve-footer charged them, running faster than the men thought possible. It closed in from behind, and at the last second, Johnny jumped one way, and Footy the other. The croc lunged, and the head came between them, jaws spread. Then it belly flopped and went skidding through the mud, while the men bounded on.

Johnny's boots were weighed with great clods, he was still half sick, and the brandy was sour in his throat. Spots pinged before his eyes. Footy got ahead, intent on the trail where it climbed into the jungle. But now two more crocs raced from the sides to cut them off.

Johnny frantically lengthened his stride, hit a patch of slick clay, and went horizontal in the air. He slammed down full-length, and all his wind was knocked out. For agonizing heartbeats, he lay unable to move, while the soldier shouted at him. At last he struggled onto hands and knees, but could not breathe.

Footy and a crocodile converged. It charged, he jumped, and the croc's jaws just missed as it went by. The thick tail swung, clipped his legs, and the Aussie did a cartwheel. The reptile turned to take him.

Johnny still could not get air, but his Springfield was in his hands. His face was covered in mud, but he forced himself to kneel and aim, sure Footy was done for. Somehow the Aussie sprang up, the croc right on him. Though his eyes were bleary, Johnny managed to shoot it, high behind the forelegs. *Spine shot!* The animal rolled and lay still. Footy tore across the last few yards and bounded into the forest.

Johnny's diaphragm convulsed, but he still could not breathe. He forced himself to stand and smeared the mud out of his eyes as he ran. He went by Footy's croc and saw that it watched him, but could not move.

But then another one skidded onto the path in front of him and turned his way, tail flicking. It was between him and the trees. He glanced back and saw the whole pack coming. He knew his rifle was not loaded and he was out of time. The croc hissed and rushed him.

But then its head bounced hard. Johnny heard the shot and glimpsed Footy, rifle smoking at his shoulder. The predator ripped a terrible burp into Johnny's face and swayed. He took a couple of steps back, counted three as he ran, and leaped high. He went over the croc's shoulders, caught a glimpse of the hole leaking blood in the back of the head, landed on his feet and pelted on.

He high stepped through the puddles and reached the edge of the mudflat. He was done in, but he ordered his burning legs to make a final push, and scrambled up the trail. At the top of the rise, he fell on his knees. He was about to pass out when, at long last, he was able to suck in a searing lungful of air.

And there was a filthy Footy, leaning on his rifle.

"G'day Yank," the Aussie grinned. "The buggers are still coming. We better shake a leg."

Johnny nodded weakly—it was all he could do. He pulled himself up on his rifle. Footy jogged ahead, and Johnny followed into the rainforest. Overhead, a cockatoo flared its yellow crest and shrieked at them. When they were sure they had outrun the crocodiles, they slowed, but kept walking.

"You should see yourself, mate," Footy gasped over his shoulder.

"You too," Johnny puffed. "You look dipped in *pookpook pekpek*."

CHAPTER 19

They climbed a jungle-clad promontory. It thrust into the Raub, falling into the water in a series of mudslides. Johnny and Footy followed the trail. Still recovering from the sickness, they were much slower than usual, and had to pause frequently to catch their breath. They soon drained their water bottles.

They were grateful when they approached the top, and the slope grew more gradual. They came to a spring bubbling through moss. They paused to slurp water and fill their canteens. They stripped, washed the mud off themselves and their clothes, and spread the wet things over the branches to dry.

Both men were hungry—a good sign, they agreed. It meant they were on the mend. The sun dried their clothes while they lay back on the vegetation and smoked.

"Blimey I'm hungry," Footy said. "I could eat a kangaroo."

"You do that?" Johnny asked.

"Shore mate," Footy said. "A 'roo's meat is dark, but good with a sauce."

"Never thought about eating kangaroos!" Johnny said. "Me, I'd go for a T-bone steak, cooked over charcoal. Seared outside, pink in the middle." His mouth watered.

"Aww, put a sock in it!" Footy moaned. "I'm so hungry I could turn bloody cannibal."

"Don't look at me when you say that," Johnny said. Footy chuckled and they lay quiet in the sun.

"What made us sick?" Johnny wondered after a time.

"Who knows in this bloody place?" Footy replied. "The last water we drank—maybe something died. But it could have been anything..."

"...the food in Mula's village. A bite from an insect." Johnny paused. "I've got malaria as well."

"Me too," Footy said, "but then, who doesn't? You still reckon a croc got the Jap?"

"I guess so," Johnny said. "It was tough enough for us with our rifles."

"And in broad daylight. Bloody right," Footy said. "I reckon a croc found him in the night and gave him a pull into the drink..."

"...and that's all she wrote," Johnny finished. He started to dress. "Still, I didn't come this far to have that Jap take us out. Let's keep our eyes peeled."

"Yes mate," Footy said, getting into his clothes. "We should have put him out of our misery long ago."

"Maybe you're right," Johnny conceded. "But he was our mission—all that was left of it. Now there's nothing to do but hump to the coast and flag a ride out."

The men hiked down the far side of the hill. Darkness came while they were at it. They ate the last food they had left, cold sweet potatoes, and slept in the jungle by the trail.

In the morning they pushed on. The storm had knocked the humidity out, and the air was fresh. Not long after, they skidded down the final incline and emerged in a field beside the river. They were both preoccupied with their hunger.

They hiked on, and at last, late in the afternoon, they found more native gardens. They had no idea whose lands they were on, and they approached with rifles ready, but the place was deserted. In fact, they had seen no one since they left Mula. They pulled up mounds of sweet potatoes and knocked off the dirt. They discarded those riddled by insects and stuffed the rest in their packs. They found beans in hairy pods and stripped handfuls of these as well.

They lit a fire and boiled the beans, and wolfed them down while the sweet potatoes roasted. When these were ready, they dragged them out with their knives. The men ate several each until they were stuffed, and saved some for the following day.

In the twilight, Johnny tied his hammock between trees and Footy spread his blanket. Even though they had seen no people, they agreed they must continue to stand watch. They took turns, Johnny first. He found it strange not to have to think about the prisoner, feed him or truss him up, but it did make things easier.

Shortly after sunrise next morning, they set off, eating cold *kaukau* as they went. They hiked along the river, ignoring the ever more numerous trails that turned inland. These, and frequent gardens, were ample evidence of natives, but there was no one around, and this was disturbing.

In mid afternoon, they approached another mudflat. They paused at the edge and gazed uneasily across. It was a lot like the place where they'd been sick, then attacked by the crocodiles. They studied the field carefully, and Johnny panned it with his scope, but they saw none of the predators. Still, they kept their rifles ready and began to pick their way across.

Up ahead was a hill with a tree on it. It was uncannily like the one they'd taken refuge on in the storm. *The one where the Jap got killed,* Johnny thought. Carrion birds circled over it, and they approached on high alert.

Their alarm increased when they saw corpses strewn in the shrubbery. They had to work their way by a number of lower intervening mounds that blocked their view. When they came around the last hillock, they saw some distance away, a long imprint in the mud. Now they noticed the footprints and heavy indentation of the body, going to the river. They followed the marks until they were close to the clear impression of a huge crocodile.

"The Father!" Johnny breathed, the hair rising on his neck.

"The very same," Footy agreed. "Unless there are two bastards this big, and the chances of that are as good as me making Pope." The men covered the field with their rifles, but there was no sign of the animal. Johnny began to measure the length. He started at the tip of the tail and walked beside it, counting his paces. Footy paused to marvel at the size of the clawed back foot. This was the very one that had almost crushed his head in Kissim.

They continued by the wide boat of the belly. They came to the hole left by a foreleg and saw there were no claw marks. Any tiny shred of doubt about the monster's identity was gone. Now they were at the head, and Johnny kept counting to the tip of the snout.

"Ten paces," he said. "At least thirty feet long."

"Blimey!" Footy said. "That's three times the length of the bull we shot back there!"

The men stared up the hillock. It was not big enough for the Father to hide, but they saw the raw earth where its claws had plowed the grass. They climbed to the torn corpses. Hawks lifted off, and the men saw native faces missing the eyes.

"They wouldn't feed if the croc was close," Footy said.

"So says you," Johnny muttered. Both men turned frequently with rifles ready. They continued through blood splashes and Footy stumbled over a torn-off head, then a leg. Blowflies buzzed everywhere. The stench of death made them retch.

They moved to the upwind side of the knoll and skirted the remains of another victim. They approached the tree. Beneath it, the ground was particularly torn up, and body parts were strewn all around. Johnny said the only way to tell how many men died here was to do a head count—literally. There were five of them.

"They're from a tribe we haven't seen before," he said. The dead men's hair was in long ringlets, woven with white beads.

"Job's tears," Footy observed.

"What's that?"

"The beads—they're called 'Job's tears,' because they grow by the thousands."

"These fellows found a lot more trouble than old Job," Johnny said. From their vantage, the men studied the mudflat. Strangely, there was only a one-way trail made by the Father, and it went to the river.

"It swam in on the flood and then walked out," Footy said. "But we must be careful. Crocs often stay near their kill."

"Let's go," Johnny said. The men walked the rest of the way across the mud with their rifles at their shoulders. They breathed easier in the forest again, and felt better when they'd put some miles between themselves and the scene of the crocodile's most recent rampage.

At last they came to another open, grassy riverbank. Again, they looked hard, but saw no sign of their hunter. Neither were there any natives.

The river was wild and beautiful. Storks and egrets hunted the shallows, and ducks careened overhead. Johnny would have liked to shoot one for dinner, but knew they couldn't waste the ammo.

Soon they found more gardens, interspersed with groves of papaya and bananas. They pulled off two of the football-size "pawpaws," as Footy called them, and ate them right there. They sliced them in half, scraped out the glistening seeds, and spooned the fruit in. They added several more, and bananas, to their bulging packs.

They hiked on, and the land grew flatter. The flood-swollen Raub remained wider than usual. They were truly in the tropical lowlands now, and the heat grew ever more oppressive. They hung their towels over their shoulders to mop the sweat from their eyes.

The path grew into a broad band of clay. It was clear that they approached another village, but still, they did not encounter a single soul. Eventually, in the distance they saw a grouping of huts and went closer.

"Still no one," Johnny said low.

"Not a dog, any animal," Footy observed.

"And no smoke," Johnny added.

They reached the houses and walked between them. They called out, stuck their heads through doorways, and found all of them vacant. Johnny ducked into one and crouched by the fire pit. He touched his fingers to the ash and sniffed.

"No one here for a long time," he said.

A dog began to howl. The men moved that way and the keening grew louder. They were approaching yet another hovel, when the dog appeared in the doorway. It was ancient, its muzzle gray, ribs standing out under loose skin. Its eyes were misty marbles.

"Blind," Footy said.

"And left behind," Johnny added.

The men kept going, and exited the village. A path went into the jungle and took them between two chest-high boulders, each crowned with a human skull. They went on through a thicket and came out in a silent, grassy clearing. It was dominated by the ruin of a giant A-frame, very much like Bumay's house.

"*House Tambaran*," Footy said. "Another men's spirit house." It was obvious some catastrophe had occurred here. Only the vertical support poles were left standing. There were about twenty of these trunks of forest giants.

"I've heard they bury a head beneath each of these poles," the pilot said. Around them lay the rest of the building, a jumble of broken beams, crushed walls and grass thatching.

The men went to the first trunk and Footy stopped beside it. It towered fifty feet up. The long ridgepole lay nearby, a backbone in the rubble.

"Look!" the Aussie said. There were punctures in the wood. "Bullet holes, I reckon. Big caliber."

Johnny stuck a finger in one and studied the angle.

"It came from above. I guess the place was strafed by fighters."

"Now why would anyone shoot up a spirit house?" Footy wondered.

"Let's find out," Johnny said. The men picked their way through the ruin and Johnny pulled up a piece of matting.

"Here!" he called and Footy scrambled over. They were looking at the skeleton of a man, and he was no native. The bones wore a Japanese helmet and uniform and there were black-rimmed holes across the chest.

"What's he doing here?" Footy asked.

"Let's see if there are more," Johnny said.

The men put down their things and went to work. Half an hour later, they'd counted thirty-four dead enemy soldiers, and a half-dozen native men. The count was complicated by the hundreds of smoke-stained skulls laying around—headhunter trophies, they guessed.

"The Japs must have been hiding in here, and somehow, our guys found out," Johnny said.

"Fish in a barrel," Footy said. "Bad magic for the *kanakas*."

"Maybe why they left," Johnny nodded, "like Kissim."

"Could be, this is the last of the Japs on the Raub," Footy said.

"I hope you're right," Johnny told him. The men returned through the village. Even the old dog was silent.

"I don't fancy this," Footy said. "Too bloody still."

"Like a grave," Johnny agreed. They came to the edge of the village and stared at the river. The glare was on the water, and the surface remained littered with torn-up vegetation.

"Let's get on to the coast," Johnny said, "I'm itching to hitch a ride out of here."

"Yes, mate," Footy said "I reckon we're through the worst of the drama now." The men cut a beeline across open land to the place the trail disappeared in the jungle once more.

The instant they were out of site, a clump of waterweeds rose in the air, borne up on a wide head. The Father had watched the enemy come out of the prey nests, and turn for the trees. And now it knew exactly where the game trail came to the water again.

At once, it splashed into the current and surged downriver. It knew it would get there first, and the smooth-headed man must come to it.

CHAPTER 20

After it killed the men on the island, the Father rested. When it had taken the first one and charged up the hill, it hurt its leg again. Savagely, the Father assuaged its suffering, throwing bodies around. It bolted its meal, then slid into the flood once more. The waters held the weight off its ruined limb. Hunger satiated, the crocodile dozed through the darkness. It sensed the flood subsiding, and dawn revealed that it stretched on a bed of mud.

It faced the hill on which its kill was scattered. Already at first light, riding the scent of death, carrion birds were circling. Their sharp eyes took note of the enormous crocodile, and they would not land.

The heat was welcome on the crocodile's back, but the incessant jab of the wound made it cranky. The Father raised its head and grunted a complaint that made eagles veer in flight. The infection was mounting a new assault, and the reptile was no longer interested in eating. It dragged itself on its belly to the river.

As always now, it watched the path of the two-legged animals, seeking the prey it truly wanted. Only killing this one would slake its fury. It launched itself into the stream and drifted downriver in the detritus of the flood.

With every bend of the Big River, the predator came to increasingly familiar haunts. Again, the light scorched the sky and the Father followed the current. Eventually, the glow dropped into the trees, and the colossus and all things flowed on through the black.

The Father's eyes on top of its head stared up. The points of light seemed to glow just above. Its leg seeped poison into its blood, and the giant became bilious. It regurgitated some of the man-flesh into the river.

With hypersensitivity, it felt every place along its flanks, on its head, and down its back, where the hot stings had ever hurt it. It shivered along its length, sending out waves, while the sensations popped and crackled along its spine and into its brain. The beast stared at the lights and saw each one as an ache in its poisoned scars. Lost in distress, the reptile stopped paying heed to where it was. Its general suffering was a discordant jangle, against which the leg was a constant shriek.

Katsu regained consciousness when his face went under water. He choked and jerked his head up, coughed and spat. He was a mere pinprick of awareness and did not know where he was, or even who he was. He was something that breathed, that was all. He attempted to puzzle it out, but only straws of disconnected nonsense drifted by.

Time passed, and he was still in the void. Gradually, he made simple distinctions. There was air—his head was in it. There was water—it surrounded his body. And there was mud—he lay in it.

Gradually a word coalesced. *Nigero! (Escape!).* He kept clutching for scraps of thought, but they made no sense. Again the thought came: *Nigero!* But from what, and to where? How had he come to be here? His head was hot, and yet he shivered. He groaned and, like a drowning man, he clutched what he could.

Nigero!

He tried to move, but all he did was twitch. At last he found arms and legs, and got on his knees, shivering and panting. He raised a hand to his eyes and both arms rose together and he felt the rope. Still, he could not see a hint of shape. At last he forced himself onto his feet and stood, strange light patterns whirling in front of his eyes.

The next thing he knew, he was floundering through water to his waist. He seemed to move with legs roped together. *They are tied as well,* he thought, and fought panic. He searched down with bound hands and found something between his knees. He tugged, and it unraveled into trousers that he pulled up and knotted the rope by feel.

On he stumbled, constantly attempting to marshal his thoughts, but without success. He toppled on his face and swallowed water that tasted of mud, came up hacking, and stumbled on. Rain struck his head and rinsed his eyes.

— ❍ —

When the flood spilled across the field, the she-crocodile stayed in the reeds and watched. The female had not fed for weeks, and she was driven by hunger. Darkness descended and she thought to explore the expanded territory in search of marooned and drowned animals. Shortly after dark, she crested the bank and nosed through the shallows. Then she heard the unmistakable sounds of a land animal in the water, in noisy distress. She turned in pursuit.

The Japanese blundered on. His feet stubbed a dirt slope and he fell forward onto thorns. He crawled out and his face and hands were torn. The crocodile heard the prey leave the water and she sped up. She, too, encountered the slope and came out. She smelled the animal and knew what kind it was.

It was close, very close.

The man ran into a wall. His hands recognized a curve of bark and broken branches. He grabbed and climbed. The fallen tree was as high as his head, and he needed both hands and feet to mount, nails tearing. He teetered at the top and fell headfirst down the far side, scraping skin off chest and shins. He broke his fall with his hands and rolled. For a moment he lay panting, then struggled on.

The crocodile rushed up and ran her snout against the wood. She heard the prey on the far side and knew she could not go over. She ran one way and found an impassible tangle of branches. She went the other, and eventually got around the roots. But by then the creature was gone, and she knew it was too far to chase. She returned the way she had come.

The man careened through the night, clawed by branches. He came to a place where he was pinned in on all sides. He fell on his belly and crawled. His knees and elbows were soon worn raw by gnarled roots.

At last his hands discovered cool, smooth columns. They felt like home and soothed his spirit. He stayed clutching them and then was oblivious. He awoke in the depths of night with a thought like a bell tolling in his mind.

I am in a bamboo grove and I am Takano, Katsu. He tried to cling to the thought, and the poles, while his mind dropped like a stone into the lake of oblivion.

☆

How long it drifted in darkness, the Father did not know. Pain brought it alert when its leg bumped a log. The giant found itself floating in blinding light. It stared around and realized it approached another gathering place of the two-legged herd. Something nudged its body and it realized it drifted beside another giant. The great tree had been undermined by the flood, and now the Father swam with its head beneath the umbrella of branches. Again, it studied the banks for any sign of its enemy.

It swept around a bend and the Father saw the prey-animals' nests. Always in its memory, the herd was thick here, but now it saw no movement. It drifted from the tree and entered an eddy. Hidden among the weeds, it waited and watched.

After some time, the Father saw something that brought its awareness to razor edge. Coming towards it from among the nests was the smooth-headed man. A companion walked beside it. The reptile watched the one-prey draw near and prepared for the reunion.

Then the prey left the trail, went across the land, and was lost in the trees. But the predator knew where the game path came to water again, and it cruised downriver. It arrived at the place and knew it was first. Here the prey animals sometimes congregated in such numbers that they had worn the vegetation away. During one of its attacks here, the crocodile had killed five in one rush.

The ambush place was a wide, shallow bay. Reeds grew in profusion. The Father slid into the bed and walked underwater until it reached the bank. The giant's arrival struck terror into its river cousins that infested the place. One minute, the bay was sleepy, reeds nodding their heads to the sun. The next, it was an explosion of lines aiming for open water. A score of river crocodiles burst onto the river and rushed away.

The Father settled until only its sly eyes were up behind the foliage. It stared at the red clay bank where the path came to it and became deathly still.

◗

The men left the abandoned village. Johnny shaded his eyes against the glare, watching the river, but saw nothing unusual. He cut directly for the jungle.

Forty minutes later, he and Footy came down a wooded hill to a field by the river. The main channel ran further out, and near shore was a vast bay, thick with reeds. They watched a heron glide in on a six-foot wingspan and splash into the shallows. It stood on one leg, dagger beak poised.

It looked to the men like this was a place where the villagers washed. The path went straight for the river, to a point of bare clay. Beyond, the trail continued between the water and the gardens.

Johnny led that way. They were passing the *kaukau* mounds when Footy stopped and turned his head. He heard something so out of place, he got goose bumps.

"Hold up mate," he called. Johnny turned. "Listen!"

The crocodile was staring at the smooth-headed man, almost within attack range, and it tensed for the lunge.

Johnny heard nothing, shrugged, and took another step toward the river. But Footy heard the eerie sound again.

"Wait!" he called.

"What is it?" Johnny grumbled.

"Listen! Over there!" Footy pointed at the inland jungle. Johnny strained his ears, and now he heard it too.

The voice was reed-thin, and in the distance, but there was no mistaking what it was. A woman was singing. Footy trotted a few steps in that direction and Johnny went after him.

The Father watched the prey retreat. It was too late for a charge, but it remained poised in place.

Footy cut across a garden and Johnny caught up. Then the breeze turned their way and both men stopped in astonishment.

"It's English!" Footy exclaimed. Johnny put a finger to his lips and unstrung his rifle. Footy did the same, and the two of them moved swiftly over the vegetable mounds, hunting the singer.

CHAPTER 21

When the men were far enough off, the Father stood and stared after them. The rising of the broad, knobbed island set frogs leaping on all sides. Water dripped from the scar across the eye and trickled from the massive jaw while the prey retreated. But it knew its ambush place was good, and it settled under to wait.

Johnny and Footy were through the gardens into a band of trees. The song came from somewhere beyond. The sound of it, a woman's voice and in English, was so out of place, their skin crawled. They continued into the woods and peered through.

They saw a sun-drenched meadow, and in the middle of it, a near-naked white woman sitting on a log. The song came from her:

"Oh where have you been Billy boy, Billy boy,
Oh where have you been charming Billy?
I have been to see my wife,
She's the darling of my life,
She's a young thing and cannot leave her mother."

The singer sat in profile. Her hair was long and honey colored in waves down her back. Her skin was a darker gold. But sun-kissed as she was, the watchers in the woods knew she was a white woman. All she wore were strands of blossoms around her hips.

On either side of her stood a young native woman, no more than teenagers. These drew bamboo combs through the blonde tresses. The dark-skinned girls were in a similar state of undress, their breasts bare, their loins scantily clad in strung flowers.

The singer continued to sing, and the men crept closer between the trees. Johnny spied four more native nymphs lying in the grass, threading blossoms onto stalks of grass.

"Struth!" Footy hissed.

"Shhh!" Johnny cautioned—but it was too late.

The woman looked into the forest and the song broke off. Johnny's gaze locked on her—the lovely body, in spite of the pink ridge of scar across her chest. He saw wide eyes in a striking face, and the woman was looking right at him. His heart beat raggedly, and he glanced at Footy and saw the Aussie's jaw hanging open.

"They've seen us," Johnny said.

"Yes mate," Footy agreed.

The singer said something and her companions stared into the shadows. The girls in the grass rose on their feet.

"We're friends!" Johnny called, "Allied soldiers."

The woman spoke again and the men heard a tribal tongue. Then she called in English.

"Come out! Show yourselves!" Johnny and Footy glanced at each other.

"What is this!" Footy rasped. "Maybe we've died and gone to heaven!"

"I doubt it's heaven," Johnny growled. "Leave your pack and knife here—take your rifle and revolver. Keep your guard up!" He dumped his pack against a tree and slipped his machete and bayonet inside. He pulled off his helmet and set it on top. Footy did the same with his own pack, Bowie knife and Dingo's hat.

The soldiers walked to the edge of the meadow and paused to face the seven women in that sun-soaked place. It came to Johnny just how rumpled and dirty they were.

The women, by contrast, looked clean and soft, and had bright hibiscus behind their ears, in addition to the flowers around their hips. They wore shell necklaces, bracelets and ankle-bands. Each woman had tattoos around her breasts, winding down her stomach to disappear into the floral skirt.

The white woman was adorned the same way, the tattoos outlining her breasts stark against fair skin. Johnny could not drag his gaze away from her. She laughed musically and spoke again:

"Come." She smiled at Johnny and opened her arms.

"She's Australian," Footy said.

"I know it," Johnny said, running his fingers through his hair.

The woman spoke in the other language and her six companions came toward the men, smiling. Their hands were outstretched, and in their state of undress, the men could see they had no weapons.

Three girls went to each man. Johnny and Footy kept their rifles in hand, but for what purpose in the face of unarmed women? Unreal as it was, they had stumbled into an oasis of comfort and bliss.

The brown girls saw the men's wide eyes and giggled. Hesitantly, they reached out and began to touch. Johnny smelled the heady perfume of sun-warmed female skin and flowers. The girls' lips glistened with some sort of oil, and their breasts and nipples grazed him, while gentle hands stroked his arms.

The truth was, Johnny and Footy were little more than boys themselves, prematurely aged by war. In spite of their misgivings, they relaxed in the caresses like men dying of thirst go into a lake of clear water.

Johnny's gaze remained on the singer. She stared straight back with arresting gray eyes, her arms still open. Johnny licked dry lips.

"There's something wrong here!" he croaked at Footy. He heard the Aussie grunt and looked over to see that a girl had pried one of his hands from his rifle and it was cupping her breast.

"What could possibly be wrong?" the Aussie sighed. He still had the Lee Enfield in one hand, but two girls were stroking the arm. The four moved like dream-walkers into the meadow.

Johnny felt a hand slip inside his shirt and stroke his chest and he shivered. Suddenly he yearned to throw caution to the wind and succumb, whatever would happen. But he had not survived three years of war that way.

Warm hands at his back gently coaxed him toward the woman waiting on the log. He glanced at Footy again and saw him with his shirt off, bathed in sunlight, the girls caressing him. He was grinning like an idiot.

"Footy!" Johnny called, "keep your guard up!"

"Why mate?" Footy said in a dreamy voice as Johnny watched a woman take the rifle from his hand. He could no longer see the revolver in the Australian's belt. A girl pulled the man's hand to the twin of the breast he already held.

"Come to me," the white woman said, and Johnny's attention swung back to her. He was just before her and she arched to show her oiled breasts, holding him in her bewitching gaze.

Johnny gaped, and a girl pried one of his hands from his rifle. Brown fingers guided it to the singer's hip. He shuddered as he touched her.

"Who—who are you?" Johnny managed. A shadow went over her face, and then she was calm again.

"We are the bridesmaids," she said. "We are here to give men their reward. Those who are thirsty, come and drink."

The soldier told him this was wrong, but Johnny's young body was swamped with desire. He stepped closer and the woman put her own hands on his hips and rose to press against him. He felt her pelvis, and the firm breasts against his shirt. She slipped her hand behind his neck and drew his face down to her own. Her lips parted and he saw a hint of tongue.

No! The shout was deep within him, and with huge effort, he turned his face so the woman's lips only brushed his cheek.

He looked at Footy and saw the girls rubbing their near naked bodies against his. The Aussie's arms were around one, and as Johnny watched, he kissed her mouth, and she kissed him back.

"No!" Johnny called, aloud this time, but the girl lay on the grass, and Footy sank on top of her. Hands were pulling down his shorts.

The white woman put her hand on Johnny's chin and turned his face to her. She had unbuttoned his shirt, and now she touched her breasts to his bare skin. It was almost more than he could bear. He was breathing hard, and felt hands tugging at his rifle. Fingers loosened his belt.

The singer lay back on the log and spread her knees, displaying herself for him. A hand lazily traced the tattoo around a breast and down into the flowers. Johnny felt on fire.

The soldier in him continued to protest, but another, stronger urge, would have what she offered. He leaned over her and pressed down. He could feel her whole length quiver, and he was separated from her by only a thin layer of cloth.

When on leave with other men, he had never used the brothels so many enjoyed. He'd even gone and taken a look, but what he saw depressed him. It was a cheat, the promise of one thing, and the substitution of another. He remembered what he'd had with his girlfriend that last year in Hawaii. The fumbling in the back of the old Packard was far more meaningful than the cash transactions he saw the whores make.

But Johnny had never known what the singer now showed him in the full light of the sun. She was a full and lovely woman, waiting for him on the log. Her arms were back over her head, hands lost in her hair.

"And the lion shall lay down with the lamb," she said. Johnny felt hands tugging at his trousers. Somehow, he still managed to clutch his rifle in his hand. Now he groaned and put it down, but kept his boot on it. He pressed on the woman again, barely noticing that two of the girls had moved back behind her. Only one remained, working at his belt.

The white woman was staring at him with those eerie gray eyes and a low chuckle escaped her. Something about that was so uncanny, all the hair rose on Johnny's head and arms, and he searched her face.

And he saw it. There was something absolutely wrong with her eyes. Gwyn's face rose before him and he saw her intelligent, thoughtful gaze. The contrast was so profound—those sane green eyes, and these eldritch gray ones—that Johnny jerked back.

The woman followed him up, bringing forward the hands that had trailed behind the log, and now they held a short stabbing spear. She put the point against Johnny's neck so he felt the cut, and the trickle of blood. Her smile disappeared in an instant, and her scowl was murderous. Then Johnny felt other points press into his back.

He felt furious and stupid, and all his desire melted away. Urgently he wanted his Springfield. He could feel the stock under his foot, but he could not reach it with the spear at his throat.

"Now see. You are the lamb, and I am the lion," the woman said.

"And you're nuttier than a pecan roll," Johnny told her, reaching a hand and buttoning his pants. He patted his belt and realized his pistol was missing. He turned his head carefully against the point to look at Footy. The Aussie was lying on the girl, shorts around his knees, buttocks to the breeze. But two girls stood over him with spears raised, ready to plunge them into his back.

"Footy!" Johnny called. The Aussie's flushed face turned his way and he absorbed Johnny's predicament. Then he craned over his shoulder and saw his own danger—but somehow, through it all, his hips continued to bounce.

"Stop!" the white woman screamed at him, but Footy's movements grew frantic, and a strange warbling sound issued from him.

"I said, stop!" the white woman shrieked. She spewed words and her handmaidens pressed the points of their spears hard against Footy's back. He slowed a little, but suddenly made a crowing, gargling sound, shivered all over, and went still.

"Disgusting little beast!" the woman hissed. Johnny saw all the women were focused on Footy. He pushed the singer's spear away, grabbed his rifle, and pressed the barrel between the white woman's breasts. His finger went around the trigger.

"Call off your girls!" Johnny barked. "Tell them to put down their weapons—or I'll kill you." Her gray eyes rested calmly on his face and she did not speak.

"I'll put a bullet through your heart!" he warned her. "This is what I do. Believe me." She stared into his eyes and returned her spear to his jugular. He felt the two points press harder behind him, and then the unmistakable muzzle of a gun. *My pistol!*

Footy rolled off the girl onto his back, and the ones holding spears repositioned them over throat and heart. The girl he'd been on got up, found another spear in the grass, and stood over him. She poised the point over his exposed genitals.

"Not there!" Footy said in horror, and covered himself with his hands.

The singer spoke in a normal voice to Johnny, as though discussing no more than the weather.

"Now—you will shoot me, and my girls will kill the both of you."

She is crazy, Johnny thought. *She wants to die. Keep her talking!*

"My friend is Australian, like you," Johnny tried. "You don't want to kill us—we're Allies! We're on the same side!"

"He's a filthy little pig," the woman said. "And we cannot be on the same side, because we are women, and you are men."

Johnny searched her eyes and knew beyond doubt she intended to kill them.

"What does that mean?" he asked.

"This is Creation," the woman said. She looked around, "and it is good. But then men come. You bring the Serpent into Eden. You put it in us, and the Serpent teaches us evil.

"We are the bridesmaids. To kill the Serpent, we kill the man." She smiled again. "You see? But I grow weary of talking. Let us make an end."

And all at once, Johnny knew who she was.

CHAPTER 22

Evil things were on Katsu. His skin was covered in them. He jumped up and saw big black ants crawling all over him. He beat at them frantically with his bound hands. They were biting everywhere, nipping his face, even inside his ears and under his trousers. He shouted and brushed them away and had to reach inside his pants, under his buttocks, to pull off the ones that hung there.

His fingernails were cracked and filthy, but as he watched them pinch off the torturers, it came to him again who he was. He even remembered some of how he happened to be here, alone in the jungle.

I am Katsu. He remembered Kissim—the crocodile, the enemy soldiers, and the trek. He thought of the fearsome cannibals, and Mula's village. The most recent event he could recall was the thunderstorm. He pushed the limits of his mind and remembered that his captors had been stricken by diarrhea.

Beyond that everything was a blank. How he came to be in this grove of bamboo, being eaten by ants, he did not know. Where his captors had gone, he had no idea either. He realized he was famished when his stomach whined.

Katsu had no weapons and no food and he was totally lost. He felt a prick of fear. At least with the enemy he had been fed! He tried to form a plan and the best he could think of was to free his hands and find the river. His mouth was parched and he needed water or he would die of thirst alone.

Katsu searched the forest floor until he found a sharp-edged rock. He sat and sawed at the rope. Eventually, he cut through a strand and peeled away the coils.

He tried to move off and found he was in foliage so dense he could make no headway. He was reduced to crawling on his belly over the roots. After a long and painful time, exhausted by his ordeal, faint from lack of water and food, he struggled into an open place in the jungle. A shaft of sunlight came down and Katsu lay in it and slept. He did not hear the wild pigs. The boar sniffed around the man, snorted and trotted off, followed by the sows.

Katsu woke in darkness and his body was a single itch. His tongue stuck to the roof of his mouth. His fingers searched out a pebble and he sucked on it. He could see nothing and he resigned himself to remaining here. The mosquitoes were a constant torment and so were his thirst and hunger. He tried to cheer himself up by thinking: *I am free—free of my captors, free to go where I will and do what I want.*

The night dragged on and he could not stop the mosquitoes feeding. When he could bear it no more, he slapped madly at himself and rubbed his hands over his skin and scratched everywhere. Then he sheltered his head with his hands and put his face against his knees. He waited out the dark, repeating fiercely, *I am free, I am free!*

The night was eternal and sometime in it, he began to say to himself, *the enemy is lying.* For years now, fighting in the foul jungle, he and his comrades had encouraged one another. *Nippon will win, Asia will be ours. We are the only truly civilized people, and we are the rightful head of the region. Nippon cannot be stopped—the Empire will win!* But now as he tried to muster the old confidence, the words rang hollow. Lost and alone, he was forced to admit the truth. He no longer believed the proud sentiments.

The news of the atomic bombing of Hiroshima stabbed through his mind like a dagger. He felt the truth of it in his bones, and he knew that Nippon's dream of expansion was undone. A voice as cold and hard as steel rang in his head. *The Empire is vanquished. In spite of our bravery and boldness, our enemies have won. We will be prisoners, even in our homeland. The world has changed forever.*

The man hated this voice that came like a faithless lover in the night, but he could not deny it. He was defenseless, nothing more than a weak boy, alone in a cruel universe. The weight of the infinite heavens pressed down so he could not breathe. He felt he would crack like an insect. There was a stabbing pain in his chest and he thought he might be dying. A sound rose in the forest. It was harsh, and came in waves, and it emanated from him. His chest heaved and water he could not spare ran from his eyes. He felt utterly defeated, and he let the mosquitoes feed unmolested.

Later during that boundless night he saw pinpricks of light. At first he thought they were hallucinations born of the illness that still wracked his body. But when they came close he saw them reflected dimly on leaves. They were fireflies! The dancing points lifted his spirits and he slept.

He awoke with the voice speaking. *The world I know is no more. We, the samurai, continue to live but in truth, we were defeated long ago. And myself, my father, and all the soldiers of the Imperial Japanese Army, have been duped. Our war leaders let their pride convince them of the lie that we could win.*

Where have they led us? To defeat. Our ships lie on the bottom of the ocean, our planes have been shot out of the skies. My countrymen lie dead by the tens of thousands in unmarked graves.

We despised each nation we conquered as "the defeated." Now we are them. We are a nation without honor or value. We have lost face before the world, and I am ashamed. Nothing in my life prepared me to face my family or my country this way! I am a stranger to the place of my birth.

But now another voice rose in him, and while it too was harsh, it had human warmth. *Yet you live, my son. You are my child and we are samurai, forever, whatever others say. That means we exist to serve the nation. Even though, by our religion, we are warriors of peace, this is wartime and you are a soldier! Your self-pity is intolerable! You will do your duty!* Katsu was grateful then for the discipline his father had occasionally beat into him.

I must take responsibility for myself. But my individual life is not important. Now there is only what I must do. He thought of his captors and decided: *I will find them and I will take back my katana. Perhaps I cannot save my nation, but I can save my sword. I will hear it sing again. That will be my story.* He felt relief and he thought, *I have become the most dangerous of men, the one with nothing left to lose.*

Gradually, he distinguished black trees against a charcoal sky. The world took form once more. In the early dawn, he saw legions of mosquitoes on his skin. They stood with legs splayed and drank his blood. He crushed dozens of them.

He stood upright, giddy with fever and urgent for water. With no path to follow, he covered his face with his arms and pushed forward, being torn by brambles. At last he stumbled across a trickle of water and knelt and drank. Now he knew he would live. He followed the rivulet, and when it formed a puddle, he pulled up handfuls of sopping moss and washed away the sting and the sweat. After that, he followed the water, ducking under giant leaves and climbing roots. The brook became a stream and, after many hours, it led him to a native path through the jungle.

The sun was a mere bright spot on the forest canopy and he could not tell which direction to go. He simply followed the trail and at last broke out of the trees and there was the Raub. He realized at once he had come all this distance in the upriver direction. His captors were traveling the other way, towards the ocean. If he wanted his sword, he must trail them.

He wondered if they had survived the sickness, and if so, what they had made of his disappearance. He hoped they thought he had been swept away by the flood or been eaten by crocodiles. This thought encouraged him, for if they thought he was dead he could surprise them.

But now he was starving and he must find food. He back-tracked along the path. An hour later he passed the same stream he had emerged on, and knelt to drink. Then he continued and broke into a trot. The enemies could not be too far ahead.

Johnny felt the prick of her spear against his neck and he knew who the singer was.

"You're Sarah!"

The woman cried out and her features contorted as if he had slugged her. She cocked her head, as though hearing a voice from far away.

"Sarah?" Her voice and spear wavered.

"Your husband is Billy," Johnny said.

"Billy? Where is my Billy?"

Johnny glanced at Footy and saw him still on his back, three spears poised over him. When Johnny returned his gaze to the white woman, he found her eyes wide with grief and remembrance.

"The Japs!" she exclaimed. "They came to the Mission and...."
She paused as the memory flooded in and Johnny saw her flinch.

"Oh!" she exclaimed. "They killed Billy!" She sagged as if something snapped inside and she began to sob. Her spear drifted away from Johnny's neck. "He is dust," she said. She raked a hand through her long hair, "and I am ashes." She was silent, and then gave a groan that wrenched Johnny's heart.

"There is a hell," she said. "I am in it."

"I'm sorry Sarah," Johnny said. He felt compassion, but he and Footy remained in mortal danger and his mind raced for a solution. *How do you threaten a person who wants to die?* And then it came to him: *you don't.*

Johnny swung the barrel of his rifle away from Sarah's chest and put it under the chin of the nearest native girl. He pressed hard so she cried out and dropped her spear. The white woman raised her eyes in alarm.

"Esther!" she said.

"Sarah," Johnny said in the soldier's voice, "put your spear down. Right now! Order your girls to drop theirs as well! Or I will blow Esther's brains out." He put pressure on the barrel and the girl choked. Johnny saw confusion, anger and fear play across Sarah's face. *This is the moment of truth.*

"Sarah," he barked, "I am a soldier and I have killed hundreds of people and I will kill Esther right now—unless you do exactly what I say. On three," he said. He tightened his finger on the trigger. "One. Two…"

"Stop!" Sarah cried, and she opened her hands and the spear clattered down. She spoke in a tremulous voice in the native language. The girls stared at her and each other and began to withdraw. Johnny saw that the one with his pistol kept it pointed at him. The native women gathered behind Sarah but did not put down the weapons.

The girls over Footy backed off as well. A few feet away, one handed her spear to a companion and picked up the Aussie's rifle, and the revolver. She turned over the pistol to another young woman and checked the Lee Enfield in a way that told Johnny she knew what she was doing. She drew the bolt to confirm there was a round in the chamber, then locked it again. Walking backwards, guided by another girl, she kept the rifle trained on Johnny's chest.

"Footy," Johnny said, "we're leaving." The Aussie got to his feet and his fists opened and closed as he watched his guns depart with the natives. The one with the revolver cocked the hammer and aimed it at him.

A girl came to Sarah and helped her to rise. Something about the way she did it made Johnny wonder who was really in charge—the mad white woman or the natives? Sarah stared at Johnny with grief-stricken eyes.

"The Japs raped me," she said. "Each one of us." She nodded at her companions. "They put us to work as their 'comfort station.' I fought back." Her fingers touched the scar across her chest. "They were too strong. I prayed to die, but I did not die." She twisted a hand in her hair and wiped her eyes with it.

"I forgot myself," she said, letting go of the hair and standing with her companions. "I am a thing that lays under men." Her voice broke. Johnny and Footy stared at her, appalled.

"I stopped fighting," she said. "Then, one day, there were a lot less Japs." She smiled and looked at her girls, then back to Johnny.

"We used sticks and rocks to kill the ones who came to us after that. We took their guns and killed more." She nodded and Johnny could not reply. He had nothing big enough to say. It was Footy who broke the silence.

"Come with us, Sarah."

"You!" she frowned at him. "Swine!" Johnny shot a warning glance his way and saw the man look both sheepish and defiant, a tough combination to pull off.

"Sarah, we can take you to your people," Johnny said. For a moment there was a flicker of hope in the mad eyes, but it went out.

"Too late," Sarah whispered. "Much too late. Who is my family?" She sighed and came to Johnny. His rifle was still pressed under the chin of the girl she called Esther. Sarah put her hand around the barrel and pushed it aside. She took Esther's hand and walked with her to the women. She murmured to the others and they moved in a knot towards the far jungle. The two holding Footy's firearms and the one with Johnny's pistol shuffled backwards, aiming at the soldiers.

"Put down our guns!" Johnny shouted, setting the crosshairs on the one with the Lee Enfield. But the women went on. He thought he would put a warning shot over their heads, but recalled how short of ammo they were.

"Shoot them!" Footy told him. "Don't let them take our guns!" Johnny sighed and lowered the Springfield.

"I've never killed a woman and I'm not going to start now!" he told Footy. "Besides, this is your fault."

The women disappeared into the forest and they heard Sarah call.

"Unclean! Unclean!" And then she started to sing again until the song faded in the distance.

"Can she bake a cherry pie, Billy boy, Billy boy,
Can she bake a cherry pie, Charming Billy?
She can bake a cherry pie
Fast as a cat can wink an eye,
She's a young thing and cannot leave her mother."

"That's the bloody world for you," Footy said bitterly. "Whenever something good comes along, it's usually too good to be true." He grabbed his shirt from the grass and put it on, then stalked back the way they'd come. Johnny followed to where they'd left their things.

Footy jammed on his hat, pulled out the Bowie knife and shoved it through his belt, then heaved the pack on. As he did so, the handle of the sword snagged his shirt and a button flew away. Footy stormed off. Johnny got his machete and knife back on his belt, swung into his own pack and went after him.

The pilot strode across the gardens towards the downriver jungle, Johnny on his tail. The men passed sixty yards inland from the place where the natives once went to wash. Johnny caught up with the Australian as they entered the trees.

"Look," Footy said to him. "I reckon we'll take turns carrying your rifle."

"What do you mean, take turns?" Johnny snapped.

"I mean," Footy said, "you keep the rifle half the day, and I'll have it the other."

"You've got to be kidding!" Johnny snorted. "Give my rifle to a man who let his be taken off him—by a girl?" He laughed scornfully and pushed by.

"And where's your pistol?" Footy yelled. Johnny shook his head.

He blitzed through the jungle and did not care if the Aussie followed or not.

CHAPTER 23

Johnny walked hard for many hours without a pause. Footy fell far behind. At last Johnny made himself take a break, ate a sweet potato and took to the trail again.

Only as night was falling did exhaustion make him stop. He chose a campsite some distance from the river where there were trees to string his hammock. Over the day, his rage had simmered to general exasperation. He felt stupid for losing his pistol, but at least he'd kept himself under control. And he still had his Springfield. Night dropped quickly as he gathered firewood. When Footy puffed up red-faced twenty minutes later, Johnny was building the fire and would not look at him.

The men moved separately into the nearby gardens and dug sweet potatoes. They laid them on the coals without speaking and sat apart. When their dinner was cooked, they ate in silence. Footy spread his blanket and muttered to the sky.

"Well, no bloody point in me keeping guard without a rifle." He lay down and turned away. Johnny was not about to argue with the fool. Instead of crawling into his hammock as he longed to do, he sat against a tree, rifle across his lap. From time to time, his fatigue overpowered him and he dozed fitfully, waking every few minutes.

Footy had rolled on his back and was snoring loudly under his patch of netting. Johnny slapped at mosquitoes and thought he might go and put his boot up the man's backside, but he did not. The night seemed interminable.

From the river, the Father watched the man in the patch of light. It had remained in its previous ambush place until it knew the prey had eluded it. Then the crocodile had gone in pursuit. It spied the enemy in the distance and trailed him, submerged like a drifting log.

As darkness came, the smaller two-legged creature came into view. The crocodile maneuvered as close as it could while remaining in the river. Its leg was sore and the pain kept the reptile from wanting to walk across land.

The predator kept watch while the night passed, but it knew this was not a good ambush place. The animal trail passed inland, and then there were cliffs. Gradually, an image grew of a better place. It was in the swampland ahead. There it had hunted frequently at a ford where all land animals that wanted to pass, must venture into the water.

The desire to take the smooth-headed man there grew in the hunter. When the stars were beginning to fade in the sky, it nosed out into the channel and swam away.

Daybreak found Johnny tired and irritated. He lit the stove and boiled water from his canteen. They were low on coffee and out of almost everything else. Johnny felt like brewing a cup just for himself, but he made two and slopped one down beside the sleeping Australian. He gulped his own quickly and stuffed his things in his pack.

As he was tying his hammock on, Footy stretched and rubbed his eyes. Johnny found he was still mad. Even the way the pilot stood and scratched his belly aggravated him. And when he hawked and spit, Johnny was ready to hammer him. He threw his pack on and strode away. Footy had to rush to get up, scramble his things together and trot, just to keep the Yank in view. He could barely get any of the coffee in his mouth.

For his part, the pilot felt it was a fine morning. His dreams had been laced with erotic images, and the euphoria was still on him. He felt badly about the loss of his firearms, but that was his problem, wasn't it? *The Yank should be over himself by now.*

It was a fresh morning, the sun a golden halo over the red-tinged forest. The wide surface of the river reflected the warm light. Water birds of all kinds were in abundance. Footy watched a kingfisher skim over the river and dive. The men passed through grasslands that gave way to wild scrub, without any sign of humans.

As Johnny walked, he peeled a yam with his fingers and tossed the black skin off the high bank into the river. Fish fed, making rings on the surface. He did not realize the Aussie had trotted close until he heard the foolish giggle. Johnny spun around and crossed his arms.

"What's so funny?"

"Aww, nothing," Footy said.

"Out with it."

"Alright then," Footy smirked. "I had a go. At least there's that."

Johnny's stare could have made icicles.

"You are *not* talking about that girl, are you?"

"Well yes," Footy said. "Cor blimey, that..."

"You lost your rifle and your pistol, you moron!" Johnny barked. "Without me you'd be dead—and all you can think about is..."

"Listen," Footy cut in. "A bloke's gotta do what a bloke's gotta do."

"Oh shove it!" Johnny said. He stalked away, but Footy wouldn't leave it alone and scuffled up again.

"Mind you, takes a cool head with spears at your back..."

"I said-shut-your-pie-hole!"

Johnny strode fast until there were a hundred yards between them once more. It was Footy's turn to be annoyed.

The bloody Yank's no better than me! I saw him all over that poor mad woman—and he lost his pistol, that's a fact. I saw him put down his rifle. Sheerest chance he got it back. Who the hell does he think he is, getting high and mighty with me? Not that I'm proud of meself. No, not the best thing you've ever done, Footy me lad. But then, not the worst either.

The miles and the hours wore away and Footy had a change of heart. He had to admit—only to himself—that he'd been stupid to lose his firearms. He was naked in the bush without them. *But I don't need bloody-Johnny-come-lately, lord-of-the-bush, to tell me that!*

When he turned sixteen his dad had said to him: "Footy, you're a man now mate—get it wherever and whenever you can. By the time you reach my age, you'll find there's never enough strange quim for a lifetime."

But wanting it and getting it were two different things, Footy had discovered that for himself. *Yes, those women had their own buggered plan—but I had me agenda. What's a bloke meant to do, turn down a sure thing? Not likely mate,* he told himself. *Not bloody likely!*

By mid-afternoon Footy had stirred himself into a rage. *Bloody Johnny, just like a bleedin' Yank—always acting like they've got the right to run the world! Forget the ruddy Nazis mate—it's the Yanks who believe they're the master race!* Footy glared at Johnny's helmeted head in the distance. *All right then, if the wanker won't talk—I won't either. Fine with me mate. Bloody fine with me!*

Footy deliberately let the American get out of sight as he plodded through the wavering heat. *I'll be glad when this is over,* he though. *Glad when the Nips and Yanks all go back to whatever hole they crawled out of. New Guinea belongs to Australia! Aus rules!*

Up ahead, Johnny's thoughts buzzed like hornets. *That dipstick is going to get us killed! Why do I always have to be the responsible one? This is just like the war. Fine talk about "Allies," but it's the U S of A that gets the job done. We beat the Japs here, by land and sea, and were the Aussies grateful? No—the opposite in fact.* Johnny remembered that bad time with the fighting in Brisbane when he'd been on leave. The memory brought a sour taste to his mouth and he spat.

He knew Footy had fallen way back and he didn't care. He had his Springfield and his food—and the last two packs of cigarettes. If the runt couldn't keep up, that was his problem.

Late in the day, having covered a lot of distance, Johnny looked for a campsite. It was real scrub wilderness now, no native gardens for a long time, but at last he found a place with a few yam mounds beside the river. He dug some and proceeded with the setup.

By the time Footy came along and rooted up his own supper, Johnny had his hammock strung. Again, they didn't speak while Footy unpacked his bedroll. They ranged out for firewood, returned with their arms full, and moved around one another with the exaggerated courtesy men give to strangers.

Johnny lit the fire with his Zippo. The fuel was drying up and it took several tries. Not for the first time, he wished he'd brought some matches from the depot. The evening was close and mosquitoes were out in force. The men placed the *kaukau* on the flames and sat in the smoke and waited. An egg-shaped moon floated into the sky. When the tubers were ready, they speared them with their knives, each careful to take only his own.

When they'd eaten, Johnny pulled out two cigarettes. After about ten flicks of his Zippo he gave up, picked up a flaming piece of grass, lit both smokes and passed one to Footy, all without a word.

"Give us a few ciggys to carry," Footy broke the silence, "if you're going to be miles off all day."

"We're almost out," Johnny said. "And besides, how're you going to light them?"

"And who put you in charge?" Footy snapped. "Trouble with you Yanks, you think you run the world." Johnny instantly regretted sharing his cigarettes and all the pent up animosity boiled over.

"We saved your bacon in this war," he said hotly. "If we hadn't, you'd be getting your orders from Tokyo right now."

"You arrogant bugger," Footy spat, "you forget you're my guest here—of me and all Australians."

"Oh yeh?" Johnny said. "Guests of Australia. What a joke. As it happens, I was there for the 'Battle of Brisbane.' You hear about that? Don't tell me how you treat your guests!"

"Were you then?" Footy fumed. "I was there as well, as it happens."

"Then you know," Johnny said. "Thousands of you Aussies—soldiers and civilians—beat up every American servicemen you could get your hands on. You had to get all liquored up, naturally. We had to barricade ourselves into our buildings and fight for our lives. It went on for days. Australian hospitality! What a joke!"

"We got tired of you bloody Yanks abusing our women, strutting around like you owned our country," Footy said.

"You jealous?" Johnny shot back. "Is it our fault the Australian women prefer us?"

"Aww, is that it Yank?" Footy sneered. "You were out with one of our women?"

"Your women? You? Huh! As it turns out, I did have a date. I was walking her home when six yahoos jumped me. Six to one!"

"Aww, you get a black eye?"

"Maybe more than that," Johnny said, "but I got my licks in."

"You know what we say in Aus?" Footy said. "There's only three things wrong with you Yanks. You're overpaid—oversexed—and over here. And at the end of it in Brisbane, it was one of our lads who lay murdered in the street. Shot and killed by a Yank in the poor bloke's own country. Yet not one bloody Yank was killed, was he?"

"Yeah? Well I saw a lot of good friends die here in New Guinea," Johnny said, "and for what? For a bunch of losers who can't even say thank you? Now I'm getting mad. You better shut up."

Footy flicked the butt of his cigarette at the ground so hard, it exploded in a shower of sparks, and stormed to his bed.

Johnny spoke to him once more that night, at midnight when he shook him awake.

"Here," he said, shoving his rifle at the pilot. "We're going to have to get along 'til we're out of here. It's your watch. It's loaded. I've got three more shells and we're out." Johnny headed for his hammock without waiting for a reply. Footy glared after him, but roused himself and stayed on watch.

Both men were up before first light. Johnny grabbed his rifle, and with ill humor, they threw their things together and took to the trail. The sun drilled down and they poured with sweat. At mid-morning, they found a stream and replenished their canteens. The land was flat and the mountains they'd come out of were far behind, no more than a distant blue ribbon under clouds. The Raub spread beside them, wide and sluggish, the banks gone to mud and reeds. It looked like a wilderness unchanged since the dawn of time.

At mid-day, the river split into the first of many branches that would spread across the flats. The men had no choice but to follow the outer arm. Another hour, and Johnny felt his hopes surge when the first seagull drifted overhead, but his spirits sank again when he saw the mangroves in the distance.

It seemed to take forever to arrive at the swamp. The trekkers were appalled by the magnitude of it as they drew close. Stagnant water flooded the horizon, choked by mangroves and waterweeds.

This place is a crocodile's wet dream, Johnny thought grimly. But if they were to reach the South Pacific, they must soldier on. He and Footy stood on the edge of the everglade, mustering the will to enter. They saw ridges of dry ground here and there, but whole sections were submerged. At last, miserable with their options and each other, the men waded in with their footgear on.

At once, Footy discovered the mud sucked the sandals right off his feet. He had to bend and feel for them, his face almost in the slime. Fortunately, he found them, held them high, and walked on. Johnny did better in his boots, but on the far side, they were full of water. He had to sit, take them off, wring out his socks and towel dry his feet. If he didn't, he knew from dismal experience that the wet leather would soon rub the skin off, not to mention the jungle rot that would eat them away. And any lame man out here was likely to be a dead one.

Soon he, too, was wading with his boots tied around his neck. The men groped with their toes through dark water. *If I step on a croc,* Footy thought, *first I'll know about it will be me leg coming off.*

They arrived at a deep ford. Johnny stopped and stared unhappily at it. They had twenty yards to traverse and crocodiles could be anywhere—in the water, or lurking among the mangroves. He waded in, rifle high in both hands. Footy followed. The water surged to mid-calf, then to their knees.

Three quarters of the way through, Johnny began to sink. He cried out and Footy watched helplessly as the Yank went down in black water to his shoulders. Gingerly, Johnny continued and was able to scramble up the bank.

Footy stood swatting at biting flies that had joined with the mosquitoes in making life unbearable. Being the shorter man, he knew the water would go higher on him. He took off his pack and balanced it on his head. When he sank into the hole, the water lapped at his chin. Footy squeezed his lips tight to keep the muck out and pushed on. Johnny waited on the bank, rifle panning the mangroves. Footy crawled onto the bank and his worry overcame his vow of silence.

"I don't like this—not a bit. Now we're truly in the Father's country. If it, or any croc, finds us in a stretch like that...."

Johnny was still angry but anxiety gained the upper hand.

"I hear you," he said. "But what choice do we have? We've got to keep going."

Footy nodded grimly and the men forged on.

CHAPTER 24

Plagued by insects and anxiety, the men toiled through the swamp. The going was difficult and the knowledge that a crocodile could be waiting at every step wore them to a frazzle. The sun fried their heads under helmet and hat, and the hours were long.

Footy slugged along in distress and at last his irritation turned inward with a vengeance. *To let that kanaka seduce me—and take my rifle and revolver! Stupid chump, Footy,* the voice taunted him. *Useless little bugger! Always doing the wrong thing. You're going to pay for it now, and you deserve every bit of what's coming to you!* These were the barbs that had wounded him as a child, words fired like javelins by schoolmates, even teachers and parents. Back then, they had cut him to the quick, and now they pierced the scars and hit the same nerves. Footy's natural cheerfulness and confidence bled away.

By the end of the day, both men were wrung out and famished. There were no gardens and all they had was what was in their packs. They would have to live on it until they found another source of food, or reached the end of their journey. Johnny figured they had enough yams for one more day, and still they'd be hungry. As for drinking water, they had not come across any since they entered the swamp.

The haze over the everglade coalesced into a rag of cloud across the horizon. In the fading evening, the men searched for a patch of earth dry enough to camp on. The light was almost gone when they saw some higher ground, but to get there, they had to make another ford. There was no point in delaying. Johnny sloshed in.

Footy had spent an absolutely wretched day. His energy was gone and he was at snapping point. The whine of mosquitoes even inside his ears threatened to drive him over the edge. He stood slapping and muttering to himself as Johnny pushed through deep water.

When the Yank was on the far side and had turned with his rifle again, Footy crossed with sandals in hand, a swarm of insects dive-bombing his head. At mid-crossing, one landed on an eyelid and plunged in its needle. Footy slapped his eye and went blind for a moment. He lost his balance, staggered sideways, and put his foot down on something sharp. He felt the deep stab and yelped.

"What is it?" Johnny asked. Tentatively, Footy wiggled the leg, but it was held fast. He panicked, gave a sharp tug and something snapped underwater.

"Bloody hell!" He limped on, pulled himself out, dropped his pack and sat.

"What?" Johnny asked again.

"Stepped on something," Footy croaked. "Cut meself." Both groaned. The Aussie rinsed the foot as best he could by swishing it in the nasty water, turned it over in his hands and inspected the sole. Johnny sank beside him and they stared anxiously at the bloody ball. There was a gash with a jagged piece of black wood sticking out. Johnny dug in his pack and pulled out his towel and the first aid kit. He used a corner of cloth to wipe most of the slime away, while Footy winced.

"I've got to get that out," Johnny told him.

"Go on, just do it!" Footy said between clenched teeth. Johnny opened the bottle of iodine and poured some around the splinter. Footy yelped and beat the ground. Johnny took the foot in one hand and pinched the stick between thumb and finger. He jerked out a two-inch wedge of sodden wood while Footy gasped.

Johnny got his thumbs on either side of the wound and pressed hard. Footy let out a string of colorful words, some Johnny had not heard. He kept the pressure on until the black flecks were gone and the blood ran pure.

He poured more iodine into the wound while Footy called down damnation on all swamps and several kinds of marsupials. When the worst of the bleeding had stopped, Johnny tipped sulfa powder into the gash.

How will I be able to go on? Footy wondered. *How can I wade through the bleeding muck like this? Hopefully, the iodine has sterilized it. If the ruddy foot gets infected mate, you'll not walk at all. I get a bit of crumpet and what—I'm forced to pay for it with me life?*

Johnny told Footy he'd bandage the cut, and they were here for the night. He unrolled the pilot's blanket for him and helped the Aussie lie down. Johnny figured he should elevate the injured foot.

He chopped a forked mangrove branch, stuck it in the mud and rested Footy's heel in it.

"How is it?" Johnny asked.

"Hurts like a bugga," Footy growled.

"Do you want morphine?" Johnny asked.

"You've got morphine?" Footy sputtered. "Bloody morphine? Why didn't you say so? Yes, dose me up mate."

Johnny selected one of the three small metal tubes called "syrettes." He broke the seal, attached the needle, inserted it in Footy's arm and squeezed the tube. The Aussie's eyes soon glazed over and he sank back.

"Better?" Johnny asked.

"Much, ta," Footy murmured.

"I'll sew it up," Johnny said.

"Take it off, for all I care," Footy said. Johnny got a needle and length of thread from his pack. He soaked both in iodine, crouched in front of the Aussie, and said he was going to begin. He got no answer and saw Footy had nodded out.

Johnny pushed the needle through the thick skin. He looped stitch after stitch, eight of them, until the gash was drawn tight. He soaked a pad of gauze in iodine and laid it over the wound, then cut strips of tape from a roll and stuck the square down. He ripped more strips and covered the patch, trying to make it watertight. He fetched his spare pair of socks—none too clean, unfortunately, but they'd have to do—and pulled them over the Aussie's feet.

Johnny gathered firewood. The fallen branches were spongy and again, he had trouble getting a flame from his Zippo. At last he managed to get a pinch of dry moss to burn. He fed it with twigs and got a fire going. Water sputtered out of the ends of the sticks, and the smoke was thick, but with the insect squadrons flying low, that was all for the best. Johnny cooked the last of the yams on the coals. *One for tonight, three for the whole day tomorrow, and that's it.*

While they roasted, Johnny gathered wood for the long night ahead. He unrolled his hammock upside down on the ground so the waterproof roof would serve as a tarp. He spread his sheet on top of that and used a spare shirt for a pillow.

While Footy slept, Johnny took a pot to the pond. He could see where their steps coming across were gray mushrooms in the black. With his hands, he parted the wiry mangroves and palms until he found a trickle of clearer water. He was able to get the edge of the pot under and filled it. He took it back to the fire and piled branches around it. When it had boiled for ten minutes, he set it aside to cool. It would be their drinking water for the day to come. When the *kaukau* were cooked, he pulled them out and ate a single one.

He lay down, still starving. Clouds obscured the stars and the ember glow was the only light. Johnny gazed into the coals as the swamp frogs sang. Something rustled through the reeds and plopped into the marsh. Johnny hadn't been able to get enough sleep for days, but he was determined to remain on guard. He was staring mesmerized at the flickering coals when he heard Footy's disembodied voice.

"About that girl..."

"That's done," Johnny told him. "Let it go."

"That was me first time."

Johnny grunted in surprise. He waited for more, but the Aussie was silent and he made out in the glow that the man was asleep. The mosquitoes were ferocious and Johnny adjusted the Digger hat over Footy's head. He pulled the square of netting from the man's pack and tented it over the hat and face. He got Footy's spare shirt and spread it over the Aussie's hands.

Johnny lay back, rifle across his lap, and thought about Gwyn. He wondered if she believed he was still alive. Many times on this journey, he'd wondered why she asked him to look for his heart. He still didn't know what to do about that. It was just the sort of thing a girl would do to torment a guy.

For a time he thought about Dingo, reminded of him by the things spread around Footy. He realized he didn't even know if the Major was married or had a family. If so, they had no idea yet that the man was not coming home.

Then Johnny thought about the Father. He had never imagined such a horrifying predator would be on the hunt for him. How could you fight something that massive and savage, and in a place like this? If it came for him now, as well it could, he was done. No man could go hand-to-hand with a brute like that.

Suddenly Johnny's head jerked up. He'd dropped off, and he shook his head and slapped his face to rouse himself. He peered into the swamp but could see nothing outside the little orange glow of the coals. He sat up, and it seemed to be forever before he saw the hint of lighter gray in the east. That was the instant his eyelids fell. He even knew for a few seconds it was happening, but he could not stop it. He fell on his side and it was too late. He was sound asleep.

He did not see the cold eyes that stared at him from the darkness. Nor was he aware when the watcher began to glide for him through the water, intent on his death.

Dawn found the Father in the delta. The river split into various branches and it chose the one most traveled by the two-legged prey. The crocodile surged deep into the marsh to the ambush place.

This ford had been haunted by generations of crocodiles. Here the topography and jungle conspired to form a bottleneck. All animals that wanted to pass from one side to the other must go through the water itself. And then they were in the domain of the aquatic reptiles. For tens of thousands of years, this had been the site of uncounted predations.

At first light, the Father arrived. In that neck of water, it sensed several of its own kind. One of them lay in the very place the Father wanted for itself. Without pause, the giant launched at the incumbent, but this was no minor freshwater reptile. It was a muscular saltwater male in its own right, and it felt the disturbance in the current and knew what it meant. Enraged, it stood through the surface and, with a territorial bellow, turned to confront the newcomer.

The Father's huge head burst up by its flank. At once, the defender knew it was undone. The challenger was at least twice its size. Bravado flipped to terror, and the smaller one tried to bolt. But the Father snatched the tail in its teeth and lifted the entire hind end out of the water, the webbed feet pedaling.

The defender corkscrewed in agony as its tail came off. The Father dropped the appendage, charged up and bit the bull's neck. Its jaws more than reached from one side to the other, and the conical teeth crushed through.

Its grip sure, the Father rolled into deeper water, dragging the victim. The whole river churned, waves slapped the bank, and the surface became a blur of scales and legs.

The combatants sank and the surface settled. Then a crimson gout shot up and the froth went pink. Again the river's surface calmed, and finally, floating up through the murk came the pale underbody of the dead crocodile. The head hung to one side, barely connected. The entire neck was missing. Belly up, the carcass drifted away, bumping its detached tail. Blood dripped from its grievous wounds, and ripples formed all around it as eels and fish rushed in to feed. The body rounded a bend in the mangroves.

The entire length of water along the bank lifted and the Father stood in the wash. It parted its jaws and roared its triumph. At once, the other crocodiles burst from hiding and flung themselves away. For several minutes, there was only frantic splashing, the snapping of branches, and the scream of watching birds.

Again the Father settled, leaving eyes, ears and nostrils exposed. It slowed its huge four-chambered heart until it beat only once every five minutes.

And so the hunter waited for the one-prey. Light and darkness came in their turn, and it did not move.

At last it heard what it craved—the unmistakable approach of the two-legged animals. The Father ducked its head entirely underwater and stared at the place where the spindly legs were bound to appear.

CHAPTER 25

A sound at his ear penetrated Johnny's sleep and he struggled for consciousness. He was on his back and his eyes opened into bright sunlight. Something loomed over him, and Johnny squinted, trying to make out the silhouette against the glare. He blinked and regained focus.

With a shock he realized it was the Japanese. He was very much alive, and he held his sword, a shaft of light over Johnny's neck. He was gauging where to strike and the blade went high for the killing blow.

Johnny's mind reeled: the sword was at the top of its arc. He wrenched his gaze from it to the Asian eyes and said the first thing that came to him.

"You owe me your life."

The man's face was fierce, his body committed to the slash, but the blade wavered and held where it was.

"You owe me your life—three times over," Johnny said. "When I captured you, I spared you. In the Mambu village, I saved you again. And when Mula's men asked for you, that was the third time."

The Japanese said nothing and his muscles bunched, but he did not strike.

A battle raged within Katsu. His enemy was helpless beneath his *katana* and he had the one deadly, beautiful act to perform. In his bones, he was samurai. On top of that, like a suit of armor, he was a soldier of the Empire. But what the Yankee said sunk into him like a steel shaft.

The problem was, it was true.

In his single-minded desire to regain his *katana* and do his duty—kill the enemy—Katsu had not considered this. But it was a fact. He owed this man his life. Now the American called for that debt to be paid.

Johnny watched the blade quiver in the light of a new sun, and he knew his life hung in the balance.

Katsu thought, *my country is beaten and so am I*. Despair fired through him and he swung the sword at Johnny's neck.

Chomi was twenty-five and he lived in the swamp. Life here was precarious. His people inhabited stilt huts beside a channel of the river. The men hunted smaller crocodiles they could snare or spear for meat and skins. When the occasional saltwater giant wandered their way, they gathered the children and pigs into the huts and waited for it to pass.

Sometimes raiding parties came their way, even the most feared of all, the cannibal Mambu. They came to kill men and take booty—women, pigs and children. When they entered the delta, the families abandoned their homes and hid in the deep swamp.

Chomi must also consider supernatural dangers, for spirits lived everywhere. Some were indifferent to humans, a few were kind, most were malevolent. Spirits inhabited every animal and tree, patch of land and pool of water. The great fierce ones lived in the sky and the river. When these manifested in the form of tempests and floods, they altered the course of the people's lives, or simply slaughtered them.

In the most recent storm, the river had risen around the houses and tugged at the stilts. Chomi and his wives rushed to get the children upstairs and then worked to save the pigs. As their relatives in each dwelling scurried to do the same, Chomi's family formed a human ladder and handed up the four adult hogs and seven piglets. He had the last two precious ones in his hands when disaster struck.

Splintering trees, a wall of water broke from the forest. Chomi saw the face of the raging spirit in it, and then it was on him, trying to pull him and his piglets away to drown. He was forced to drop the little ones and hang on with both arms while his wives, children and the other pigs screamed overhead. Chomi climbed the ladder like a half-drowned swamp rat, but the little pigs were swept off.

Throughout the night the storm raged, and the people and their animals huddled together and comforted one another. But then, in the dawn, when it seemed the worst was over, an uprooted forest giant struck across the stilts.

For several minutes the houses shuddered, and then the support poles gave way. People, pigs, and possessions, rained into the torrent. Chomi managed to grab the baby and another child as he fell. Humans and animals of his clan were swept away, everyone shouting, and he held the baby and grabbed a branch. The other boy clutched his neck. Chomi clung on and waited for the flood to subside, not knowing who lived or died.

Eventually, the clan found it had lost one man, two women, four children, and nine pigs. It was clear they had offended a powerful spiritual force. The place itself had turned on them. They could no longer remain here. It had become taboo.

Chomi knew at once he must guide the clan to another site, but the group discussion raged for two more days. This was interspersed with the search for the lost and the rituals for the dead. The human corpses they tied in the trees. Three freshly drowned pigs, they ate. Other corpses, including a woman and two children, they never found. These, no doubt, had been eaten by crocodiles.

Chomi was the best hunter in the clan, and he knew the swamp for miles around. He must take his immediate family to a new place, then return and lead the others to safety.

This was how Chomi, accompanied by all his wives, children and animals, found himself journeying through the everglade. The place he was taking them to was dry ground on which they could build. It had room to plant a garden. Wild Sago Palms grew in abundance, which the women would beat and wash to remove the poison before they could eat the starchy paste. A spring of clean water flowed there, rare in the swamp. The surrounding trees were strong and tall. They would make good stilts for the new homes.

Most importantly, a branch of the river flowed by the land. It was their hunting ground and provider of life. From the first time he saw it, Chomi felt it was a place where the inhabiting spirits would permit the people to live.

In order to reach it, however, they must cross the one place Chomi feared above all else. This was a ford where the big *pook-pook* lay in wait. Even saltwater monsters lurked here. Over the years, Chomi had witnessed three full-grown warriors taken at this crossing. It was terrible to watch a crocodile kill a man.

Now he led the way with a son on his hip, and the young boar around his neck. In Chomi's fist was his prize possession, a metal machete he had traded a pig for. Behind him came the young wife and the baby, and she led the boar on a vine rope. More children and pigs followed and the senior wife walked at the rear.

She was strong and carried a stout pole, and Chomi had confidence in her. The sow she pulled came grunting, head down, harassed by three large offspring. These pressed against her, trying to suckle, but this the sow would not permit.

The family had crossed water several times. At each pool, Chomi stopped the others well back while he went on alone. He looked to see if any large *pookpook* waited there. When he saw dung and tracks, he noted how fresh they were and if the animal was present. Several times, he saw the eye bumps of smaller crocodiles and entered the water to drive them off.

At one ford, he spied a big crocodile lurking in the reeds. This *pookpook* was twice as big as Chomi and he did not even try to confront it. He returned to the family and they backtracked around the danger.

Traveling with children and pigs slowed Chomi and he was anxious and irritable, shouting at the little ones when normally, he was the most tender of fathers. The reason was that he wanted to cross the most dangerous place in daylight. But by the time they got there, evening already dimmed the forest. His apprehension peaked when he considered being stranded here in darkness. Then the crocodiles could take them at their leisure.

The new home site was not far off. Chomi planned to sleep there this night. But the perilous water stood between him and safety.

When they approached the ford, Chomi told the family to wait. He took the stick from a wife and trotted to the water. His worry increased when he saw the droppings and footprints of large *pookpook*. He prodded the vegetation and nothing erupted. He turned his attention to the water and poked the pole there. Again, nothing.

Cautiously he waded in, working the stick ahead before each step. When he made it to the other bank he gasped with relief. It was almost dark now. He had minutes to get the family through before the horror of the night would be on them.

He ran back and urged his family towards the dark water. The people drove the pigs up and surrounded them to prevent them from running off. The swine milled around complaining. They smelled the crocodiles and they knew the humans were going to force them to swim. The people felt very much like the pigs, on the verge of blind panic.

Chomi took the boy on his hip again and put the young boar around his neck. He knew he must be decisive or everything would be lost. He ordered all to follow and waded in, again prodding with the stick before him. The water came to his waist and the boy clung to his father as they pushed through.

Chomi trembled with relief when he climbed the far bank. He put the boy down and returned to the channel. He took the baby from the young wife and hauled the swimming boar bodily along by an ear. When the woman and the first group were safe, he went back into the pool to help the older wife and the rest. Now he beat the pigs through the water.

A piglet panicked and broke for the wrong bank. Chomi called a warning and the oldest girl lunged after it into deeper water. She caught the animal by the leg and brought it out.

Chomi breathed easier when everyone was across. Rapidly, he led them away from the place that turned his bowels to water.

The Father lay submerged, its snout where the people and animals had just passed. When they were in the water, all its instincts screamed to attack! During its long years, this was how the dominant bull had fed its vast body. But something profound had changed in its appetite. It had waited here only for the smooth-headed man.

The crocodile watched the creatures pass. It could taste the fear coming off them in the eddies of warm urine. It knew how the bodies bursting in its teeth would taste. But it did not attack. Even when the little pig swam overhead and the small female kicked the Father's head, it did not bite.

Now the noisy prey were gone, the crocodile stood up. It felt a turmoil of conflicting urges and it parted its jaws and roared its frustration.

A hundred paces further along the trail, Chomi heard that and shivered from head to toe. He knew how big the predator must be to make that sound, and it came from the water they had just crossed.

The children and swine heard as well and they squealed in terror. Chomi ordered the younger wife to lead. She ran while he fell back, urging the family on.

"Run! Run for your lives!" They virtually flew along, pigs with their tails high, people rolling their eyes at every shadow. Chomi came last, and every few strides he whirled, machete ready.

The predator was far too agitated to remain here. Again, it rumbled its frustration and abandoned its ambush. It swam downstream aggressively, its foreleg throbbing. Without interest, it swept by the corpse of the cousin it had slaughtered.

It swam as darkness came, and then into the night. With each hour that passed, it grew leaner, harder, and hungrier. But this hunger was for one food only—the one-prey. It even ignored the juicy, coarse-scaled fish that swam right in front of its snout.

The water turned brackish with the rising tide. Salt tingled around the reptile's teeth and burned into the wounded limb, but this hurt was welcome. The Father grew eager for the ocean.

The South Pacific was calling its child to come home.

CHAPTER 26

The samurai sword flashed down at Johnny's neck and he did not know if he lived or died. Now the enemy's hands were locked, the blade out of sight. The swordsman held still, muscles like ropes. Then he stood, lifted the weapon away and stepped back.

Johnny's hand flew to his throat and he brought fingers up to see if he was cut. There was no blood, and only then did he know he was unharmed. He sat, staring warily at the other man. The Japanese deliberately touched his thumb to the razor edge and a line of scarlet appeared.

"When I draw the *katana*," the soldier said in the clearest English Johnny had heard from him, "it must taste blood." He wiped the thumb on his trousers and slipped the *katana* into its scabbard.

The man was outlined in sun and Johnny saw him in that moment with hyper-clarity, as though for the very first time. In the gift of his life continuing, the perception flooded him: the Japanese was lithe, centered, and each movement was precise, controlled. For the first time, Johnny did not see an unattractive foreigner. He was a man born of another race and tradition, certainly, but he was a warrior of artistry, even grace. Johnny received the insight in a flash, at a super-conscious level, beyond his ability to articulate.

Jap, Nip, Slant, Slope, the words chased their tails through his mind. *We call them that to make them subhuman, to make it easy to kill them. But here is a soldier like me, who fights because his country sent him.* In the hours and days to come, the realization would fade, but it would never be entirely lost.

"I owe you my life. I forgot that," the Japanese told him. The man sat on the ground, crossed his legs, and spoke again.

"It is an old thing you call on, much older than this war. But it is true—yes, I owe you my life." Johnny stared back at him.

"Now I have paid that debt, or some of it. I have given you your life. Beyond that, I believe the atom bomb is real. Nippon is lost, for who can fight such a catastrophe? And if my country is lost, my life has no value. You say I owe you my life—I give it to you. Kill me or not, it is the same to me now."

The scabbard was at hand and he slid the sword into it. He held the *katana* in both hands, bowed his head, and placed it on the ground in front of the American. Johnny saw his rifle was out of reach as well. The Japanese had moved it. Now the man put the Springfield beside the sword and sat back. Johnny looked at him searchingly and saw that this time, the enemy had truly surrendered.

"What the bloody hell is going on?" Footy asked, voice raw with sleep. The pilot was raised on his elbow, hair tousled, hat and netting pushed aside. Johnny found he was very glad the Japanese had not hurt Footy and he grinned.

"Look what the cat dragged in."

Footy was unhappy. Johnny explained what had happened, about the Japanese coming back and then surrendering again. The pilot was too distracted by his pain to ask many questions. He saw the socks on his feet and did ask about that.

"I sewed your cut while you were out from the morphine," Johnny said. "I hope you can walk, but you can't go barefoot. I got the injury taped, but you're going to have to wear my boots."

Footy knew he should be grateful to the Yank, but he was in a filthy mood. He asked himself why, and apart from the obvious injury, it was something he couldn't put his finger on. *It has to do with the Jap, but what?* He tried to puzzle it through, but it eluded him.

Johnny brought his boots and the Aussie pulled them over the socks. They were too big and he laced them tight. With the Yank's help he got up to his feet and tried his weight on the hurt leg. The pain was sharp. Footy grimaced but forced himself to take some steps.

"It'll do," he muttered. His head felt thick and he realized he was hung over from the morphine. As soon as he thought it, he wanted more and asked for it.

"Better not," Johnny said, "if you can bear it, Footy. There are only two more doses and you might need it worse—later on." Footy saw the sense of that, and gave a curt nod.

"Right you are," he said. *One more thing the Yank's in charge of*. He turned his bloodshot stare at the enemy and then back to Johnny. *It's something there.*

Johnny packed his gear and poured the boiled water into the bottles. He tied his machete and bayonet-knife to the outside of his pack. He didn't want to get them wet when he had to wade. Once more, he missed the feel of his .45 on the belt and had to let it go.

The only food they had were the three potatoes he'd cooked last night. He gave one to Footy, then looked at the prisoner and at the two *kaukau* he had left. *I could eat six myself*, he thought.

"Here!" Johnny said gruffly and gave one to the Japanese. The man nodded thanks and bit in ravenously, not bothering to strip the burnt skin. Johnny ate the other one.

Footy watched the Japanese shovel it in, resenting every bite. *Johnny can play bloody saint if he wants, but not me mate, not me. The Jap's the enemy and he's eating our food.* The blighter was dirty and scratched all over. He'd even lost his shirt somewhere. *Almost naked,* Footy thought. *Bloody monkey!*

"Look," Johnny said to him, "we can't be far from the ocean. The Jap surrendered and I believe he means it. I'm not going to tie him up anymore. He wants to run, let him go. We've got your foot to deal with. Let's try and get out of this alive!" Footy glared at the captive.

"No bloody way he can go free," he said. "I don't trust him." Johnny stepped to the prisoner and stared in his face.

"I want your word you will not hurt us," Johnny said "If you want to leave, I won't stop you. But if you come with us, you're our prisoner. You obey our orders. Do we have a deal?" The prisoner gazed back and nodded.

"Say 'yes,'" Johnny told him.

"Yes," the Japanese said.

"Ok," Johnny said, and turned away.

"Bloody hell!" Footy exploded, "you're going to accept that?" The Japanese turned and stared hard at the Australian, but said nothing.

"Ok," Johnny said to Footy, "how would you do it?" The Aussie frowned at the Japanese.

"Swear on your Emperor's life that you won't harm us," he said. "These bloody people believe the Emperor is a god," Footy said to Johnny. The prisoner thought, nodded, and spoke.

"This is an unusual request, but I swear on the life of Emperor

Hirohito I will not harm you." The man was clearly serious, and even Footy was somewhat mollified.

"Ok," Johnny said. "Here's how I see it. We've still got a lot of croc country to cover. Let's move out! You come behind me," he told the Aussie. "You need help, I'm right in front. You come last," he said to the Japanese, "You carry Footy's pack and water." The Japanese nodded. Footy was unhappy to have his things in the prisoner's hands but he knew what the Yank said made sense. Johnny picked up the sword and balanced it on his hands.

"Now," he said, "what are we going to do with this?"

"No way the Jap's having it," Footy barked. "You can't trust him with that! It's mine."

"Fine," Johnny said. "I'm not going to hump it. You?"

Footy limped over and snatched the thing. *I'm not going to let the Jap behind me with this bloody pig sticker! The Yank forgets what the bugger did to those cannibals!* More than that, he was not going to give up his samurai souvenir for anyone. He already pictured himself showing it around the taverns in Cairns.

The Japanese watched but said nothing. Johnny shrugged, put on his pack and picked up his Springfield. Footy wore his boots, so now Johnny's own feet were bare. The marsh stretched away on all sides. It was not even pools of water, but more like a wide and putrid lake, standing with mangroves.

Johnny waded into the rank liquid. The edges were tangles of roots. When he was up to his waist, he saw something move in the shadows and whirled with his rifle. A snake, body thick as his arm, undulated through the stalks and disappeared. Johnny shuddered and pushed on.

He climbed out on the bank, turned with the Springfield ready and called for Footy to come. The Aussie limped slowly through, having trouble as his booted feet sank in the thick ooze. The sword waved in his free hand. The prisoner followed, carrying Dingo's pack.

They got across and continued, wading more often than walking. Footy's pace was agonizingly slow and Johnny had to stop frequently and wait. He got an idea and began to study the vegetation. When he saw what he wanted, a mangrove that forked at shoulder height, he chopped it down. Johnny tried the crutch under Footy's arm, trimmed it to fit and padded the fork with his towel. Footy passed the sword to Johnny and took some steps as rivulets of sweat streamed down his face.

"Footy, that's better," Johnny said, "but what are we going to do about this?" He waved the sword.

"You carry it mate," Footy puffed.

"No way," Johnny said. "I've got enough as it is."

"Give it here then," Footy glowered and Johnny handed it over. The prisoner's eyes flashed between the men. The Aussie gripped the crutch in his right hand and the sword in his left. Johnny shrugged and strode away. The Japanese waited for the Australian to move and trailed him. They went on like that for several hours. Footy did better on the crutch, but still went at a turtle pace.

Finally, and for the first time, the Japanese spoke directly to him.

"I will carry the sword."

"Not a prayer in hell," Footy frowned.

"That has been in my family for three hundred years," the Japanese said. "It has been handed from father to son all that time. Please—you cannot get it wet. And you are unable to carry it."

"I will bloody well do what I like with it!" Footy barked.

"I have surrendered," the prisoner said. "I have promised not to hurt you." He took a breath. "The sword has a name. *'Katsumushi-maru.'* I ask you—please keep *Katsumushi-maru* dry. Its value is beyond price."

"I'll soak it in sheep-dip if I want," Footy shouted, shaking the sword. "It's mine! " Now Johnny was irritated.

"What does it matter if we don't get through? This is crazy! Let's get out of this swamp!"

Johnny marched to the next ford. It was another deep one. He raised his rifle and went in. The murk smelled like a sewer and swirled up to his chest. When he got to the far bank, once again he covered the other men while they crossed.

Footy reached the halfway point, the Japanese a pace behind. Then the Aussie's crutch stuck deep in the mud and pulled out from under his arm. Footy started to fall and the sword swung wildly. He would have gone facedown if the prisoner hadn't rushed up and grabbed him. Footy half turned, still falling. For a long moment they did a slow dance, the sword circling wildly. Then the Australian brought the scabbard down hard across the other man's head. The crack made Johnny wince.

The prisoner steadied Footy with a fist in his shirt while his other hand shot out and snatched the sword. Blood trickled from the gash above his headband. When he was sure Footy was steady, the Japanese let him go and went back for the crutch. He pulled it from the mud and shoved it at the Aussie.

"Take it!" he said. Footy squinted at the man's split scalp.

"Crikey!" He said.

"I will carry the sword across," the prisoner said. The pilot stared at him. "Then you can have it."

Without waiting for a reply, the Japanese lifted Footy's free arm and shoved his head under. He put an arm around the injured man's waist and extended his other one holding the sword for balance. The twosome moved towards Johnny. Footy's right hand worked the crutch and he was forced to put his own arm around the prisoner's shoulders. He was struck by the physical reality of the captive, solid in his reluctant embrace. The two came through foul water up to their necks.

When they were safely beside Johnny, the Japanese pulled away from the Australian. Johnny saw each man brush at the place where the other's hands had touched him. Footy was panting and streaming with water.

"Give it back," he said. The prisoner looked him over, nodded, and handed him the sword. The Aussie grabbed it and glared.

"Come on!" Johnny said and led them across a dryer stretch of mud. The day was sweltering, the insects remorseless, and the men were famished.

And as it turned out, it was the sword that was Footy's downfall. Each time they entered water—and that was every few minutes—he had to hand it to the Japanese. When they came to dryer land again, he insisted he take it back. And so it went, on and on. When they were not in the water, Footy shoved the scabbard through his belt. The snarled mangroves caught it and made it thump across his shins. Finally it wedged against a branch and tripped him up. All his weight came down on his throbbing foot and he fell on his face.

"Blast it all to bloody hell!" he shouted. He scrambled up and jerked the sword out of his belt. "I'd like to throw this far, far away!" The other men were watching him.

"Footy, you're a drag on us," Johnny told him. "Either do throw it away, or let the prisoner carry it. He said he'd give it back when we're out of here."

"Not on your life," Footy snapped. "He'll kill us with it, mark my words."

"Maybe we should stop talking like he wasn't here," Johnny said. "You!" he said to the Japanese. "If we give you the sword, you promise not to hurt us?"

"I already promised," the Japanese said. "I will not hurt you."

"Give him the sword!" Johnny shouted, "Or we're going to have to leave you behind. We've got to find food!"

"All-bloody-right!" Footy snarled. "Here, take the blasted thing! But when I ask you for it, you give it back at once! Agreed?"

The two men stared until the Japanese spoke quietly.

"I am your prisoner. When you say, I give it to you."

Footy shoved the scabbard into the man's hands and turned away, fussing with the crutch. The Japanese held his sword once more and Johnny saw the barest hint of a smile.

"Sheesh!" Johnny said and headed off. Footy limped after him, and the Japanese came at the end.

Stupid bloody turn of events, Footy fumed. *Bloody Jap behind me with that carving knife!* He thought of the way the prisoner removed those heads in the Valley of the Cannibals and he shivered. He took another step while the crutch jarred him under the arm.

The bloody Yank! He shot a murderous look at the back of Johnny's head. *He's taking sides with the Jap! Yes, exactly mate*, it came to him, *what's bothering me. The Yank is siding against me with the friggin' Jap. What's it coming to?*

Stupid hairy ogre, the Japanese thought, watching Footy's back. *You are goshu-yaro, a rude peasant. I speak English better than you know. And you? You will never even begin to understand my language or the ways of civilized people. I could remove your head from your neck before you could turn around. But I will not do it because I have promised. You live, not because you deserve to, but because of my word, my honor.*

I am sick of both of them, Johnny thought. *I am sick of this place, the Father, and I am fed up with these men. I am stuck in the middle of nowhere while my unit goes to invade Japan without me! And I'm so hungry I could eat a shoe. I'd give anything for a burger on a toasted bun. I want a thick meat patty running with juice, lettuce, sliced tomato, pickles and catsup. I'll have a plate of fries and a frosty vanilla shake.* He saw the vision so vividly, his stomach whined. He clamped his empty jaw shut and made the hallucination go away by sucking in a lungful of rancid air.

The men toiled across the sodden landscape. Always, they watched for crocodiles. Many times they saw them, but these were smaller ones they could scare away by yelling and smacking the water. *Where is the Father?* Johnny wondered for the thousandth time.

They came to an especially perilous ford. It was long and deep and had numerous channels into the mangroves. Johnny crossed on high alert, but reached the far bank without incident. He clambered up and turned with his rifle.

"Come!"

Once again, Footy and the prisoner put their arms around one another and entered the water. They got halfway across before Johnny saw what he'd been half-expecting, but hoping not to see.

A massive scaled snout came out of a channel. Head caked in sludge, lines of yellow teeth showing, it sped silently at the men. Johnny saw at once it was a massive saltwater crocodile, but he could not see if the eye was scarred.

"Croc!" Johnny yelled and aimed for the heart, into the body behind the foreleg, and shot. The bullet flew true and the swimmer shuddered as though hit by a sledgehammer, but kept on coming.

His shout and the clap of the shot made the other men flinch. In unison they swung their heads where the smoking rifle pointed and saw the crocodile coming for them. Instantly they ran, but in slow motion, impeded by deep water. The predator slid across the surface.

They won't make it! Johnny inserted another shell as some scorekeeper in his head began to call. *One gone, three bullets left!*

The brute might be big enough to be the Father. Johnny couldn't tell with the mud on it. Now it was almost behind the men. In seconds, their bodies would shield it as it maneuvered to attack from behind.

Johnny shot again and hit the jaw in front of the eye. The attacker hissed and kept coming. Johnny chambered another shell as the scorekeeper called—*two left!*

Footy and the Japanese ran on, faces contorted. Footy held his crutch out of the water while the Japanese raised the scabbard on the other side. The croc was almost behind the prisoner and it dove as Johnny fired again. The bullet whistled by the captive's arm, glanced off the top of the rock-hard skull and ricocheted away.

One left! The scorekeeper screamed as Johnny loaded it.

Footy was taking long strides and the Japanese almost carried him. But the croc was too fast, right behind them now, and they were still fifteen feet from the bank.

Johnny felt the first urge to run and let it go by. Urgently calm, he peered through the scope but all he could see was the men, and the wake of the croc behind them as it rushed to attack.

CHAPTER 27

"Get aside! Dive!" Johnny yelled at the men in the water. It seemed to take forever for his words to reach them, and even longer for them to grasp his meaning. At last Footy and the prisoner let go of one another. A space opened between them and Johnny put the crosshairs there. The Japanese ducked under Footy's arm and pushed the Australian towards the bank, while he fell aside, trying to maintain his balance and keep his sword from getting wet.

Johnny's crosshairs found the croc's head and he squeezed. He heard the clap of the shot and the instantaneous crack of bullet striking thick bone.

Footy twisted, fell onto his back in the slop, and ran up against the bank. The crocodile rushed him with open jaws. The Japanese fell into the dark water and his head went under, but he kept the *katana* dry. He sprang to his feet and drew the blade. Johnny had no bullets left, and he put down the rifle and pulled his machete.

Jaws lined with jagged teeth surged up Footy's body. With his crutch, the pilot stabbed into the dark mouth. The point struck the reptile's palate so hard the vibration hurt the pilot's arm.

One hundred billion synapses fired randomly when Johnny's last bullet twisted through the crocodilian brain. The long jaws slammed shut and pulverized the crutch. But the snout kept coming until it slammed Footy back and pushed against his chin. He was pinned against the bank, unable even to turn his head. The water swirled a last time as a croc leg kicked underwater. The death sigh blasted into Footy's face and he choked.

The Japanese stood with his sword ready but the crocodile was dead. The crack of the shots still carried across the swamp and a thousand water birds lifted in a wide circle and flew away.

"Get the bastard off me!" Footy wheezed beneath the weight. In its final rush, the water had washed the scaled head and there was no moon scar. Now it was not moving, Johnny could see it would measure about twenty feet.

"It's not the Father," he observed. He left his machete and crouched behind Footy.

"It's friggin' heavy enough!" the Aussie sputtered. "Get the bastard off me!" The Japanese put his sword down and kneeled beside Johnny. They grabbed Footy under the arms and pulled hard, but he did not budge.

"We'll have to lift the head," Johnny told the Japanese. They entered the water on each side of the croc and got their fingers under the edge of the lower jaw. Johnny saw that the skull was about as long as he was tall.

"Lift!" Johnny called and the two put their backs into it. The head floated just a little and Footy tried to jerk his body out, but could not get free. Neither could the men hold up the weight, and it settled back on the pilot.

"Bloody hell!" Footy gasped. "By all the bleedin' saints, try again!" Johnny wiped the sweat from his eyes and took a breath. Already, blowflies were gathering on the croc's wounds and eyes.

Once more they bent. Again they lifted with all their strength, tendons standing out on necks and arms. Footy grasped the snout, wedged his fingers between the teeth and pushed up. He worked his feet out on each side of the jaw, and then was able to crab up the bank. Johnny and the prisoner let the head splash back in the glop and climbed out as well.

"On top of everything else, we're out of ammo," Johnny told a shaken Footy. "If the Father comes now...." He shrugged, picked up his machete and gave a wolfish grin.

"At least tonight we eat steak!"

— O —

On the beach near the mouth of the Raub River, Captain Cleveland Karsh of the United States Marine Corps strode among his men. They jumped to meet his orders, the way he liked it.

This, Karsh knew, was a truly momentous day and he had a celebration planned for his marines. But first, he would see to the completion of their task. This morning the Captain brought fifteen men ashore. The launch, skippered by Karsh himself, came in from the ship. Now it bobbed at anchor while two smaller tenders with outboard motors were pulled up on the sand.

Before he'd selected this site, Karsh had the boats run in both directions along the beach and the delta mouths of the Raub River. They'd searched for any sign of the men he'd been sent to find—three Allied soldiers and two civilians. *Priests, of all things*. The men had gone missing far up-river, in the unexplored interior of the island. It had been an Army scheme gone wrong, Karsh had been briefed. Now the men were MIA and presumed KIA. Karsh's assignment had been described to him as a long shot. *Still, whatever we can do for our boys.*

In fact, Karsh would rather be headed north to observe one of the most momentous days of the decade, even of the 20th Century. But, as always, Cleveland Karsh did his duty competently and with a positive disposition.

His attention was on the cache of goods they'd brought—emergency supplies in case the missing men got this far. He'd picked the logical place to leave it, near the widest branch of the Raub. Beneath a shade tree so tall it would be a landmark in every direction, he had the marines spread the tarp. On it, the men had piled an assortment of items.

The Captain's two aides stood beside him, both 2nd Lieutenants. The tropical sun was fierce in spite of the breeze off the Pacific. Karsh tugged off his cap and ran a handkerchief over his egg-bald head. He folded the square of cloth and returned it to his pocket, then stood at ease, powerful legs apart, hands clasped behind his back. The cache was almost ready. Karsh checked his watch and told his aides to call a break.

It was midday and the Captain had arranged for lunch on the beach. He brought the cooks and materials on the launch and now the meal was ready. Karsh and his officers returned to where the Commander's tent had been pitched. They sat on folding chairs at a folding table.

The cooks served them first—china plates piled with pot roast made from frozen Texas beef, canned peas and instant mashed potatoes swimming in gravy. Not far away, the enlisted men sat with Gunny on the sand. They would enjoy the same fare, served on metal plates. This was one of the Captain's rules. *My men eat what I eat.*

The sun blazed in the brilliant sky, the South Pacific sparkled and the coconut palms swayed. Most of the men had stripped to the waist. After they plowed through their chow, they lay back and smoked, or simply suntanned.

At 16-hundred hours, three hours from now, the Captain was due back aboard ship. Karsh would be there early, as always. The motto of the marines was *"Semper Fidelis*—Always Faithful." The Captain added his own: *"Semper Promptus*—Always Early."

"Bring me pen and paper, and the waterproof pouch," he ordered. His senior aide was Alexander "Chip" Calder. Chip had been with the Captain for two years, a lifetime out here. The other young man was Blair, who'd been with them a month. Now Chip nodded at the younger man and he trotted to the tent and fetched the requested materials. Karsh took them, uncapped his fountain pen, and prepared to write.

"What was the name again?" he asked. Chip had his notebook ready.

"The officer in charge of 'Operation Teeth' is an Australian, Major D. Hawsey. The American is Sergeant John Willman. Then there's another Aussie—the pilot, former Corporal Glen Carmichael."

"August 17th, 1945," the Captain read as he wrote. "Attention: Sergeant J. Willman, and Party." He went silent.

"These things are for you," the pen scratched across the page. "Try the radio. The request to look for you came from Colonel Waters in Port Moresby." Below this he wrote a few more sentences, then signed his name with a flourish.

"Here." He handed the paper and pen back to Blair. "Put this in the pouch. Write Willman's name on the outside."

Karsh and Chip returned to the tarp. Gunny saw them coming and brought the list. Karsh personally double-checked the items as they were read off.

"Should we add guns and ammo, Sir?" Chip asked the Captain when that was done.

"No son," Karsh responded. "We hope it's our men who find this, but that's doubtful. We don't want to arm any hostiles—Japs or natives."

The Captain had the men hold up the corners of the tarp and they lashed it to make a big waterproof sack. He had them tie a rope to it and sent a man up the tree. The marine climbed thirty feet and threw the rope over a branch. Other men hauled the sack high, wrapped the rope around the trunk and tied it off.

"The pouch," Karsh said. Blair handed it over and the Captain wedged it through the coils.

"That's that," Karsh said. "Gather the men, Gunny. Pass out a beer to each one, but tell them to wait for my word."

There were two wooden crates stamped "Anheuser-Busch, St. Louis," heaped with ice chips in the shade. The men had heard the bottles clink when they brought them ashore. *Budweiser from home!*

When the marines were ranged before him, a cool bottle in each hand, the Captain accepted one himself and spoke.

"Men, it's official. Japan has surrendered! We've beaten the bastards!" An enthusiastic cheer went up. The marines had heard rumors of this. You couldn't keep such momentous news under wraps, but it hadn't been official until now. Karsh held up a hand for silence.

"I've been told that yesterday, the Japanese Emperor himself went on radio to tell his subjects the news. That was a first, they say. The Japs had never even heard his voice before.

"Now every one of our available ships is steaming for Tokyo. The greatest armada of the war will assemble to accept the official surrender. There'll be a grand ceremony where the Nips will sign the documents. Unconditional surrender, men! And we're going to the party!" Another cheer broke out.

"Here's to the United States of America!" Karsh called, raising his Bud. "Here's to victory!" They lifted their bottles high, the Captain took a long swallow, and everyone did the same. There was laughter and marines clapped one another on the back. Some put thumbs over the necks, shook, and sprayed their buddies. It might not be champagne, but it was sweet!

Grinning broadly, Karsh told Gunny to set four men with Tommy guns as sentries, and the others could relax until further notice.

Captain Karsh ducked into his tent and emerged a few minutes later dressed in his bathing costume. It was a conservative affair that covered the chest. It had been a gift from Lois, his wife of twenty-one years. She pointed out that the blue color matched his dress uniform. It was not the trunks the younger fellows favored these days, but it showed the Captain's manly physique to advantage. At forty-two, Cleveland Karsh worked diligently to maintain his musculature. He had a set of weights in the basement at home and swam three times a week at the Y, fast laps an hour at a time. In the field, unless in battle, he did a hundred push-ups and two hundred sit-ups before breakfast.

The marines watched as their Captain marched to the sea, strode into the crashing surf and dove into a wave. He came up beyond it, swimming strongly. When he was in deeper water, he began to parallel the shore, arms rising and falling in a fast crawl. After fifty strokes, he reversed and swam the other way. His aides sat and watched and Chip shook his head in admiration.

"He's something, the Old Man," he said. "The South Pacific's loaded with sharks. You wouldn't catch me out there for a million bucks."

"Our fearless Captain," Blair smiled. They shaded their eyes against the reflection. A breaker went over Karsh, then the watchers saw the gleam of his head again.

Chip had been given instructions and he went to the tent. He checked that everything was in order with the Captain's uniform on its hanger, then knelt by the wooden trunk and fished out a set of keys. He selected one and turned it in the lock, opened the lid and noted the personal papers and photos of Karsh, his wife and three children. Chip had seen these before and he was looking for something else.

He found the velvet sack and brought it out, loosened the drawstring and extracted a bottle. It had a coating of fine dust and he wiped it away and read the label: *Glenmorangie—Highland Single Malt Scotch Whisky.*

Chip was twenty-two years old and did not know single malt from bar bourbon, but he knew this was something special. He relocked the case and returned to the beach. Blair had prepared three glasses on the table and an ice bucket.

Cleveland Karsh swam hard, eyes closed against the salt. Unseen by him, forty-five feet below, the reef was a riot of colors. It was a wonderland of hard and soft corals, thronged with thousands of species of fish. When the aquatic creatures looked up, they saw a dark spot on the ceiling of the world.

For millions of years, any creature churning the surface was a dying fish or an animal in trouble. In either case, it was food. The vibrations made by the swimmer radiated through this atmosphere and in deep water, they attracted a colossal predator. Instantly it was speeding to the source.

The Tiger Shark soared in, sunlight rippling over its stripes. It moved its head slightly from side to side, searching for the meal with its eyes, and the electrical sensors in its skin known as "Ampules of Lorenzini." The hunter flashed along, scattering clouds of reef fish.

It saw something slapping the surface and honed in. But then, just ahead of it, a long length of the reef itself detached and floated up, casting a shadow.

Suddenly, the Tiger Shark realized what it was looking at. It saw huge eyes staring back, and a row of teeth as long as its body. The fish turned violently, voided its bowels, and rocketed back to the depths.

Unaware of the activity below, the Captain swam on. The clock in his head told him it was time to get out and he ventured a glance at the beach, then struck out that way. He bodysurfed the last roller in and burst out on his feet. He took some running steps and, aware of the eyes of the men, marched up, smiling broadly.

Karsh accepted the towel Chip handed him and glanced with approval at the bottle of Glenmorangie. As he'd instructed, a bucket of fresh water stood on the sand. The Captain held it over his head with a muscled arm and sluiced off the seawater. Toweling his chest, Karsh walked to his tent. He stepped out of his bathing suit, dried himself and donned khaki slacks and shirt, but kept the jacket with its decorations aside. He would put it on just before they went back on board.

He added socks and shoes and buckled on the belt with the holstered pistol. It was an M1911 .45 automatic in nickel finish with a wooden grip. He had cleaned it the previous evening and knew the clip was full. Karsh was already sweating and he ran the towel over his shaved head once more. Then, cap in hand, jacket over the forearm, he stepped back into the sun. Marines were stretched out on the sand. Some shot the breeze with their buddies, some slept, and there was a card game going. He called over.

"Gunny, give the men their second beer."

"Yes sir!" the Sarg responded. He had no shortage of volunteers to hand around the bottles.

Karsh joined his aides. The Lieutenants stood from their chairs as he approached. He told them to sit, then walked to the ocean side of the table, hung the jacket over the back of the chair, put down his cap and faced the younger men. He picked up the bottle of scotch.

"Gentlemen," he said, "our work together is almost done." He held the amber liquid to the sun.

"This is a special bottle for a special day. This is twenty-one year old single malt scotch. It was aged by the distiller for almost the length of time you've been alive, young man," he said to Chip. "And—well, since before you were a twinkle in your daddy's eye," he told Blair.

"It was a gift from my own father some years ago. He told me I'd know when to open it. He was right."

He cracked the seal with a nail, twisted the cork and it came out with a musical pop. He put his nose to the neck and sniffed. He smiled, and poured two fingers of scotch into each tumbler, pushed the glasses toward the young men, and picked up his own. His aides added ice, while the Captain did not.

"Chip, Blair," he said, "as you know, the war is over, but I propose a personal toast. To the end of our war! Semper Fi!" He held up his glass.

"To the end of our war! Semper Fi!" the aides responded and clinked their glasses against the Captain's. Each took a swallow. Karsh closed his eyes and savored the buttery burn. It was a moment of bliss, suddenly broken.

Karsh heard shouts and turned sharply. Marines were on their feet, pointing at the ocean. The Captain spun and could hardly believe his eyes. A gigantic crocodile charged out of the waves and it seemed to be looking at him. Karsh took in the curved scar across the head, and the malformed front leg that made the animal's shoulder dip as it ran. It loomed larger with every step and he stared at the prehistoric-looking head and all the teeth.

Cleveland Karsh got an adrenaline rush. Still, his hand set his glass smoothly on the table, then unsnapped his holster and drew the .45, and racked the slide with the other hand. It had only been seconds, but the brute was almost to him and he fired. He saw a divot of scales fly off the head but the crocodile did not slow.

He shot again, and the beast was on him.

CHAPTER 28

Captain Karsh dove away at the last minute but the crocodile turned with him and caught his leg in the air. Karsh felt his bones shatter. Then the Father turned and ran for the ocean.

Karsh felt the implacable strength and as he fell, he fired into the head again before his back struck sand. His left leg was entirely in the reptile's mouth and the other dragged as the crocodile plowed him down the beach. He felt no pain but he knew his leg was crushed. The crocodile ran as though his own two hundred and thirty pounds were nothing. Karsh reached with his left hand, grabbed the jaw and raised his body. Jolted as he was, he shot the side of the head.

Karsh went backwards into the ocean as he heard the stutter of automatic fire. He saw bullets shudder along the flank. A wave rushed around him and another line of slugs kicked sand and pounded the crocodile's body.

The Father staggered under the onslaught and fell onto its misshapen foreleg. Karsh heard something pop as the Father thumped onto its belly and slid into the ocean. The man was thrust into a roller that loomed overhead. He kept his eyes open underwater, staring into the crocodile's scarred eye. As the wave drew back he gasped air, aimed his soaked .45 and pulled the trigger. It fired, and he got off three shots before he went under again. The wave boiled over and the crocodile dove into it and swam. The man's arms scraped along the sand and the pistol was torn from his grip. In the sudden silence, the crocodile undulated down fifty feet.

The Captain held his breath and felt the pressure mount in his head. He moved his jaw and his ears popped. The crocodile let go of his leg and Karsh had an irrational burst of hope that he might yet escape, but it only was repositioning him. Karsh felt the teeth scrape across his chest and back, and the horrific penetration.

He knew then his personal war over.

Still, he tried to hurt his attacker. He ran his hand along the jaw until his thumb found the eye and he gouged in. At once, the reptile rolled. The Captain was flung around, salt burned up his nose and he breathed water. He had a moment of terrible panic and then it faded away.

The crocodile felt the prey go still. It came out of its roll and swam deeper.

For an eternity of heartbeats, Cleveland stared up at reversed waves passing far overhead, and the sun beyond. He had never seen anything so electric blue and sublime in his life.

The Father had escaped the explosions, but its head and side burned. The pain in its foreleg, however, had suddenly eased.

It had the smooth-headed man in its teeth and it knew the savage satisfaction of having killed the one-prey.

☆

Chip was facing it when the crocodile erupted from the waves and came at them. It ran fast, with a rolling gait. He saw the Old Man shoot the monster and then it was on them.

Chip found he was moving, leaping through the air. He glimpsed the monster bite the Captain, then he hit sand and rolled. When he looked again, the crocodile was racing back down the beach, tail raised. He heard shouts and the clatter of Tommy guns. He saw the animal get hit as it entered the water. It fell on its weird leg, the foot buckled back, and something squirted out. The croc rolled on is belly and slid into the surf.

Chip saw a wave crash over and fall away. Captain Karsh rose up in the jaws and fired into the head. It sounded like a cap gun, but he saw the pistol jump. Another breaker surged over, and when it was gone, so were man and beast. Chip felt he was in a waking nightmare.

The predator was gone, but so was his Captain. Gone, gone! Yet the ocean sparkled merrily and the sun beamed down.

Chip saw marines run to the water. He heard a sob and there was Blair sprawled out, lower lip bleeding, an empty glass in his fingers. His own was nearby, half filled with sand.

He stood up and on the table was the Captain's special bottle, beside the glass the Old Man's own hand had set down only a minute before. The liquor still trembled. Chip lurched to the table, grabbed the bottle and drank deeply. His gullet and eyes seemed to catch fire. Still clutching the neck, he stumbled down the sand, gaze fixed on the thing that had burst out of the creature.

He got close and saw a gelatinous mass laced with yellow and red, black at the core. It looked like a dead jellyfish, but it had come from the leg and he prodded it with his toe. It was hard. A wave swirled around his boot and when it retreated, some of the goo was gone. He was looking at a shaft of black wood. One end was a sharp point, the other in splinters.

Again Chip tipped up the bottle and his Adam's apple bobbed. Heat spilled from his eyes and the world melted. His arm fell and his fingers went slack. He heard the thud of boots and the surf sizzled like hot grease.

Strong hands grabbed the young officer just as his knees gave out. His eyes rolled back in his head as the marines dragged him up the beach.

Ten minutes before, it had been an idyllic scene out of some South Pacific movie. Now it was pandemonium. Men ran waving firearms. Some leapt into the tenders and yanked the motors to life. They roared back and forth, staring helplessly into the water.

Eventually, the thirty-seven year old Gunnery Sergeant took charge. The young lieutenants were no help. He saw no option but to return with the men to the ship, and there report the bizarre death of the Captain.

Once more, the beach was deserted. At the surf line, a clear object tumbled. Each time it moved, some of its amber contents glugged out. Another breaker rushed over it, and fine single malt scotch mixed with a far more ancient vintage. A big breaker caught the thing and hurled up, then sucked it back again. As it rolled, picking up speed, it struck something hard in the sand.

Cleveland Karsh's victory bottle and the business end of Chief Bumay's war spear clinked together in the surf.

Johnny was terrified, running through putrid mud that crawled with maggots. The stench of death was thick in his nostrils. His legs pumped furiously, but he only sank deeper.

The Father was coming.

It slid at him across the mud and Johnny redoubled his efforts but he could not move and the crocodile knew it. Its jaws curved in a tooth-studded smile. Johnny stared at the crescent scar that was livid red and oozed blood. The yellow eye in the center of it stared back with hostile intelligence.

Johnny raised his rifle and shot the Father in the eye, but it only clicked. He heard the scorekeeper's cheery voice:

"No bullets left!"

The Father came and it spread jaws strung with saliva that gaped and kept going. The red moon filled the sky and the maw was wide enough to swallow the entire stinking swamp. The teeth grew like mountain ranges.

Johnny heard agonized cries and saw living human heads wedged between the teeth. The faces were stacked on each other and the cries came from them.

Chief Bumay was there. His eyes were white and terrified in his black face, his black teeth exposed, and his death scream went on endlessly.

Then Johnny heard a voice he knew far better. In dread, he searched for the source and found it. There was Footy's face with the others. The eyes were wide and he was urgently trying to tell Johnny something, but the words were lost in the howl of the damned.

And then the Father's jaws came slamming down. It was like the sky falling. It crashed onto Johnny and the long teeth shot through him.

Johnny woke and smelled the dead crocodile. He saw the Japanese in the firelight, staring at him, and realized he'd been making noise. *I put him on watch,* he remembered. He saw Footy, asleep. Johnny took deep breaths and waited for this new nightmare to dissipate.

Fingers trembling, he found a cigarette. He did not even try to use the Zippo. It had taken a lot of shaking, flicking and coaxing to get the fire going. He touched the cigarette to a coal. He smoked it half down and handed it to the Japanese, who nodded and puffed.

Johnny got up and told the man to sleep on his bed. He sat on the dirt and stared into the ominous darkness of the swamp. The fire gave a glimmer that outlined the head of the hulking saltwater crocodile.

As night had fallen, he and the Japanese had worked the machete and Bowie knife through the tough scales on the back.

Johnny asked the prisoner to use his sword—it was sharper—but the man refused. Johnny asked why, and was told it was not right to use the *katana* for that purpose. He had not forced the issue.

They got a flap of tough hide peeled back and they carved steaks. They skewered these on sticks and roasted them over the fire. Then the men had a meat-fest, eating until they were gorged, and cooked more for the trail ahead.

Johnny pulled the boots off Footy's feet and tended to the cut. He removed the bandage and was pleased to see the site was relatively clean. The ball was swollen and purple, the lips of the cut red between the stitches, but it did not look infected. Johnny doused it with disinfectant and taped it.

Footy was in considerable pain and Johnny asked if he needed the morphine. Through gritted teeth, the Aussie said yes, but not yet. Footy lay quietly until he fell asleep. Johnny told the prisoner they would share sentry duty, and he could go first. There was no point giving the man an unloaded rifle, but he did have his sword.

Johnny took over from him in the middle of the night. He was concerned the dead croc would attract big feeders, but fortunately, none showed up. The cloud cover lifted and Johnny watched stars that faded at last into the lightening dawn.

Seagulls drifted overhead, coming from the north. As the morning light intensified, Johnny saw a far off ridge of trees. It had been too dim to make it out the previous evening.

His spirits lifted—*palm trees mean solid ground!* He woke the others and shared the good news. Even Footy managed a smile.

"Let's get out of this hellhole," the Aussie said.

"Things will get better there," Johnny promised.

"They have to."

CHAPTER 29

The Father swam through the balmy sea. The cyst in its foreleg had burst and saltwater stung, but the hurt was good. The crocodile carried its kill to the bottom. The body leaked from its punctures and the reptile was bleeding as well. Underwater, both kinds of blood appeared green.

A festive crowd rushed up from the reef. All the fish, even the tiniest, had a significant advantage over the reptile. They could eat in this world, but it could not. It could bite, but it could not unseal its throat flap and swallow.

A frenzy of feeders as bright as stained glass formed a ball around the crocodile's head. Local reef sharks rushed on the blood scent, and a squadron of big Silvertips came in from the ocean. In its excitement, one extruded its jaws as it did to bite, and nervously pulled them in again.

But the big fish stayed back when they saw the crocodile. The pelagic Silvertips knew they could not compete, and swept away, while the territorial Blacktips remained—at a distance. The Father approached the reef while a shoal of a thousand Barracuda drifted overhead, undershot jaws lined with daggers. They swam in cylindrical formation, head to tail, and stared down at the master and its kill.

The Father cruised majestically on, ignoring all the lesser creatures. Its instincts directed it to store its meat and it swam to a place it knew. It swooped into a coral canyon and swam to an overhang. It settled on the reef and a million coral polyps fired their stingers without effect against the heavy armor.

The Father pushed its head into a cave and observed the hole in the back wall. It had used this larder before and it nosed the carcass in. The prey's crushed leg, still wearing a shoe and dress sock, sliced off and spun to the sand.

The Father pulled back and stared at its victim. It saw the smooth head, the staring blue eyes, the purple tongue protruding, but it no longer perceived the one-prey.

Earlier, the Father had been resting on the reef when it was startled to observe the smooth-headed man swimming above. At once, consumed by its obsession to kill, the giant rose. The prey tried to escape onto land, but that did not deter the predator. It pursued the man across the beach and took him down.

But now in the cave, the Father no longer saw its enemy. Seething and unsatisfied, the crocodile withdrew, rose from the canyon, and surged across the reef. It went over the drop off and sank down the wall. It watched the waves pass a hundred feet up. It turned its head and looked down, and saw the sharks that cruised the sandy bottom another two hundred feet below.

The instant the crocodile had pulled out of the cave, a thousand fish rushed in. They raced to the carcass and tugged at the ribbons of flesh. Now that the master was gone, the reef sharks dared approach. One ventured under the overhang but did not like the tight quarters and pulled out. The second noticed the joint lying on the sand. It went far enough to take it in its teeth, backed out and shot away, all its kin in pursuit. A tug-of-war ensued, great bodies charging in and out of the haze of blood and tissue. One bit off the foot, sock, shoe and all, and swallowed it whole.

As if with a single mind, the shoal of barracuda circled over the cave. The lower ones peeled off and swooped under the overhang. Small fry obscured the corpse as the first barracuda fired in and struck. It plucked out an eye and zoomed away. The second one slashed off the nose. The third got the tongue, and all the brethren followed. The smaller fish surged aside each time, then rushed for the newly exposed flesh. Soon they were inside the skull and chest, then the pelvis, feasting on organs.

Within the hour, it was only a skeleton that loomed from the hole, arms hanging out, skull in a permanent grin that glinted gold at the back. With the buffet gone, the crowd drifted off. Only the diehards remained, picking over the gristle.

An octopus flowed across the canyon floor, emotions flickering like light over its skin. It slipped under the overhang and when it perceived what was in the back wall, it went bright blue, then mottled green. It unfurled its tentacles, grasped the ribs and pulled up. It oozed between bones, and stared out from the ribcage. It flared scarlet and then faded entirely away. To the fish, it simply seemed to disappear, all except the black vertical bars of its eyes.

Beside the coral wall, the Father hung weightless. It parted its jaws as Cleaner Wrasse, shrimp, and other small fish fanned over its body. Some nibbled at the edges of the wounds while others pulled off parasites. An entire bouquet of feeders flared around the anus. Others even dared to enter the mouth where they cleaned up the palate, tongue, and around each tooth. The crocodile was careful not to harm them.

The most frantic feeding occurred at the foreleg. A hole gaped in the center of the clubfoot. Some fish stripped away the flayed flesh while tiny Wrasse wiggled inside to feed in the slick darkness.

— ☾ —

After Johnny had seen the palm trees on the horizon, it had required still a full day's march to get out of the swamp. But that night, the travelers slept on *terra firma*. Johnny cut a new crutch for Footy, and he was able to walk in his sandals again. Johnny got his boots back.

They headed out, following a defined watercourse once more. The sandy delta was covered in creeping grasses and minute flowers, and the men wandered between palms and new kinds of coastal trees.

The first morning out of the marsh, they passed another empty village. They guessed the people had been gone a long time, because the huts were broken down and smothered in creepers. To their relief, there were some overgrown gardens. Footy rested, while Johnny and the prisoner gathered *kaukau* and all the vegetables they could find. Again Johnny struggled to light his Zippo. He shook and coaxed it for half an hour before he got a tiny flame and lit the tinder.

The ravenous men cooked all they could eat, and then more for the trail. The last of the croc meat had gone off and they were forced to discard it.

They went on over open land. Johnny and the Japanese toiled under packs weighted with vegetables, while Footy had enough to do just to haul himself along.

If I can only make it to the Pacific, the Aussie thought as the crutch jammed relentlessly into the bruise under his arm, *everything will be jake mate! One foot in front of the other, that's the way.*

On and on they toiled across a deserted landscape. Another day passed and they made camp. That night, Johnny could not get the Zippo to fire at all, no matter how hard he and the others tried. In addition, they were out of cigarettes. The men ate the last of the cooked food, and in the morning, they were reduced to gnawing raw tubers.

They continued. The skies clouded over and it rained on them, but it was a warm downpour that was as good as a shower. Unfortunately, the mosquitoes got worse.

At noon they came to a wide and puddled plain. Johnny led off and heard snapping under his boots. He crouched and studied the pale shards. He pulled a rib up and threw it aside. They were human bones.

"We're on a battlefield," he said.

"Yes mate. We're walking on dead men."

Does anyone even remember this place? Johnny thought. *In the overall scheme, did it make a speck of difference?*

Poor bastards, Footy thought. *Part of the mud forever.*

How terrible to be lost so far from home, the prisoner thought as he hobbled on bare feet over the bones. *But at least they did not know defeat.*

They saw bits of uniform, rusted rifles and helmets and broken down artillery. At last they got off the killing field and that was a relief, but the ocean remained tantalizingly over the horizon. They slogged the day away, passing burned out trucks, armored vehicles and even downed aircraft. They detoured by one to see if there was anything useable, but found nothing.

That night they camped near a crashed Japanese "Betty Bomber" matted with jungle. Again they had to choke down a raw dinner. The potatoes were too hard to chew, but at least they managed the green beans. They slept hungry and when breakfast was more of the same, Johnny decided their bleak situation had become intolerable.

"Footy," he said, "we can't even cook. I'm sorry, but we're going to have to leave you. The Jap and I will go for the ocean—or at least try and find help. We'll come back for you." Footy gave the Yank an anxious frown, but he'd arrived at the same conclusion.

"I'll wait here," he said. "The rest will do my foot some good. You blokes get along—find us some food."

They had camped beneath a shade tree near a spring. Johnny

left his hammock strung and told Footy to use it. He placed the pilot's pack of raw vegetables close by, and filled all available containers with fresh water. For defense, Footy had the Bowie knife, and Johnny handed him his rifle as well.

"We've got no ammo, but if someone does come, they won't know that. It may not be loaded, but you take care of it, hear?"

"I'll be right, mate. Not to worry."

"We'll be back soon," Johnny told him. "I'll be gone a day, two at the most. Then I'll come back, no matter what. Don't wander off."

"On this leg?" Footy snorted. "Get on with you."

The two men departed. Without the pilot slowing them down, they made good time over flat land. In the early afternoon, a dense patch of jungle blocked their way, and they began to hike around it. They noticed something bright winking within, but could not make it out.

"Let's go see," Johnny decided. He swung his machete and they worked their way in. Twenty minutes later, the silver patch was larger, and obviously metallic. They forged past a bamboo grove, stumbled into a clearing, and there it was.

A crumpled wide-bodied aircraft lay pointed their way down the hillside. It had flattened the jungle when it crashed, although the foliage was making a comeback. Behind it was a swath of felled trees and the broken off tail section.

They worked their way along the fuselage and Johnny noted the US Army insignia. The craft had been part of General MacArthur's Air Force. They continued by the jagged place where a wing had ripped off. The one on the other side poked into the trees, the propeller blades bent back.

The men came to the torn end and stared into the dark interior. The metal circle towered over their heads and vines covered the opening. Johnny slashed through, and he and the Japanese walked up the metal ramp. Their eyes adjusted to the gloom and Johnny whistled.

Two jeeps were lashed there. They were held in place by straps, and vines curled around these and almost covered the vehicles. Johnny pulled a load of foliage out, watching for snakes and spiders, and dropped his pack in. He left the Japanese checking the vehicles, and went forward to the cockpit. He stepped through into harsh sunlight and was momentarily blinded.

Then he saw the pilot. *Or at least, what's left of him*. It was a skeleton, skewered through the chest by a splintered tree that lay over the instrument panel. The man wore a flyer's cap and a jungle rotted bomber jacket. Johnny made out the US flag on the shoulder. The pole continued through the smashed windshield.

He turned to the other seat and saw the co-pilot, a heap of bones and clothing on the floor. The prisoner came up behind and grunted in surprise.

Johnny had the distasteful task of checking the aviators' pockets, but the damp and rot had destroyed anything useful. He did collect one each of their ID tags and pocketed them. He'd turn them in when he could.

"Let's get the jeeps running," he said. "I've done enough walking to last a lifetime." The vehicles faced the torn end of the fuselage. They opened the hoods and checked the oil. Both were topped up. He sat in the metal driver's seat and saw the key in the ignition. He turned it and was not surprised when nothing happened.

"Flat battery," he said. "We'll have to push-start them." He wiped webs off the dashboard and saw the fuel gauge at about half full. "We've got gas. Let's get the straps off. You drive a stick-shift?" The Japanese nodded.

"Ok," Johnny said. "You take the other one. Give me a hand with this. Then we'll get yours going." The men dropped all tie-downs but two, one on each side. Johnny took a seat again and pumped the accelerator until he smelled gasoline. He pulled the choke, turned the key on and put the transmission in second.

"Drop the ties," Johnny said, "then push!" He kept the brake on while the Japanese removed the last hooks, ran to the back and put his shoulder to the spare tire. Johnny let up the brake and pressed down the clutch.

The vehicle started to roll. When it picked up enough speed, he popped the clutch and the transmission clunked in. The engine caught, quit, started again, backfired, and began to chug. Johnny cheered and ducked his head as the jeep rolled through the creepers. Outside, he put the stick in neutral and worked the gas. The engine sputtered unevenly and blue smoke belched from the exhaust pipe, blowing out insects. Gradually, he increased the pressure until it was roaring. He drove it to one side and left it idling.

"Ok," Johnny said, "let's get yours." The men returned to the aircraft, and this time the Japanese got in the driver's seat while they repeated the process. Soon there were two jeeps purring in the sunlight. Johnny climbed into his again and put his helmet down.

"Let's get Footy," he grinned. He gunned the engine and shot off through the brush, weaving between the trees. The Japanese came after him and soon they burst onto open country. Johnny spun the way they had come and the Asian sped up beside him. They glanced at one another and smiles split their unshaven faces. They drove fast, and ate up in an hour what had taken them all day to walk.

Footy was dozing in the Yank's hammock when he heard the motors. He struggled out, got up on his crutch, and gawked open-mouthed as two jeeps raced up and skidded to a halt.

"Like a ride?" Johnny drawled.

"Crikey mate," Footy crowed, "it's the bloody Jungle Express!"

CHAPTER 30

Johnny and the Japanese piled out of the vehicles and quickly broke camp. Footy limped to the passenger seat of the Yank's jeep and climbed in. Shortly, all the gear was stowed in the back and the drivers got in. Footy's mood improved enormously. He even spoke to the prisoner.

"How's it going then?" The man responded with a small smile and a nod. Johnny gunned the engine and the wheels spun, heading north. The Japanese came on his tail and they raced among the trees, eating up the miles. The wind whipped Footy's hat back, pulling on the tie under his chin, and dried his sweat-soaked hair. Johnny shouted an explanation of how they'd found the vehicles.

"There are wrecks all over New Guinea," the pilot observed.

"They'll never get them all cleared away," Johnny said.

"Well, good for us mate. Our luck has changed!" The fact was, he'd spent the day fretting he'd never see the Yank again. He had to admit—only to himself—that he'd seldom seen anything as good as the Yank, cruising up in that jeep.

"The Father can eat our dust!" Johnny shouted.

The jeeps sped between the palms, sometimes splashing through streams and dodging around deeper gullies. They went by a patch of jungle, and Johnny yelled this was where they'd found the jeeps. They were by in a flash, and he thought how lucky they'd been to see the glint. A slight change of light, and they would have missed it.

The hours blew by and the men's desire soared to see the Pacific. The Japanese thought the same ocean washed his homeland, only a few hundred miles to the north. Footy longed for the South Pacific that lapped his doorstep down in Queensland.

Johnny was flooded with memories of his younger life around this ocean. The closer they came, the more vibrant the images that washed through him. *I learned to swim off the beaches of San Diego. In southern Cal and especially Hawaii, I surfed its breakers.*

Johnny thought he could smell the ocean and it brought his boyhood exuberance sweeping into him. It even cracked the shell of the tough soldier he'd become killing men in these jungles.

Johnny was distracted by his memories as he rushed up too fast on a deep channel of water. He was forced to stand on the brake and the other vehicle fishtailed behind him. They skidded to a stop and almost ran over a beefy basking salty. It hissed and flung itself down the bank into the water.

"Better up here than down in the mud with it," Johnny said.

"When you're right mate, you're bloody right," Footy grinned.

The Aussie called the slough a "billabong" and said it was a loop the river had cut off. The jeeps turned and went around it.

The terrain changed again. The soil was sand and there were new trees. Then they began to run through orderly rows of coconut palms. Thousands of the nuts were strewn on the ground and when the tires hit them, they shot out like cannon shells. After a few near misses, the Japanese dropped back and they went single file.

It was afternoon and the light went golden. Seagulls dipped over their heads, crying in the breeze. Then, ahead through the palms, Johnny got a glimpse of shimmering blue. He gunned the jeep up a sand dune, hit the top and got air. He and Footy saw the ravishing South Pacific. Both men cheered and there was a shout from the other jeep. Rich blue filled the world, and gigantic rollers marched towards them as far as they could see.

They blasted out of the last of the trees and were churning deep sand. Now there was nothing between them and the water and the jeeps drifted across the beach. With the front wheels on a smooth band, Johnny killed the engine. The other jeep pulled up.

And there was the South Pacific Ocean. At last, they had arrived! A breaker ten feet tall swept at them, fell on itself, and foamed up. They heard the roar of water, the hiss of the foam, and the call of gulls.

Johnny and Footy shared a delighted smile and then Johnny was running for the surf. He stumbled out of his pants, threw aside his filthy shirt, and wearing only his boxers, he raced into the water. He dove in and swam a long way underwater. He burst up to breathe and turned shoreward. The jeeps sat side-by-side on the dune and the prisoner was already in the ocean, a bobbing black head.

Footy was just limping in, wearing only his briefs and a grin. A wave knocked him down and then he was swimming strongly out to Johnny. The men luxuriated in the warm seas as it washed away the marsh stink, and the long journey. They swam side by side and began to splash each other. At the ocean at last, with his weight off the leg, Footy was in high spirits. He came up behind the Yank and pushed him under. Johnny grabbed back and they both went down. They played like the boys they'd once been, only on opposite sides of the world.

The Japanese flipped onto his back and floated in blessed relief from the itch, and the stench of both the swamp and the hairy *gaijin*. He was caressed by the water and it brought potent memories of his childhood in his seaside city.

Johnny and Footy splashed one another until they could barely breathe. Then Johnny caught sight of the Japanese floating peacefully off by himself. At once he dove under and swam. He came up below the prisoner and grabbed his leg—*a little something we call 'shark attack.'* Johnny heard a shout cut off in bubbles as the man came down. His eyes spread wide, and he saw the Yankee and kicked at him.

Johnny shot up to breathe and saw outrage in the other face. He laughed and dove away as the Japanese lunged for him. He twisted out of his grasp time after time, but the man was relentless. At last the Asian got an arm around Johnny's neck and choked him. Johnny found there was sand under his feet. He towered up with the soldier on his back, pried the arm away, and the smaller man crashed back in the surf. A big wave sent them both tumbling, then withdrew and left them beached.

Johnny staggered up the hot sand and flopped onto his back. Footy came out chuckling and threw himself down. The prisoner stood and adjusted his ragged trousers. An unusual feeling came over him and he trotted out of the water as the noises burst from him. For the first time in months, he was laughing.

"You know something?" Johnny said to him. "I don't even know your name. What do they call you?"

"My family name is 'Takano,'" the Japanese said. "My name is 'Katsu.'"

"Cat-soup?" Footy asked.

"Ketchup?" Johnny said.

"Kat-su," the Japanese told them. He lay down and turned

away. The mirth passed out of him.

He felt the blaze in the sky and, like a nightmare, he saw the cloud of a great bomb churning over Japan. He watched a city of people stare at the manmade sun, and they all burned away like blades of grass. He lay with the sunlight blinding him and pinched his eyes as saltwater leaked to mix with the sea on his face. Gradually, mercifully, he drifted to a hazy place somewhere beyond both pain and pleasure, and for a time, he knew no more.

Sprawled on a wild and empty South Pacific beach, three men slept like babies.

Part 3
The Beach

☽

"Forgive your enemies, but never forget their names."
– President John F. "Jack" Kennedy

●

"I, Ishmael, was one of that crew…Ahab's quenchless feud seemed mine. With greedy ears I learned the history of that murderous monster against whom I and all the others had taken our oaths of violence and revenge."
– Herman Melville, Moby Dick

☼

"To do right is heavy as a mountain but death is lighter than a feather."
– Emperor Meiji, Imperial Edict for Soldiers & Sailors, 1882

↔

"Gi wa sangaku yorimo omoku shi wa komo yorimo karushi."

Chapter 1

Johnny's face was in the sand and he sat up and spat. He brushed off the salty stubble and squinted at the sunset blazing in the western sky. He saw Footy on his back, staring up. The Japanese was further off, turned away.

"How's the foot?" Johnny asked.

"Hurts like a bugga," Footy said cheerfully, "but it's better than a sharp stick up the bum."

Johnny nodded. "Pretty soon we'll call you 'Hopalong Cassidy.'" Johnny was thinking of the limping cowboy from the books his dad had read to him when he was a kid. "Hopalong" had gone on to be portrayed in a series of movies, although some Hollywood dim bulb had removed the limp, a sore spot with his father.

"Aw yeh," Footy said, "The cowboy. The Yank makes a joke. You feeling better then?"

"Sure!" Johnny said. "I'm glad to be off the river, out of the swamp, and at the beach! Did I tell you I lived in Hawaii?"

"Is that home then?" the Aussie asked. "Is that where your parents are?"

"My folks are dead," Johnny said curtly. He got up. "It's getting late. We'd better make camp."

"Sorry mate ..." Footy began as the American offered him a hand and pulled him up.

"Not your fault. Hey!" Johnny called to the Japanese. "Hey... Kato!" The man rolled over.

"My name is 'Katsu,'" he said.

"Cat-soo, let's go!" Johnny called.

They gathered their clothes as they went. Johnny stepped into his trousers and rolled up the legs. The Yank was thinner than when they'd started, Footy saw—all lean muscle, not a lick of fat. Footy pulled on his stained shorts. *I'm a bit stringy meself.* Johnny strode to the jeeps and the Aussie hopped on one leg to keep up.

Hopalong, he thought, hoisting himself into the passenger seat.

Could be mate. Except not a Yank—never in a million years! The Japanese climbed into the other jeep and they started their engines. Johnny aimed for the line of trees that marked the river's course.

"If anyone's still looking for us," he told Footy, "they'll search around the mouth of the Raub."

"Yes mate—bloody big if."

Johnny tapped the gas gauge. The needle banged the "empty" post. The Japanese drove alongside and the jeeps ran together.

Fifteen minutes later, not far from the fringe of jungle, the men saw an arrow on the beach made of coconuts. The sand around it was pocked by bootprints. Someone had been here! The jeeps slowed and the men scanned the palms where the arrow pointed. Footy saw it first.

"There!" An enormous shade tree towered over the palms and something dangled from the branches. The vehicles pulled up below, and the men gazed at a bulging canvas bag, tied by a rope around the trunk. There was something stuck in the coils. Johnny jumped out and went over. He tugged out a canvas pouch.

"What? You're not going to believe this," he called. "It's got my name on it!" He held it up and the others saw "WILLMAN" in big letters.

☾

The men sat smoking Lucky Strikes, the tarpaulin spread open displaying a treasure trove.

"Read it again," Footy said. Johnny had the letter on his knee and he read the last part first.

"'The Japs have surrendered. The war is over. Good luck and God Speed.'" He looked up. "That's what it says."

"Japan has surrendered," The prisoner repeated in wonder.

"And the war is over?" Footy added. "Bloody cryptic. Could have given us a few details."

"That's all there is," Johnny said. "It's signed 'Captain C. Karsh, US Marine Corps.' Sounds like someone who should know."

"What else?" Footy asked, lighting a fresh ciggy from the butt in his fingers.

"'The request to look for you comes from Colonel Waters in Port Moresby,'" Johnny read. "Colonel Waters—I guess Chambers is gone."

"When was it written?" Footy asked.

"August 17th," Johnny said.

"What date it is now?" Footy asked. "I've been trying to keep track. I reckon it's August 21st."

"I've been doing the same," Johnny said. "But I think it's the 19th. 'Course I might have lost track when we were sick. Any idea?" he asked the Japanese.

"What bloody good will that do?" Footy hooted. "Nine hundredth day of the year of the pig?" But the prisoner was counting on his fingers.

"*Hachigatsu*," he said. "I believe it is *hatsuka.* You do not know we use the same calendar in Nippon?" he said scornfully to Footy, and turned to Johnny. "That is the 20th day of August. But also—I may be wrong."

"Well, whatever, we missed the rescue," Johnny said. "But at least we've got food and all the rest!"

Slower now, the men sorted through the cache. Footy had gone directly for the cigarettes, then found the big box of matches. All three were grateful for that. Not being able to cook had been the last straw. There was no ammunition, Johnny saw, and that was a disappointment, but the rest made up for it.

There were boxes of canned food—stew, soup, rice, potatoes, various kinds of meat, including a full cooked ham, wieners, chicken, green beans, corn, carrots, baked beans, and more. There were cans of fruit and desserts and packages of hard tack biscuits, and several bars of chocolate. There was even a percolator coffee pot with a glass knob and inner metal filter, with three big cans labeled "coffee," "sugar" and "powdered milk."

Wrapped inside a half dozen new Army blankets was a kerosene two-burner stove, cans of fuel, assorted pots and pans, metal plates, and cutlery. There were bars of soap and terrycloth towels. They had spools of fishing line and hooks. There was a large medical kit and various bottles containing water purification tablets, Atabrine for malaria, and morphine tubes and needles.

The *pièce de résistance* was the radio in four wooden crates with batteries for it.

"Look at how small they're getting!" Footy exclaimed. "Two men could carry it. Imagine!"

They turned to their pressing priority—something to eat. The prisoner fueled the stove and lit it. Johnny and Footy opened four cans of beef stew and two more of baked beans and dumped them all in the biggest pot. They put it on the heat, but as soon as the steam started to rise, the smell was too much. Johnny grabbed it and slopped the contents onto plates. As fast as he could pour, the others shoveled it in.

The prisoner wiped the stew pot clean with his fingers, licking every last bit. Johnny opened three cans of cling peaches. Each man took one and slurped down the slices. The Japanese volunteered to make coffee using water in their bottles. When it was ready, he poured the fragrant brew into the new enamel mugs and dosed them with powdered milk and sugar. The men dunked sticks of chocolate in the steaming liquid.

Satiated at last, they lay on the sand and smoked. The sun had set and the sky blazed with stars.

"I still can't believe we're here!" Johnny sighed. "I'm beat. I vote no watch tonight. We haven't seen any sign of life for a long time, and we left the crocodile way back."

He barely had the energy to rope his hammock between palms while the others spread new blankets on the sand. Within minutes, they were all sound asleep.

Monumental waves curled in and Johnny was on his favorite surfing beach. Hawaiian music played, ukuleles plinking over steel guitars. And there was his father! Dad wore swimming trunks and he came dancing to the music, a hibiscus flower behind his ear, which was not like Dad at all.

His father smiled and whisked from behind his back a platter. It bore a whole roast piglet with baked pineapple rounds all over, a maraschino cherry spiked in the center of each one. Johnny's mouth watered.

And here came Mom! She was doing the hula moves she'd learned in class, wearing a grass skirt, bikini top, a flower lei and sequined sunglasses.

"Here's our gal!" Dad grinned. Mom held out a steaming mug.

"Coffee Jo-Jo?" she asked, using her private nickname for him.

"Mmmumph?" Johnny mumbled.

"Coffee?" Mom asked, and her voice changed.

"What?" Johnny protested.

"Coffee?" Mom asked in a deep voice with an accent. Her skin went yellow and black hairs sprouted on her lip. Johnny grunted awake and there was Cat, holding a mug.

"Coffee?"

Johnny sighed, slid out of the hammock and accepted the cup. He sipped while the Japanese returned to the stove and brought back a plate. It was piled with corned beef fried with canned potatoes. There was a pile of fresh clams, open and steaming, and fruit cocktail with wedges of coconut. On top was a purple jungle flower. Johnny shot the man a look of astonishment.

"What in the world...?"

"Breakfast," he shrugged and handed Johnny a fork. Footy was just sitting up and the prisoner fetched a mug and another portion for him.

"Hells bells," Footy croaked, "It's the bloody Cairns Hotel!"

After the men had cleaned their plates, there were second helpings and more coffee. The prisoner brought the cigarettes. The sun was already hot and all three were shirtless. The Japanese fetched his own plate and ate on the sand.

"Where did you learn to cook like this?" Footy asked.

"Cook?" The Japanese said. "No, this is not cooking. This is only opening can, and..." he made a sound and mimicked pouring.

"And the shellfish? My boy Tojo!" Footy said.

"Not Tojo," the Japanese objected. "My name is 'Katsu.'"

"Cat," Johnny suggested.

"My boy Cat," Footy said.

The prisoner sighed. "Katsu" was a noble name denoting "victory," but given his circumstances, he would not insist.

How like the gaijin to shorten a man's name! A "cat," he knew, was a small creature, but at least it had sharp claws.

After they'd eaten, Johnny got the new medical kit and set it by Footy.

"You should clean your foot and change the bandage," he said. "Meantime, me and—Cat—we'll go find drinking water."

"I know where," the prisoner told him. "I found it this morning." They left, going into the trees, and Footy went to work. He turned the sole over and peeled the old bandage off. The ball was purple and swollen, but the gash had knitted. He used the tip of his knife to cut the stitches, pulled out the bits of thread, and wiped the area with iodine.

Johnny and Cat carried the containers through the trees. The prisoner led to a place thirty yards from the campsite. There, a trickle of water ran from a clump of shrubs. Taking turns with the machete, it took half an hour to clear the brush away. They exposed a bank down which water dripped onto a bed of stones. There was a puddle there, and Johnny tried a handful and found it sweet. He drank his fill and Cat took a turn.

A stand of bamboo grew nearby and Johnny cut a thick column three inches in diameter. He split it lengthways and knocked out the walls. He cut forked sticks and wedged them between the stones. He took his bamboo trough and shoved an end into the sodden moss where the spring emerged. He and Cat used the sticks to hold it in place, and shored them up with rocks.

Water flowed along the tube and splashed into the pool. They filled their water containers and rinsed themselves under the spout.

When they got back to camp, Footy was operating the radio. Wires were strung between the boxes, and the dials and the tubes glowed. He had on headphones, and had a microphone and Morse key plugged in.

"S O S," Footy said into the mike. "S O S. This is Footy Carmichael and Sergeant Johnny Willman of the Allied mission 'Operation Teeth.' We are located on the ocean at the mouth of the Raub River. Come in, over. Come in, over." He changed the frequency and repeated the whole thing. Then he tapped away in Morse code. He left the radio on for a response, but there was only static.

"I reckon I'll put out our call each morning and night," he said. "I'll leave the radio on a half hour each time, but we must conserve the batteries."

It was broiling hot. Johnny figured he was done with the jungle. He took his knife and cut his pants off just above the knees. He'd made the long-legged shorts called "Bermudas." He got his shirts and sliced the arms off at the shoulders, and put one on. He fetched his boots and cut the leg tops away, and carved out the toes, sides and backs, leaving straps. Now he had sandals and he tried them on.

"Hey, I'm a beachboy again!"

"So I see," Footy observed. "Ruddy fashion plate."

Cat asked to use the knife. He slit the legs off his own trousers and had shorts as well. The prisoner no longer even had a shirt and Johnny threw him his spare.

"Try that," he said gruffly. Cat put it on. It was too big, but the man could have passed for one of Johnny's friends from Waikiki.

"You both look utterly ridiculous, of course," Footy observed.

"Sure Footy," Johnny said. "Now, with that leg, you better stay and keep an eye on things. Cat and I will take a look-see around the neighborhood."

"This is an old plantation, mate," Footy said. "There might be a house."

"We'll make the rounds," Johnny said. He stuck his machete and bayonet knife through his belt.

"Bring the sword," he told Cat. The prisoner nodded and got it, glancing at the Australian.

"Yes, go on then," Footy called after him. "I lend it to you."

The two walked along the beach toward the river. The line of jungle ended in another enormous shade tree that dominated the point. The men wandered under its wide branches. Beneath the fallen leaves was a rutted road. Johnny cut through hanging vines and chest-high weeds, and after about ten yards, they broke into the open, and there was the Raub once more.

They stood at the mouth where the cloudy water poured into the blue sea. Thousands of water birds paddled or hovered along the swirling edges where the brown and blue mixed. Stately trees grew along the bank, and the trail ran beside them. The men stared upstream, looking for crocodiles, and they saw one. Seventy yards up, a fifteen-footer slid into the water.

The men followed the trail. It ran about sixty feet and turned back into the jungle. Johnny made out croc tracks on it, but none that were fresh. He saw truck tires set in the water along the bank, spaced every few feet. A worn rope connected them and went to trees fifty feet apart.

"For boats," Cat observed and Johnny nodded. Tall grass had sprung up on the old road and where it turned into the trees, they disturbed a huge python. When it saw the men, it sucked in a breath that swelled it to double its girth, and let it all out in a menacing hiss. It flung out of its coils and squirmed into the brush.

They followed the track back into the jungle. They came to a clearing, and the road disappeared. There was only the undisturbed forest floor, littered with leaves and palm fronds. The place looked serene, but something triggered Johnny's inner alarm.

He took another step as he puzzled it through, and then he saw it. On the other side of the clearing, the ruts picked up again. Just as he noticed that, his foot went through the earth as if going into quicksand. He lost his balance and began to fall forward. He yelled and would have gone on his face, if Cat hadn't grabbed his belt from behind. For long seconds they stood there—Johnny tilted forward, the prisoner trying to hold him back with all his weight on his heels. But Johnny outweighed the Asian, and he continued a slow motion fall, dragging the captive with him.

But then Cat crouched, jerked hard, and Johnny tumbled back. They both sat hard on the ground.

"What the...?" Johnny exclaimed and scrambled forward. He shoved a hand through where his foot had gone, but instead of solid earth, his fingers snarled in something that had bounce.

He realized what it was—a camouflage net, cleverly placed. Branches and fronds obscured the edges, and scattered with leaves and grown over with creepers, it was virtually undetectable. But now that Johnny knew it was there, he could see the shape, ten or twelve feet square. He and Cat grabbed the rope edge and raised it so they could look underneath. Johnny gave a whistle and air hissed in through the prisoner's teeth.

"Now you owe me another life," Cat told Johnny.

CHAPTER 2

Johnny and Cat stared into a pit six feet deep that bristled with sharpened bamboo spears. The points were poised just under the net, fifty or more fixed in the earth. Johnny got a sick feeling just looking at what he had almost fallen onto.

"Yes," he said to the prisoner. "I owe you another life."

"But I owed you three," the other man said. "Now you owe me two. I owe you one more," he sighed.

"Forget it! Who's keeping score?" Johnny said. "And thanks."

"Who made this terrible thing?" Cat asked.

"Soldiers—your side or ours," Johnny said. "Let's go around."

The men pushed through the foliage around one side of the booby-trap and rejoined the trail. Shortly, they were out of the jungle and into the plantation rows. The tops of the palms were heavy with nuts and the ground was covered, green ones on top, dark husks below.

"There's been no harvest for years," Johnny said. Cat tapped his arm. A building loomed ahead. The men crept closer and saw the ruin of a house, constructed of palm trunks stacked log-cabin style. There was a dark entrance, the door lying in the scrub. It would be impossible to get in that way, Johnny saw, because the roof had fallen in.

The house stood in a clearing choked in weeds. It was silent except for the hissing of cicadas. It didn't look like anyone had been here for a long time, but Johnny put a finger to his lips and motioned for Cat to go one way, while he went the other.

The Japanese was approaching the corner when there was outraged squawking and a bird exploded up, shedding feathers. In a heartbeat, the sword was out and slashing. The head spun one way, while the body went another, and Cat trapped it with his foot.

"Sheesh!" Johnny said in a normal voice, no need to be quiet any longer.

"Sorry," Cat said. "It jumped and I...." He shrugged. He cleaned the sword on the vegetation and sheathed it again, then lifted the bird by the feet. It was skinny, but a real barnyard chicken.

"I will cook," Cat smiled.

"Alright, let's keep going."

The men went opposite ways around the ruin. Johnny passed a woven reed wall laced with bullet holes. It was torn at one end and he saw into the room. The pole rafters were intact and he went in. Light streamed through gaps in the grass thatch. The room's dirt floor was littered with shell casings and dark stains that he knew were blood.

He continued into the last room. It had another vacant doorway that looked into the overgrown backyard. Windows were cut into the log walls and Cat appeared in one.

"No one here," Johnny said. "This is where the plantation family once lived."

"Then soldiers come," Cat replied.

"I think a lot of men died here," Johnny said.

There was a fire pit in the center of the room and the remnants of broken up and partially burned furniture. Against a wall stood a makeshift bed with a rag of a blanket still on it. Johnny took a closer look and saw it had once been a massive desk, the splintered drawers buried in the clay. He pulled the cloth off and saw the soiled top carved with words in English and Japanese. He read one: "Davey was here, 1943."

"The plantation got its supplies from the river, but there must be a way through the coconut grove."

"Yes," Cat nodded at the door.

As they suspected, the trail led them through the rows of palms. They saw the jungle was reclaiming it. Wild trees and underbrush almost smothered the path in places. They continued, and heard the crash of the surf.

They found themselves entering a banana orchard. The trees were heavy with several types of the fruit—long and short, red, green and yellow. They cut two bunches and each slung one over a shoulder. Their path intersected with another going to the beach and they took it. They passed their pool of water and emerged at camp. Footy was busy with the radio. When he finished, Johnny filled him in on the house.

"Anything good there?" the Aussie asked. "Anything to get?"

"Not much except these bananas," Johnny said, "and Cat's

surprise." The Japanese held up the chicken.

"A chook!" Footy observed.

"*Wakadori*," Cat said. "I will cook."

"This place saw action, but now we're alone," Johnny said. "Let's have a meeting."

The three hunkered down. The first thing Johnny wanted to talk about was where they should set up camp. Footy wondered if the house might not provide decent shelter.

"It's too far back in the trees," Johnny said. "We might miss any ship or plane that does come by. Besides, a lot of people died there. Maybe the natives are right about things like that."

"Very many insects," the prisoner spoke up. "It is better here." Footy shot him a look. *When did the Jap get a say in things?*

"Alright," the pilot said. "I agree we have a better chance of being spotted out here."

Next they talked about food. Johnny figured they had enough for two weeks, but much longer, if they augmented it with what they could find in the area. Cat spoke up again. He said he would like to organize the kitchen and do the cooking. The other two were only too happy to let him have at it.

Footy said they should build a big stack of wood on the beach, ready to light the moment they saw a chance of rescue. Johnny said they'd get to it the next day.

"Next order of business. We need to wash our stuff."

"Right mate," Footy agreed. "I'm about to pass away from me own stink."

"Yes," the Japanese agreed. "Very bad smell."

They gathered all the clothes, old blankets, bars of soap, and went to the spring. First, they took turns lathering themselves and rinsing off, then they washed everything else. They carried the things back to camp and spread them on the branches to dry.

That evening as another tropical sunset drenched the sky, Johnny offered to look at Footy's cut. He removed the dressing and was pleased to see it had healed over, but the ball remained livid and swollen. He pressed on it, and Footy exercised his vocabulary.

"I think it's abscessed," Johnny said. "You need a doc to open it up."

"Yes mate," Footy said. "And while you're at it, how about dancing girls and a lorry load of beer? But at least I can walk."

Cat went into the forest. During the hungry years in this country he had found some edible plants. He recognized one and pulled it up. Its ribbed roots tasted like peppery ginger. He discovered a patch of grass with a lemony taste and harvested a handful. He returned to camp with an armload of green coconuts. He had shaken each one to make sure it sloshed. The milky liquid made a refreshing drink, and he would use some to flavor his cooking.

He went back for brown coconuts. These he husked with the machete and cracked them in two. They were almost solid with white flesh. He scooped it out and chopped it fine. He searched along the beach and found a large, flat stone that he brought to camp. On this he piled the shredded coconut. He selected a fist-size rock and used it to grind the nutmeat. Oily liquid emerged, and he poured it into an empty can.

Cat plucked and cleaned the chicken. He made a fire, split the carcass, and roasted it over the coals. He boiled the organs, strained out the meat, and made a soup with canned tomatoes and other vegetables. He fried yam slices, spiced with wild ginger.

As the men ate, the swollen ball of the sun struck the horizon and squashed flat. The clouds turned mango and tangerine as the sun disappeared, and the sky went purple, then black. Points of light began to gleam through, and the heavens took on infinite depth.

Cat made coffee, and Johnny and Footy lay on the sand and stared up. Each set of eyes focused on a small, brilliant constellation.

"The Southern Cross," Footy pointed. "That's Aus, mate. That's our flag."

"Above the equator, sailors navigate by the North Star," Johnny said. "Down here, they use that one—also called the 'Crux.'"

"See the bright cluster inside?" Footy said, not to be outdone. "That's the Jewel Box."

The prisoner came with mugs of coffee and sat. He gazed at *minami-juji-sei* as well. It was not visible from his home in the north, but it was a familiar companion from the hundreds of nights in New Guinea.

Then a brilliant white streak shot from one side to the other. Within minutes, another followed, leaving a ghostly trail. Apart from murmurs of appreciation, the men did not speak. Johnny reflected that the term, "meteor shower" did not come close to doing justice to what followed. This was more like cosmic fireworks against a backdrop of a billion suns, with a soundtrack courtesy of the South Pacific.

Eventually the show tapered off. In silence, unwilling to break the spell, the men crept off to their beds.

They slept and Planet Earth added another measure to its passage through forever.

CHAPTER 3

Johnny woke again to fragrant coffee and hot breakfast. Once more, Cat was up early. The men talked while they ate and agreed that this morning, they would build their camp. Footy tried the radio, again without response.

While he was occupied, Johnny and Cat climbed the trees with the tarp that had held their cache. They roped it between the big tree and palms to make a roof. Beneath it, Footy and the prisoner laid out mattresses made of several blankets. Each had a crate for a bedside table. Johnny was happy to stick with his hammock, enormously improved by a washed and sun-dried sheet.

Under one end of the tarp, they set up their kitchen. Cat had seen a round from a felled tree back in the palms, and he and Johnny rolled it out and laid it flat as a worktable.

Cat said he would do the rest. He made a shelving unit from crates and boxes, and lined up the cans. He put everything perishable into a box he could raise on a rope. He hung the bananas from a branch.

Johnny and Footy went a few feet down the beach and built their fire pit. They scooped a hollow and lined it with rocks. They set boulders and logs around for seats. By noon, the camp was shipshape.

After lunch, Johnny said he and the prisoner would build the signal fire. Footy, hampered by his leg, said he had another job. He wanted to spell a giant "S O S" with coconuts that could be seen from the air. Johnny and Cat collected armloads of nuts and piled them for him on the beach, including the ones that had formed the arrow. Footy began by marking letters with a stick, then laid the lines of coconuts.

Johnny and Cat scoured the plantation for deadfalls and dragged them out. They made a waist-high cone of branches stuffed with dry moss and twigs. On top of this, they leaned larger branches. As they worked, Johnny considered his future.

If the Marine Captain is right, the war is over. So what will I do? Once it had seemed clear. He would be a career Navy officer, like his father and grandfather before him. But now, Johnny knew that wasn't his future.

As for the Army, Johnny had sworn he was in the fight against Japan to the finish. He'd been convinced this required the invasion of the enemy homeland. The truth was, he hadn't expected to live through that, and so he had made no plans for the future. But now he had to grapple with life in this brave new world. He remembered a quotation his father liked: "peace shall destroy many."

Johnny's hometown was San Diego. But his family had left, and now his grandparents were dead, the house sold. He realized that was a closed chapter. His mom's family was from Colorado, and while Johnny had visited as a boy, he felt no connection there.

What about Hawaii? Johnny had spent a year on Oahu when he was sixteen. He'd learned to love the island. *Or at least until the end,* he thought. But because of that, he had a powerful aversion to the place. *I'll never go back.*

So what about the States? Most of his life, he'd assumed he'd end up somewhere in the U S of A. Once he'd dreamed of life in the big northern cities he saw in the magazines—*Chicago or New York. Glamour, babes in hot fashions.*

But no, he decided. That had always been a vague daydream. Truth was, he loved the outdoors. Living crammed on top of millions of others would not work for him. In fact, the war had shown him a bigger world.

Johnny and Cat went back to the grove, looking for fallen palms.

I've learned to like hot climates. The fruit is sweeter, the flowers and birds more colorful. Everything is bolder in the tropics! What about something totally different?

Johnny spoke some Spanish he'd picked up from his Mexican amigos in Southern Cal. He got a picture of himself trekking up the Amazon River—or maybe hunting in Africa like Hemmingway. He'd carry his rifle and wear a hat like "Idaho Jones."

Johnny and Cat leaned the tall poles against each other like a teepee.

What am I qualified to do? What are my skills, he wondered seriously. *I can surf,* he thought. *And I can shoot men.* Neither struck him as a reasonable way to earn a living.

Maybe I will sell life insurance! He'd had a war buddy who bragged on how much he could make doing that. Johnny hoped the poor fellow had bought himself a good policy, because he hadn't made it home. But the harder he thought about selling door-to-door, the more it seemed about as much fun as latrine duty.

Maybe cars! He felt more enthusiasm about that, because he liked automobiles. With the war over, the government's ban on manufacturing was bound to be lifted. By heart, he listed the great companies. *Buick, Cadillac, Chevrolet, Chrysler, Dodge, Essex, Ford, Hudson, Jordon, Lincoln, LaSalle, Mercury, Nash, Oldsmobile, Packard—my dad's favorite. Plymouth, Pontiac, Studebaker and Willys.* They were constellations in the car-manufacturing firmament, and Johnny figured they'd always be there. With the war won, they'd be raring for business again!

But then, Johnny recalled the man who'd sold his dad his last sedan. The twelve-year-old Johnny had tagged along. The salesman had a loud voice and an even louder jacket. Johnny figured, from the way the man acted, that he was good friends with his dad. But later his father told him he didn't know the fellow. He said he was the kind of man who would clap you on the back with one hand, while his other rifled your wallet. Johnny guessed all salesmen weren't like that, but when he tried to see himself spending a life under the flapping flags, waiting for the next sucker—*err, customer*—it just didn't turn his crank.

The problem was, it came to Johnny, once you'd spent your days fighting for your life, everything else seemed too tame. More than a little boring. *Strange*—during the years of fighting, there hadn't been a day when he didn't wish it was over. Now that it was, he didn't know what to do with the long road of years that suddenly stretched ahead.

The signal fire was done. Johnny and Cat helped Footy finish the "S O S."

Cat's entree that night was the ham, simmered with potatoes and fresh beans, flavored with lemon grass. Dessert was custard folded with sliced bananas, coconut, and chunks of chocolate.

Again the men slept with full bellies. They were fast recovering from the extraordinary exertions of their trek, although the Aussie's foot still gave him grief.

Over breakfast, Footy had a plan.

"Let's go fishing!"

"Sure thing!" Johnny said.

"I go too," the Japanese said. They dug out the spools of fishing line and counted ten hooks on a card.

"We need to make lures," Footy said, and they tore strips of brightly colored paper and foil from their growing garbage pile.

Johnny had done a lot of fishing, both fresh and salt water, but not without a rod. At the water's edge, Footy showed him how. They tied bits of broken coral to the end of the lines for weights, and knotted on their hooks a yard or two up. Over these, they wove strips of paper to cover the barb.

The men spaced themselves facing the ocean. Johnny watched Footy strip line off his spool and lay loops on the sand. The Aussie whirled the weighted line over his head, gradually paying it out, and let fly. The weight spun over the waves and splashed down. Cat cast in a similar way. Johnny watched them retrieve, tugging rhythmically. When the lures were close to shore, he admired the way they flashed and danced.

Johnny made his first attempt. He got the line spinning, but when he let loose, somehow it made an enormous snarl that barely hit the water. He spent the next twenty minutes unraveling the mess.

Cat gave a yell and jerked a little silver fish from the brine. It flipped on the sand until he pinched its head. He came to Johnny and asked for his clasp knife. He cut the fish into strips, leaving a bit of tail on each one.

"Now we catch big ones," he grinned. He left a couple of pieces for Johnny and gave some to Footy. Johnny replaced the paper with a fish wedge. He got the weight whirling again and let it go. This time it went about twenty feet before it plopped in the water. That was not as good as the other men, but it was a start. Johnny retrieved and cast again, and each time, his technique improved.

Fifteen minutes later, it was Footy who whooped. His taut line danced across the water. He brought it in little by little, getting a good fight. Johnny and Cat wrapped in their lines so they wouldn't tangle and went to watch. There was a flash in the shallows. Cat ran in and held up a fish as long as his forearm.

"Trevally," Footy said.

"Naw, that's a Jack," Johnny called. He'd caught ones like it in Hawaii.

"Trevally mate," Footy said. "Don't bloody tell me about fishing!"

"Oh, I wouldn't try to tell you anything," Johnny replied. "But that's a Jack."

Footy collected his fish from the Japanese and whacked its head with a stick.

"Well, now it's supper," the Aussie grinned. He got a piece of banana leaf, soaked it in seawater, and wrapped the fish in it.

An hour later, Johnny was casting as well as the others. He let one burn out and the weight dropped into the swells. At once there was a strong hit and Johnny got the heart-leap that is the fisherman's addiction. The line pulled tight and Johnny could feel every tremor between himself and the living thing on the other end. He hollered, and it was the other men's turn to get their gear out of the way and watch.

Johnny was pulling in steadily when the fish burst through the surface. It looked like something from another planet—white, covered in polka dots. It submerged and jerked away, but Johnny brought it in. Footy waded out and grabbed it.

"Barramundi, mate!" he exclaimed. "A young one."

"I'll take your word for it," Johnny said.

"Nice fish!" the Japanese called.

Johnny took a break and smoked while the others kept casting. Then it was the prisoner who yelled.

"You're on!" Footy said, and pulled in his line. The Japanese hauled away, but suddenly his arms jerked and the filament burned through his fingers. *A second strike!* Just as fast, the line went slack.

The prisoner muttered anxiously and kept retrieving. There was something silver in the shallows and then on the sand. It was a fish head, the mouth gasping, but only a stump of spine behind.

"Hit!" Johnny exclaimed.

"Shark?" Footy asked.

"Goni-kamasu!" the Japanese pointed.

The men saw the dark shape flick into deeper water.

"Barracuda!" Johnny said.

And that was the beginning of the end of fishing that day. Everything they caught came in chopped up. Then Footy's line was cut and he lost his hook. Now they had nine.

"Better give it up," the Aussie said. The men wound in their tackle. Next time the 'cuda found them, they'd quit right away.

Cat said he'd clean the fish. He went close to the breaking waves, sliced open the bellies, scooped out the guts and flung them into the sea. Where they dropped, the water rippled with feeders. He scraped scales off and was silver to the elbows. He filleted the catch with sure strokes.

He carried the fish to his kitchen, lit the stove and poured coconut oil in the pan. He scraped in a spoonful of white fat he'd saved from the stew. When it was sputtering, he slipped in the meat. He drilled the eyes of a green coconut with a knife and splashed in some liquid. He sprinkled on ginger root and lemon grass.

The smell was bewitching and the men's mouths watered. In less than five minutes, Cat handed around the plates. Johnny saw white flesh swimming in marinade. He took a bite that fell apart in his mouth.

"That's the best I've ever tasted," he said fervently.

"Cor, mate, fair dinkum," Footy managed. The men forked it in while the prisoner's eyes flashed between them. Then Cat ate as well.

Life is not half bad, Johnny sighed, *since we left the Father behind*.

CHAPTER 4

The following morning, Footy again put out the call on the radio while Johnny rinsed the breakfast dishes in the ocean. Cat came with him and said they would make some salt. They carried a little water back in the bottom of the pans and set them in the sun. Eventually, Cat scraped up the residue and put it in a twist of paper.

Footy finished up with his S O S and wanted to fish again.

"There's no pub and no women," he said. "We might as well enjoy the next best thing." Cat prepared his gear but Johnny said he'd had enough of the twirl-and-throw method. He told the others to go ahead.

Johnny was tired of the beard he'd grown on their odyssey. He sharpened his clasp knife against a shell until the blade could take the hair off his arm. He warmed water, made suds and spread it over cheeks and chin. He had no mirror so he stuck Footy's Bowie knife sideways in the tree and peered in. He went to work with his blade, pulling and nicking some, but he got the hair off.

Johnny returned to the bamboo thicket and cut a thin pole ten feet long. He tried it and liked the whip. He took a stick and inserted it to knock out the sections out of his bamboo so he had a hollow tube. He wrapped fishing line tightly around the outside of the tip to prevent it from splitting.

He scoured their garbage dump and chose a large tin can. He washed it and tied it sideways on the thick end of the pole. Now he had a primitive reel. He threaded his fishing line through the hollow rod and wrapped the excess around the can. With paper for a lure, he headed down to the beach.

Johnny hiked to the place where dark blue water came close to shore. This was a drop off and he figured the bigger fish were down the wall. He tied on a weight, dressed the hook and stood at the breaking waves. He pulled line off the can in spools at his feet, pinched it between finger and thumb of his left hand and cocked the pole back.

He whipped it forward and released. The weight soared high, by far the longest cast any of them had made. Footy and Cat were watching and the Aussie crowed. Johnny pulled the line through his pole and wrapped it around the can. He worked the rod's tip to make the lure dance.

After a dozen casts, he was rewarded with a heavy strike. Johnny fought the fish towards shore. Again the other two brought in their tackle and came to help. The tip of Johnny's rod quivered like a live thing. At last he worked the fish into shallow water and Cat wrestled it out. It was more than two feet long, shaped like a mackerel, but with blue bars down its side, and had an undershot jaw like a 'cuda.

"It's an 'Ono,'" Johnny said, using the Hawaiian name.

"Oh, no mate, that's a Wahoo," Footy told him. It must weigh at least fifteen pounds, at least they agreed on that.

Once more they had an excellent dinner. The men were starting to put flesh back on their bones. Maybe the Japanese had been the most starved, because the change was most obvious in him.

The next day, Johnny helped the others make their own bamboo rods. By midday they had as many fish as they could eat and quit.

Hanging around camp, Johnny was restless. There had been no sign of a ship or plane, and it had been so long since he hadn't been fighting for his life in battle, or hospital, he didn't know what to do with himself.

I need a project, he thought, *but what?* He cleaned his rifle, and even though it didn't need it, he organized his pack. He came across the brandy. He'd almost forgotten about it.

What did Footy say about a pub? The others were napping in the shade when Johnny brought the bottle over.

"We can't help the lack of female company," he smiled, "but at least the bar's open." He took a swallow and passed the bottle to the Aussie.

"Crikey!" Footy croaked, sitting up. "I wouldn't say no." He took a drink, studied the prisoner for a moment and passed the bottle to him. Cat sniffed it and took an experimental sip. He swished it around his mouth and swallowed.

"Oh, good!" he said, and took a long drink. The men lit Lucky Strikes and continued to pass the brandy. It took an hour to accomplish their task, but they drank it dry.

"Why didn't you bring that out before, mate?" Footy asked, sprawled on the sand, eyes a little unfocused. "Trouble with you Yanks—too cautious."

"Cautious?" Johnny sat up, nettled. His eyes went to the jeeps in front of them.

"Too cautious?" he repeated. "Can you drive a car?"

"Of coursh—course," the Australian replied. "I can drive or fly anything built by man."

"With that foot?"

"Bloody right," Footy said, also sitting bolt upright. "Born mechanic and operator, that's Yours Truly."

"You ever play 'chicken?'" Johnny asked.

"Chicken?" Footy said, blinking reddened eyes. "Here chook, chook, chook!"

"Naw," Johnny said. He stood, swaying a little. "Chicken. With vehicles." Footy just stared at him, so Johnny explained the time-hallowed American tradition.

"You got it?" Johnny asked.

"Bloody right," Footy said, also lurching up, fire in his eyes.

"Alright pal," Johnny told him. "You drive that way, I'll go the other." He pointed down the beach. The Japanese listened, totally bewildered. Perhaps it was the strong drink, but the *gaijin* had stopped making sense. Footy strode barefoot to a jeep. Johnny noticed he walked without a limp.

"How's the cut?"

"Don't feel a bloody thing," Footy grinned. He climbed in and turned the key. The engine roared to life. Johnny came over, folded the windshield flat and hooked it down. He did the same with the other vehicle, got in the driver's seat and fired it up. His head was spinning as he stared at the Aussie.

"May the best man win!" he called and drove off, spewing sand.

"I'd like to thank me ma and pa," Footy began, rehearsing his winning speech. He ground his jeep into gear and burst in the opposite direction.

About seventy yards apart, they wheeled to face each other.

Johnny goosed his engine. Footy did the same. Johnny slammed the jeep into first and drove at Footy, fishtailing.

"Coooo-eeee," the Aussie screamed and his jeep lurched into motion. He aimed at the Yank and floored it. They hammered through the gears. The Japanese stared.

What are the crazy red men doing? Footy saw Johnny's jeep come at alarming speed, but steered straight at it. Just when it seemed they must crash, Footy jerked the wheel over. At once Johnny turned the other way and the vehicles narrowly missed. The drivers fought for control and stopped.

"You turned first!" Johnny bellowed with laughter. "You're the chicken!" Footy's face turned beet red.

"Come on Yank!" the Aussie shouted, "go again!" Johnny waved derisively, headed down the beach and turned as he had before. Footy did the same.

Again the vehicles faced one another. Again, the men gunned the motors and came at each other as fast as they could. This time, at the last second, it was Johnny who veered off and the men pulled up.

"Now who's the chook-chook-chook?" The Aussie cawed. Johnny pointed his finger like a gun.

"Pow!" he said. "Go again!"

The men made several more close passes. They were high on booze and hormones, yelling insults and having a great time.

On about their eighth pass, their fenders touched and one of Footy's headlights exploded. A shard of glass flew back and cut his eyebrow. He wiped it and when he looked up, the Japanese was standing directly in his path, waving his arms. Footy had to stand on the brake in order not to run the man over and pain shot up his leg.

"Are you bleedin' thick?" he shouted.

"My turn," Cat said. Johnny had stopped some distance off.

"What's he say?"

Footy wiped the blood from his eyebrow.

"He wants a go," he shouted.

"Let him," Johnny said and roared off. Footy shrugged and got out of the jeep.

"Alright, let's see if you're the one Oriental who can drive.'"

Cat climbed behind the wheel and Footy noticed the crazed look in his eye.

Johnny spun his vehicle and waited. The Japanese got to where Footy turned around and did the same. From a distance, the drivers stared at one another. Then the prisoner shoved his jeep in gear and the tires spun. Johnny jammed the stick in first and shot down the beach as well. They put the pedals to the floor and the engines screamed.

The vehicles picked up speed, throwing up rooster tails of sand. They shifted gears, hit top speed and came on. Footy stood at midpoint and watched them howl together. Cat half stood, shook a fist and screamed.

"Banzai!"

Johnny raised himself as well and shot up a fist.

"Geronimo!"

The grille of Cat's jeep filled Johnny's vision and then, too late, he knew the man was not going to turn.

He wasn't even going to try.

Desperately, Johnny yanked his wheel hard over, but Cat saw what he did and turned in the same direction.

It was all over in a split second.

CHAPTER 5

It was like a bomb going off. The jeeps hit dead on and Footy watched both men fly through the air. Johnny's jeep got instantly shorter while the other one tipped on its nose.

One second Johnny was behind the wheel and the next he was airborne. There was the blur of the other man going by and then the back end of the jeep was rising to meet him. He just cleared it and was soaring over the sand, the tremendous bang ringing in his ears.

And that was all he would ever recall of his brief solo flight.

The next thing he knew, he was staring into Footy's face. The Aussie was glaring at him as Johnny discovered he was on his back on the sand. He tried to sit up and it was as if a wrecker's ball swung into him. He was knocked flat, his arm went over his eyes and he groaned.

"You great bleeding idiot!" Footy shouted. "You could have killed yourself!"

"And the Jap?" Johnny asked.

"No idea," Footy said. "Probably dead."

Johnny sat up and checked himself over. He rotated his head gingerly, felt his neck and decided nothing major was broken. He cranked around and looked at the jeeps. He could see only the exposed chassis of the one the prisoner had driven. It stood on its nose, one back wheel spinning, the other missing entirely.

With help from Footy he was able to get up. Leaning on the Aussie, he staggered to find Cat. They came to the jeeps and Johnny knew both were totaled. The hood of his was squeezed like an accordion and the smoking engine sat in the front seat. He looked for the wheel missing off the other one and saw it bouncing far down the beach. Johnny put out a hand and patted his jeep.

The body was lying some distance away. They hobbled to it. The prisoner sprawled face down, at a bad angle, an arm bent beneath him.

"Cat!" Johnny croaked, falling on his knees. "Katsu!"

The Japanese lay like a corpse and Johnny put a hand on him, expecting the worst. Suddenly the man sat up. He put his hands to his head and twisted and there was a rippling crack. Sand was caked down his face and he dug a little finger in his ear and shook out a shower. Then he leaned over and spat out a bloody tooth. He stared at it in dismay, picked it up and put it in his pocket.

Slowly, a wide smile split his battered features. He looked triumphantly at Johnny.

"Now who is the chicken?" he asked. "Hey? Who is the chicken now?"

"You bloody fool!" Footy shouted at him. "You wrecked our jeeps!"

Johnny frowned severely at the prisoner and shook his head.

"That is not how you play chicken!" Johnny lectured him. "You hear me?

"C'mon Footy," he turned to the Aussie. "Let's go."

Leaning hard on each other, they staggered back to camp. Sunset stained the sky blood red. They sat at the fire pit and lit cigarettes with trembling fingers. Johnny felt like he'd been on the losing end of a prizefight. They smoked in silence as a monster hangover crept over them.

Some time later the prisoner shuffled up, dragging his leg. A mottled bruise covered one side of his face and chest and he clutched his side. He stopped in front of the men and bowed.

"Sorry," he said. "So sorry."

"The point is to miss, not hit!" Johnny griped. "Sheesh! That is not how you play chicken!"

☼

Hurt as he was, Cat insisted on making dinner. The men ate in silence. All were suffering the aftereffects of the brandy, and Johnny and the Japanese were badly beaten up. They bedded down shortly after dark.

Cat lay on his blankets aching all over. There was a stabbing pain in his neck and his head pounded. He lay awake and smelled the breeze off the ocean and at once, he was transported home.

Of course, he thought. *This air was over my city only hours ago*. He imagined his wife and family and was flooded with longing.

Eventually he drifted to sleep and found himself in a recurring dream.

Katsu the dreamer, saw his younger self standing in an elaborate garden. Trimmed trees and blossoming shrubs ranged around a grand home. This was the gracious estate that had been in his family for generations. The dreamer looked to the pond where the white swan swam.

The man he saw there was a younger, more confident, handsome version of himself. His thick hair was brushed back from his clean-shaven, unlined face. His body was muscular, not thin as he was now. He was outfitted in a crisp officer's uniform, with its decorations and the insignia of a Captain in the Imperial Army. The younger Katsu held a crystal glass of golden liquor and ice, and around him were his fellow officers, each with a drink.

Senior officers stood to the side and the dreamer searched for a particular face. He saw the stern features and the white hair at the temples. His father was in uniform, his chest ablaze with the Golden Kite, the Rising Sun, and the Order of the Sacred Treasure.

Katsu saw the women in their splendid kimonos, his mother with her heavy hair and sweet smile. But his eyes were for Koto—his wife was so lovely! He drank in her pale, flawless skin and the long neck. Her shining hair was coiled up, adorned with the mother-of-pearl combs he had given her on their wedding night. The dreamer's heart swelled as he saw their children beside her—Ryo, his nine-year old son and his five-year old daughter, Yuriko.

In the dream, Katsu's father spoke in his authoritative voice.

"The war has come! The Takano family is samurai and we have waited all our lives to serve the Empire. A toast to our beloved Emperor and his family! A toast to Nippon and our sure victory!"

With the others, the young Katsu raised his glass and drank. The liquor was his father's favorite—Talisker Whisky from the United Kingdom. It was very expensive and now impossible to come by, but his father had visited London before the war, and had brought several cases home.

The dreamer watched his father enter the house and go to an alcove. Here a priceless heirloom rested on its stand. This was the most precious of the family swords in its scabbard, and the man picked it up. It was the *katana* called *"Bizen,"* but by the men of the Takano family, *"Katsumushi-maru."*

In his dream, as in life, Katsu's father returned outside where the guests waited. He approached the younger Katsu and held out the *katana*.

"My son," his father said, his voice solemn. *"Tomorrow you leave for battle. Take Katsumushi-maru. It is the spirit of our ancestors. Now it is yours."*

His father offered the sword and Katsu, overcome with the honor done him, accepted it and bowed low.

"Use it well. Protect Katsumushi-maru and it will protect you. Never forget this. You are a Captain in the Imperial Army. But more than that, you are samurai in the service of the Emperor. Obey your orders. May you honor your heritage and the uniform." His father turned to the assembled guests.

"My fellow warriors, my family, honored friends. I present to you my son, Takano Katsu—and Katsumushi-maru!"

There were broad smiles and calls of appreciation. The men drank again, this time to him.

Then in the dream, Katsu was alone with his father in the room where they displayed the five suits of full armor of their ancestors. Ancient paintings hung on the walls, some done by the warriors themselves. *Katsumushi-maru* was in Katsu's hands as his father spoke.

"Many families would not send a priceless heirloom like Katsumushi-maru into battle. A soldier would take an inferior blade so that the katana would not be lost. But to think that way is to defeat your warrior heart before the first blow!" His father studied him and went on passionately.

"With Katsumushi-maru in your hand, victory is the only acceptable outcome. You must teach the enemy the tune Katsumushi-maru sings."

The dream changed again, and Katsu was entering the bedroom as he removed his clothing. His heart rose to find Koto waiting for him, naked in bed, all her lovely hair spilling over her shoulders. Katsu lay beside her, wrapped her in his arms and smelled the scent of her skin. He clutched her beloved form to him, as he had that very last night before he sailed for war.

The dream was so heartbreakingly vivid Katsu awoke, his hands embracing sand. Koto was gone and he was alone, terribly alone. His cheeks were wet with tears and he yearned for her so strongly that if he could not have her, he desired death. But that respite, once again, would not come.

He rolled on his back and looked into the cold countenance of the moon. Koto filled his heart, as did his children Ryo and Yuriko, and all the people he loved. He wondered if they were staring at this very same face of the night. Perhaps they asked it if he, Katsu, was somewhere under it, or had died long ago. There had been no communication for so long.

His hand went to the *katana* at his side and clutched the hard comfort. It was the last shred of his pride, the one thing that connected him to his family and tradition.

It occurred to him then, even though he had made a solemn promise otherwise, it was impossible to go home without *Katsu-mushi-maru*. Yet he had given his word. He had promised the Australian that when the time came, he would surrender it to him.

The cosmic light allowed no lies. Katsu admitted he no longer hated Footy, but at the same time, he was *gaijin* and unworthy of a prize he could not understand. Katsu imagined the sword hanging on the wall of a peasant house, dusty and unloved. He saw Footy grown old, handing the rusted blade to profane hands as he recounted his threadbare war stories.

Katsu rolled over and stared at the man himself, a sleeping form outlined in moonlight. How easily the *katana* could reach over and stroke the life from him! But even as the thought came, Katsu was flooded with the certainty that his war with these two men was finished.

Unthinkable as it was, he had promised to surrender *Katsu-mushi-maru* to the Australian, and this he must humble himself to do. *But not before the time—not until the last second,* he promised himself. *After that I may live, but my warrior heart will be dead.*

Sleep had deserted Katsu and he sat up. The South Pacific had grown gentle in the night and it seemed to steal softly like a lover to kiss the beach. He saw the path the moonlight made across the water and was struck by the fancy that he could travel it. He would run and never stop until he was home.

But as Katsu's yearning eyes traveled that wavering light, they were tripped up by darkness. Out perhaps three hundred meters, a wedge of blackness moved across the beam and broke it into fragments.

It might simply be the ocean tossing in his sleep. But perhaps something huge moved out there, that was more than a trick of the light. He strained his eyes, but could not make it out. And now the moon sank into the water, and the path home was gone.

What was it? Was it the crocodile? The ocean of stars continued to glimmer, but it was not enough. Sharply, he recalled his first confrontation with the Father. It had taken his rifle from him and batted him as a man would strike a fly. He had been knocked unconscious, and that is how the soldiers had taken him without a fight.

I have not finished with the beast, he thought.

He stayed awake for some time and smoked a cigarette. He was unsettled, because the monstrous animal frightened him. That was the only sane response to such a dragon of the deep. But now he became aware of his pains. His body throbbed from the crash, and his brain was bruised by the brandy. He yawned hugely and lay back on his side.

He put his hand on *Katsumushi-maru* and at last he slept.

Katsu woke when the stars were fading in the east. He had forgotten what he had dreamed, except that Koto was in his mind. She retreated as his consciousness returned, and he ached with her absence. He cherished the memory of her as he rose and began to prepare breakfast.

In Katsu's home, there had been servants to prepare the food, but since he was a boy, his secret passion had been to cook. He had haunted the kitchens and the workers had indulged the master's son. Now here with his former enemies on the beach, the humble work gave him something practical to do, in a world that was almost too much to bear.

In truth, he was in agony this morning, and walked like an old man. This was the legacy of the very serious American game called "chicken." Its object, colored by the strong drink, had seemed obvious to him. The combatants only turned away because they were afraid. And Katsu had known he was no longer fearful, not even to die.

At that moment yesterday when he left the jeep, he had flown toward the end with something like gratitude. It was with regret that he awakened with sand and a loose tooth in his mouth.

Then, as Katsu limped to put the coffee on, he remembered the moving darkness that had carved the moonlight. His eyes flashed to the ocean, but all he saw were the eternal waves, rising in the dawn to do battle with the land once more.

Katsu cooked and watched the play of the ocean. Gulls rose in the breeze to hover above it, while others huddled in groups on the sand, preening their feathers.

He was in the fleeting moments when it was not night, but not yet day. Katsu saw the other men sleeping. *They are my captors and yet I am free!*

He picked up Johnny's clasp knife, and took soap, a towel, and the largest cooking pot. He made his way to the pool of water. There he filled the container, then sat and scrubbed himself thoroughly under the spout. He had seen that Johnny had shaved, and now he lathered his head and face and did the same with the blade, over his scalp, lip and chin, using touch to tell him when the skin was smooth. He brushed his teeth with a twig and returned to camp.

When breakfast was ready, he woke the other men. This morning's new offering was fried bananas. Johnny climbed out of his hammock and groaned. He, too, hurt all over. Somehow he had gashed both shins and his body was covered with bruises and abrasions. The wound in his chest hurt again, but at least it had not torn open.

Footy hunched by the fire pit and Johnny dragged himself to sit nearby. Cat brought coffee and plates of food and the men ate in silence, staring at the day.

Johnny tried not to look at the wrecked jeeps, although they loomed large. Cat ate with them and Johnny saw his hangdog look. It hadn't been the prisoner's idea to play "chicken," but his own, and the Asian could hardly be blamed for not knowing how it went. Even the brandy had been Johnny's idea.

"Thanks for breakfast," Johnny told him.

"Yes, ta," Footy mumbled.

The captive nodded and gathered up the dishes. Johnny and Footy went to the radio where the Aussie broadcast the call for rescue.

After that, the men went fishing. It was not for sport. They needed the meat. The sun seemed particularly harsh this morning, glaring in their eyes. They cast for a couple of hours, but with the surf up, nothing was biting, and they gave it up. Johnny's stomach was queasy and he thought Cat looked half dead. All three had headaches and they returned to camp and tried to sleep it off.

In mid-afternoon, clouds drifted over the sun. Johnny got up feeling only marginally better. Barefoot, wearing his shorts, he took his pole and went to fish the wall. He prepared his lure and began to cast. Eventually the other men awoke and came down to watch. They sat some distance apart, their shadows stretched long down the beach.

They sat for an hour before Johnny got the huge strike. His rod bent double and he shouted and spilled line as his catch hauled out to sea. It felt like he'd hooked a tow truck, and he knew he had to slow it or it would take his whole spool. To keep from burning his fingers, he pinched the line in the material of his shorts and squeezed. Footy and Cat called and pointed as the filament cut across the waves.

Finally Johnny managed to slow the creature, but when he glanced down, he saw only a few loops left around the can. Using the rod as a lever, he dragged the weight in, dipped the tip and wrapped up the slack.

He'd muscled the fish in twenty yards when it launched another rush, and he lost everything he'd gained. Over and over, he and the fish repeated the contest of strength and wills.

Finally, Johnny dragged it over the drop off and caught his first glimpse, a dark shape hovering in the water. Worn out as he was, the sight gave him strength. But the fish got a second wind as well. Again, the pole slammed over, and Johnny could not spill off line fast enough. It hummed and he knew it would snap at any second.

He ran into the ocean up to his chest. For long moments he fought the swimmer, muscles bulging, locked in a standoff. Then, foot-by-foot, he levered it in. Gradually, he was able to back onto dry land.

Then the glorious fish jumped. It came up dark green, flashing water and light. It tossed its massive head with the prominent hump, and tried to shake the hook out of its lip. The men shouted hoarsely, and the fish splashed down and pulled hard away. Johnny was forced to pay out line.

"Did you see?" Johnny called. "Napoleon Wrasse!"

"Maori! Maori Wrasse mate!" Footy yelled. But Johnny knew this fish. When a Hawaiian fisherman caught one, he could trade it for a stack of dollars at the best restaurants in Honolulu. And they got big. Johnny had seen one on the scales, six feet long and four hundred pounds. The one he'd hooked was not a Goliath like that, but it was giant enough.

"Napoleon!" Johnny called back. "See the hat on its head?"

"Maori!" Footy insisted. "See the tattoos on its face?"

Another half hour, and Johnny was played out. But so was the fish. It finned on its side in four feet of ocean. Johnny's arms quivered, but he kept the pressure on.

Footy and Cat went in after it. The fish saw them coming and made its last break. Again, Johnny ran into the water while his rod went berserk. He mustered all he had to drag it back into the shallows.

The Wrasse rolled sluggishly. Footy and Cat approached from each side and rammed a hand through the gills. They half carried, half dragged it out. A wave broke over its back and left it stranded.

"It must weigh five stone—about seventy pounds, mate!" Footy crowed. Cat grabbed driftwood and cracked it over the hump. The great fish quivered and died. Johnny sat down, panting. Footy rolled it on its side. Cat slit it, anus to jaw, and began to haul out the substantial guts, arms in to the elbows.

"Jolly good show!" a British voice called behind them.

"Now, kindly turn around—and be so good as to raise your hands."

CHAPTER 6

Johnny looked sharply over his shoulder and saw a man in khaki shorts and a loose cotton shirt. He wore an old bowler hat and had a patchy, curly black beard. A kerchief was knotted around his neck and oriental sandals with curled toes set off his ensemble.

The newcomer's most conspicuous feature was the revolver he held. Johnny raised his hands. Footy and the Japanese stopped their work and put theirs up as well, Cat's draped with fish guts.

"Splendid," the newcomer said. "Who's in charge?"

"I guess I am," Johnny said.

"Let's have the introductions, shall we? You first."

Johnny turned to face his interrogator.

"I'm Sergeant John Willman, US Army. The Aussie is Glen Carmichael, formerly Australian Army, now private citizen."

"And the Nip?" the Englishman asked.

"He's our prisoner, an enemy officer we captured up the river. His name—say the whole thing again, Cat?"

"I am Takano, Katsu," the Japanese said.

"We call him Cat," Johnny said.

"Cat, I see" the Brit said. "And your purpose here?"

"Allied operation," Johnny said. "Rescue mission to Kissim at the headwaters of the Raub. We were to find some priests and neutralize any hostiles. He's the only one left."

"Name of your assignment?" the man asked.

"Operation Teeth," Johnny said.

"Alright then," the man said, lowering his pistol. "Who I expected—the chaps on the wireless." He turned to the Australian. "That would be you, Footy, from your voice."

"Right you are," Footy grinned. "Wireless Op."

"And who are you?" Johnny asked.

"Yes of course. Charles Rutherford, formerly Captain in the Royal Marines, at your service." The man gave an ironic salute.

"Or rather, formerly with the British Forces. Demobbed—all that. You can call me 'Chas.'

"I came here by way of Asia, and at present I reside at my plantation, inland several days. You've brought me on quite a chase. I served his Majesty most recently in Burma. For the last few months, I've been what the Aussies call a 'Coast Watcher.' I report on the nefarious activities of his crowd," he nodded at the Japanese. "We've been quite busy. You know the war is over?"

"We heard," Johnny said. "We dropped some new bomb on Japan and they surrendered. But that's all we know."

"Quite right," Chas said. "The atomic bomb. At this very moment, gentlemen, the greatest Allied armada of the Pacific War is sailing for Tokyo Harbor to accept the formal surrender of the Japs. The war is over and the new American Emperor is on his way to Japan," he said. "By that I mean your Douglas MacArthur," he winked at Johnny. "His High and Mighty Supremacy, long may he live."

"The war is over?" Katsu asked. "This is certain?"

The Brit looked at the prisoner. He did not realize until now that the man spoke the King's English.

"Yes." Chas spoke directly to him.

"Today is August 25th. About ten days ago, your Emperor Hirohito went on the wireless and told the nation Japan had surrendered. I heard the translation on the news. He said something to the effect that should Japan fight on, the new bomb would result in the extinction of civilization.

"There are tens of thousands of your countrymen still in New Guinea," he told the Japanese. "Mobs of them in the Wewak area. But now, no doubt, the unpleasantness will draw to a close. I imagine you'll be joining your fellows on the ships home.

"I've just returned from a walkabout with my *one-talks*, spying out enemy activity. It's clear some refuse to believe Japan has lost. I returned to my village only to hear your cry for help on my wireless. *Voilà*—here I am. Rutherford to the rescue."

"How about staying for dinner?" Johnny said. "As you can see, we're having Wrasse."

"Very kind—yes, let's talk." Chas holstered his pistol and Johnny gathered his tackle while the other men finished cleaning the fish. Cat sliced off the wide head and the men piled the guts on it and carried it between them into the waves. They heaved the mess out and there was a furious swirl.

"Don't mean to tell you your business," Chas called, "but I wouldn't do that."

"Not do what?" Footy asked.

"Throw offal in the ocean," Chas said.

"Why's that?"

"This is saltwater crocodile country, gentlemen." Chas said. "If you like large visitors, by all means, carry on."

"Bloody good point, mate," Footy said. He and Cat shared a look.

Johnny and Rutherford sat at the fire pit. The Brit nodded at the wrecked jeeps.

"Bit of a story?" he asked.

"Ahhh..." Johnny started. "A lack of road signs," he finished.

"Rather not talk about it?"

"Just as soon not," Johnny said.

"Well, well, I see."

"Hey," Johnny said, "do you have any thirty-aught-six ammo? I'm out."

"Sorry—Johnny, is it?" Chas said. "I've got my one revolver with me. I have a rifle in the village, but wrong caliber. What other firearms do you have?"

"None," Johnny said. "We lost the rest on the river."

"Seems odd. Again—rather not discuss it?"

"Right," Johnny said. "It's a long story."

"And your business," Chas nodded. "Never mind."

Cat and Footy arrived with heavy fillets draped over their arms. Cat went to work in the kitchen while Footy washed up and came and sat down. They recounted what they knew of the death of the Kissim priests and their adventures on the river.

Cat heated oil in the frying pan and slid in the Wrasse meat. He opened cans of potatoes and distributed these around the fish. He did his magic with his spices. The odors permeated the campsite and the men's stomachs rumbled.

Soon Cat was ready to serve and they passed around the plates. Cat had cooked the last of their fresh beans to go with the fish and potatoes. The men tucked in and nothing was said for some time. The Wrasse was drenched in its marinade. It came apart in flakes, so tender it made their eyes water. When every plate was scraped clean, the men laid on the compliments to the chef. He nodded and brewed coffee.

"You were here before the war?" Johnny asked their guest.

"Correct," Chas said. "I was born in New Guinea and grew up here. The plantation was my father's," he explained. "He was a British subject. This place…" he indicated the coconut palms around them, "…belonged to friends of my father's, although I never met them. I was at school in England.

"When the war came, dear old Dad abandoned the place. 'Not worth dying for,' he wrote in a letter I received in England. He left my mother in the village—she's indigenous, you see. Now she lives with me. The family that had this place thought they'd stay on. Thought they'd be safe. They were killed. There was a lot of fighting in these parts at one time, and up the Raub and Sepik Rivers, of course.

"I myself wouldn't have this place for all the tea in China. Too many of the big crocs, you see."

"If you don't mind me asking, why'd you come back?" Johnny asked. "The men I fought with, not one wanted to see New Guinea again."

"In England I got along, but just barely," Chas said, leaning back on an arm. "I was what my schoolmates kindly called 'a mongrel bastard from the end of the Earth.'

"Here, however, I'm a 'Big Man,' an important rank in New Guinea. I'm the son and heir of Master Rutherford. My father, by the way, never made it back to the old country. His ship was sunk by the blasted Krauts. So I own the plantation.

"I have three wives and seven children there, with another two on the way—wives that is."

"Bloody hell!" Footy exclaimed. "You've gone native, mate."

"Well Footy," Chas said mildly as he pulled off his hat to reveal tight black curls, "I am native, you see. Foot in both worlds. But not to concern yourself. I live like a king. I've got a house with electric lights and a diesel generator. I've got a kerosene refrigerator. I have a thousand acres and will soon have copra and coffee going again, and I'm planning to expand into peanuts. I believe there's a world market." Footy offered the cigarettes and the Brit accepted.

"I believe I'll try tobacco as well," he said.

"When the war came along, I joined the Royal Marines. I saw action in Asia—Burma in the last year. Got a few stories to tell."

"All right," Johnny said. "Let's hear one."

"Yes mate," Footy chimed in. "It's not like we don't have the time."

"Hmmm. Well, one might interest you—involves crocodiles."

"In Burma?" Footy asked.

"Right," the Brit said. "Place was ours before the war. Japs grabbed it. Short story—we took it back.

"Any rate, I was with the engineers. In association with our British India troops, my last assignment was to help clear a God-forsaken island by the name of 'Ramree.'"

"Never heard of it," Footy said.

"Not a surprise. Middle of nowhere, all bog and pestilence. There were perhaps a thousand of your countrymen there," he nodded at Cat. "We had 'em surrounded. As we saw it, they had two options. Death by our guns, or surrender."

Cat sipped his coffee and listened.

"The Nips were in a pickle. Through our Burmese translators, we gave them the opportunity to surrender. Yelled into the marsh—'throw down your arms and come out.' But the Japs made a third choice, one we had not anticipated. Retreat through a ten-mile swath of swamp.

"What we didn't know was that hellish place was home to an entire colony of saltwater crocs. By our reckoning, a thousand Japs went into the water. Then, like now, the night came on."

The sky over the camp had gone dark and stars winked along the ocean. A wave crashed and sighed up the beach.

"In the dark we could hear the Japs pushing through the water." Chas paused to light a cigarette and the match showed his face.

"Then a gun fired and we heard the first scream." There was silence and he continued.

"Occasionally I heard a crocodile move—the sound of a heavy body rushing through the mangroves, and the splash as it entered the water.

"Most particularly, we heard it when one of the brutes discovered a soldier. On my soul—the scream!" Again he paused.

"In extremis, men sound the same, whatever language they speak, whatever tribe they're from." Footy lit the fire and the yellow light flickered over the men.

"In the morning, we had no trouble rounding up the last of the Japs," Rutherford continued. "There were only twenty of them.

Twenty, out of a thousand! Of course, I have no idea how many made it through the swamp. Could have been most of them, could have been none. All I can tell you, we watched the crocs feed on corpses until we left the place. That was February of this year."

Johnny then told Chas about the carnage they'd seen just one crocodile inflict in the Valley of the Cannibals. Rutherford listened with keen interest.

"You men came through the Valley of the Cannibals? And you and this big *pookpook* killed the *Mambu-ato* himself! By Jove!"

"Do you think a croc will track a man over a considerable distance?" Footy asked.

"Certainly," Rutherford nodded. "I've become a reluctant expert on crocs of all kinds, particularly the saltys. My people have a saying. Goes like this: 'by the time a *pookpook* chooses you, you are already dead.'

"Your croc waits for his victim. It watches him—or her. It sets its ambush, and when the time is right—it strikes." He clapped his hands and Johnny jumped.

"The mouth of the Raub is notorious for saltys. I must tell you, there's an especially enormous one in these parts. It's the dominant bull of the entire region. And you, gentlemen..." he spread his arms, "...have set up camp in the heart of his territory."

"Is this the Father—the one with the moon scar on its head?" Johnny asked.

"Ahh, you've heard of him," Chas said. "Quite right. Notorious on the Raub. My people tell me it disappeared during the war, but now it's back."

"That's the bugga that killed Bumay in the Valley of the Cannibals!" Footy said.

"Indeed!" Rutherford said. "Your story grows ever stranger. But you should know, the Father's been seen in these parts, very recently."

"Go on," Johnny said.

"On my way here, I came through a village that was mourning a fisherman. He'd been in his canoe when the *pookpook* swamped it and killed him. Strange thing—the Papa didn't eat him. Left him floating."

"Did the natives notice anything unusual about it?" Johnny asked.

"Apart from its extraordinary size and the scar on its head?"

"No, not the scar. Its right foreleg," Johnny said. "I shot the foot off."

"No one mentioned that," Chas said, "but then, the croc was in the water."

"I believe the Father has been stalking Johnny," Footy said, "ever since he shot it at Kissim."

"Is that right?" Chas asked.

"It's possible," Johnny admitted. "But we haven't seen it lately."

"Well, I'm here to tell you, the Father has returned. I advise you to leave," Chas said.

"Suits me," Johnny said. "And that's where you come in. We need a rescue."

"Right you are," the Brit said. "Soon as I get home, I'll get the word in. I have a powerful radio, powered by my generator.

"Now I'd like to sleep, if it's alright by you. I've been on the trail here for days, and I will leave at first light. Perhaps you men should consider coming with me? Leave the Father's territory?" The others thought about it.

"In my opinion, thanks, but no thanks," Johnny said. "Now that we're finally off the river, I'd like to keep it that way. And I don't think Footy can handle a hike."

"Not on mate," the Aussie agreed. "And from a pilot's point of view it makes sense to stay here. Easier to find at the mouth of the Raub."

"There's merit in that," Rutherford acknowledged. "As you wish."

The men gave him a blanket and Chas lay down with his back to the fire and promptly fell asleep. Footy stretched out, propped his injured foot on a log and drifted off as well.

Johnny and Cat sat up a few minutes longer. The moon rose, almost full, and its cold light made the ocean ghostly. The men stared at the glittering darkness and thought about the great crocodile. Still, they'd seen no sign of it.

They hoped it would stay that way.

Chapter 7

Johnny woke to the sound of voices. He peered through the hammock netting in the early light and saw Chas Rutherford with a group of natives. There were five armed men, three women and some mixed-race children. Chas had his arms around a boy and a girl and another little one clung to his leg. Johnny got up and went to the kitchen where Cat poured him coffee. Footy lay near the fire pit, sipping from a mug.

"Looks like our Pommy friend has the wives and *pikininis* here," the Aussie said. Chas and his entourage came closer. The native men had white beads woven in their hair, cowrie shell necklaces, a pair of bound croc teeth through their noses and their bows and spears.

The Brit made the introductions. These were some of his wives and progeny, and the warriors were his clan *one-talks*. The group of them had camped inland, Chas explained, while he came alone to reconnoiter the situation. He had expected to rejoin his people up the trail, but, well, they came to find him.

Cat filled every available container, including some empty cans, with sweet coffee and the people passed these around. Johnny took the men into the jungle to cut bunches of bananas for their journey. They brought back leaves as well and Cat cooked and wrapped more Wrasse. The warriors accepted the food, but stared at the Japanese with dislike. Cat observed that and stayed in the kitchen.

Rutherford announced they would leave. He reaffirmed he would radio for a rescue aircraft as soon as he got home. If he was lucky and the weather was right, he'd talk directly to Port Moresby. Otherwise, he'd relay the message through Wewak, Madang, Mount Hagen or Goroka.

"However it must go, I'll get the message through. Although, of course, I can't say how long the authorities will take to find you.

"By the way. Any issue with me salvaging your jeeps at some point? I may be able to make one good one from the two."

"Help yourself," Johnny told him. "Though I guess they're not ours to give away."

"I'd like a word, mate," Footy said. "I'm setting up an air cargo business. I lost my aircraft at Kissim—pranged beyond all hope, unfortunately, but I'll buy another. Your plantation will need my services, am I right?"

"Right you are," Rutherford agreed. "When you're ready, Footy, reach me by wireless. We might make a few pounds together."

At last the farewells and handshaking were done. As always in New Guinea, that took time. Rutherford noticed Cat hanging back in the kitchen, went to him and offered his hand. They shook.

"The war is over," Chas said. "Difficult as it is, we must let bygones be bygones. Cat, I wish you luck on your return to Japan."

"Thank you," Katsu said, and bowed.

"By the way, I visited Japan with my father. What city are you from?"

"Beautiful port city," the Japanese smiled. "Do you know Nagasaki?"

"Nagasaki?" Chas repeated, with sudden strain in his voice.

"Yes—Nagasaki," Cat said. "You probably have not heard of it. It is not well known."

Johnny and Footy had wandered over and were listening.

"Oh, I've heard of it," Rutherford said. "The whole world has heard of it. Do you know Nagasaki was bombed?"

"Bombed?" Cat repeated. "I imagine many Japanese cities suffered bombs." Rutherford's silence made Katsu unbearably anxious. There was something very wrong with the way the Englishman was staring at him.

"You've not heard," Chas said at last.

"Spit it out, would you?" Johnny told him. Rutherford nodded.

"Yes, right. As you say, many Japanese cities were bombed, including Tokyo. But that was with conventional ordnance. Cat, I am very sorry to be the one to tell you this, but there were *two* atom bombs dropped on Japan."

"We heard about one," Footy said. "On—what was the place?"

"Hiroshima!" Cat said, not taking his eyes off Chas.

"Yes. That was on August 7th.

"Then—on August 10th, the Americans dropped another atom bomb. On Nagasaki."

"Nagasaki!" Cat exclaimed, thunderstruck. "This is true?" He looked at Rutherford's face and read the reality.

"This atom bomb, what does it do?" he asked urgently.

"Afraid I can't tell you precisely," Chas said. "But the news reports say those cities are destroyed. The people—well, most of the people are gone. Simply—atomized."

"My family," Cat said in horror, "my wife, my children, my parents..."

"I'm dreadfully sorry old chap," Chas said. Cat's face showed such naked anguish the others looked away.

"Thought you knew," Chas said lamely. "Thought you'd heard."

"We heard about the one—not the other," Footy repeated. On the beach, one of the children called for his father.

"Look Chas, there's nothing you can do about it." Johnny took Rutherford's arm and guided him toward his group. Chas nodded, shot Cat a final look and rejoined his party. With a last wave, they disappeared into the trees behind the camp. The Japanese sat with a hand over his eyes.

"Listen," Johnny said to him. "You can't know what happened there. With the war over, you'll be sent home with the other P O Ws. Then you can find out for yourself. Maybe your family is ok."

"Johnny's right," Footy said. Cat looked up at the men with shock and grief on his face.

"Please," he said, "leave me alone." He lurched up and stumbled down the beach, head bowed. The others let him go.

Things had been bad for the prisoner, but now they were infinitely worse.

Cat was gone for many hours. Footy went fishing but Johnny did not. He watched Footy limp far down the shore, then sharpened his knives and straightened up camp.

Eventually Cat returned, looking as downtrodden as a man could get. He did not look at Johnny and slumped at the fire pit.

Johnny eyed the man and knew what kind of anguish he was feeling. He recalled that terrible morning when he was sixteen. In some ways it seemed a lifetime ago, but in others, it was as fresh as yesterday.

That horrific memory was buried within him all this time, agony he could not fix, so he had shoved it aside and hoped it would go away. While that had allowed him to cope, it had not dealt with the problem.

What Gwyn had asked him to do had bothered him all the way down the river. Add that to the news the war was over, and the core of anguish was coming closer to the surface. It was an emotional wound that was worse in many ways than the physical ones he had endured. They had been treated, and had healed. But this had simply grown a tough layer over it, while beneath, it remained a festering sore.

Johnny sat beside Cat and saw the depths of his suffering, and his heart went out to him. He lit two cigarettes and nudged the man. The prisoner took one without looking up. Then Johnny started to talk, and once he got going he could not stop.

"Maybe you've heard me say I lived in Hawaii," he began. The Japanese gave no sign, and Johnny went on.

"My family moved there when I was a teenager. I grew up in San Diego, a Navy town on the border with Mexico. My Grandfather was a Rear Admiral who retired before the war. He died last year. My father was a Lieutenant Commander of a battleship. In early 1941, Dad was assigned to a new ship. It had just been refitted in Washington State, and was sent to join the fleet stationed in the Hawaiian Territory.

We moved—my parents and I—to the island of Oahu. I didn't like it. All my friends were in the States. But I'd tried surfing in California, and Hawaii was 'surfer-central.' You know what surfing is?" Cat gave a perfunctory nod and Johnny went on.

"There were lots of surfers around Honolulu and Diamond Head. They called them 'beachboys,' and the beachboys got the prettiest girls. That seemed good to me. I talked my folks into buying me a second hand board. It was wood, twelve feet long. Every chance I got, I was on the waves. I made new friends. I got good at it, finally good enough even to ride the enormous breakers at Sunset Beach and Waimea Bay on the north shore. I started to like Hawaii."

Johnny might as well have been talking to himself. The Japanese was focused inward.

"December rolled around. Christmas was coming up and my parents promised me a new board if my grades were good.

"Dad's ship had been out at sea for exercises. On Saturday, it came back and he got shore leave for the night, but had to return aboard first thing next morning.

"That night, my parents had a barbecue at a friend's house, but came home early because Dad had to be up at 0-6-hundred hours. The plan was, Mom would drive Dad to the harbor at 7:00. At 10:30, she wanted me to go to church with her.

"Usually I went with my mother to see Dad board. I liked to look at the ships, and I knew all their names. But this time, I had other plans. I wanted to go surfing. Having to come back for church was a pain, but I figured I'd be able to get in two or three hours before I had to return.

"I was up at 6:00. I was sixteen, and my parents had started to let me drive the old car. We called it the "Woody"—it was a Packard, like all my dad's cars.

"I was rushing out and Mom was cooking bacon and eggs. She said wait, I should eat with them." Johnny's voice slowed and now Cat was watching him.

"I remember. She was wearing a blue dress with yellow sunflowers on it. I didn't see my dad, but I heard him moving in the bedroom. He'd be getting his uniform on.

"I told Mom, no, a friend was waiting. But she forced me to sit while she made a peanut butter sandwich. I grabbed it and ran." Johnny paused. Katsu was listening now.

"I didn't say goodbye to Dad. What did I know? It was just another Sunday morning.

"I was surfing at Diamond Head when I heard aircraft coming. And then the sky was full of them. I couldn't understand it. Dad said the carriers were out of port, so what were all these planes? I figured it must be a flight from the States. Even when I saw the red circles, I didn't get it.

"Then a fighter dove and went right overhead. At home, we had a book of military aircraft silhouettes. It was a Mitsubishi 'Zeke,' also called 'Zero.'

"I actually saw the pilot and he was a Jap. He waved.

"Then I knew where they were going. But still, it was like a bad dream. It couldn't be real—even when I saw the black smoke over the hills. It all happened so fast and then I was moving.

"I paddled for shore and I remember, there was a radio playing, some happy tune. I just left my board on the beach and ran to the Woody.

"Diamond Head to Pearl Harbor is twelve miles. Normally I'd do it in half an hour. I think I made it in fifteen minutes. There were only a few other cars on the roads, all racing somewhere.

"I could see the planes, bombers and fighters, lots of them. They dove on the harbor, and I saw the sun on the wings as they came up. And then I could hear the screaming engines. They were all yours, and none of ours.

"I drove right to the harbor. The guard gate was empty. No one stopped me."

Now Cat was staring at Johnny.

"It was crazy, sailors running everywhere. The planes disappeared and the whole harbor was on fire. All the ships were burning. I saw one with its hull in the air." Johnny stared into the cold fire, lost in that other time.

"I saw dead men. The first ones I saw. Americans. I ran to the water and stared out where my dad's ship should be, but I couldn't see it. It was all smoke and flames and men shouting. The harbor had changed. I couldn't recognize anything.

"I saw a sailor shooting his rifle in the air, at nothing I could see. I asked him, 'where's the 'Arizona?' The USS Arizona was my dad's ship. He pointed and I saw burning water and twisted metal towers. That couldn't be my father's battleship! But it was.

"I saw men burning out there. There were bodies floating and sailors covered in oil crawling out, some with their skin coming off. The screams! I remember the screams. I looked everywhere for my father and never found him." Cat lit two cigarettes and passed one to Johnny.

"I ran to the parking area and saw Dad's car," Johnny said. "His blue '37 Packard Touring Sedan—his 'pride and joy.' He bought it brand new and had it shipped to Hawaii. Then I knew my mom still had to be there. I ran to the lookout where she watched him board." Johnny's voice cracked and he took a deep drag.

"I should have been there! But I wanted to surf. I saw a crashed fighter. I saw the 'meatball,' on it, your red sun. I saw my first dead Jap—the pilot, hanging out of the cockpit.

"Then I saw blue cloth, under the wing. I went closer. It had sunflowers on it, and it was soaked in blood."

Johnny stopped because his throat had seized. He dropped the butt onto the sand and angrily wiped his eyes with the back of his hand. At last he turned a raw stare on the Japanese.

"My parents died just after 8:00 o'clock, December the 7th,

1941. You people murdered more than two thousand, three hundred Americans that morning, my mother and father with them. We weren't at war with you! You attacked in peacetime!"

Cat cleared his throat. Johnny locked gazes until the other man looked at the sand.

"And then there was the second attack by your aircraft," Johnny went on. "I could shoot a rifle, better that most of those sailors. Someone gave one to me and I took my first shots of the war. Men were yelling that the Japs were about to invade Hawaii.

"Much later, I ended up at home. I sat in an empty house with a loaded rifle for two days, until the Navy sent someone by.

"They shipped me to my grandparents in San Diego. That was a bad Christmas—the worst. By New Year's, I'd made a resolution.

"I was going to kill Japs. I made a promise to my parents. I was going to kill as many as I could to pay for their murders, and I would fight until Japan was finished, or I was.

"My Granddad approved of my desire to fight, but said the battle in the Pacific would be a Navy show. He knew Admiral Nimitz. It might take years, but first I'd finish school, take officer's training and get on a ship. As if I'd go back to school!

"I wouldn't wait. And I wouldn't sit out at sea and lob shells at an unseen enemy. I wanted to look at the men I killed. I left a letter and ran away. I joined the Army. I was seventeen.

"I've been killing Japs ever since."

Johnny stopped talking. The minutes dragged by and at last Cat nodded.

"I see why you hate us," he said. "I understand. I would feel the same."

"I've never told that to anyone," Johnny said. "Keep it between us."

"Yes," Cat said. "I agree.

"Did you ever wonder where I learned to speak English?"

"Well, I figured you studied it at school," Johnny replied.

"I learned it at my church."

"Your church?" Johnny asked. He assumed the man must mean some kind of temple.

"My church," the Japanese emphasized. "I learned from a priest. I am Christian."

"You? Christian?" Johnny was flabbergasted.

"Yes, me," the Japanese nodded. "How long has there been an

America?"

"Well, I remember from school. The Declaration of Independence was written in 1776."

"Oh—less than a hundred and seventy years?"

"I guess," Johnny said.

"My family has been samurai for five centuries," Cat said. "And we have been Christian for four hundred years. Yes, Christian," he repeated, seeing the incredulity on Johnny's face.

"The Europeans came to Nippon long ago. Many important families in my area became Christian. But the Shogun—the leader, like your President—outlawed Christianity. In my city, he crucified twenty-six Christians.

"To survive we became *'kakure Kirishitan'*—the hidden ones. But finally the ban on our religion was lifted, before I was born. In my neighborhood of Nagasaki, called 'Urakami,' there is—if it is still there—the biggest, most beautiful cathedral in all Asia.

"But if your atom bomb has demolished Nagasaki, America has destroyed the center of Christianity in Japan! You have killed who knows how many hundreds of thousands of my countrymen, and also, tens of thousands of Christians. You have slaughtered all the people I knew—my family, my wife, my children!"

Tears welled in Cat's eyes and he looked away. It was Johnny's turn to find nothing to say. Cat blinked his eyes rapidly and choked back a sob.

"I am very sorry about your parents. Of course, I was not at Pearl Harbor. But my family—my father and I, and our friends—we supported the war. As a Japanese, I accept responsibility.

"But now, Nippon has paid the price. I, myself, have paid the price." Johnny saw Footy returning along the beach.

"If peace has come—you and me, what do we do?" Johnny asked. "I've hated you so long I don't think I can quit."

"I do not know," Cat said. "This is a difficult thing. Here there are tribes that kill each other generation after generation. Maybe we will do the same. My problem is, I no longer know how to live."

"I know this," Johnny said slowly. "I have killed and killed, and my parents are still dead. Revenge felt good, but it didn't fix my loss."

Katsu nodded. He, too, saw the Australian coming. He took his towel and went to the forest. When he returned, he cooked without speaking and handed around the plates.

CHAPTER 8

Johnny and Footy figured it would take a day for Rutherford to get home before he could send his radio message. And then? With all the monumental events the ending of the war must have put in play, would they get any attention?

The following morning they took stock of their supplies. They were doing well at augmenting the canned food with what they could catch and pick. As for coffee and cigarettes, they had enough for two more weeks, if they restricted themselves to two cups and three cigarettes per man a day. Footy grumbled half-heartedly about including the prisoner in their rations, especially with the tobacco, but Johnny insisted.

"We're all in this together now," he said. "Everyone gets a share."

Fishing was a daily necessity, and a subdued Cat joined the others in the morning's effort. They went barefoot into the surf, casting over the drop-off. Within hours, they had enough. They napped through the midday heat. Later, when a cooler breeze drifted off the ocean, Johnny walked for miles along the beach. Footy limped into the forest in search of more bananas.

Alone, Cat cleaned the fish. After what the 'Engli' had said about crocodiles, he scraped a hole in the sand back in the trees and buried the guts. He poured himself the dregs of the coffee. He would have preferred green tea, but that was a far off memory. He smoked the second of his day's cigarettes and stared at the ocean.

His attention was drawn to a flock of screaming seabirds over agitated water. The gulls dove repeatedly and rose with fish flipping in their beaks. There was a ball, he realized, just under the surface. They leaped like handfuls of tossed coins and the group surged in another direction. *They try to escape the fish below*.

Then he saw the big torpedoes come. He counted six sharks, distorted through the water. They rushed at breakneck speed into the bait ball. The activity grew even more frenzied. Now it was not only the smallfry that got airborne, but big ones with yellow fins arced up as well. The gulls shrieked and fanned away as shark heads lunged up. The activity boiled one way and then the other.

Then suddenly it was over. The baitfish melted away and the seabirds rose complaining. The sharks vanished and the sea was placid once more.

It is a paradise, he thought. *But it is a paradise that becomes a bloodbath in an instant. Death lurks just beneath the skin of beauty, and this is also the truth of creation.*

The whole world is at war! Cat thought. *It is not just men. Always, something kills and eats something else. The difference with men is that we do not do it for hunger, unless you include the cannibals. But like them, we "civilized people" also do it from tribal hatred. We do it for pride. We kill for an idea. And we are so clever, we slaughter even women and children with machines, from far off.*

This is what makes us civilized, he thought bitterly. *We have become so advanced, our machines can rain death on ordinary people from the sky. My nation is not innocent. We were the first to mass bomb civilian cities. But now, with their atom bomb, the Americans can destroy the world. And so, have they become gods? No!* The answer shot back. *Only God makes life. Humans can only take it. This is the absence of God. This is evil.*

He gazed at the scene. *The world is so beautiful!* His eyes drank in the tawny beach and the growing jungle, the rise and fall of the ocean's breast under the dome of heaven.

In his mind's eye he saw his parents, his wife Koto, Ryo, his son, Yuriko, his daughter, and Yuji, his older brother and his family. He pictured them, and his relations and all his friends in Nagasaki. He saw Father Valenti, the priest who had been so patient while he wrestled with the impossible foreign tongue called 'English.'

Each of the cherished faces came like a living photograph, but as it drew close, it erupted in fire. Katsu closed his eyes and wished he would sleep and never awake.

If I were truly a man, I would commit seppuku, the honorable suicide of the warrior, by slicing my belly. But, equally, I am a Christian, and I am forbidden to kill myself. My samurai spirit is at war with my Christian soul and my war will never end! At last he drifted into a ragged and unsatisfying sleep.

Footy returned laden with bunches of bananas to find Johnny cooking at the stove.

"Where's the Jap, then?" he asked.

"Shhh!" Johnny pointed to the prisoner, sleeping on his side with his hands between his knees.

"What's the story?" Footy whispered.

"Think about it," Johnny said, turning the fillets. "He just found out his wife and kids and whole family are probably dead—most likely dead. What would you do?"

"Fair dinkum," Footy said. "I actually feel sorry for the blighter."

"Open that, will you?" Johnny asked. Footy picked up the baked beans and worked the opener. Johnny dumped the contents in a pot on the heat. He poured three mugs of coffee and dished the food, with a plate for Cat left cooling on the stove. He and Footy moved further off and sat on rocks near the ocean.

"What are you going to do when we get away from here?" Johnny asked between bites.

"The air cargo business, like I told the Pommy," Footy said. "And you?"

"I don't have a clue," Johnny said. "I was seventeen when I joined up. I only know how to do two things."

"Wanking, there's one," Footy said, "and the other?"

"Speak for yourself," Johnny said. "One, *surfing*, and, two..." he raised his hands like a gun. "Pow! Don't think that'll go over big in the States, unless I start knocking over banks."

"There's a thought, mate," Footy said. "That's what you Yanks do, isn't it? Shoot one another. At least that's what I see in your movies. Wonder there's so many of you, really.

"On the other hand," Footy continued, "maybe there'll be another war—with the Russians. If the Germans couldn't beat the buggers, maybe you Yanks can. There's work for you."

"Maybe," Johnny said, "but with this bomb, it'll be over fast."

"Ahh," Footy said. "Yes, of course. Boom—there goes bloody Moscow. Bye-bye Joe Stalin. Well, first things first. When we get back, I'll have an ice-cold beer, or a truckload. I've got a bird to see in Moresby…" he winked at Johnny. "Then I'll hop a plane to Cairns. Me parents are gone and I need to take care of things. I've got to find another aircraft. I expect there'll be heaps around, with the war over."

"We'll turn Cat over to the authorities," Johnny said. "They'll be shipping the P O Ws home. And I've got a girl to see myself. I can't wait to leave the croc behind—and the mud..."

"...and the bloody jungle..." Footy said.

"...and the mosquitoes..." Johnny went on.

"...and the cannibals." Footy added.

"Right," Johnny said. "And the mud. Did I say the mud? I'd like a platter of barbecued ribs and..."

"Awww, put a bung in it, mate," Footy protested. "Red meat! Cor! I may drown in me own spit."

The men returned to camp. Johnny went to Cat, shook his shoulder and put the meal beside him.

"You need to eat," Johnny said. The Japanese forked the food in, then rolled in his blanket and slept again. Johnny and Footy washed the dishes, smoked their last cigarette of the day and bedded down.

☆

They were in the habit of rising with the dawn. Again, Cat had food ready. He handed the men their plates, took his own and sat morosely by himself.

The three fished and caught enough for dinner before the barracuda raided their lines. After a lunch of pan-sized perch, Johnny spoke up.

"I need a project," he said. "I'm going stir-crazy. I'd like you both to help with something, but no questions 'til I'm done."

"What is it?" Footy asked at once.

"You'll see," Johnny said. "Come to the old house, ok?"

He led the way through the plantation. Footy's leg had kept him from exploring when they first got there, and he was intrigued. The trail was thick with ferns and littered with deadfalls. Eventually they emerged in the ruin's backyard.

The men entered and Johnny went to the bed that had once been a desk. The marred wooden top was a rectangle of thick planks, eight feet long and four feet across, attached to the splintered drawers.

"Help me carry this to camp," Johnny said. He faced away and hoisted an end. Footy and Cat each took a corner. They pried it out of the earth, got it outside, and began to walk.

It was heavy and the men were sweating. Footy grumbled it was too much work not to know what it was for, but Johnny just chuckled. The Japanese plodded doggedly with his head down. They stopped to rest several times, but at last they were back in camp. They set the thing upside down near the fire pit.

"I'll take it from here," Johnny said. The other two watched while, with a kitchen knife, he removed the screws holding on the drawers. He put the shattered wood aside and fetched his machete. He leaned the desktop against his knees, grasped the blade between his hands and drew the edge towards him, spilling off a curl. Beneath the ruined surface, the wood was sound. A pile of shavings formed at his feet.

Footy went to fish. Cat wandered aimlessly down the beach and Johnny saw him sit and stare at the ocean. *That's the direction where Japan lies*, Johnny thought. The sun beat on him. Johnny got his helmet and fashioned a brim from a broad leaf and poked it through the netting. It shaded his eyes, and he continued carving, finding a rhythm.

Maybe because of what he'd told Cat, today his mind flooded with memories of his father. During the war, he'd done everything he could to keep these from coming. They hurt too much, and the hard voice told him such mooning would get him killed. But this morning, it was as if a dam had burst. Johnny's hands moved, and the man who had loomed large over much of his life became as real as if he was beside him.

He and his dad had shared a love of stories. During the long weeks his father was at sea, he told his son he spent his free time reading in his bunk. He said he could disappear into the worlds he carried between cardboard covers. Every time he left, Dad took several tomes in his duffle. His favorites were the great seafaring yarns—"Moby Dick," "Robinson Crusoe," and anything by Conrad. He also had a good selection of Robert Louis Stevenson, Rudyard Kipling, Jack London, and Ernest Hemmingway.

When Johnny was young and his dad was in port, bedtime meant passages read aloud from whatever book the man was reading. When Johnny was about seven, his dad included him in the process. First, he'd read a chapter aloud and then Johnny had to stammer through a paragraph or two. His father told him this would set him up for school, give him the literal taste of fine prose, and prepare him for a life in public.

By the time Johnny was nine, his father was lending him books to read on his own. As always with his father, there were rules. Books except gifts were a loan. His father required that they be returned in the same condition in which they had been lent. Folding over a corner to mark a page, for example, was forbidden.

When Johnny was done, he was expected to be able to discuss the story in an intelligent manner. But it was never like the book reports he had to write for school—mostly about getting the characters names spelled right and outlining plot and theme.

With Dad it was different. They chewed over the story, and discussed whether the author was worth his salt. Did he know the world he talked about, and did his yarn hang together? His dad was fascinated by what motivated characters, both human and animal, and whether their behavior was consistent with the personality the author had bestowed on them.

His father always carried a Bible, a collected works of Shakespeare, and some Dickens. His father said the Bible was packed with conniving and nefarious characters, and fantastic tales most sanctimonious preachers didn't have the parts to tell.

"'How about this?'" he once asked Johnny. "'Eglon, King of Moab was a very fat man. And Ehud put forth his left hand, and took the dagger from his right thigh, and thrust it into his belly. And the haft also went in after the blade, and the fat closed upon the blade, so he could not draw the dagger out of his belly. And the dirt came out.' How about that for graphic action?"

He told his son that most literature was written by authors steeped in scripture, and if you didn't know the source, you couldn't get the reference. Many of the best quotations were either the Bible or Shakespeare, he said, and one of his games was to quote something, and Johnny had to guess which it was.

"How sharper than a serpent's tooth it is to have a thankless child," he'd said. "Dad!" Johnny protested. "Proverbs?"

"Shakespeare. King Lear," Dad told him. Now as Johnny's blade carved the wood, he heard his father's voice:

"They sow the wind and reap the whirlwind." *Hosea,* Johnny's mind shot back. *Well, that Sunday in Hawaii, Japan sowed the wind. And with the atom bomb, the enemy Empire has reaped the whirlwind.*

Johnny recalled the slaughter of his parents and the old hatred welled up again. He found himself panting, and had to clench his teeth against it.

Justice has been done, he told himself. *Japan has been more than punished. The enemy nation has been clubbed to its knees and kicked onto its back.*

He realized that he had to find a way to let the hatred go, or it would eat him alive.

Maybe that's part of what Gwyn meant when she said to look for my heart. First, I have to get through the hatred.

Johnny's hands continued to draw the cutting edge. He had cleaned an entire section. He smelled the fresh wood and wondered what forest it had grown in.

Footy was coming back with his pole over his shoulder. He arrived in camp and hung his string of fish in the kitchen. Later Cat appeared, soaking wet, with an armload of shellfish.

"Where'd you get those?" Johnny asked.

"I dive," Cat shrugged.

"Not afraid of sharks?" Footy asked.

"No," Cat said shortly. He spilled the shells into a pot of water and fired up the stove.

"What kind are they?" Johnny asked.

"I do not know in English. *Hokkigai*," Cat said.

"What you said," Johnny replied.

By early-afternoon Johnny had shaved the entire top. He turned the wood over and started on the other side. It was not as damaged and the work went faster. By late afternoon he had it smooth. He turned the rectangle on an edge and began to round off a corner. Finally as the western sky lit up again he stood and stretched.

"Let's go for a run."

"What mate?" Footy asked. Cat looked up.

"You know—a run," Johnny said, "something you do with your feet."

"Yes, and what about my ruddy foot?"

"What about it?" Johnny asked. "Come on, I'll take it easy on you. I played football in high school. A little workout is just what the doctor ordered."

"Football?" Footy said. "You're going to teach me, mate? Why do you think they call me 'Footy'? I'm a runner. But now..." he shrugged.

"Come on, have a little backbone," Johnny said. "You too Cat."

"Do what?" the Japanese asked. "Does it involve a collision?'"

"No! I'm talking about a run—on the beach," Johnny said. "Sheesh. Do I have to spell it out?"

He headed off and the others followed.

CHAPTER 9

In bare feet, wearing only their shorts, the men walked down the beach to the wet sand. Johnny broke into a jog and Footy and Cat followed. After a dozen steps he turned and ran on the spot.

"Move it!" he shouted. Cat went by, arms pumping. The Aussie came gamely enough, favoring his bum leg.

"Come on Hopalong!" Johnny said and ran off.

"I'd show you bloody 'Hopalong,' if not for this bloody leg," Footy fumed. When Johnny and Cat got too far ahead, Johnny led them back and they literally ran circles around the Aussie. Then off they'd sprint again, while Footy lurched grimly along. The men covered two hundred yards before Johnny turned.

"Ok!" he called, "The other way!" He and the prisoner passed Footy forty yards back and he went with them. Johnny got a burst of high spirits. He went into the surf and ran with knees up.

"Like this!" he called. Cat came behind him, getting soaked.

"Way to go Cat!" Johnny said. "Footy, get with the program!" But the Aussie had stopped and was leaning with his hands on his knees, face scarlet.

"Bloody foot, mate," he puffed. "Not on me game." He lay down in the shallows on his back. Johnny and Cat continued to run around him. Finally the American pointed down the beach at the enormous tree on the point.

"There!" Johnny said. "The 'Finish Tree.' Get up Footy—fast as you can, no excuses!" The Aussie groaned and pushed himself to his feet. The other men were off, running full tilt in their different styles. Johnny bounded along, the dark hair that was getting long, blowing back. The shorter Japanese pumped behind him, his center of gravity low, legs churning. Footy took off after them.

The men sprinted the last hundred yards and Johnny came to the Finish Tree first. He flung an arm around the trunk, spun and fell onto the carpet of leaves. A second back, Cat slammed his hands against the bark and fell panting as well.

It was a few minutes before Footy limped up, slapped the tree, and pitched out full length. The men lay, talking idly for half an hour, then sauntered back to camp. Cat made steamed clams and fish, poached in coconut milk.

Johnny and Footy awoke to Japanese shouts. They scrambled up and looked where he pointed into the plantation. In the early light, they saw a column of invaders. Gigantic crabs followed each other across the forest floor. The crustaceans' backs were up to three feet long, and they stood at least a foot tall. They looked like lobster musclemen. The men watched the leader hoist a coconut in its massive claw and squeeze. The coconut cracked like a Christmas nut and the crab picked up white shreds and began to feed. The others spread out to do the same.

Cat grabbed up a stick and ran at the big one. As he came close, it dropped its meal, stood on its hind legs and raised its claws for battle. Then it actually rushed the man! For only the second time since they'd met him, they heard the prisoner laugh.

"Kani!" he shouted delightedly. He swung his cudgel between the claws. The carapace cracked and the crab fell on its back. Cat grabbed it from behind and held it up, massive claws swinging.

"Good eatin' there!" Footy observed, searching for a cudgel of his own. Soon he and Johnny were crab-bashing as well. Their opponents might be smaller, but they were feisty and well armed. Pincers that could split a coconut could take off a finger, even a hand.

Johnny had never had crab claws and legs for breakfast, but they were superb. They gorged themselves on the tender boiled meat, dredged in coconut oil, salt and lemon grass.

When they could not eat another bite, Footy and Cat went fishing. Johnny nursed a coffee and returned to his project. Soon he was in shavings to the knees. He got one corner carved in an arc. He turned the board over and began on the opposite side.

By mid afternoon, his hands sore and cramped, he took a break. He saw Footy fishing a long way off. Cat, however, was nearer, and he was drawing with a stick on the sand. Curious, Johnny went down to him. Cat was on the wet sand above the waves, scratching Japanese characters.

"What's that?" Johnny asked.

"Nothing. A poem."

"You're a poet?" Johnny asked.

"No," the man said. "Yes—sometimes."

"What's it say?" Johnny asked.

"You will not understand." The prisoner looked at him.

"Try me," Johnny said. Cat shrugged.

"Meigetu ya," he said,
"kuni moetukite,
kagayakinu."

Johnny stared at him.

"In English?"

"I will try," Cat said. "Forgive my poor translation." He thought it through, nodded and spoke:

"Since my country burned down,
how clearly
I see the moon."

He looked at the Yankee. "You understand?"

"Hmmm," Johnny said. "It's got something, I'll give you that. It's mournful. I'll think on it."

"As I said," Cat shrugged, "it is Japanese—what we call 'haiku.'" Johnny nodded and went back to his project. Footy returned near sunset and looked at what Johnny had carved.

"It's a boat. Give it up, mate. Too small. You'll never get to Bora Bora that way." Johnny pinched tired eyes and set the wood aside.

"You're a card. Ready to run?"

Cat nodded. Footy griped but went along. This time, although the Aussie still reached the Finish Tree after the others, his time had improved.

That night, Cat's entree was savory seafood soup, featuring crab claws and chunks of Grouper, with canned corn, tomatoes and coconut milk. The result, Johnny thought, was better than any thing he'd tasted in a restaurant. For dessert they had fresh bananas and fruit cocktail. Afterwards, the men relaxed around their fire under the stars, and smoked.

It seemed to the men that the beach was deserted and they were alone, but in fact, a thousand creatures of the forest and ocean watched their every move. And on this particular night, as on several before it, they had a very large observer.

Just after nightfall, it emerged from the river and drifted out into the saltwater. It rounded the point and now floated fifty yards off the beach, the waves sliding over its back.

This witness had sharp senses. It was no longer impaired by confusion brought about by infection. The giant hung just beneath the surface and watched its enemy in the fire glow.

The Father had not eaten for weeks and it was cranky with hunger, but only for this, the one-prey. It watched him and thought where to attack. It had developed an aversion to a charge over open land. The last time it did this, it killed the animal, but had been badly wounded as well.

It reverted to the age-old instinct to lay in ambush. Now, under cover of darkness, it floated in the ocean and fixated on the men. The crocodile knew it could not hide here by day, because the prey would see it in the clear water. Eventually, it swam back into its river. Now, in the new light, it crawled through the jungle. It crept until it was behind a thin veil of leaves, and watched the men again.

It was troubled. It was not sure of its attack because sometimes it saw the smooth-headed man with two others, but other times, there were three of the furry-headed ones.

The Father continued to watch and learn.

It observed that each day when the light grew dimmer, the animals loped along the beach and then basked in the jungle. It watched this behavior for two days, and on the third, once the animals had departed, the crocodile stole to where they had lain.

The huge head slid from the undergrowth and hovered over the place. It sniffed the unique spoor of each man. One of the spots inflamed its senses. Here it drew in the very body signature of the smooth-headed man.

The predator eased through the trees. It stopped when its snout touched the sand. It saw three figures in the flickering light. Eventually, it slunk to the river.

In the morning, the hunter crawled out to watch again.

— ☾ —

As the sun came over the sea, the men rose and searched for the coconut crabs. There were not as many as yesterday, but enough for a decent crab-whacking. After another breakfast of claws, Footy and Cat went fishing. They were not natural companions and unless Johnny was with them, they kept their distance.

The Aussie had been wandering further away each day, while Cat liked the nearby wall.

Johnny put on his sunshaded helmet and continued with his project. He had each of the long sides of the tabletop curved. One end came to a point while the other was blunt. Johnny would work on one side for an hour, then turn the wood over and match the other to it. He began to round the edges.

For lunch he ate cold crab and bananas, and carried a plate to Cat. The man had a pile of fish wrapped in banana leaves. Cat wound in his line and consumed the food.

"Where do you get the clams?" Johnny asked.

"You want to see?"

"Yes," Johnny told him. Cat led along the beach to a place where the coral bed came close to shore. The top was so near the surface, it damped the wave action.

"We have to swim," the Japanese told him.

"Let's cool off," Johnny said. Cat went into the waves and Johnny followed. They swam thirty yards beside the coral shelf, the sandy bottom ten or twelve feet below. Cat upended and breast stroked down. Johnny breathed deep and went after him.

Footy was a further fifty yards along the beach. He'd discovered a hole the barracuda didn't seem to frequent. He saw his companions splash into the ocean, swim out and disappear. He shaded his eyes and stared after them.

Are they daft, that far out with the Father and his mates about? In the euphoria of their arrival at the beach, Footy had gone swimming. But since then, he'd noticed too many sharks, and while he'd not seen a saltwater croc, that did not mean they weren't there.

Rutherford said the Father was back—and what is that shadow in the water? His heart tripped and he squinted against the glare. He began to walk towards the men, wrapping in his line.

Submerged beside the coral head, Cat picked up a stone from the sand. Johnny was beside him with eyes open. Unlike the fish, he could see only a blur. He watched Cat pull himself to the clam colony on the side of the coral head and strike with the stone. He tugged off loosened shells and handed them to Johnny, who clutched them in an arm.

Suddenly Johnny felt that spooky sense of something watching him. He stared into the blue. While he couldn't make it out, he saw something gliding from the deep.

Cat clunked with his stone and continued to load Johnny up. Now he chipped off an armload himself. Johnny felt the desire for air burn in his lungs. He pointed for the surface and pushed that way, Cat right behind. Then, from the corner of his eye, Johnny saw something dark coming fast, and kicked harder.

Footy saw the big shadow in the water, dropped his rod and ran. The men broke the surface and swam hard for shore, on their sides, leading with one arm.

Something was chasing them.

"Bloody hell! Faster!" The Aussie screamed, hands cupping his mouth. Johnny peered down and found he was looking into the fierce eyes of the predator. A pointed head with big teeth was right below him in the water, looking up.

"Move your arses!" Footy bellowed.

Johnny kicked like a madman, Cat beside him, and his feet touched sand. They dashed out of the waves just as Footy got there.

"'Cuda!" Johnny gasped. "Huge!"

"You bloody dunderheads!" Footy stormed, "You about gave me a stroke!"

Johnny laughed and looked at the Japanese. They had been spooked, but neither had been willing to drop his clams. Cat chuckled as well and then they laughed.

"Aww, yeh," Footy said, arms crossed. "Right—it's a bloody joke. But you keep playing silly buggers, you'll get what's coming to you." He stormed back to his fishing.

Johnny and Cat carried the clams to the kitchen and put them in fresh water. Johnny returned to his carving and Cat went to the forest to wash, and haul drinking water.

Footy returned in the heat of the afternoon. He had a brace of Grouper that he set in the kitchen, then lay down in the shade for a nap.

"I'm sorry," Johnny called to him. "I know the ocean's dangerous! When I saw the size of that 'cuda, I about walked on water."

"Come on mate," Footy said. "You've got to realize, this is no joke! Tell you what Johnny—I'm not going in again. You want to, it's your funeral."

"Maybe you're right," Johnny said, "but the ocean's always felt like home to me."

"Not here mate!" Footy said, "This is bloody New Guinea!

"Stupid to survive the war, only to end up in a croc or shark belly."

"You're right," Johnny conceded, shaving another spiral of wood.

He worked until the sun plunged for the ocean, then called for another run. With all the good food, fresh air and exercise, they were getting stronger by the day.

This time Footy changed his style of running. It was more like a skip, with a long hop off his sound leg. While Johnny still managed to hit the Finish Tree first, the Japanese crowded him, and Footy was on their tails. Again they lay on the leaves and caught their breath.

Johnny was on his back, looking up into the branches when he got that eerie sense of being watched again. He sat up and stared around, but saw nothing unusual in the quiet clearing.

"What is wrong?" Cat asked.

"Yes, what's up mate?"

"Nothing—I guess," Johnny said. Then there was an unearthly scream. The men's hearts hammered and something large lifted in the branches. The three sprang up and ran to the beach and saw a huge fish eagle flapping away.

The men went back to camp. The catch of the day was the steamed clams.

"Alright then," Footy said, popping another succulent morsel in his mouth. "If you blokes want to die getting these, carry on. They're that good."

"I hope Chas made it safely home," Johnny said as they smoked contentedly by the fire.

"And we see a plane any day," Footy said. He turned to Cat. "Not long and you'll be back in Jap-land."

"What will you do when you get home?" Johnny asked. The Asian was silent a long minute.

"I do not know," he said.

"What do you do? What's your job?" Johnny asked.

"I am a career Army officer," Cat replied. "But now I will find other work."

"Well, there'll be money to be made," Footy said, "you've got a whole country to rebuild." The Japanese turned on him fiercely.

"With my family dead? Burned to nothing? My city gone? And you think about money?" There was an awkward pause filled by the crashing of the surf.

"Sorry, I meant no harm," Footy said stiffly.

"He was just talking," Johnny added. "There'll be millions of people in the same boat as you." This time the silence stretched so long, the conversation died.

During the afternoon, the waves rose higher. Now they were enormous rollers that hurled at the beach. The wind whistled, and the tarp cracked like a whip.

Finally the Japanese spoke.

"I am sorry," he told the others. "This is not your fault. But I do not know if I can face this new Japan.

"I think defeat takes more courage than war."

CHAPTER 10

The following day, the palm heads tossed and the ocean climbed higher. Johnny kept carving and the shavings tumbled down the beach. Footy and Cat tried to fish the booming breakers, but caught only a few perch, which the men had for lunch.

In the afternoon the Japanese brought his sword and sat beside Johnny. He had a rag and coconut oil and he drew the blade from its scabbard. He set it across his knees and for an hour, he scrubbed the metal until it gleamed.

He stood, holding the grip in two fists, and made sweeps through the air. Johnny studied the man's stance—legs widespread, the committed face, the sure moves. Johnny admired the long curve of steel. The point was formed by a forty-five degree angle across the end. Behind the sharp edge, a wavy line ran the length of the blade.

"That is a fine thing," he said.

"When I was home," Cat said, making another pass, "six days a week I must practice with a sword. At first it was bamboo, later metal, never *Katsumushi-maru!*

My father was a master—he taught me himself, although I had another *sensei* as well." He made a particularly deadly slash.

"Mostly we drill. Practice, practice, practice. Then, when I was good enough, my father and I started cutting *makiwara* together. These are straw bundles, about as thick as a man's neck. It was a long time before I could sever one with a single stroke! My father did it every time." He paused for a moment and studied Johnny.

"My father and I did not agree on some things. He was very critical, very strict. Now I think our happiest time together was when we were cutting *makiwara*.

"A warrior's sword is a living thing," he went on as he turned on a heel and carved the air. "We call it a *'katana'* and this one has a name, given to it by one of my ancestors after a great battle. It is called *'Katsumushi-maru.' Katsumushi* means 'dragonfly.'"

"Dragonfly?" Footy said as he came and sat down. "Sounds

girly." Cat suppressed his irritation and ignored the Australian. He finished his routine and took a seat.

"For us, the dragonfly is 'the invincible one,'" he said to Johnny. "It means both war, and victory." He displayed the sword.

"*Katsumushi-maru* was forged three hundred years ago, and has been in my family all that time. It has killed more than five hundred men—and the story of those victories, I know by heart.

"It took thirty men at a place called 'Bizen' to make this sword. They were under three masters. One made the steel. The second forged the sword. The third polished and finished it.

"The blade itself has two natures. You see where the metal joins?" Cat held the *katana* so the light caught the wavy line behind the cutting edge. Johnny stopped working to listen and both he and Footy nodded.

"The edge is very hard—very sharp. This is necessary! But the sword must also be flexible so it does not shatter when it strikes. The genius of the master who made it was to marry the two steels, the two personalities." The prisoner turned to stare at Footy.

"I hope when you take my *katana* to your home, you will understand its value. You will treat it with respect."

Footy was tempted to make a scathing retort, but something in the prisoner's earnest stare gave him pause.

"I will," he said seriously. Katsu dipped his head and returned the blade to its scabbard.

☆

The day ended with another run. As they approached the point, Johnny was once more in the lead, but then he tripped. The Japanese stepped in front of him and was first to the Finish Tree. Johnny came second, with Footy breathing down his neck.

This evening, the sun on the western horizon turned the clouds to pink cotton candy shot with bright lemon. The color bled away and the rising wind drove a curtain of dark clouds across the sky.

The men ate, and lit their fire, but the wind sucked the sparks toward the trees. They kicked sand over it and went to bed. Johnny lay in his swaying hammock, while the others wrapped themselves in blankets and turned their backs to the driving sand.

Katsu heard the wind in his ears, but that was not why sleep evaded him. He was troubled by an inner storm. Perhaps it was triggered by the sword practice, but once again he felt the conflict between his lethal warrior nature and his peaceful religious one. Samurai tradition required that he be ready to kill himself for honor at a moment's notice. Christianity forbade it and said he would forfeit his eternal spirit. How could he resolve this? How had his ancestors done it? It was like trying to piece together the two types of steel for the sword.

He pondered it like a Buddhist *koan*, a conundrum or contradiction that held a kernel of enlightenment. His father had taught that the essence of a samurai was to be of service, to give absolute loyalty to his lord. In addition, Katsu had grown up in a Christian family. He had been baptized in the cathedral as a baby, and confirmed as a teenager. In a way, he had no choice. It was the family tradition, and Katsu had not questioned his father, or the priests. It was the Takano family way.

But the furnace of war, and now defeat, had melted all that was not essential out of him. Now, as he tried to fit what remained of himself together, he found there was a hard core after all. If this atom bomb on Nagasaki had destroyed the *Urakami Tenshudo*, the Cathedral, then it was all gone—the Latin mass, the incense, the ornate robes, statues of the saints, and of course, the politics of the priesthood. Oh yes, Katsu had observed that this was also a hierarchy of men, jockeying for position. But all stripped away, he saw the Christ at the center. And now as he looked into that life, he could see one thing. Service.

The God of the universe, on his knees washing the feet of peasants. Katsu had an epiphany. *That is it!* Jesus was forever feeding the people, healing the sick, comforting sufferers. Two thousand years of human intervention had turned him into something else, perhaps an icon of gold high in a temple, but at the true heart was humble service.

I have been blind! My warrior nature and my peaceful soul come together in this! I was made to serve.

Nippon was overwhelmingly Buddhist, Katsu thought, and did not both the Buddha and the Christ teach peace? And were they not the spiritual teachers of both Japan and America? But in spite of that, the nations rattled their sabers, dressed their sons in uniform, and rushed to war. *How is that possible?*

Katsu felt a glimmer of hope. *My family may be dead, my world is in ruins, but perhaps I can serve my countrymen.* His hand touched *Kasumushi-maru* and he sent a thought to it.

Perhaps it is best that I give up you, spirit of my fathers, my warrior heart. What has this prideful nature done for Nippon? It has destroyed us. When I must, I will surrender you. I made a solemn promise. But not yet! No, not yet.

That night the crocodile did not watch from the tossing ocean. It wormed to the edge of the jungle and stared at the men. When the light winked out, the Father crept back and slid into the shallows. The wind could howl, but it was submerged in the silence of the river, only the nubs of its nostrils up in the storm.

It had selected its place of ambush and now it could rest.

The men awoke to tumultuous seas and clouds scudding across an iron sky. The coconut crabs were gone and they spent the morning huddled in camp, watching the waves mount in fury.

Johnny did the math and figured it was the seventh day since Chas Rutherford had departed. He went back to his project. It was almost done. He'd carved off a third of the wood he'd started with, and what he had left did not resemble a desktop in the least. The stains and cuts were long gone, and the flat surfaces and the rounded edges were fresh and golden.

The others ventured to try their luck at fishing. They needed the food. After some hours they returned with a meager catch, a single cod the Aussie had landed.

Johnny was done. He stood his creation on end and rose beside it. It came to a point over his head, flared to its widest at his shoulders, and narrowed to the rounded butt on the sand.

Johnny caressed the sleek shape and was well pleased.

"A small boat," the Japanese observed.

"No mate," Footy said. "I know what it is."

"What's that?" Johnny asked.

"I've never seen a real one," the Aussie said. "But it's a surfboard."

"Head of the class!" Johnny told him. "It's the first one I've carved, but not the first I owned." He turned it, admiring the grain.

"It's about eight feet long, and that's short, but it's all I had to work with."

"I knew some time ago, but I didn't want to spoil your fun,"

Footy said. "But mate, you're actually going to surf this bloody ocean? If so, you're as *longlong* as that crazy woman, Sarah."

"I haven't decided," Johnny said. "It was something to do."

"It is ready?" The Japanese asked. "I would like to see 'surf-board-ing.'"

"'Surfing,'" Johnny told him, "and it's not quite ready. I'd like your help to waterproof the wood. I need coconut oil, lots of it."

Cat collected seasoned nuts, split them and chopped the meat. Footy wanted to help and the two took turns crushing the nutmeat against the flat rock until they had a can of oil. Johnny rubbed layer after layer into the wood. After each coat, he let it dry. Half an hour later, the surface would be matte patches and he'd do it again.

Late that day, he had the wood saturated. The men studied the shining grain. Even Footy had to admit that the Yank had made a handsome thing.

It was time for their run. The three jogged through strong wind to their starting place.

"Ready?" Johnny asked. They crouched. "Set—go!" Footy and Cat got a pace ahead and Johnny leaped after them. For the first hundred yards, he followed the Japanese. The man ran in his vigorous way. Footy was next and ran with hardly a limp, making up for the slight lag of his right leg with longer leaps of the other.

With a hundred yards left, Johnny rushed into the lead. With the point fifty yards away, Cat caught up and they pounded neck-and-neck.

Then Footy seemed to fly by them, running faster than Johnny had seen him go since Bumay's cannibals were behind them. Both Johnny and Cat stretched after him, but for the first time, it was the Aussie who slapped the Finish Tree first.

Footy jogged in a circle, face tomato red, shaking victory fists. Johnny and Cat came in together and dropped. Footy tottered around the clearing, threw himself down at the jungle's edge and leaned against a log.

"I won!" he crowed. "I won, I bloody won!" His grin wouldn't quit. Johnny and Cat's chests heaved and for a time, there was only the sound of gasping. Some minutes later Johnny rolled on his side and smiled with genuine pleasure at Footy. The pilot had such a blissful look as he leaned back, eyes closed, chest still heaving.

Johnny put an elbow under his head and he, too, closed his eyes, awash in the euphoria that followed all-out exertion. But somewhere in the back of his mind, a jangle of alarm sounded. It was something he couldn't put his finger on, but the warning wouldn't go away. On the contrary, it got steadily more urgent until it was screaming for attention.

Johnny's eyes snapped open. It was absolutely serene under the shade of the huge tree. But there was something wrong, and he could not see it.

And then it struck him. Footy was sitting near a puddle of water. It had not rained.

Johnny's eyes fixed on the Australian. He sat with his legs straight out, leaning against a log in the foliage. But it came to Johnny—there was no log in that place.

Johnny sat bolt upright.

"Footy!" he hissed, "get up!"

"Why mate?" Footy said dreamily, eyes still closed.

"Footy," Johnny said and jumped up, his voice rising. "Get away from there!"

Footy glanced to his right and then his left, peering at the dense leaves, and Johnny saw his face change. Through the caked mud, he saw the rows of scales.

And then the log breathed.

Cat was watching as well and jerked to his feet. Johnny took a step toward Footy as the Aussie sprang up, trying to get away from the thing that waited in the quiet woods.

There was an eruption of branches cracking, and chunks of mud flying. And the unmistakable, murderous, blunt-arrow head of the Father swung into the clearing. The men absorbed the massive skull, the greenish eyes with the black slits, one marked with the dark, curving scar.

But it was the teeth that riveted Johnny's attention, the long rows along the indented jaws.

"Run!" Johnny's mind screamed, but like one of his nightmares, he did not say it and his feet were rooted to the spot.

The Father stood up off its belly and stepped fully into the clearing. A branch of a tree broke like a gun report, and more clay cracked off.

It opened its jaws and roared. The sound shook the men to the core. They gasped in terror and sucked in the crocodile's rotten breath.

Footy was closest to it. He still had the impression of the scales on his hands as he tried to leap away.

But Footy had expended all his energy on the race. It had taken an extraordinary effort to beat the other men. His injured leg dragged back, and the predator was swift. The Father bit him.

Cat and Johnny saw the teeth clamp on Footy's leg. There was the crack of bone and the scream. The Father shook its head and the man whipped like a rat in the jaws of a Rottweiler.

The Japanese finally made his legs move. He turned and ran away.

Johnny was frozen by warring impulses—run for his life, or fight for his friend. So it was he who saw the crocodile lash its head and Footy's leg come off at the calf. The man hurled through the air and crashed upside down against the Finish Tree. The sound leg wedged between the branches and the body hung down, arterial blood spurting from the stump. His eyes were fixed open, seeing nothing.

Johnny looked at the Father. The crocodile was so close, he could have touched its snout. In ecstatic rage, the crocodile glowered at its enemy. The body scent of the man was unmistakable.

This was the one-prey.

Johnny saw the great throat contract and realized the reptile had swallowed Footy's leg. Something twisted inside him. Blind fury exploded, and he no longer wanted to run away.

He glanced around for a stick or a rock—anything to beat on the beast that had murdered his friend.

Chapter 11

The Father faced its enemy and the urge to kill was immense.

Before dawn broke, the crocodile had dredged itself in mud and crept up the bank. It moved like the stalker it was, careful not to betray its substantial presence. By midday it was in place. Through a veil of leaves, it watched. With its sharp hearing, it listened. With sensitive nostrils, it tested the air. In a motionless fever of anticipation, it waited.

In the cool of the day, it had its reward. The two-legged animals galloped down the sand toward its place of ambush. The crocodile heard the raucous cries and part of it relaxed, while another part tightened like a great coil. The three animals approached together. The hidden predator watched them come. The distinct odor of the one-prey speared into its brain.

The predator bit the first man because it touched him and tried to run. That was all instinct. Then the Father faced its true goal. The small creature before it had fur on its head, but the reptile sucked in its scent and knew it was in the very presence of its enemy.

The crocodile stepped to the one-prey, so close its snout brushed him. It rumbled so its throat and belly vibrated and saw the creature tremble in its breath, fur lifting on head and chest.

Johnny glanced around for a weapon and spied a heavy branch the croc had broken off. Normally it would have been too much to handle, but now he snatched it up like a sapling.

The scarred eye was in front of him as the crocodile sized him up. With every ounce of strength Johnny had, he swung the club over his head and brought it down. The wood cracked the reptile over the eye knob, so hard Johnny's feet almost left the ground.

Always, the scar had been sensitive. The blow did not damage the thick bone or the eye itself, but the pain was searing. The Father flinched and was flooded with killing fury. It hissed in the prey's face. The man jumped back and raised his stick again. The reptile parted its jaws and came for him.

Again, Johnny swung his club like an axe into a woodblock. It struck the crocodile between the eyes and all down the snout to the nostrils. The Father recoiled and air hissed through its teeth. Being hit like this was a novel experience, not one it enjoyed. Its wrath expanded beyond all bounds.

Johnny saw the head go sideways in the same way the Father had taken Dingo, the jaws opening to engulf him. He jumped backwards as it lunged. The edge of the lower jaw struck him. He somersaulted and dropped his branch. The beast realized it had bitten air as Johnny scooped up the club and cocked it over his shoulder like an overgrown baseball bat.

The reptile grunted as it saw the creature at bay, prepared to make its last stand. During all the years of its life, the Father had seen uncounted animals in this ultimate predicament. In the prelude to their death, they bared their pitiful claws and teeth.

Again, the crocodile roared. Johnny felt his whole body vibrate. The brute shoved its huge head out from its hulking shoulders and fixed the man in its most ferocious stare. Johnny was almost mesmerized.

But the man was a killer himself. In his mind, he had never stopped attacking. Now Johnny swung his club with all his might, aimed at the eye again, the only vulnerable spot on the armored creature. Seemingly without effort, the Father cracked its jaws and caught the stick. It jerked, and the wood ripped from Johnny's fingers, stripping skin. The crocodile crunched the branch like a toothpick, dropped the splinters, and stepped so close its front teeth rested against him.

"Uh oh," Johnny said. Gwyn flashed into his mind and he felt a stab of regret for the things they would never do, and that was all the time he had. The Father spread its jaws and Johnny looked into the dark tunnel he was about to enter.

There was a blur of motion from the side. Cat ran at the crocodile, sword in hand. He stepped up the malformed foreleg and leapt astride the neck.

The crocodile experienced another novel sensation. It had never been ridden before. It turned its head sharply, trying to see what was there, but could not. It swung its head the other way and Johnny barely managed to jump back. The great snout just missed him. The crocodile peered over its shoulder and saw a man shape.

As Katsu had raced to camp and snatched up his *katana,* he

tried to plan. The best technique with the sword was the slashing cut, but the monster's skull would be such heavy armor, he must improvise.

Katsu rode the Father's neck and raised *Katsumushi-maru* in both hands, pointed down. The crocodile hissed and launched straight into the air, trying to throw the rider off. Johnny watched the head shoot up, so high the forelegs came off the ground.

Katsu rode the reptile almost standing, knees pressed to the scales, belly against the rock skull. The Father went ten feet among the branches, then slammed down with such force, the earth bounced.

Somehow the Japanese kept his seat. Johnny saw the intensity of his focus as he adjusted the *katana* slightly to one side.

Katsu shouted and stabbed. The sword slid into the Father's moon-eye. Liquid popped and the steel went through bone, shot into the mouth between the top teeth, and pierced the floor of the lower jaw. It stopped when it jammed into heavy bone there. Cat's face was a fierce mask.

The crocodile's jaws flew open and it bawled pure agony. Johnny stared into the gaping mouth and saw the red-stained steel at the back.

The Father spun and ran for the ocean. Johnny threw himself flat to escape the tail that swung over him like a tree trunk. Trees toppled as the colossus broke them down and charged for refuge. Johnny ran out behind it and saw Cat ride the brute down the beach and into the surf. Unbelievably, the Japanese was still committed to his task, his weight raised, twisting on the sword.

The Father rushed into the water and rolled. Cat was thrown off and a wave broke over them. It withdrew and Johnny's heart fell to see the Father, still with the sword in its eye, but the man in its jaws. Cat struggled vigorously until the crocodile gnashed its teeth. From thirty yards off, Johnny heard the bones shatter, and another wave crashed in.

When the foam pulled back this time, the Father stood with the man hanging limp. Johnny saw the blood pumping from the moon scar and spilling into the sea. It remained that way as several more waves broke over it.

The crocodile opened its jaws, let the body fall and stood awash in the South Pacific. Again it bellowed its abject suffering. The Father turned its head, and with its one good eye, it stared at

Johnny. Then it swung its head, scattering scarlet drops, and looked across the ocean.

The beast lumbered deeper, stopped, wobbled, and crashed over. Another roller surged along the vast body as if swamping a shipwreck.

Johnny ran to Cat. He found the man in the shallows with terrible puncture marks all through him. Cat was crushed, but somehow, he was still alive.

Johnny crouched and lifted him. The man's eyes were open, staring at him. He struggled to say something. Johnny leaned closer.

"We are even," Cat breathed, and went still.

Blood spilled from the corners of his mouth, and from all the holes in his chest. Johnny had seen thousands of dead men, and this was one more. He pounded a fist on the sand.

Johnny carried Cat's body out of the water and put him on the beach. The hulk of the Father had not moved. Johnny ran back to Footy. He found him hanging upside down from the tree, the blue eyes wide open and blind. Blood still flowed from the stump of the leg. Again Johnny was flooded with anguish, fists opening and closing. *Do something!*

He went to Footy, grabbed him and lifted, and the leg came out of the branches. The torn off calf and exposed bone by his face sickened him, but Johnny did not let that stop him. He laid Footy at the tree roots. With a sinking heart, he saw the puddle of blood by the trunk and realized how much of it his friend had lost. Johnny thought he was looking at another corpse and his eyes teared up.

But beyond all hope, Footy moved. His chest heaved and he gasped air. He groaned and blinked, and his eyelids closed.

Johnny knew that if Footy had any chance, it came down to what he did in the next few seconds. He undid the man's belt and yanked it through the loops. He wrapped it tightly around the thigh of the ripped leg and buckled it.

Johnny picked up Footy and ran to camp. He laid him on a blanket, lit the stove and heated the blade of his machete in the ring of fire until it glowed orange. Footy was tossing. His eyes flew open and he sat up. His gaze went to his cut-off leg and he screamed.

Johnny ran to him holding the smoking machete and shoved him down. He sat on him facing away, seized the bleeding stump in one hand and put the flat of the blade to the torn flesh. It sizzled and Footy shouted. His body arched up and then went slack as he passed out. Johnny was grateful for that.

He turned the blade, seared another raw section and kept scorching until the metal cooled. He returned to the stove, heated it again and continued until the stump was completely cauterized. The flesh was blackened, reddish fluid seeping through.

A sharp end of bone protruded and Johnny needed to do something about it. He propped the leg on a log and raised the machete three or four times to gauge where to strike.

He swung hard, the blade hit true, the bone broke cleanly off and sailed away.

Footy was starting to come to again. Johnny raced to the medical kit and grabbed a tube of morphine. He broke the seal, screwed on the needle, jammed it into Footy's arm and squeezed in the drug. The man went limp again. Johnny stared into the stricken face.

He's a hair from death—what more can I do? Footy desperately needed expert medical help, and all he had was Johnny.

Keep trying! Johnny got the iodine, spilled it on a pad and swabbed the stump. He opened the sulfa powder and poured it on. He loosened the tourniquet and was relieved to see the worst of the arterial squirting had stopped, although it still bled. He waited a minute and tightened the belt.

For ten minutes, Johnny watched the pilot's waxen face. Each breath he took was a fight for life. Then Johnny loosened the belt again, let the stump bleed, and cinched it back up. He'd seen men lose limbs because the tourniquet was left on too long. After half an hour, he pulled out rolls of gauze and wrapped the injury. He ripped strips of tape from the roll and stuck down the bandage. At least once the stump was neatly wrapped, it looked better.

For the first time since the attack, Johnny had a moment. Another surreal sunset blazed across the west and it struck him like a blow.

This time yesterday I sat here with Footy and Cat. Now Cat is dead and Footy is close behind. The Father found us at last, and with a vengeance.

Johnny's gaze flashed to look at the crocodile, but it was gone. For a crazy minute he wondered if it was behind him and he jumped up and spun all around, but it was not there. In growing consternation he stared at the ocean. Night was falling fast now, and the breakers were huge. It was hard to make out anything.

Then he saw the birds. A hundred yards out, the gulls were gathering. Beneath them, the swells broke strangely. Something wallowed like a drifting log.

It's the croc! The birds began to land on the carcass and peck at it. It was time to adjust the tourniquet again and Johnny bent to his task.

The Father is dead, he thought, *killed by Cat.*

CHAPTER 12

It was dark. Johnny remained near Footy and made a fire. He was too distraught to be hungry, and he lit a cigarette that disappeared in a few drags. The Australian began to mutter and toss. Johnny brought water, raised him up, and dribbled some between his lips. Footy choked but swallowed, then sagged again and Johnny felt for his pulse. It beat faintly.

Johnny wondered when to give him more morphine. He counted how many doses were left. With the syrettes in the cache, added to the ones they'd conserved in the swamp, he had nine tubes. He did not know how often to administer the powerful opiate. Too much would kill his friend. He decided to wait until he knew Footy had to have it. *If he lives.*

A waning moon sailed into view. Johnny stared at the waves, but could no longer see the Father's remains. He kept vigil over Footy all night. At regular intervals, he loosened the tourniquet. Every hour, he tipped water in his mouth and hoped he swallowed some.

Now I'm a nurse, he thought. *So this is what Gwyn did for me.* Caring for another in this way was both intimate and somehow impersonal, both powerful and humbling. Johnny gained a new level of appreciation for Gwyn and all the others who had nursed him. Then he remembered how badly he'd treated them as he recovered, and felt ashamed.

In the middle of the night he realized Footy had urinated on his bedding. Johnny made another bed using two blankets. He folded one to go under Footy's upper body, left a space for the hips, and placed the other to cushion his legs. Gently as he could, he stripped Footy's shorts off, easing the cloth over the terrible injury. His patient whimpered but did not come to.

Johnny placed him on the fresh bed. At least now when Footy must void he would do so on the sand. Johnny hung the damp blanket on a branch to wash another time. The night was warm, but Footy was cold to the touch, and Johnny got his sheet and covered him.

Time passed and Footy's breathing grew more labored. *He needs so much more than I can do!* Johnny thought despairingly. *Where's our rescue? Did Chas even get the message through?*

The night wore on, and Johnny felt supremely alone under the cold stars. *This is why you can't coddle your feelings,* the soldier warned him. Another thought arose: *I'd give about anything to have Gwyn here, just for a few minutes, just to talk.*

Johnny's spirits sank even lower. He expected Footy to die at any minute. In the darkest hours of the morning, the pilot let go a rattling breath and Johnny thought it was done. He grabbed the man's wrist and found no pulse. He threw handfuls of twigs on the coals for light, and held the blade of his knife over Footy's lips. When a faint mist formed, he got a lump in his throat.

The sky over the eastern sea turned from coal to ash. Morning dragged in at last. Footy began to shout and thrash. Johnny shot him with morphine and held him down until he passed out.

Gradually, Footy's breathing grew regular. Johnny stared at the haggard face. The Australian seemed to have shrunk and aged ten years overnight. Johnny removed the tourniquet and saw that no more blood came through the bandage. He set the belt aside.

Finally, Johnny could think about his own condition. He forced himself to eat bananas and brewed coffee. *I have to keep strong for Footy's sake*. He felt a little less hopeless in daylight, but still desperately sad. It came to him that he was mourning. *For Cat,* Johnny realized. *He should be here, busy in the kitchen.*

Dumb! His killer mind chastised him. *He was just another enemy, one more Jap! Not long ago I would have shot him as soon as look at him.*

At least Footy rested peacefully and Johnny began to think about the task he did not want. He drank more coffee and smoked and put it off, but at last he stood. He walked down the beach, passed the jeeps he and Cat had wrecked and the signal bonfire they had made together. There was Footy's S O S, for all the good it had done them.

Johnny came along the surf and saw Cat's corpse partially buried in the sand. He half-wished something had dragged it off in the night. He shaded his eyes and studied the ocean. There was no sign of anything floating, but it would have drifted with the tide. Gulls stood around Cat's body and Johnny raised his arms and shouted at them. They scattered and he knelt by the corpse. With revulsion, he saw small crabs feeding on the torn flesh and he snatched up a stick and drove them back to their holes.

Johnny picked Cat up in his arms and walked the route they had run together. He carried him to the Finish Tree and laid him on the ground. Here Johnny would bury the dead, but first he must tend to the living. He jogged back to camp, gave Footy more water and held his head up until he quit sputtering and slept again.

Johnny cracked a wedge of board from the discarded desk drawers and went back to the Finish Tree. He felt exhausted, but the thing must be done. He brushed away the leaves, drew a rectangle on the sand and began to dig with the wood. His hands became raw and he persevered. He grew blisters and went on.

The job was especially slow because every twenty minutes, he must check on Footy. Usually the patient was passed out, but sometimes he was semi-conscious, eyes flickering beneath the lids. Johnny tended to him and went back to the burial.

His arms ached and still he dug. The blisters burst and he went deeper. By the early afternoon, he stood in a pit up to his chest and considered his labor. The hole was about five feet deep and it had started out wide enough, but the sides kept caving in. He sighed and shoveled some more.

At last it was ready. Johnny looked from Cat's body to the grave. He steeled himself for the task of putting him in and could not begin. He was appalled by his weakness. During the war, he'd walked away from his own dead countrymen countless times. He'd passed enemy corpses without a second thought. But now he must put Cat in and throw dirt on his face, and he could not do it.

What is wrong with me? And then it came to him. *He was my friend.* The realization shocked him. When had the prisoner stopped being his enemy and crossed into this new territory?

Johnny postponed what he had to do and went back to camp. He found Footy had soiled his bed-site. Johnny made up another one, washed him with soap and a pot of water, dried him and moved him again. Footy tossed and moaned and Johnny shot him with painkiller and waited until it knocked him out.

Johnny untied his jungle hammock, pulled on his helmet and returned to the gravesite. He spread his bed beside the corpse, cut a piece of rope off an end and put it aside. He opened the zipper and slid the body in. He rolled Cat in the material and roped the makeshift shroud.

Quickly, before he could think about it, he pushed the bundle into the pit. He turned his back and scraped the dirt into the hole, then packed the mound with his bare feet. He cut two saplings and used the piece of rope to tie a cross. He stuck this in the soil at the head of the grave.

It was done, but not finished. Johnny thought he should say some words. He pulled his helmet off and searched for something fitting.

Dad would have a quotation. Johnny wracked his mind but came up empty. At last he recalled a phrase from San Diego. They'd learned it from the Mexicans, and it had become a family tradition. It was the last thing his parents said to one another before his father went to sea.

"Vaya con Dios, Cat," Johnny said gruffly. He placed his helmet on the top of the cross, nodded at the grave, and walked away.

Footy seemed to be sleeping and Johnny took empty pots and soap and went to the stream. He stripped off his shorts and sat in the pool, head under the spout while the water splashed over him. He filled the containers and returned.

Johnny opened a can of stew and ate the chunks with his fingers. He poured the broth into another pot, added water, and heated it. When it was lukewarm, he took it to Footy.

The man was white as paper, muttering nonsense. Johnny sat beside him and raised Footy's head on his leg. He put a spoonful of soup to the man's lips and tipped a little in. Footy coughed and shook his head. But then, Johnny was encouraged to see, he swallowed and licked his lips. Johnny got about half of it into him, while the rest went down his chin. He cleaned the patient up and Footy slept again.

The day drew on, and at last it came to Johnny that this was when the three of them would have gone for their run. Again, he was wracked by sadness and sat listlessly as night fell. He roused himself, lit a fire, smoked, and kept watch.

In the middle of the night, the Australian began an unintelligible conversation with unseen companions. The hours dragged on and Footy progressed through a number of states. Sometimes he lay still as death. Other times, he tossed and raved.

Johnny heard a scream and sat bolt upright. He realized he'd nodded off and in the faint glow of the coals, he saw Footy face-down in the sand. He had rolled off his blankets and banged his poor leg. Johnny rushed for another tube of morphine and stuck it in him. At last Footy stopped writhing and went limp, and Johnny placed him back on his bedding.

He lay awake, staring at dark patches of clouds drifting across the stars. What did it all mean? He'd been raised in church, like he'd told Doc Mac, and he'd once believed in a loving God. But three years of brutal war had about beaten the faith out of him.

His first day of fighting, the day Walt died, he'd realized bone-deep that no supernatural force was going to step in and stop the bullets—not the ones coming at him, or those he'd sent at other men. War was all projectiles and trajectories, the physics of death.

Somewhere along that journey, Johnny stopped believing in a loving presence behind it all. But now as he stared into space, he remembered what Doc Mac told him. *"God does not require your belief in order to exist."*

The soldier voice said the world was all violent chaos and blind chance. At school, they said everything was a mindless explosion of matter, and no one knew how it got started or where it was going. Johnny pondered that as he listened to the thin evidence of human life, the ragged breaths of his friend.

Gradually a conviction grew in him, the tiniest flicker of hope. The theory this was all merely a cosmic accident was just that, a theory. Johnny stared at the billion suns across the sky and thought it took a greater leap of faith to believe all this had "just happened," than that it was a work of infinite imagination and intelligence.

If there is a God, why did he make it so hard to figure out? And it struck him. *You can't "figure out" the awesome presence that can conjure up a universe.*

So how could a puny creature like he was know how to get by? *"Live by the code,"* he heard his father's voice. *"Do unto others as you would have them do unto you."*

But that had all been kicked in the ditch by the war. In the jungles of New Guinea where the tough soldier emerged, Johnny came up with a new rule.

"Kill the enemy before he kills you." It was not a belief, not an

article of faith. It was a daily necessity.

The only reason he was even here to think these things was because he had followed that rule to the letter. But now he hurt deep inside, like something was breaking. He was bereft, with only the unconscious and the dead for company.

Johnny put a stick on the fire and lit another cigarette. He was no longer rationing.

What if all this is a design—some great scheme where my life is only a snap of the fingers?

What if we've been given everything we need? Paradise is here, all around us. But then there's this little thing called "free will."

None of this took a leap of faith, Johnny decided. Anyone could see it. *We are free to love or hate. The Uhuli and Mambu—America and Japan—it's the same, just on a different scale. Now our tribal wars tear up the Earth and the slaughter is counted in millions.*

And where is God? There is a fact and this is it. If God does intervene, it's only here and there. This life saved, that one let go. On the big scale, God does not step in. God does not save the millions. The silence says, "You are free. Here is the world. Make it heaven or hell, live like angels or devils, it's your choice."

Maybe God asks us a question, Johnny thought, *and history is our answer.*

Footy cried out and Johnny went to him. As he adjusted the leg, he saw the depths of his friend's suffering and it devastated him.

Later, as the sun was coming up, he had another thought.

Maybe we break God's heart.

Day dawned and Footy still lived. Johnny mashed bananas and stirred in coconut milk. He lifted the Aussie's head and spooned the sweet concoction into his mouth. Footy's eyes stayed closed but he was able get some down. Finally he spoke.

"Ta," he whispered. It was the first intelligible thing he'd said since the Father's attack and Johnny got a lump in his throat. *What's happening to me? Don't turn into a pussy!*

Footy's teeth chattered and Johnny tucked a blanket up to his chin. He was overly emotional, even tearful this morning. *I've been through a lot,* he told himself. *I'm just tired. I need sleep, and soon, but then who will look after Footy?*

He wished he had a book to read. "*The Man Who Would Be King,*" or "*White Fang.*" But there was no book, and he sat by Footy while the clouds unraveled across the sky.

In the afternoon, Johnny pulled off the bandages and inspected the stump. He was relieved to see no sign of infection. A scab had formed over the seared flesh. Johnny swabbed it with iodine, smothered it in antibiotic powder, and wrapped it again.

"You are doing great pal," he told Footy in a hearty voice he did not feel, even though the Aussie was out cold. "A few more days of R and R and you'll be good as new." Footy mumbled and raised a hand. Johnny gently pressed it down. *You desperately need a doc, but at least you're eating.*

That day and another night dragged by. In the new morning, Footy was suffering, and Johnny drugged him again. He changed the bandage in the afternoon and was encouraged to see patches of pink showing through the scab. He boiled a towel, wrung it out, and washed the man from head to toe.

The sun was a bright patch behind roiling clouds. The seas were wild and wind tossed the foam. In growing admiration, Johnny watched the rollers come in. Gradually, a sense of longing rose within him. The water giants called him to play, and his eyes flashed to the sleek thing he had made. He had the urge to escape into the tumult, mount his wooden wing and never come back.

Footy groaned, and Johnny abandoned his pipedream and returned to his caretaker chores. The day went by, and the weather grew worse.

That night, Footy's babbling became hysteria. Johnny put a hand on the patient's forehead and found him burning up. He dosed him with morphine and that quieted Footy, but the heat came off him like a furnace. Johnny wanted to soak him down but found he was out of water. He pulled a burning branch from the fire and took a pot into the jungle.

He was walking fast on bare feet, hardly paying attention, when he almost stepped on the snake. The Death Adder reared up and struck and Johnny barely managed to dance beyond its reach. He shoved the torch at the viper's head and it recoiled and slithered off the path.

Johnny's track and field events had been sprints, hurdles and the long jump. He backed up a few paces, pot in one hand and the stick in the other, took some running steps and leapt over the place the snake might still lurk. He jogged to the pool and returned with the water, waving the smoldering stick in front of him, but the serpent was gone.

Johnny soaked Footy down, and while the evaporation cooled him, the skin was soon burning again. Johnny kept at it for hours. His arms ached and his body begged for sleep, but he persisted. Day broke, and on he went.

At last his patient began to cool. In a final burst of sweat, the fever broke, and Footy's breathing became deep and regular. Johnny saw that his skin color was returning to normal. The Aussie began to snore, really going at it, and for once, Johnny welcomed the sound. He stretched out on the sand and slumbered.

He awoke in the full glare of the afternoon sun. He sat up and saw Footy. The Aussie's blue eyes were open, staring at him.

"Johnny," the pilot rasped, "where's me bloody leg?"

CHAPTER 13

"Footy," Johnny began. "I've got a lot to tell you," but the patient's eyes drifted shut and he was gone again.

Johnny roused himself, washed his face and made coffee. He felt better for the rest. He opened a can of spaghetti and ate it cold. He sat by Footy and smoked, and watched the mounting seas. There must be a storm out on the South Pacific. Jumbo waves tumbled in that reminded Johnny of "Pipeline," his favorite run on Oahu's north shore.

Eventually Footy had a fit of coughing and raised himself on his elbows. His eyes came open and stayed that way. Johnny brought him some water and he drank the whole cup.

"Hungry?" Johnny asked and Footy nodded. He opened a can of fruit cocktail and brought it back.

"What happened?" Footy asked in a cracked voice.

"Not yet," Johnny said and sat beside him. "Eat first." He held the Aussie's head in the crook of his elbow and fed him the fruit and all the syrup.

"Now," Footy said when that was done. "I can see me bloody leg is gone. Talk."

"Do you remember being attacked by the crocodile?" Johnny asked. Footy closed his eyes.

"Ahh, the Father," he said. "No..."

"The run," Johnny said, "the Finish Tree..."

"Ah yes," Footy said, cracking an eye. "I won..."

"It was there," Johnny said. "The Father was there, waiting for us. It attacked you. But you're going to make it."

"Ahh?" Footy breathed as he raised his head and looked at the bandaged, shortened leg.

"No more bleeding," Johnny said. "No infection."

"Ahh," Footy said in a lost voice. Johnny took a breath.

"Cat is dead."

"Dead? How...?" Footy's gaze fixed on the Yank.

"The Father killed him," Johnny said.

"And where's that bloody croc now?"

"Dead as well. Cat killed it," Johnny said, "with his sword."

"Ahhh," Footy said. He lay back and passed out.

Johnny drew his surfboard against his legs. He stroked the warm wood, fingers tracing the grain, while he watched the tempest. The gulls rode the wild wind and he marveled at the way they dipped and soared. The rollers were incredible, and the surf hammered the beach. Every so often, Johnny woke Footy up enough to take water. For lunch, he fed him mashed bananas and pudding. The Aussie slept again.

Late in the afternoon, Johnny was wandering back and forth in front of the campsite when Footy called.

"I need help, sorry to say. Toilet," he explained. "Help me sit up. There," he pointed at a log. "Get me on it." Johnny lifted the man from behind. Footy held his stump sticking out so it wouldn't get bumped, while his other heel dragged in the sand. Johnny put him on the log and walked away to give him privacy. He went to the dump in the trees and chose a big can. He filled it with water and set it beside Footy so he could wash himself. When the Aussie was ready, Johnny helped him back to bed.

"Give us a ciggy," Footy said, "there's a mate." Johnny lit it for him.

"Now," Footy breathed through the smoke, "that's better. Make a latrine close by, would you Johnny? I'd like to take care of meself."

"Ok," Johnny said.

"And bring me clothes." Johnny helped him get into a roomy pair of Dingo's shorts. Then he dug a deep hole in the sand and rolled a log near it for a seat. He stood a few cans of water nearby.

That evening, the Aussie insisted on feeding himself. Johnny propped him up and gave him a plate of stew. Footy ate most of it, but he was in pain. Finally he pushed it aside and clutched his thigh, sweat popping on his forehead.

"Hells bloody bells! Morphine!" he gasped.

"Ok," Johnny said. "We've got three tubes left. That's all there are. Three—you want one?"

"Give me half a dose mate," Footy managed. "Right now!" Johnny slid the needle in and squeezed a portion of the tube. The pilot gasped hard, but after a few minutes he calmed down. He grabbed the cigarettes and smoked four in a row, lighting one from the end of the other.

"Struth mate," he said, "in the war I worried about getting killed, but this is worse."

Sometime after the drug kicked in, Footy dragged himself to the latrine. Johnny got up to help but the Aussie waved him away. It took Footy ten minutes crabbing on hands and a foot to get there and sit on the log, but he managed. Afterwards, he grunted his way back to his blankets.

Johnny put a box of cigarettes, matches, and a bottle of water beside Footy. He also set the half-dose of morphine at hand.

"Anything else I can do for you?" Johnny asked.

"A pistol and one bullet," Footy groaned.

"Besides that," Johnny said. "I need sleep too. I've been up most of the time since this happened. You want something, you yell until I wake up." He rolled out a blanket, and for the first time since the Father's attack, he slept the entire night.

Johnny awoke to a gale blowing and saw Footy sitting against a log, cigarette butts stuck all around in the sand.

"'Mornin', mate," Footy said, "but I can't say it's good."

"Bad night?" Johnny asked.

"The worst," Footy said, "I gave meself the morphine. I'm ready for more."

"Ok," Johnny said. "There are two tubes left."

"Bloody hell," Footy gasped. "Give me another half."

"Right away," Johnny said and he got up. "From here on, it's up to you to tell me when." He gave Footy the shot. "I'll put on coffee."

"Make it easy and just chop me friggin' head off," Footy wheezed. Johnny brought him a mug of the brew, then heated beef hash and cooked the last of the bananas. He told the pilot he had to provision the camp. This morning, he'd haul water, get bananas and go fishing.

"Go on mate," Footy told him. By late morning Johnny had bunches of bananas in the branches and a pile of green coconuts, one cut open by the pilot to drink. All the pots were full of water.

Johnny took his pole and went to the ocean. It was tough casting into the roaring waves, and he caught nothing for an hour, then hooked six pan-size Snappers in rapid succession.

When Johnny got back he found Footy asleep and was glad to see it. To be awake was to suffer. Johnny fried the fish while his stomach grumbled. He ate three, covered another for Footy's lunch, and saved two for dinner.

That night, he was forced to give the Aussie another half dose of morphine.

"One more squeeze and we're out," Johnny warned.

"Alright mate," Footy said. "Don't leave it near me or I'll use it for shore. But the pain's lessening a bit."

"That's good news."

Next time Johnny was conscious, there was rain drumming on the canvas. He listened to the water running and the endless growl of the breakers.

When next Johnny awoke, clouds were blowing off a clear sky. The sun had made a comeback and bright blue rollers fifteen feet tall washed in from the horizon.

Footy was awake and Johnny got up and cooked. The morning passed with the patient drifting in and out of awareness. Johnny got the oil and rubbed another coat onto his board, then sat staring at the South Pacific.

"Why don't you go on then?" Footy's voice came to him. "I take back what I said before—before everything." Johnny looked at him.

"To tell the truth, Johnny," Footy said, "I'm overly cautious around the water. Always have been. We had crocs and sharks where I grew up. I've been hearing about swimmers being taken since I can remember. But don't let me stop you. With the Father dead, you give it a go."

"I'd like to," Johnny told him, "but no way."

"Why?"

"You," Johnny said simply. Footy thought about it and nodded.

"Right," he said. "I see—sorry."

"Oh come on," Johnny said. "That's just the way it is. You'd do the same for me."

"Don't be so shore," Footy answered.

"Sure you would," Johnny nodded. "That's what friends are for."

"We're friends?" Footy asked.

"Yes," Johnny said.

"Good mates?" Footy pushed it.

"Best of mates," Johnny affirmed. "Now shut up!"

Footy lay back with a smile. Johnny put the surfboard aside and got him fresh water. Then he went fishing and landed a single cod. He fried it with coconut for lunch.

During the afternoon, Footy had a nasty pain attack and begged for another shot. Johnny warned him it was the end of the very last tube. Footy sweated bullets and said he must have it.

Johnny injected him and waited. When Footy was able to lie back, he went and fished the giant seas some more, but the weather seemed to have scared off the catch. All he managed were two small perch, and that was it for dinner.

Later on, Johnny fetched his Springfield. He might not have any ammo, but his life had depended on it so long, caring for it was second nature. Already, due to the salt air, there were rust patches. He kicked himself one more time for not bringing a cleaning kit. *Of course, it was supposed to be a three-day mission.* But at least there was Cat's coconut oil. Johnny soaked a piece of his cut-off pant leg and rubbed each spot smooth.

As he worked, he had an unpleasant thought. With the end of the war, the Army would want his Springfield. *And that's not going to happen,* he decided. *It's mine. I paid for it with my blood.*

He put the scope to his eye and panned along the beach, and another realization came over him. *I will never hunt another man with it. Never.*

He hadn't expected that, and he was surprised by the intensity. It was something more than the war being over. It was like a key turning in a secret lock.

I am done killing men! Something seemed to untie inside him, a knot he didn't know was there until it let go.

I have done my part. How did General MacArthur put it? Duty, honor, country. I've served all three.

Then an incredible realization struck Johnny. It was so big, he could hardly take it in. *The atom bomb will put an end to war!* It hadn't hit him until just now.

How can soldiers, even nations, fight this thing? The answer is, they can't. The mere threat of it would make a new Hitler throw up his hands and quit.

That's it! he thought with wonder. *Because of this terrible bomb, war is finished!*

A ray of hope lit Johnny's heart. This strange new world, reborn in peace, might be a better one after all.

Five days passed. Footy's leg continued to heal. The skies stayed blue, the breeze was stiff, and the waves were immense.

On the morning of the twelfth day since the crocodile's attack, Johnny unwound the bandages from Footy's leg while the patient sat on a log and watched, both fascinated and repelled.

"Give us a good gander," he said. "I can bear it now."

Johnny did as he was asked, turning the stump this way and that. The scabs were falling off and the skin underneath looked raw, but whole.

"Ugly as a wombat's arse," Footy observed. "Hell of a thing to have to show the Sheilas. But at least the bloody croc got the leg I hurt in the swamp. Always look at the bright side, that's what me old Pa said." He offered a ghastly smile.

"You did a good job, Johnny. Thanks mate."

"Forget it," Johnny said. He bandaged the stump again, then boiled a pair of his socks, wrung them out and let them dry. He took one and rolled it over Footy's rounded calf. It made a neat cover.

"Help me up," Footy asked. "I need to start walking again, or as near as a crip like me can manage."

"Sure you're ready?"

"Shore I'm shore. Give us a hand."

Johnny got Footy balanced on his sound leg. Then, as Cat had done in the swamp, he put his head under the Aussie's arm and helped him take a few steps. Footy started gasping, his face sagged and Johnny settled him back on his blanket.

"That's a good start," Johnny said. Footy turned away.

"I'll try again tomorrow," he muttered.

The following morning, he did. With Johnny half carrying him, he managed a dozen steps. Then he needed to lie down again.

Johnny decided to make another crutch. He searched the forest until he found the ideal forked sapling and cut it. He tore strips off an old blanket, wound a thick pad over the crotch and tied it tight. The next time Footy wanted to walk, Johnny got him up and tried it under his arm.

"This feels too bloody familiar," the Aussie grimaced, but he was able to move about on his own. Then he lost his balance and started to fall. Johnny jumped to him and held him up.

"Crikey!" Footy gasped. "I'm seeing firecrackers." Johnny carried him back to bed.

"Leg's thumping like a drum."

"But that wasn't bad," Johnny encouraged him.

"You'll be your old self in no time."

Three more days, and Footy could walk around camp on his own. He went back to broadcasting their S O S and hailed Chas Rutherford directly, but got no reply.

By Johnny's count, it was seventeen days since the Father's attack, and twenty-two since the Brit had gone. The skies were clear, but now the wind blew all the time and the waves continued high. It seemed to be a change of season, one that had a negative effect on the fishing. Johnny was forced to devote long hours to the attempt, and just managed to land enough to keep them going. He lost three more of their hooks to barracuda.

There came a morning when Johnny woke to find Footy on his crutch behind the stove. He'd made coffee and was cooking "brecky," chunks of fish fried with crumbled hardtack.

After they ate, the two men sat and smoked and watched the day. Again, Johnny found himself holding his surfboard. The breakers frothed shoreward in dangerous mountains whose tops curled over on themselves. *The barrel!*

Johnny laid the board on the beach and stood on it, practicing his stance. The wood was slippery with oil and he took handfuls of sand and roughed the places where his feet would grip.

Footy watched all this and spoke again.

"Look Johnny, give it a go mate," he said. "I can see how much you want to. I insist. The truth is, I'd like to see surfing."

"Are you sure?" Johnny asked. Footy smiled broadly.

"Shore I'm shore. If a bloody great shark, or even the Father's brother, gobbles you up, I'm right now. No worries. I don't need you."

"Thanks," Johnny said dryly.

"No mate, I'm serious," Footy insisted. "Get on out there." At last, Johnny gave in.

"Ok!"

"Off you bloody go, sport," Footy grinned.

Johnny was already barefoot in weathered shorts. He smiled broadly, white teeth in a deeply tanned face with a dark line of stubble. His curly hair was streaked by the sun. He whooped, grabbed his surfboard and ran for the ocean. Footy noticed that the Yank had filled out since they got to the beach.

Johnny ran into the surf, turned his back and crashed through a wave. As soon as he was deep enough, he dove onto his board and shot up the incoming swell. It broke over his head and he was underwater, assailed by doubt.

Will it float? Will it carry my weight? And then—*do I even remember how to surf?* It had been four years since he'd been an ocean rider. He hadn't been on a board since December 7, 1941. That morning, he'd run towards Pearl Harbor, and he never saw his board again.

Johnny exploded into sunlight and realized with joy that the board carried him high.

Footy sat on his log and watched the Yank disappear into the wild and windswept South Pacific.

CHAPTER 14

The water rose and Johnny rode it like an elevator. The nose of his board cut through the top of the wave and he spilled down the other side into the trough. Every nerve tingled and he felt fully alive. He raised his chest and paddled. He was thrilled by how light the board floated.

Footy watched the Yank go out of sight, and there was the lad again, drifting up the face of the curve. Johnny paddled on and was out of Footy's view much of the time.

Johnny felt a rush of eagerness. He'd almost forgotten this, the twined cables of fear and excitement. The anticipation grew for the sweet instant he would stand and race away. During the war, all this had been left behind, but now he was immersed again.

The Pacific was a living thing, a body that embraced the world. He was a mere speck on water that washed New Guinea, Hawaii and California all at the same time. He thought of the ocean as female, and he was separate from, but joined to her, and connected through her to all things.

Footy watched Johnny become a dot on the rich blue. The Yank was out a hundred yards now.

Over deep water, Johnny turned the point to the beach. He rested, hands gripping the edges, ready to stand. He looked over his shoulder, waiting for his ride. A giant swell flung him up and he let it pass. He studied the march of waves, knowing he'd recognize the right one.

And there it came, churning in from open ocean, a bearded giant above the others. It frothed toward Johnny and he saw sunlight along its flanks, glowing all turquoise and sapphire within. A mane of foam licked the top edge. Thirty yards away, it curled over and spilled down its face.

The curl! Johnny's heart beat faster as the water titan picked up and tossed him at the sky. He stood and at once was moving. The board shot away as he balanced himself over it and came to his full height. He adjusted his feet on the wood and raced along the wave.

The board responded to the slightest pressure and Johnny laughed with delight. He bent his knees and found his rhythm. He was moving fast, whipping through the wind, the water frothing along the edges of his board. He held himself loosely, one foot forward, arms bent, hands out to either side.

Johnny used his feet to turn the nose up and he climbed the wave. Just below the crest, he leveled out and rode the giant. All the emotion of the last days burst out of him in a wild yell. He stood twenty feet above the trough, the strength of the Pacific in his legs.

Johnny glanced behind and saw the liquid tunnel, big enough to stand in. He stepped on his back foot, the board slowed and he drifted into the curl. The light went green and water whooshed over his head. Bathed in mist, Johnny reached out a hand and trailed his fingers through the rising brine.

He shifted his weight and shot into sunlight. He stepped back and was in the curl once more.

Footy watched the huge wave come, and there was a tiny shape flying on it. The breakers rolled shoreward and Johnny grew in size. The Yank hovered high, near the white-crowned peak, and disappeared. The wave rolled on and there was no Johnny. Just as Footy began to worry, the surfer came out as if shot from a liquid cannon, and he darted and dipped along the face.

Footy had never been more impressed with Johnny than he was now. The Yank's ability with a rifle was something to see, and the Aussie had admired that more than he'd let on. On top of that, Johnny was a good bloke in the bush, or a tight spot like the Valley of the Cannibals.

But the skill Johnny demonstrated on his stick of wood put him in an entirely new league. In spite of Footy's situation, his heart lifted. He watched the Yank ride that wave and a cheer broke out.

"Good on ya mate!" Johnny rode with sureness, even a cockiness, which dazzled Footy. For these few minutes, his own suffering was forgotten.

Johnny saw the beach get closer and there was Footy in the distance. As the breaker thundered over the shallows, the curl began to collapse.

Time to get off this train, Johnny thought. A stab of regret went through him. It had been a perfect run. He scooted his board along the breaker until it was merely a hill, turned over the top and sank down in the sea.

The wave unrolled its water carpet along the sand. Another fell on it, and churned back out. Footy saw the dark head on the waves. Johnny waved and paddled away.

An hour flew by while the Aussie watched his mate make run after superb run. It was a treat to watch.

Johnny was entirely absorbed in making the board dance. Time disappeared and the war washed out of him. Temporarily, at least, the South Pacific restored his lost youth.

One of the things Johnny loved about surfing was the concentration required. He needed all his focus to remain in the bright world. One distraction, and the dark power would suck him down and grind him along the razor coral. The knife-edge between ecstasy and terror was what made the ride so sweet.

Johnny only noticed the time when he felt all his muscles trembling. Sunset was painting the sky. He bucked the last water bull ashore, tucked his board under his arm and jogged to camp.

"Crikey mate!" Footy crowed. "Don't get a fat head, but you were brilliant out there!" Johnny chuckled, grabbed a towel and went to rinse off the salt.

He developed a new routine. Johnny fished in the morning and surfed away the afternoons.

Footy, left at camp, forced himself to walk a little more every day. It was an arduous and painful process, and often he returned discouraged. After the latest effort, a half-hour grind that left him panting and sore, he slumped on a log and raised his stump.

"Bloody hell," he muttered, staring at the foreshortened limb that used to kick goals. "I'll never be 'Footy' again."

"That's where you're wrong," Johnny said from the kitchen. "You're truly 'Footy' now."

The Australian put on a good front, but he was seriously depressed. He had to spend most of his days lying down, or at least propped against something. He had too much time on his hands and he spent a lot of it grappling with his future. The problem was, everywhere he looked, a one-legged cripple stared back at him.

His one respite was watching Johnny surf. When Yank-gazing got to be too much, he found himself searching the skies. *Where is our bloody rescue? Will it ever come?*

And then what, mate?

I'll get meself to Aus, visit the family. Get fitted for a false leg. You can still fly a plane, he encouraged himself, *don't let anyone tell you different. You can do the cargo business—you've just got a better excuse to let others do the loading.*

With Cat gone, Johnny had become the cook, on top of every thing else. Now Footy insisted he lend a hand. Still, try as they both did, neither came close to Cat's culinary creations.

When it came to cooking, the prisoner had been another kind of artist.

☆

Johnny was home. It was the three-bedroom bungalow covered in flowering bougainvillea. When the warm rains came, there was a delicious scent of blossoms and lush growth, and Johnny smelled it now.

He entered the house and saw himself as a teenager, sitting at the kitchen table. He was sun-browned, dressed in shorts and an unbuttoned Hawaiian shirt, sandals on his feet. His mother was at the stove, making French toast. She put a plate in front of him, with a bottle of real Vermont maple syrup. Johnny spread butter and poured it on.

Dad entered the room. Johnny had almost forgotten how impressive he was in his crisp uniform, bars of decorations on his chest. He was an executive officer who commanded thousands of men, and he looked it. He was freshly shaved, and his hair was short, clean around the ears and neck. Dad took off his cap, set it on the table, and breathed deep.

"Ahh!" he said. "Heaven! And how are the two most important people in the world this morning?

"Wonderful, Darling," his mother smiled. "Come and sit." Dad came to Johnny and put his hands on his son's shoulders. He smelled of soap and aftershave.

"And what is my number one son up to today?"

"Your only son," Johnny told him. "I'm going surfing—to the north shore."

His mother turned from the stove.

"Oh, I wish you wouldn't!" she said. "I heard in Honolulu—there's been another shark attack." She paused in her work and looked at him.

"Mom!" Johnny said. "That was on Maui!"

"Come here," his dad told her kindly. She brushed her hands on her apron and brought another plate of toast that she slid onto the table. She came up beside Johnny and put a hand over her husband's on their son's shoulder.

"I worry about you, Jo-Jo, that's all."

"Now, Honey," his father said, "who do you see sitting here?"

"My little boy," she said.

"I think you better look again," Dad said. "I see a man at our table."

Johnny watched his teenage self sit up straighter and positively glow.

"Hard as it is, it's time for us to start letting him go," Dad said. He slipped his arm around his wife's waist, as he often did, and bent to kiss her. She turned into him, a hand on his chest, and their lips met. It was only a moment, but Johnny saw how much love was in it and his heart ached.

"I guess you're right," Mom said and turned back to her son. "But you'll always be my baby. It's a big world—you be careful out there!"

She bent and planted a wet one on Johnny's cheek.

"Mother!" the teenager protested.

Johnny opened his eyes.

"Sorry mate, I'm not your Mum," Footy told him from where he lay on his blanket. Johnny looked at the one-legged man, sunburned nose, reddish-blonde beard on his face.

"Sheesh!" he said. "You can say that again!"

☼

A week since he'd started surfing, and almost a month since the Father's attack, Johnny was on the water when fear swept over him.

His sea legs were strong. He'd made six exhilarating runs and was waiting for the seventh. He was a long way out, watching over his shoulder for a wave, when fright surged up.

Fear was always the surfer's dark companion. Sometimes the primordial terror that a mouthful of teeth rushed from below got the better of everyone. Johnny had felt it often enough. It was nothing to be ashamed of, the Hawaiian surfers told him.

"Fear of the Landlord," that's what they called it. Maybe today was the day he'd come to collect his due. Some days, the jitters got so bad, a fellow had to call it quits. *Try again tomorrow*, that was the only remedy.

Why the shivers got him now, Johnny didn't know, but he couldn't deny it. He looked into the depths and saw his legs undulating against shafts of light that went to a point far below.

Get going! Catch the next wave! Sometimes when he got up on his board, the trepidation faded and he could keep surfing. Other times, the uneasiness became near panic and he had to get out. *What will it be?*

Footy squinted against the light, trying to see the Yank on the enormous waves.

Johnny let a swell break over him and the jitters got worse. *Ok,* he told himself. *Take the next train in and get out.*

He was staring out to sea, and Footy was too far away. Neither saw the silver ball come gleaming from the sea. It was solid and it parted the water. It came shedding drops like gems to reveal a collar on a silver shaft that rose steadily against the blue. A trick of the light made the water's surface opaque as mercury, reflecting and distorting the rising band.

The bright thing began to move. It sliced across the deep at the floating man. Still Johnny faced away and did not see it.

Ten yards from him, it went down like a periscope. Now it was merely a silver ball that rolled across the surface, then a bright spot underwater, trailing bubbles.

Over his shoulder, Johnny saw the monster he'd been waiting for.

CHAPTER 15

Johnny held his board ready while the breaker rushed up, shedding foam. He gauged the distance and tensed to rise.

He was looking into the aquamarine light within, when it was eclipsed by darkness. Something black moved into the wave and sucked out the light. Then the roller was looming over Johnny in the trough.

The ocean threw him up like a cork. He got on his feet, looked up and was stabbed by fear. The top of the wave was a waterfall, and rising out of it was the samurai sword. It was steady in the liquid chaos and Johnny was transfixed, but his board was moving and he must look to it.

He carved the concave wall. The instant he could, he glanced back and saw the sword come slicing down after him. He got a thrill of horror when he saw the immense darkness that loomed behind it.

Johnny had to look forward again, and the next time he chanced a look back, it was to see the gleaming, gargantuan head of the Father surging through the froth. Cat's sword stood in the empty eye socket, and the one good eye stared at him, enraged.

Johnny worked his feet to fishtail away, but the crocodile moved above him on the wave, water splashing through its scutes.

The Father unsealed its nostrils, sniffed and it knew him. This was the one-prey, the only thing it still wanted. It lunged at the man and its teeth crashed together as the creature dodged away. The reptile surged across the surface, its mammoth body sweeping in arcs.

The crocodile was more at home in the ocean than the man would ever be, and it was faster and immeasurably stronger. The row of teeth slid up beside the surfboard.

Footy sat grinning on shore as he watched the magnificent wave rush at his mate. He knew from its size that this was the one the Yank would choose. Sure enough, the tiny surfer stood and began to cut it up.

"Good on ya!" Footy shouted. He lost sight of Johnny behind other waves and there the Yank came again, going like a kangaroo at full hop. But in an instant, all the joy drained out of Footy when he saw the great black thing on his tail.

In horror, he recognized the Father. Footy's stomach went into freefall. He leapt to his feet, forgot there was only one of them, and fell hard across a log. Agony shot through him, but he ignored it, rolled on his side and strained to see. There was Johnny, being chased by the brute. Footy grabbed his crutch and beat on the log.

"Come on, mate!" he shouted, "Faster! *Much faster!*"

He saw Johnny fight desperately to stay in front of it, like a fly trying to outrun a charging bull. Again and again the surfer scooted his board away, but the Father was not to be shaken.

"Come on Johnny," Footy fretted, "come on!" He struggled up on his crutch and there was Johnny, a nose ahead of the predator. Footy had watched the Yank through scores of runs, but never anything like this. Johnny made the most incredible turns, using the entire face of the wave.

Johnny saw the crocodile just behind and he aimed straight down and dropped. Almost in the trough, he rocketed away, but the croc was right there. Suddenly Johnny turned up, crouched, and shot in front of its snout. His wake washed over the crocodile's head and it instinctively closed its underwater eyelids. In the ruined eye, the membrane sliced on the sword. The burn fired into the predator's brain and it lost sight of the prey.

Johnny zoomed to the top of the breaker, ducked into the curl and disappeared. The Father missed the move. It raised its head and quested from side to side.

Johnny's view was reduced to a greenish cone with a bright oval ahead. He caught his breath, but when he looked down, fright blasted through him. An enormous shadow was rising below.

Johnny fired out into sunlight as the Father's head came up behind him, jaws gaping. It bit and the teeth struck the back of the board. Johnny's arms swung wildly as he fought for balance. He turned hard just as the crocodile snapped again. It missed, but the sword almost gashed Johnny's leg.

Footy watched the jaws open as high as Johnny. At the last instant, the surfer seemed to jump out of the Father's mouth and the jaws slammed empty.

"Great hairy bollocks!" Footy screamed as an intervening wave cut off his view of the chase.

Johnny had played every trick he knew, and it was not enough. A flick of his eyes showed fifty yards to the beach. *Too far!* The sword swept up beside him in the boulder of the Father's head. The single eye glared and the croc swung its snout, banging the surfboard again. Johnny teetered, stood on one leg, almost lost his balance, and barely managed to recover. *If I fall, it's all over but the chewing.*

But the truth was, the crocodile was too great a foe. Johnny could not outrun it. Again, it jostled the surfboard and he had to drop to his knees and hang on. That slowed him, and the crocodile came up behind and went under. Through the water, Johnny watched the giant head ripple below. The sword scraped against the edge of the board. Then the Father began to rise and Johnny made a last-ditch move.

He stood, stepped hard on the back of the board, and spun a hundred and eighty degrees. He was so close to the blade, it carved off a shaving. Then Johnny was flying the other way, toward the tail, surfing the crocodile's blind side.

The Father came up through the surface expecting to lift the prey, but it was gone. Again, the reptile raised its half-blind head and swung it in exaggerated motions as it tried to find the man.

The wave came closer to the beach and Footy saw predator and prey get bigger. He watched the crocodile rush Johnny and the Yank get on his knees. For a minute, it looked like Johnny was riding the great head. But then he spun around and went skimming down the flank.

"Yes!" Footy shouted.

Johnny's legs were trembling. This was the most challenging run he'd ever made, and it wasn't over. He had to cut hard to get away from the croc's tail as it swung his way. After that, the wave was all chaotic falling water that would knock him down, and he was forced to turn again. He found himself going the same direction as the croc once more, above it.

The reptile had not yet seen him. Johnny reached the massive shoulders and any second he'd be spotted. Again he turned up, shot to the wave's crest and cut into the decaying curl. It was smaller now, less defined, and he had to crouch. He guessed he had only a minute until the breaker crashed onto the beach and spilled him out—right with the Father.

The land would be no respite. The crocodile was as at home there as he was. Johnny furiously searched for a plan. What he came up with was simple, and started with one word. *Run!*

Footy watched the breaker carry the Father to shore. Johnny was nowhere in sight. The wave leading the big one smashed onto the beach.

"Where the hell are you mate?" Footy fumed. The roller was ten yards out and falling apart. The top became a ribbon of spume as it rushed the shallows.

Then, at the last possible instant, Johnny shot out of the mist. Footy's anxiety crested as the Father surfed up behind him. Johnny spun the board for the beach.

"Go!" Footy screamed, "don't look back!"

Johnny heard him. The ocean spat him out and his board ground on the sand. He leapt off just as the Father got there, jaws parting. Johnny kicked the board and it flew between the teeth. The Father felt something enter its mouth and bit hard. It tasted wood and splinters, not the warm flesh it expected, and it grunted and gave chase.

Johnny knew Footy was helpless at camp and he raced in the opposite direction along the beach. The Father stood up and ran after him at full gallop. Its clubfoot was clumsy, but the reptile was frenzied.

For short distances the crocodile could outrun any man. Johnny felt its breath on his legs, and like the pass receiver he'd been, he dodged to the side. The croc turned that way and its four thousand pounds of inertia forced it along. Johnny deked back the other way and gained a second. The jungle loomed and he poured it on.

Footy watched Johnny dash into the trees, the crocodile right behind. *Now what mate? Slap the tree and tell it you won?*

Johnny found he was sprinting by Cat's grave and, on impulse, he snatched his helmet off the cross. He crammed it on and kept running. Now the Father not only smelled the smooth-headed man, it saw him, and its desire to kill crested.

Johnny burst onto the riverbank and skidded into the turn. The

Father piled after him and almost fell in the water it its attempt to change direction. Its huge weight caused the bank to collapse, and Johnny gained another few seconds as it floundered. But now there was nowhere to go but straight ahead, and the reptile caught up with him.

The Father swung its head into the man's side and bowled him over. Johnny shouted in alarm, and Footy heard that. The pilot guessed the worst had come, and called down damnation on the croc.

Johnny, scraped all over, bleeding from his cuts, turned to confront his attacker.

Since its foot had been blown off, the crocodile had been in constant pain. But the stab through its head amounted to screaming torture. When the sword put its eye out, the agony was so intense, the reptile barely killed its attacker before it passed out. It had been sucked out on the waves. Eventually, it came to and tried to swim, but the effort caused such piercing anguish, it went unconscious again.

It came to in anguish, stranded on a coral head, and lay near death for days. Little by little, it regained a portion of its senses. In its distress, it wanted the refuge of its river, and it pushed into the waves.

And then as the crocodile approached the estuary, it encountered the very creature that was its suffering. It tasted the man's body musk in the water, knew who he was, and its wrath overwhelmed its wretchedness.

Now, at long last, the smooth-headed man stood before it at bay. The crocodile opened its jaws for the kill.

But then the prey moved.

It pulled off his head and struck the Father with it, and thunder and lightning clanged all through its brain.

CHAPTER 16

Johnny pulled off his helmet and slammed it down on the sword in the Father's eye socket. The blow made the reptile's mono-vision jitter. It blinked rapidly and blood welled in the cave.

The crocodile hissed and came at Johnny. He showed it his helmet, then lobbed it one way, while he went the other.

The Father turned for the smooth head and caught it in its teeth. It put all its pent up fury into that bite.

The M1 helmet was solid steel that could deflect a bullet. But the enormous jaws of the saltwater crocodile possessed more crushing power than that terror of the ancient world, Tyrannosaurus Rex. Its muscles clenched, exerting an incredible six thousand pounds per square inch of irresistible force. The steel helmet did bend, but the reptile shattered a tooth on it. The shredded nerve stabbed directly into its already overwrought brain. The Father's mouth jerked open and the thing spilled out.

Johnny got two steps before the croc came after him. It gained rapidly, and there was nowhere left to go.

Johnny started to count. *One, two, three!* He leapt up, arms flailing. The Father lunged to seize him in the air. Johnny kicked forward, going for maximum reach. The crocodile was five times as long as the man, and it rose on its muscled tail.

Then man and beast were falling. Johnny's toes stretched an extra inch and gripped earth. He hit and tumbled forward, sprawling full length. He was facedown in the dirt, unable to move.

Four thousands pounds of furious predator came down on his heels. Johnny glanced over his shoulder. He saw the Father's forelegs wheeling, one a blunt club, the other with claws extended. Then the massive head slammed just behind him—and kept going.

Forest floor sprang away like gossamer. A phalanx of spears was revealed and the crocodile slammed onto them with all its weight.

Johnny had just managed to clear the pit of death under the

camouflage net, but the reptile had not. It landed with such force, Johnny heard the hide pop as the spears burst in. Air whooshed from the crocodile, as close to a groan as it could make.

It felt to the Father as if it had fallen into the jaws of an even greater predator. The cruel teeth bit all through its long head, into its neck, and its chest that contained its heart and lungs.

The Father was impaled.

Johnny crawled on his knees to the edge of the pit and saw the beast stuck fast. He stared in awe at the huge head, so close. In turn, it stared with its one eye at the man, unable to look away.

Johnny brushed himself off. He was badly banged up, but that was forgotten as he gazed at the nightmare that had tracked him all the way down the Raub River.

The Father could not move its head and torso, but the back legs churned, tearing up the road. The ridged dragon tail thudded from side to side.

Johnny sat near the transfixed head and hung his feet into the pit. The crocodile continued to jerk, trying to escape the torture, but every shake only drove it further onto the spears.

During his years in New Guinea, Johnny had seen every kind of arrow the tribal warriors made. For shooting men, they carved backswept points that once in the flesh, could not be pulled out. For birds, they employed barbs splayed like fingers to knock them out of the air.

When they hunted wild boar, they used arrowheads of sharpened bamboo. Even a well-shot pig would run, but with a tube stuck in it, the wound could not close. The boar would bleed out, and somewhere along the blood trail, the hunters would find it.

Now in the booby-trapped pit, the Father flailed on similar bamboo points, only of a much larger caliber. Johnny heard running liquid, and saw the blood gushing into the bottom of the hole.

Through its one eye, the reptile continued to gaze at the prey, while the points slowly entered the inner sanctum of its body. From time to time, a razor tip penetrated a particularly sensitive mystery, and the creature shuddered and hissed so that all the spears shook.

Some time later, the Father's upper jaw flew open as if on a spring. Johnny peered into the gore of the mouth and saw five bamboo points coming through. At the back was the wet steel of

Cat's sword stuck through the palate.

He noticed something was happening along the Father's neck and back. Peaks were forming. Johnny realized the skin was being pushed up by spears that raised it like tent poles.

He heard a familiar voice.

"I thought the bloody Father had croaked you, mate, but it's the other way around!"

Johnny turned. Footy had come through the plantation, and he was flushed and sweating, leaning heavily on his crutch. Johnny gave him a nod and a tired smile.

"You're in time for the end," he said. "Take a seat."

Footy limped closer and stared down on the ruin of the Father. His gaze went all the way along the broad back to the tail that still twitched and jittered on the road. The Aussie sat down by the Yank on the edge of the pit.

The bellows' breaths grew more labored and the body convulsed, making poles crack. The Father shuddered along its length and a fresh wave of blood pumped through its nostrils and sprayed around the teeth.

Johnny was fascinated by the eye. It was bulging up. Suddenly it popped, and a bamboo spear poked through. The Father's head slid down it and it gurgled out a great sigh. The tail lifted and swung a last time, uprooting a palm tree. It crashed over and coconuts spilled across the road.

Cat's sword shivered in the dark moon scar and the body clenched hard and went still.

"Hell's—bloody—bells!" Footy breathed. "You've killed the Father!"

"And this time," Johnny said, "I believe it's really dead."

CHAPTER 17

A fat-bodied Empire Flying Boat soared along the New Guinea coast. The pilot manned the controls while the co-pilot handled navigation. Two crewmen sat in the lower passenger compartment and looked out through the windows. The plane had refueled in Wewak within the hour and now, flying low, it approached the delta. From a long way off, the aviators had spotted the muddy stain on the South Pacific that marked the egress of the Raub River.

The aircraft had seen action with the Royal Australian Air Force during the war. Recently, it had been returned to its owner, the Queensland and Northern Territories Aviation Service, better known as "Qantas." With the coming of peace, the airline had been frantically busy, but at last it had responded to multiple requests for assistance by the Allied Army in New Guinea.

The crew had been given the day to get to the Raub and retrieve three survivors of something called "Operation Teeth."

"There's the Raub," the co-pilot shouted. "We're to look for the biggest branch."

"Right," the pilot said and banked the four-engine plane so he could see down through the side window. "That's where the Coast Watcher said the men would be."

"There!" the co-pilot called. A column of smoke spouted over the trees. The plane shot across the band of river and a strip of jungle, and there was the beach. A glance showed a bonfire, what appeared to be two crashed jeeps, and an S O S on the sand.

The Flying Boat thundered over, then the pilot banked it over the ocean and came back for a closer look. From a hundred feet up, the aviators saw two men waving, one at the fire and another near the palms.

Again they went by. A flash of green, then muddy water, and they turned. This time they came at treetop level and were treated to a startling sight. An enormous skeleton stretched along a road in the jungle. It reminded the pilot at once of a dinosaur he'd seen in a museum. The co-pilot could look below and saw crocodiles scattering from the carcass.

The plane shot through the plume of smoke and they saw the men. One bare-chested bloke stood by the fire, furiously waving. The other lad was beside the canvas roof in the trees, shaking a stick. *Looks like the poor bugger has only one leg.*

At the sound of engines, Johnny had dropped his fishing pole and rushed to light the signal fire. Footy was napping at camp and struggled up. Both men were frantic to be seen.

Soon it was clear they had been spotted. The plane made several passes, then roared over the ocean, banked, and came back. The waves were still huge, but had settled somewhat in the last week. The aircraft came skimming at them and then it fell in. There was a great splash and Johnny and Footy lost sight of it. But here it rose, engines roaring.

They went down to meet it. The Aussie was better on his crutch now, and the two arrived together and stood, grinning broadly.

The pilot slowed near the beach, waited for the next wave and rode it in. Two crewmen in white shirts and shorts jumped barefoot out a door and pushed on a pontoon. The engines died and four propellers stopped turning. The pilots sat in the doorway to pull off socks and shoes, let down a set of stairs and climbed out. The flyers came to greet the castaways.

"You're a sight for sore eyes!" the tall one said.

"About time!" the one-legged man beamed. "What the hell took you so long?"

"G'day mate," the pilot said, offering his hand to Johnny and then Footy. They shook enthusiastically. "We heard you might be looking for a lift. But aren't there three of you? We were told to expect a prisoner."

"He didn't make it," Johnny said shortly. The pilot nodded and introduced the crew.

"You blokes have a lovely spot here and I hate to rush you, but with this sea we can't stay," he said. "You better shake a leg. May we help with your things?"

"I spotted an enormous carcass by the river," the co-pilot put in as they walked to the camp. "Know anything about that?"

"That's what I want to talk to you about," the dark haired man said. "We do have some luggage, and we need your help."

"No worries, mate," a muscular crewman said as he slapped him on the shoulder.

"We've got heaps of room. How many bags can you possibly have?" All of them laughed.

The Flying Boat's engines labored as the aircraft lumbered over the Owen Stanley Range, on course for Port Moresby. On the far side of the mountains, it tilted into the long descent. The pilot turned the controls over to his colleague and walked back from the flying deck to stretch his legs. He came down the steps to the lower area, passed the crewmen playing cribbage, and stood studying his passengers.

The Yank and his one-legged mate were sprawled across the seats, asleep. Both had wild hair and stubble on their chins and looked about as sun-cooked as two men could be.

The Yank wore ragged shorts and an unbuttoned shirt with the sleeves missing. Around his neck was a chain with his metal tags, and an enormous crocodile tooth. Across his lap was a rifle with a scope on it, and he wore two knives in his belt, one a long cane cutter.

The Aussie, too, was bare-chested. He had a brimmed hat hanging back on the string, and he wore faded shorts, a huge knife through his belt as well. The stump of his leg, covered in a sock, was propped on the cushions. His homemade crutch rested on the floor beside two packs.

The wood-framed one had a Japanese sword, of all things, sticking out the top.

They look like bloody pirates, the aviator thought. *My word, I'd hate to run into them on a dark street late at night.*

Coiled behind them, nearly filling the compartment, was the skin. *What did the Yank—Johnny, it was—call the croc? The Father!* Beside it was an even more macabre item, the enormous skull of the brute itself, all bones and long teeth. The two men had told a wild tale of the croc chasing them down the river. It killed their prisoner, they said, and took Footy's leg off. After that, Johnny said, the brute had come after him one last time. He'd managed to lead it into a pit full of spears.

It had taken a week to skin the beast, and another to partially cure the hide in saltwater and sun.

The head, Johnny said he'd chopped off with the samurai sword. With some help from Footy, he'd somehow rolled it on palm rounds to the ocean. He'd tied ropes on it and sunk it there. The fish and crabs had done the rest.

The things smelled worse than low tide and the pilot had been reluctant to take them aboard. The stink would linger, and he'd get an earful back in Aus. But what was he going to do? The blokes wouldn't come without their treasures. It was the strangest load the pilot had carried, but he was a boy from the outback, and such interesting items did not put him off.

The aviator smiled, gave his head a shake, and returned to the business of flying his aircraft.

☆

As the light played through the cabin, Footy drifted in and out of awareness. He'd been dreaming of the gorgeous bird he knew in Moresby, the one he'd been after these two years.

A bloke couldn't help but fall for a beauty like Gwyn!

In the last months, even though she hadn't come out and said it, he'd gathered she was going to stay on in New Guinea. The nurse had made it clear to him early on that she would not have a military man. Since he'd become a regular bloke again, he reckoned he had a better chance with her. Just before this buggered mission, he'd put his case before her once more—and she'd shot him down.

Of course, he hadn't said a word about her to Johnny, and that was why. But as he'd recovered from his injury, he'd had plenty of time to consider his options. Now he was convinced he had another chance with her.

Gwyn is a nurse, and I am a bloke in need of care. Instead of a handicap, this bloody leg may just be your ticket to her heart, mate.

There on the beach, Footy had renewed his determination to build his air cargo business. And while he had enjoyed his bachelor years, hanging about and drinking with his mates, eventually a bloke had to do the right thing.

He would make his home in the Territory of Papua, on the ocean outside of Port Moresby. With the war over, the capital would revive a lively social life. There'd be ever more people, more stores, more of the comforts of home. Some of his mates, old Dingo included, had jawed about getting a horse track going. *That'd be beaut!*

All of it meant there would be increasing demand for goods to fly up from Aus, and plantation produce to fly back. For Footy, that indicated it was time to set up house and take a wife.

I need someone who can get along in this place, different as it is from life in Aus. And who better than a Sheila who's already here, someone who knows the ins and outs? Someone who's got her own friends, and enough to keep her busy. Being a pilot, he'd be away from home half the time. He couldn't have a woman always at him for not being there.

Gwyn is the ideal choice—if only she'll have me!

Talk to Doc Mac, he counseled himself. The medical man was a mate Footy respected. Better yet, he was friends with Gwyn.

Listen now, he advised himself. *Don't be too proud to play the sympathy card. Do whatever it takes! Gwyn is worth every bit.*

The engines droned on. Johnny dozed and sometimes came to, still having to pinch himself to believe they had really been rescued. Operation Teeth was over, and much more importantly, so was World War Two.

Continually now, his thoughts were on Gwyn. He couldn't wait to see her, but now they were actually on their way, he was nervous. The truth was, he was unsure how things stood between them. Everything had been left up in the air.

We were supposed to be gone three days. Instead, it's been what—more than two months! She asked me to look for my heart. What can I tell her?

I know this. My war is over. A Jap, my sworn enemy, became Cat, my friend.

What will peace bring? Do I have any hope of a normal life? What is that, anyway?

When he was a boy, Johnny's future looked straight ahead. He'd grow up to be a Navy career officer, like his forbearers. As they had, he would fall in love and take a wife. He would do what his country commanded. And where he was, there would his family be also.

But on the beach, Johnny had learned that path was not for him. He would be the first in generations to choose a different course, but he was done with war.

The question remained. As a civilian in peacetime, what would he do? Johnny had tried to part the veil of the future, peering at a score of possibilities. But he found now that every path he looked at had Gwyndolyn on it. When he tried to imagine any one of them without her, it turned into a long, bleak haul with no joy in it.

Or love.

He formed the word gingerly. For the first time since Pearl Harbor—or maybe it was the first time—he let the idea of real love, deep love, bloom as a possibility for his own life.

"Love." He said it deliberately in his mind. Could a man who had done what his country had required him to do, who had taken the lives of so many other men—could he claim love for himself?

The pilot adjusted course and Johnny felt it through the fuselage.

It struck him again that he was flying to Gwyn. He felt a flutter in his gut. The soldier told him to smarten up. He could not let go like that! But now Johnny ordered the warrior to stand down.

The nascent feeling in him had the thrill of surfing, but this sea was his life itself. Knowledge grew in him. He did want love, he wanted it with Gwyn, and he wanted it more than anything else.

Johnny's eyes were closed, but he was alert. *How blind I've been!* How could he not have seen this desire growing?

And then he grasped it. It was because of the solemn promise his sixteen-year-old self had sworn. In the dark shadow of Pearl, and the deaths of his parents, he had vowed to avenge their murder, and the betrayal of his country.

I swore I would kill every Jap I could, and not stop until they were dead, or I was, or they gave up.

That promise had left no room for Gwyn. But now he had fulfilled his promise. And that allowed new possibilities to take shape.

The Flying Boat creaked in the winds over the savage island. Johnny's ears popped as the aircraft went into its final descent. Again, he felt that flutter. And now Johnny made another promise, formed as intensely as the first.

I am not sure who I am anymore. But I will find out who Gwyn thinks I can be, and I will become that man.

A crewman came back to see if the passengers needed anything. He saw two men at rest, a smile touching each set of lips.

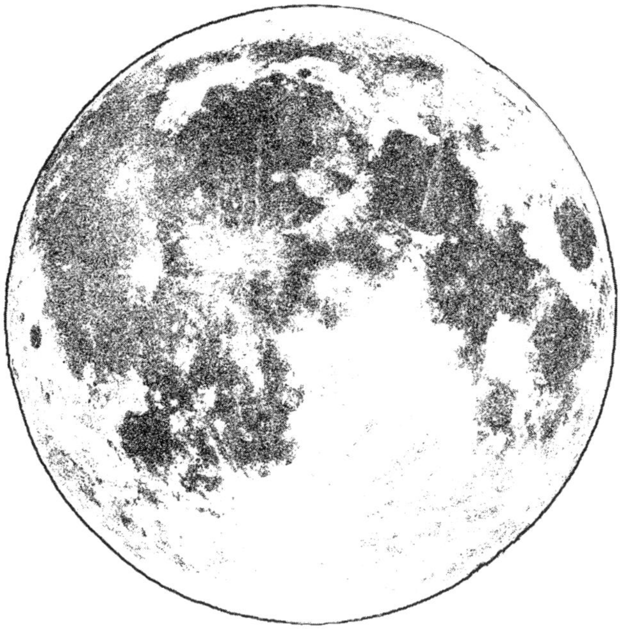

A long sweep of empty beach. Faded canvas between trees. Blankets half buried, sand sifting over charcoal.

On the point where the Raub River flowed into the South Pacific stood a stately tree. In the dappled light beneath it was a mound strewn with leaves. Beside this was the eroded indent of a massive clawed foot, half full of water.

At the head of the grave was a cross made of sticks. On it hung a crushed soldier's helmet, netting torn, paint scored in rusted ridges.

Behind this, of all things, stood a hand-carved surfboard. The splintered end was buried in the earth. The nose pointed skyward.

On it was carved, letter by laborious letter:

Katsu
Samurai and Soldier of Japan
Died Sept 2, 1945

And below this:

Since my country burned down
How clearly
I see the moon

AFTERWORD

And there, Dear Reader, you have it, as Colonel Chambers might say.

***TEETH** will be followed by **SKINS**, the sequel, and then one more book to complete the New Guinea trilogy. The next two books exist in draft, although they are rough blocks in need of sculpting.*

My first thanks go to you, oh Faithful Reader! Without you, this novel would be no more than a response to the Zen koan, "what is the sound of one hand clapping?"

The book you hold began at least two years ago when, with the encouragement and support of my wife, Deborah, I gave up all else, and began to write full time. All thanks to you, Deborah, for your unflagging support and assistance! Who else would have read the manuscript, word for word, so many times? Who else would have been so complimentary of the good bits, and so kindly and constructively critical of the rest? And who else would have experienced with me, every pang and ecstasy of the birth?

*But hold the presses! Maybe this book truly began in the 1990s when, on one of my return visits to Papua New Guinea (PNG), I found the picture of "the Father." I was busy filling journals with notes and buying locally produced books. One was a photographic record by Mike Coutts of South Pacific Magazine. It was called "Invasion," a pictorial record of the war, but on the penultimate page, I encountered a photo that would change my life. It was the gigantic Saltwater Crocodile pictured at the beginning of **TEETH**.*

From that moment, "the Father" began to swim through the murky recesses of my mind. Imagine, I thought, men confronting the world's largest reptile on its own turf! And what if they were stripped of their firearms, so they must face this force of nature with nothing but hand weapons and wits?

We know that neither whales nor sharks hunt individual humans for weeks on end. But, Dear Reader, crocodiles do. They are intelligent predators that choose their victims and plot their attacks. So, lost on its river, how would our heroes escape a great hunter of the

Father's magnitude? And what if these modern men must also confront the headhunters and cannibals of New Guinea?

What of tribal wars, the coming of Christianity and materialism (the "Cargo Cult"), and the people's introduction to "civilization" in the form of world war? What of first contact between pristine tribal culture and the outside world? What about tribal clashes on a global scale—the hatred and enmity between America and Japan, from Pearl Harbor, to the only use in history of atomic weapons? And if the world could find peace at last, how about Johnny and Katsu?

Back when I first ran across the Father, I was on one of my world "walkabouts." It had taken me once more through Hong Kong, to Japan, Australia, and then PNG. I knocked about the island, going where I would, moving on when I wanted.

I visited my hometown and found to my surprise, many expat childhood friends. Ukarumpa is in the Eastern Highlands, where my parents founded the Wycliffe Mission in the 1950s. Most missionary kids, of course, had "gone-finish." But who remained in force were the natives. These are my "one-talks," the Gadsup people of the river. My boyhood playmates were now the leaders of the village. What hugs and tears! What a reunion and feast!

(I would return a year later with a television crew to film an international documentary—see my website).

I spent a few weeks that time exploring the Sepik River. I traveled primarily by dugout canoe (see author cover photo, with a tagline ubiquitous during the war: "Somewhere in New Guinea").

The Sepik is the inspiration for the "Raub River," but I did not want to give offense to the real inhabitants of the Big River by ascribing to them behavior and a history not theirs. So I created the Raub, a mythic river.

You people of the Sepik River, I hope you enjoy this story, and get a good laugh at the pikinini from Ukarumpa!

To return to my quest for origins: it is possible this book began in the 1980's when I was Head Writer and Literary Producer of the Vancouver Show. This was a live, primetime two-hour television magazine I would ultimately Executive Produce. I recognized a cannibal when I saw one! That TV monster chewed up bright young people by the dozen, sucked them to the rind, and spat them out. Somehow, I lasted five years.

It was during my sojourn in Vanity Fair that I met renowned author and movie producer, James Clavell ("King Rat," "Shogun," "Tai Pan," "Gai Jin," and many more). I produced an interview about his latest, "Noble House," and James and I hit it off. He was kind enough to mentor me. We shared a fascination with Asia and the South Pacific. He read pieces I had written on places I lived, including New Guinea and the Philippines, told me I had talent and to keep on and never quit—and perdition on the naysayers!

"A writer writes," he said. "You can't call yourself a writer if you are not writing." James, from wherever you look down, domo arigato, sensei. I owe you much. And thanks for the stories, and the advice about women.

But maybe it truly began when I was a boy growing up in New Guinea. From a young age, I camped in the wild, cooked my kaukau in the fire, stripped sugar cane with my teeth, and loved sleeping in jungle hammocks. I learned to swim in her rivers and hike her jungles and kunai fields.

I grew up on stories. My father read C.S. Lewis's "Narnia" books aloud to the five Dean children (something I enjoyed doing myself years later for my own daughter, Tara. And thank you, kiddo, for encouraging your dad to keep spinning his yarns).

As a boy, I was a voracious reader of everything I could get my hands on. I recall a much-thumbed set of Dickens novels. In addition I read the books attributed to Johnny's father, including the works of Conrad and Kipling. Now, I know these two giants have fallen somewhat out of favor due to their "colonial views." However, I say that a novelist is in many ways the true journalist of his times, and we ought not to shoot the messenger. If we toss out all those whose views are not in lockstep with the "politically correct" opinions of our own era, we will have no history from which to learn.

I had to wrestle with the issues of tribalism and racism in order to write ***TEETH****. I grew up in a world where white men were called "Master," and I also had the pleasure of seeing the practice disappear. Native women did display their breasts, and it was foreigners who taught them this was wrong, or at least, unseemly. (Even anthropologists bring their cultural bias and alien influence).*

The same thing happened to warriors and penis gourds. Again, outsiders pressured them to adopt Western garb. The result was often an undignified compromise—a man with his tribal covering protruding through a pair of shorts! Having experienced the New Guinea of my youth, when the people walked proud in their bilas, I am discouraged to see crowds of native people in their one pair of pants and T-shirt emblazoned with Western products and slogans.

I hope we can still learn to celebrate tribal cultures. I hope at the same time that we can continue to let go of the tribal and racial prejudices that exists, truth be told, just under the skin of most of us. Perhaps this is naive, but I hope we can do it while holding onto the best aspects of our heritage—our unique dance, music, dress and food that make the various peoples of our planet so interesting. I rue the day when the whole world is one big strip mall flogging the same fast food and retail chains—a global homogenized mediocrity of the lowest common denominator.

There are two other gigantic presences in the room I want to recognize. One is Homer, and the other, John Bunyan. **TEETH** *is, to the best of my ability, an homage to "the Odyssey" and "Pilgrim's Progress."*

For any skill in bringing the crocodile to life, I once more acknowledge my debt to C.S. Lewis—and Richard Adams, author of "Watership Down," "The Plague Dogs" and many more, whose creation of the great bear "Shardik" was a marvelous thing. Before that, I cut my teeth on my father's made-up tales about Uncle Wiggily and friends, running from the wolf in the Black Forest. With apologies to Howard Garis—Dad, your stories were the best!

Of course, there was the Bible. As the child of missionaries, I was immersed in the scriptures. Then there was a long period where I wanted desperately to fit in, and I "forgot" my origins.

It was not until I began to study literature at university that I realized what a profound advantage I had been given! As Northrop Frye wrote in "The Great Code," "a student of English literature who does not know the Bible does not understand a good deal of what is going on...."

There was another New Guinea book I read as a boy that had a lasting impact. This was the first-hand report by Russell Hitt of the interaction between intrepid missionaries and the New Guinea nation known as the "Dani." That book was "Cannibal Valley," and came complete with powerful chiefs, sorcerers, intrigue, vendetta wars, and the consumption of human flesh. That was the long-distant inspiration for the Mambu and the Valley of the Cannibals.

It was around the time I first read Hitt's book, when I was about eleven, that I had my own first story published. We Ukarumpa kids hiked to the one-room school in nearby Aiyura, presided over by the formidable Mrs. Schindler. But by this time, I was attending school by correspondence with Australia.

A horror story I wrote was picked up by the school magazine. I no longer recall the title, but I do remember that it involved a boy much like me. He is home alone one night, quietly reading, when he looks up to see a sorcerer with wild dreadlocks leering at him through the screen window! The boy sits petrified by terror, hour after hour. He knows that if he even dares turn a page, let alone glance up, he will be killed, and very likely mutilated. He reads the same paragraph ad infinitum, ad nauseum. At last his parents return, and at once the wicked warlock transmogrifies into an ordinary mop leaning against the window. And so the evil one waits, until the next time he can catch the boy alone.

I imagine that story went out across the Australian outback to terrorize dozens if not hundreds of rural youngsters. Now that I think about it, I do believe **TEETH** *began there!*

What I can tell you for certain is that the South Pacific island made a huge impression that has remained strong all these years. The wild topography, the colorful trade language, the WW2 aircraft wrecks that were our playground, the pulse of the singsing drums, the big-hearted people, the mighty rivers, the crystalline oceans in which I have plunged as a scuba diver, outlandish insects, and animals that include the saltwater crocodile, have long inhabited my personal dreamtime.

I have never forgotten New Guinea. (I'm sorry, but I will probably call PNG "New Guinea," even though I know it is not politically correct, until I climb the great tree of the dead myself. This is because I grew up in the then-Australian Trust Territory of New Guinea, with Papua to the south, and Dutch New Guinea to the west).

In truth, the realities of PNG—which went from the Stone Age to the Space Age in one generation—are often far more bizarre than fiction. A novel has the challenge of being credible. First and foremost, this is an entertainment for the 21st Century.

I want to throw a rose as well to the great movie and documentary makers, a pantheon too legion to name. (I spent most of my first career as a creator of television documentaries and other programs). On the docu and book side, I must mention "First Contact" by Australia's Bob Connolly and Robin Anderson, featuring the priceless photographs and film shot by the Leahy brothers in the 1930s. Bob kindly supplied historical footage for my own documentary on New Guinea, "Return to the Stone Age" (see my website).

In ***TEETH****'s genre, Steven Spielberg's "Jaws," the only good shark flick, and the "Jurassic Park" movies, were influential. Mr. Spielberg taught me that the lulls between the monster's attacks are at least as important as its appearance.*

I am also grateful to another genius of the silver screen, Mel Gibson. His epic productions stand head and shoulders above the crowd. I learned much from his work about the courage to tell big stories, and about construction of set up and payoff.

I've read that Francis Ford Coppola took two essential items to the jungles of Asia when he filmed his epic, "Apocalypse Now." One was a dog-eared copy of Conrad's "Heart of Darkness." ("The horror. The horror"). The other was a list of more than 600 things about the Vietnam War he simply must work in.

In ***TEETH****, I had at least that many topics to include about the place, the people, and its history. In addition, I wanted to illustrate a fact I think is fundamental to any hope of finding peace on Earth. We are all connected, even (or perhaps especially), sworn enemies. To that end, the book has many parallels. Johnny is an ambush hunter: so is the Father. There is Footy and his foot, and the crocodile and his foreleg. And more. For better or for worse, this is my attempt to weave that tapestry. I hope you enjoyed the result.*

To the survivors of Pearl Harbor and their descendants: my apologies for taking the liberty of placing Johnny's father as a Lt. Commander and Executive Officer of the USS Arizona. In fact, there were seven Lt. Commanders of the warship as of Dec. 1, '41, two of whom, P. Register and J. French, were killed in the bombing, along with Captain Franklin Van Valkenburgh. The actual Executive Officer, Ellis Geiselman, survived. In the interest of keeping alive the memory of Dec. 7, I beg your indulgence.

Also, to the survivors of the only atomic bomb attacks in history, the "hibakusha" of Hiroshima and Nagasaki. Please forgive me for the fictional use of your terrible ordeal and suffering. Again, the purpose is to make these things real for new generations. Also, I did want to emphasize the horrific irony of the inadvertent destruction of the center of Christianity in Japan and the Urakami Cathedral (located at Ground Zero of the explosion over Nagasaki). However, by no means do I mean to imply that any group of Japanese was or is more important than any other.

A word about facts: while a great deal of reading and research went into this, and I am grateful to the authors of more than a hundred books on various aspects of history, ethnography and more, and to everyone who shared their knowledge and expertise, all errors are my responsibility.

When describing real people, and events ascribed to them, I have tried to be accurate. For example, the speech attributed to General MacArthur on the occasion of his return to the Philippines is what he said. The radio report of the dropping of the atom bomb on Hiroshima is from an actual broadcast of the time, and so on.

In regard to dates, as Newt Gingrich and William Forstchen noted so carefully in "Pearl Harbor – A Novel of December 8th," on the other side of the International Date Line, all dates are a day later than in North America.

One of the trade languages of New Guinea is pidgin English, spelled in-country, "tok pisin" (talk pidgin). It would have been easy to get carried away with (to me, fascinating) pidgin expressions, but this would have made the book laborious for most readers. I have parted company with the official spelling of some of the vocabulary. Of note is the word for "crocodile," which I render as "pookpook" (rhymes with "book"). The official spelling is "pukpuk," but when most readers made it sound like Hawaiian hockey, I went phonetic.

There are more people I hasten to thank. One is Yasuyuki Kasai, a Japanese of samurai descent whose father was a soldier in WW2. While researching ***TEETH****, I came across the Guinness Book of World Records report of "The Greatest Disaster Suffered from Animals." This was the Ramree Island Saltwater Crocodile attack on Japanese soldiers in February, 1945. My Chas Rutherford is a "witness" to the event.*

On that trail, I found "Dragons of the Mangrove" by Mr. Kasai, a well-researched novel from the viewpoint of the Japanese soldiers who had to enter the perilous swamp. Yasuyuki disputes how many actually died during that crossing. Mr. Kasai was kind enough to read my manuscript at an early stage. He has generously given a great many helpful observations about the story, and in particular, the Japanese characters, martial arts, and the samurai and their swords.

The poem Katsu writes in the sand was inspired by a book I read long ago—"Zen Flesh, Zen Bones" a translation into English of ancient Japanese writings. At least, that is where I think I read an old haiku similar to the one I gave Katsu. The original involved a house, not a country. I wrote my version, and Yasuyuki was kind enough to translate it back into Japanese. Thank you, Yasuyuki! Your encouragement and friendship have been a delightful bonus to all this.

I thank Sharon and Tom. They took time from an always-insane schedule to travel across the US so that Sharon could read the manuscript. She has been consistently strong in her encouragement and support. Heartfelt thanks to both of you.

Then there is my brother, Dave Dean. He, too, lived in New Guinea, and almost died there (but that is another story). He and I have shared favorite books for decades. I so enjoyed having him read ***TEETH****! He made many insightful suggestions that improved the book. Thanks, brother.*

Cover art rules! Deborah and I saw Dwight Kirkland's Africa paintings and were entranced. "What if we could get him," we dreamed, and we did. Thank you Dwight.

Another enthusiastic reader was Donna Wooten, M.A. and teacher. Thanks, Donna! Then there was Montessori teacher and professional proofreader, Julie Price. Julie, you're a peach.

I give a final tip of the hat to all you friends and strangers who shared your advice, insights and encouragement along the way.

See you later, alligator. In a while, crocodile.
Behind me looklook, pookpook.

Timothy James Dean

"Somewhere on Planet Earth," November, 2009

Don't be a stranger!
www.TimothyJamesDean.com

WORLDERS™

www.worlders.net

The first 500 to register will be listed as the founding members of Worlders.

Did you grow up so many places, you're not sure where you are from, or where you belong? Well, there's a tribe you do belong to, and we gather at ***worlders.net***.

"Where in the world are you from?" If you're a "Worlder," that's a tough question. People like me, who grew up with cannibals, and had lived in six countries by the time I was eighteen, learned early to dodge that one.

Some Worlders (like me) are the children of missionaries. Others I went to school with in places like Kodaicanal in South India, are the offspring of diplomats, scholars, industrialists, aid workers, and the military. We share many attributes.

Launched with this book is a new virtual "coffee shop" where you are always welcome! Make new friends—share your story.

Deborah, my wife, is a "Navy brat." And while she didn't necessarily hop countries, she moved a lot. We share a joy in exploring our planet. Neither of us would trade our experiences, and the people we have met, for any of the benefits no doubt enjoyed by the "stay-at-homers." Of course, there is a darker side to growing up disconnected. More on that as we get to know one another.

Many Worlders have a lively interest in the furthest-flung corners of the world. Our friends are generally a well-traveled lot. Many of us work in communications. Quite a few are writers.

We Worlders may be rootless—we often feel like we don't belong anywhere. At the same time, we are equally at home everywhere. We are not necessarily rooted vertically—planted in one place. We are rooted laterally—that is, to people and other places, and even our memories. Many of us carry "sacred objects"—a box of photographs and a particular painting that when you hang it, you're home (again).

We Worlders really got going in a big way after the Second World War. Aircraft shrunk the planet. The pace of the global diaspora picked up.

We have been called other names (yes, those too!). The late Ruth Useem, an American sociologist, took her kids to India. She observed that they experienced two cultures, and created a third from the mix. Thus, in the 1960s, she coined the term, "Third Culture Kid."

Some years later, my old friend and fellow Kodai alumnus (who, sadly, recently left the planet), Norma McCaig, coined another term—"Global Nomads."

I've never been entirely comfortable in the skin of either expression. For one, I lived in far more than two countries, so "third culture" is more like seventh. (Nor have I been a "kid" for some time). And while "nomadic" describes how I've lived, there are those Worlders who had a much-traveled childhood, and then settled down.

To me, "Worlders" is apt. Planet Earth is our home, even if we are just a-passing through. If you relate, come participate.

Moreover, it doesn't matter if you merely grew up in Missouri and moved to Montana. If you have the peculiar sense of not belonging anywhere, of being the chameleon who blends in but isn't of the crowd—if you are searching for ways to find a community into which you fit by definition, then **worlders.net** may be for you.

What we are *not* is a political organization. Like Thoreau, most of us who have to get through borders agree, "that government is best which governs least of all." (No, we are not denying that terrorists exist. We are simply saying that personally, we want it easy to get from here to Timbuktu).

Neither are we a religious gathering. We each, no doubt, bring our spiritual beliefs, and Worlders come from every faith and walk of life. The only thing of which the site is intolerant is hatred of any other tribe, and intolerance itself.

Welcome you Worlders, you members of the Planet Earth tribe!

See you online.

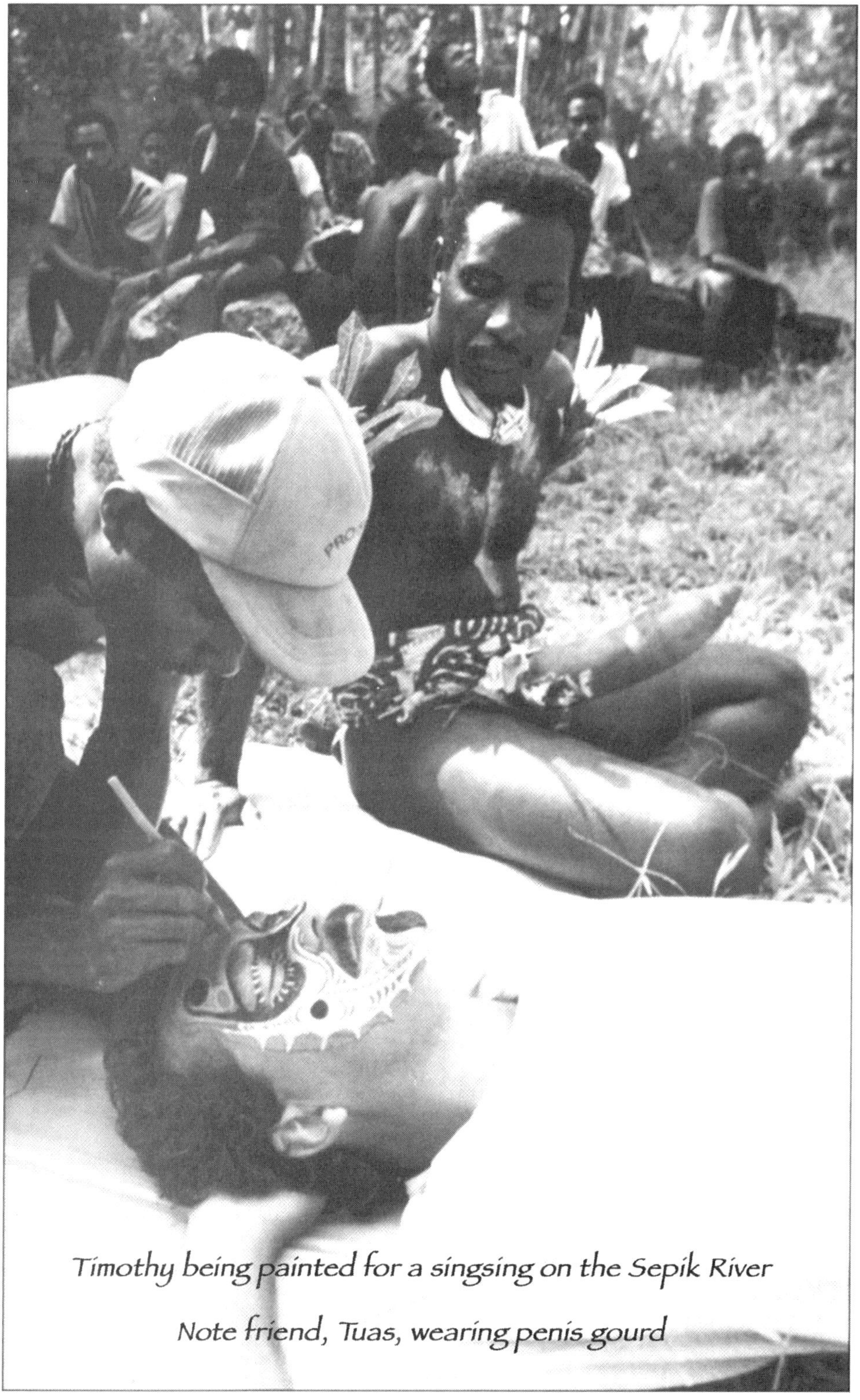

Timothy being painted for a singsing on the Sepik River

Note friend, Tuas, wearing penis gourd

Timothy and *"one-talks"* of the Gadsup tribe, Ukarumpa, Eastern Highlands, PNG

"My childhood friends are the elders of the village"

The Author as a boy in New Guinea in the 1960s

Photograph by Deborah Dean

Author Timothy James Dean